TAKE HIM A NATION

A Novel of Independent Scotland

Robert Morris

ב"ה

Take Him A Nation is the generous gift of
GEOFFREY SIMMONDS
on the occasion of the Friends of The Hebrew University
Annual Burns Night Supper, January 24, 2002

Make their *consequence* thy care

from *For the Future Be Prepar'd* by Robert Burns

To you, my dear reader, bonny best wishes,

Robert Morris

Robert Morris

Your gift is a special pre-release copy of
TAKE HIM A NATION: A NOVEL OF INDEPENDENT SCOTLAND
Scheduled for publication April 10, 2002

IUMIX Limited
www.iumix.com

TAKE HIM A NATION
A Novel of Independent Scotland

First eBook edition ISBN: 1 84320 004 X
Paperback edition ISBN: 1 84320 010 4
Hardback edition ISBN: 1 84320 008 2

Cover art by Sharon Ratheiser © 2001

Published by Iumix Limited
http://www.iumix.com
Set in Times New Roman

Iumix Ltd., P.O. Box 179,
Totton, SO40 8YD,
United Kingdom.

A CIP catalogue record for this book
is available from the British Library.

To my loving Ruth, for her good taste

Acknowledgements

The current Chief Rabbi of Britain, Jonathan Sacks, unwittingly fired my imagination with an early morning radio spot he broadcast some nine or ten years ago. Half asleep, I have no memory of what he said. But I clearly remember asking myself, "What if..."

In that same period of my life, Prof. David Craig of Lancaster University kindly accepted this mature student into his class of undergraduates, and inspired me to write a novel. Much appreciation goes next to our Jerusalem writing circle — Moira, Leon, Helena, and Vivienne, who died far too young — for their straight-shooting criticisms, advice, and encouragement. It was my privilege to know Rabbi Eli Munk and Reverend Joe Russon, two angelic spirits no longer with us, whose teachings and influence have contributed significantly to the character and content of my life and fiction. No words can describe my gratitude to Ruth, my long-suffering editor-in-residence. No one I know has a better eye for spotting the "clunkers," or a more uncanny feel for the correct English idiom. I am sorry that I cannot personally thank my parents of blessed memory, who instilled within me the freedom to write. Finally, I wish to thank Edward Waite, without whose bold initiative, *Take Him A Nation* would never have emerged from its cocoon.

**

The quotation from Uri Zvi Greenberg's poem "Ma'asei BiYerushalmi" which appears on page 182 is excerpted from *A Treasury of Jewish Quotations*, edited by Joseph L. Baron, and is reprinted by kind permission of the publisher, Jason Aronson, Inc., Northvale, NJ, copyright Bernice Baron © 1985.

About the author

Robert Morris is the pseudonym of a writer and photographer born in England, raised in America, educated in Scotland, working in Israel, and wherever he is, living in another world.

CONTENTS

Part Three: Winter Night

Part Four: Spring Morning

The more perfection anything has, the more active and less passive it is; and contrariwise, the more active it is, the more perfect it becomes.

Ethics, Baruch Spinoza (1632-77)

*

"Weel, Tam, what's the news the nicht?" would old Geordie Murray say, as Tam entered with his *Josephus* under his arm, and seated himself at the family fireside.

"Bad news, bad news," replied Tam. "Titus has begun to besiege Jerusalem — it's gaun to be a terrible business."

Memoirs, William Chambers (1800-83)

Take

Him

A

Nation

Prologue

My academic career in the Geography Department at Edinburgh University was running entirely to schedule. I went up to university full of promise, and was soon earmarked for the scholarly life. Invited to stay on after my first degree, I completed my doctorate in a record two years. Nine years ago I was appointed Professor of Social Geography. Looking down the road, I saw myself continuing to lecture, research and write in my chosen field to the end of my working days. It was not an exciting life, but I was successful, well regarded, and quite content.

However, life took an unexpected twist on September Ninth, Twenty ninety-two. I arrived at the department to find an unsolicited packet in my pigeonhole. The stamps indicated it was sent from the State of Israel. There was no return address.

The string-tied parcel slightly larger than an A4-size page contained loose-leaf sheets that were brown-edged and brittle, bound only by a blue ribbon. The manuscript, for that is what it was, turned out to be some four hundred and twenty-nine pages.

Initially, I was rather peeved that someone should take the liberty of sending me so long a document without so much as a please or thank you. And since it was the beginning of the academic year, a season always fraught with administrative duties, my negative response to the anonymous sheaf before me was appreciably amplified.

I asked myself, whom did I know in Israel. Naturally, I had contacts with colleagues, particularly at the Hebrew University in Jerusalem and Ben-Gurion University of the Negev at Beersheba. But these were strictly formal and academic for reasons all too well known and documented. Relations between the Jewish State and Scotland remain discernibly cool to this day, sadly, even in academic circles.

Though I had little time that day, intellectual curiosity got the better of me. I scrutinised the first page. The document was quaintly handwritten in a looping, easily deciphered script. The manuscript was written in a non-academic style, not normally my cup of tea. I am a man of facts. Yet, from the very outset, I saw in the treatment an immediacy, an honesty, a genuineness that I could not resist. At once, the handling of the subject matter compelled me. A large part of the intrigue was that the manuscript appeared to have been written at the time that the events described therein unfolded.

As I had pressing work to do, I forced myself to close the parcel. But closing my mind was less easy. Leaning back, I lapsed into an ill-affordable moment of reflection. Why me? True, I thought, I had recently written a surprisingly influential paper on Edinburgh's ancient sewer system, and its role in the city's social history. The twist in my hypothesis was an attempt to show how certain historical events effected changes in attitudes towards sewers in general, and Edinburgh's sewers in particular. In the course of my paper, I did briefly refer to the Brew Moray affair. On reflection, I decided that my reference to Moray, the then Chief Rabbi of Scotland, had been couched in rather sympathetic terms. Today, few Scots possess even a passing acquaintance with the "Black Year of Twenty o-nine." Perhaps that was why, of all people in Scotland, the manuscript landed on me.

The next day, when I had more time, I untied the ribbon. Without removing the sheaf from the bottom of the box, I flipped over each delicate page into the top as I read. The text purported to cover one fateful year in the early history of Scotland's re-emergence as an independent nation-state. My first reading took a week. It thrilled me. A rare reverence overcame my ordinarily sceptical self.

Under the last page, the sender had placed an envelope. My name was written on it in rather shaky block capitals, which I presumed were indicative of old age, unaccustomed difficulty in writing English script, or both. I looked at the envelope with some inexplicable trepidation before opening it. Inside was a brief, enigmatic note in the same hand as on the envelope, but clearly different from that of the manuscript. The writer, who gave neither his name nor a date, challenged me to seek out the manuscript's true author.

I was sucked in. Every minute I could spare I devoted to my newly appointed task. Only lectures and unavoidable duties kept me from my assignment.

First I undertook the monumental task of validating the manuscript's authenticity. I began listing the titles and authors of the mountain of literature that has accumulated over the past eighty-two years concerning the events of Twenty o-nine and ten. I limited my research to works originating from Jewish, Israeli and Scottish sources alone. Next, I systematically organised, cross-referenced and read the books, papers and bibliographies I had collected. By the end of the year I had satisfied myself that "my manuscript" was authentic, a genuine one-off. Furthermore, and more exciting still, its existence appeared to be unknown in the literature.

As my investigations progressed, I kept asking myself over and over again why me, why a Scotsman in Scotland. One answer, apart from my previously mentioned sympathies, may have been the language of the manuscript — English. The Israeli finder/sender might simply have decided that a "native" English speaker, and preferably one familiar with Scottish nuances would best serve the redaction of a manuscript in English. Clearly, he understood the significance of the manuscript to both Scottish and Jewish history, but in the waning years of his life lacked the strength to continue delving into an event that took place so long ago and so far away. After all, what concern are those distant happenings to the people of Israel today?

Willy-nilly, the direction of my life was changed. I asked the university authorities for a sabbatical the following year, Twenty ninety-three. In the end, the task of editing the book has taken four years to complete. While the work was going on, I read widely on all aspects of Jewish religion, history and culture. Utilising Edinburgh University's Divinity School library to its fullest, I acquainted myself with the rudiments of Hebrew, Aramaic and Yiddish. Since there are no Jews living in Scotland today, my task was the more difficult. I used mail-com, net-post and e-ddress extensively to glean information on the more obscure and arcane questions arising out of the editing.

The text the reader is about to encounter is true to the original, complete and unaltered, except where clarity demanded it. The manuscript's punctuation left something to be desired. Also, the writer (the handwriting was graphologically uniform throughout) had the annoying habit of leaving out words. But the omissions, mostly the articles "a" and "the", generally explicated themselves from the context. The dates at the beginnings of and sometimes within the chapters have been converted from the Hebrew calendar, hence their placement in square brackets.

I have lightly annotated the text where I believe the Scottish reader, in particular, is likely to require a crutch of understanding. Also, for the benefit of the modern audience, I have appended expository remarks at the end of a number of chapters. In Dr Samuel Johnson's words: 'I have endeavoured to be neither superfluously copious, nor scrupulously reserved, and hope that I have made my author's meaning accessible...'

Professor Evlyn Tennet
Edinburgh, Twenty ninety-six

PART ONE: SUMMER AFTERNOON

Chapter I

'A Vision of Living Light'

[Monday morning, July 27, 2009]

Her hand reached out for him under the sheets.

'Brew Moray?'

Hardly opening her eyes, she found him sitting by the window. Slow-breaking daylight outlined the curve of his back. A book on his knee served for a desk. He was writing. He worked in dreamy bursts, as if taking a dictated message that would not be repeated.

To her surprise he was still wearing his prayer shawl and phylacteries.[1] One white sleeve was rolled up above the elbow. From the black box on the bare muscle, the thong coiled down his left arm, ending in a knot around the hand. On his forehead the second leather box poked out square between the eyes.

'Brew Moray—' Even in half-sleep she said his full name. She liked the music of those three syllables, which over the years she had learned to say with near-infinite variation and richness. She liked being married to him, a rabbi, a chief rabbi, the Chief Rabbi of Scotland. At their very first meeting she had told him, 'You have a face like fire, changing all the time.' The young rabbinical student, then beardless, touched his blushing cheek, and chuckled, 'Feels more like a hot flush.' Even when he made a silly joke, his voice never lost its pure rounded baritone. She called it the voice of a true Scotsman.

'What are you doing up so early?'

'Sorry, Debs, must get this down—'

Deborah wanted to ask, 'What is it that can't wait until a civilised hour?' but thought better of it. She was soon asleep again.

Brew finished. As he ran his pen over the lines, he struck out two words, and changed another for clarity. On the first, silent reading, he tested transition and continuity. For the final proof, he stood up straight, a short, but robust, wiry man. His voice rose and fell in modulated cadences that graced his speech with assurance and sincerity. As if there were a pendulum inside him, he rocked slightly in perfect time to the rhythm of his delivery.

Deborah woke up again. Brew was gently unwinding the thong from his arm. 'What was it you were doing so early, your sermon for this week?' she asked.

'No, my radio talk for this morning.'

'But I thought you'd written that days ago—' Deborah pulled away the covers. She washed her hands from the bowl by the side of her bed, and said the blessing.

Brew waited for her to finish. 'I had to rewrite it.'

---

[1] Phylacteries (Heb. *tefillin*), pointing inward on the arm and outward from the head, are perhaps best described as prayers created to wear. See Ex. 13.9,16; Deut. 6.4-9, 11.13-21. If a man is wearing his phylacteries when he hears a drowning child cry out, he is commanded not to lose time taking them off. To delay might cost the child its life. Babylonian Talmud, Tractate *Sotah* 21b; Jerusalem Talmud, Tractate *Sotah* 3:4, 19a.

'But why, Brew? It was a fine talk that you wrote.'

'I had a dream.'

'A bad dream?'

'No, not bad. But frightening. A vision of living light. It finished with a verse from the Torah. I woke up saying the words.'

'What did it say, the verse?'

'I can't tell you. You know, I cannot repeat dreamt verse, to anybody.'

'But why not?'

'Our Debs, it's too complicated—' he began, sounding sorry he'd mentioned it.

Another woman might have frowned at the "our" before her name, but right from the start of their togetherness Deborah liked it. Calling her "our Debs" made her a part of him, and an equal partner in their imaginary family. 'Brew Moray, I know when you're trying to fob me off,' she said in a bantering key.

'What I can tell you is my dream.' He rubbed his beard. 'A dream like I've never had before.' I saw a mountain on a wide plain. The mountain stood completely alone against a dark blue sky. The plain was a flat stretch of desert, as white as salt. In the next instant, I was close to the mountain. It was like I was zooming in. I saw myself climbing. The way up was hard and rocky.' Brew Moray held back before going on, as if entering deeper into his vision. 'Near the top, without warning, the way opened up into a cleft in the rock. It had been completely hidden before then. From where I stood, everything in it looked green and lush. It was like heaven, cool and bubbling with water. At the centre was a single stone, like a sepulchre. I could see letters written on it in fire, but could not make them out. I went closer to read the inscription. That's when the verse from the Torah woke me—'

Deborah's eyes, ordinarily shuttered under half-closed lids, had widened to full circles of blue. 'What does it all mean?'

'For one thing, it meant I had to write a new talk for the radio this morning.'

'I don't understand.'

'You will. The message is clear.'

'May I read it?'

'Perhaps not. Just tune in at five to eight.'

'Live?'

'That's the way they like it. More spontaneity, they say. More human. I agree.'

'Breakfast?'

'No, I'd better go to Salisbury Road,[2] just in case we have the prescribed ten bodies.[3] They'll need me to read the Torah.'

'There's hardly been a weekday service for nearly a year now.'

'I know. That's why I said my morning service here as a congregation of one. But I keep hoping.'

'When will I see you? Have you got the shopping list?'

'It's right here in my jacket pocket. Promise, I won't lose it. I've written my talk on the back.' She could visualise the concentrated compression of his tiny handwriting. 'I'll be back with the groceries around nine-thirty, ten. I have a speaking engagement with the students in Glasgow this afternoon. Always a challenge doing battle with sceptical young minds. How's your day look, our Debs?'

'More of the same. The full whack. Jabs, blood test, ultra-sound, consultation with the gyn. Brew—' He sat next to her on the bed. Always in the back of her mind, she wondered

---

[2] The site of the Edinburgh synagogue.

[3] The Orthodox Jewish tradition requires a quorum or minimum count (hence the Hebrew word *minyan* meaning "count") of ten Jewish men in order to hold a full service.

just what it was he saw in her. She saw herself minutely reflected in his gaze. Her face was pleasantly round, but featureless. Natural loose curls, like a whipped chocolate topping, were so easy to cut that Brew was her hairdresser. Half-hooded eyes made her seem permanently sleepy. Her bittersweet smile drew people to her, but her small talk almost always seemed insufficient to bring on the next stage, the deeper confidences she craved. She had no close friends, outside of Brew. 'I should be coming with you,' he said.

'No, that's not it. I'm a big girl now.' Deborah looked around searching out new words for old uncomfortable thoughts. 'It's just that, I don't know, not having children is like not having an arm or a leg. And people are so inconsiderate; they go on about how wonderful their kids are. It's like talking to the blind about going to "see" this or that. People don't think.'

'But we have Sophie's little ones around sometimes. We're a good aunt and uncle.' Brew squeezed her hands, and gave them a slight warming rub.

'That's just it. It feels like we're auntie and uncle to hundreds of children...and mother and father to none. Auntie Deborah and Uncle Brew. Every kid in the congregation, not that there are so many any more, is a child of ours. I know that I'm feeling sorry for myself, but it's our third try. I don't mind the physical pain, or even the ops. It's the feeling that I'm a recipe, a scientific experiment — and if they get the chemicals right, we have a baby. If they don't, it's disappointment. There's so much disappointment.'

Brew let his head hang.

'Don't you go feeling sorry for me. That's not what I want,' she said sharply.

'Debs, that's not it at all. I was bowing to you. What you're doing is so hard. And it all falls on you. It's you suffering for the both of us. We'll have kids of our own. I know it. I see it.'

'But if we can't—?'

'You know I won't leave you.'

'You say that every time. But deep, deep down, I know you could divorce me. I mean, if I were you, I might divorce me. You're a rabbi. And now a chief rabbi. The Law is on your side, if you decided to end our marriage. Rabbis are supposed to have children, their own children to teach.'

'C'mon, Debs, who else would marry *me*?' The ironic smile that glinted in his eyes was always the same, every time he said the now worn-out line. 'Children. So precious are they. And yet— Adam and Eve had two. And what happened? One quarter of the world's population destroyed another quarter. What do we make of that? Would it have been better if Cain had not been born, or Abel? Maybe that's why we don't have— Maybe something dreadful would happen to them or, worse, they would do something — unspeakable.'

'So then, why do we keep trying? Why frustrate ourselves? Why raise our hopes, every time we—?'

'Our brief in life is not to give up, not to waste life giving up. It's as simple as that.'

'It's so easy to say. Brew, you're not talking to the students or a congregation here. You're talking to me. This is our bedroom.'

Brew got up, and walked around the bed, as though for the first time. 'Curious place, the bedroom. Where most babies are conceived, where most folk die, or at least used to. There's no other room like it. No other place where there's so much worrying, so much dreaming, and hoping, hoping for new life, hoping against death. In a way it's a little temple of hope. Wouldn't you say? And when it comes to hope, we two here in our little temple have more to hope for than most. Our Debs, we're lucky. We have a corner on the market. Think about it. If in our prayers, we as a people can entertain hope for the dead to live again, then surely we, you and I, have no right to give up the hope between us for a child.' Brew looked at his watch. 'Oy, the time. Must be away.'

His rolling, supple stride had already carried him halfway out the door as Deborah called out, 'Brew, if you remember, buy yourself a box of *matzoh* crackers to munch. It's not on the list, but you're almost out.'

'I'll try not to forget,' he answered, his voice disappearing down the stairs.

Deborah stared an indecisive moment at the chair where Brew had sat. His prayer book lay on the seat. She saw no reason to get up. The radio was set to wake her as usual at five to eight. Putting her head down on the pillow, she turned away from the window for another hour's sleep. But sleep did not come.

* * *

The plight of the childless couple is nowhere more painfully enshrined in Jewish teaching than in the story of the Prophet Samuel. The Hebrew Bible makes it clear that Samuel's mother Hannah 'cried and did not eat' (I Sam. 1.7) not only because she could have no children and so her husband could divorce her, but also because her barrenness was cruelly taunted by Peninnah, the mother of ten children.

In his commentary on everyday life, The Book of the Pious, *the twelfth century Rabbi Judah the Pious wrote with perceptive concern, 'Parents are urged to refrain from kissing and hugging their children in public, because to do so is to show insensitivity to childless adults, who might see this and long further for the child they do not have to hug and kiss, and to orphaned children, who miss having parents to hug and kiss them.' E.T.*

Chapter II

The Handshake

Prime Minister Angus Montrose was up and waiting behind his desk. An altogether extra-large man. Tall. Wide. Fleshy. Thick-necked. Huge-headed. Everything about him was big. The signature. The gestures. The booming voice. 'Chief Rabbi, Rabbi Moray, this is...the first time, I believe, that I've had the honour.' Montrose thrust out a broad, open hand to underline his words. 'A great pleasure to meet you.'

Is it? Brew asked himself. He did not come forward to the shake the hand. Instead, the Rabbi slightly inclined his head and said, '"For them that honour ME will I honour—"'[4] Still Brew did not move. Montrose made alternative use of his empty hand, pointing to an empty chair. 'Please, Chief Rabbi, no need to stand.' Montrose seated himself. Gabled grey eyebrows furrowed his forehead. He gave the silver-white bristle over his upper lip a thoughtful rub. Brew raised his head and took his place in the proffered chair before the Scottish premier's desk. Montrose said, 'I hope that my bringing you here at such short notice hasn't inconvenienced you unduly.'

'Not at all, Mr Prime Minister. It'll delay the wife's shopping a little, that's all. Now, what was it she wanted me to add to the list?'

'Good. My driver will return you to you to the car-park at Scottish Broadcasting House...the moment our little chat is concluded—' As soon as Brew had left the soundproof studio, he was waylaid by his producer. Flustered and worried, she told him that the Prime Minister's Bureau was sending round the PM's private driver. Angus Montrose wished to speak to the Rabbi, immediately, this morning. On the way over, Brew tried to imagine the conversation—

Montrose said, 'I won't take much of your time, Rabbi—'

Brew leaned forward. 'Mr Prime Minister— Have you ever noticed that the older people become, the more their chins seem to protrude?'

At the Rabbi's suggestion, Montrose rubbed his own lower jaw. 'I honestly cannot say that I have.'

'Sorry. You haven't brought me here to hear a rabbinical lesson on chins.'

'No, but even a Gentile might—' Montrose let his thought be interrupted by the butler's entrance behind a rattling trolley, heavily laden with a silver salver, a matching silver tea service and a fine set of gilt-edged china cups and saucers. 'Coffee or tea, sir?' he asked the Rabbi.

'No thank you, neither.'

'Are you sure, Rabbi?' asked Montrose. 'The state can afford it.'

'I'm fine, thank you.'

'Hamish, my usual. Thank you.'

---

[4] I Samuel 2.30.

The butler poured half a cup of coffee, then added sugar. While stirring, he topped up the drink with a heavy-scented whisky from a crystal milk jug. The Rabbi keenly followed the ritual.

'The papers say I have a drinking problem,' said Montrose. 'Highland coffee, the perfect balance of stimulation and inebriation. Try it, Rabbi.' Hamish started to pour a cup for the Rabbi.

'Nothing for me this morning, thank you. And in any case our Sages teach us that to combine two pleasures is to enjoy neither.'

'As you like. But you don't mind if I do?' Montrose drank half the contents of his cup. 'Hamish,' he said, choking a little, 'please ask Mrs Jamieson to hold all my calls for the next twenty minutes or so.' The butler bowed from the waist with a 'Very good, sir', and departed. 'Now, Rabbi, where were we?' asked Montrose, replacing his cup on its saucer.

'I believe,' the Rabbi reminded him, 'you were mentioning something about "Gentile might".'

Montrose swallowed a stillborn smile. Abstractedly, he took up the copperhead hammer lying on his desk, and began slapping the heavy tool into the palm of his hand.

'There must be *some* story behind that,' Brew remarked. The blunt mallet seemed to possess a life of its own.

Montrose looked at the hammer. 'My working life began in a brewery — a small-town independent, long since gobbled up by the big boys—' He gauged the Chief Rabbi through watery sky-blue eyes before continuing, 'I was a big lad already then. The brewers used to call me "a one-man growth industry". Anyway, the water pipes ran high overhead. I could reach them without a ladder. It was an old-fashioned operation, even for those days. But the beer was good, the best. The piping there was all copper, with brass connections, like wing nuts. I'd have to give the connections a good tap with this hammer to loosen them, then swing the pipes around over another vat, and rejoin 'em. This copper mallet here...was the brewmaster's. He gave it to me with some good advice. "Angus," he said, "you're still young, an' a clever lad. Go back to school. Go to university. Make something of yourself. And when you get to the top, let this old copper mallet be there so you don't forget how far you've come." I did just as he said, and now his hammer's a paperweight on the Prime Minister's desk.' Montrose continued to study the hammer, as if it were a rare jewel. The edges of the barrel-shaped head were curled back viciously like teeth gone wrong. The wooden handle was short, thick, and shapeless.

The slapping started again. 'Rabbi,' he said, 'let's talk about your radio spot this morning—' Brew braced himself. If Deborah had heard his radio talk before he went on air with it, she'd have cautioned him— Impractical. Crazy. Downright dangerous. 'It was, according to the programme producer, a "radical departure" — her words — from your original text, which I understand was submitted and editorially approved days ago.'

'Correct.'

'You're an articulate, responsible man, the spiritual leader of your small but esteemed community. A community, might I add, that our society values very much in its midst. So I ask you, Rabbi, why? Why?'

'Small word, big question.'

Montrose began again. 'Right, then, Chief Rabbi. Scotland. Free. Democratic. Independent. The year — Twenty o-nine. Is the Jewish community here and now under any form of threat?' A potent wave of his hammer blocked any response but Montrose's own: 'None, absolutely none.' He put the hammer down, and leaned back. 'Scotland has an enviable record vis-a-vis its minorities, the Jewish community in particular. The Jews here have prospered. The practice of your rites and religion is protected by law. Your social and economic lives are unhindered. Jews are welcomed in the highest echelons of the nation's academic, medical and commercial establishments and, of course, the government and its institutions. Judith Levitt, my honourable Minister of Justice, as I hardly need mention to you, is a member of your faith group. Furthermore, as I'm sure you're perfectly aware, Scotland has excellent diplomatic and cultural relations with the Jewish State. Our ambassador to Israel, Mr Muriel, is one of your own. We have venerable institutions in the Holy Land — the Scottish Hospice on the Sea of Galilee, the Tabetha School in Old Jaffa and, right in the heart of Jerusalem, St Andrew's Scottish Church and, bang next door to the church, Dunhoorn Castle, our proud embassy. So, humour an old man, Rabbi. Why?' Montrose pulled himself forward; he renewed the beat of his hammer.

The Rabbi answered, 'There are two kinds of Jews: those who are home,[5] and those who are on the way.'

'Yes, Rabbi, but there's only one kind of Scot: the kind who stays in Scotland. The spirit of your call on the radio this morning was divisive. It was a call for disunity. Now what are *we* going to do about it?'

Brew was not comfortable with Montrose's "we". He took up the challenge. 'The day after we won independence from England, Jewish leaders met in Edinburgh, in our synagogue in Salisbury Road. I was elected the first ever Chief Rabbi of Scotland. I felt very proud to be Scottish that day.'

'But now, Rabbi, now where is your heart?'

Brew Moray, black eyes glinting, put his right hand on his breast and said, 'My Scottish heart is right here.'

'That's not what you were saying on the radio this morning.'

'At the risk of sounding impertinent, Prime Minister, when you were in my position with respect to His Majesty's government, did you not say similar things on the radio?'

'The things I said were a matter of national self-preservation. Scotland was nothing more than a provincial frontier with a national football team. The English would have destroyed us, if we'd let them.'

'Exactly. And I claim the same right of self-preservation for Jewish people that you claimed for the Scottish people. I'm simply asking for *our* future. No more, no less. Prime Minister, this country would not be where it is today without your vision and able leadership. You have a grateful nation behind you, including the Jewish community, if I may say so. But...we're a tiny community. We're cut off. Scotland's independence has marginalised us Scottish Jews to the point of extinction.'

'You do realise, Chief Rabbi, that you could be prosecuted. That's not a threat, but hypothetically speaking — there are grounds—'

'Mr Prime Minister, for the Jew there is no higher law than the law of the land. But, in any conflict between the Scottish Constitution and Jewish survival, I—'

Again, the hammer stroked the air imperiously. 'I want to understand you, Chief Rabbi, but you've got to understand *me*. Frankly, your comments were potentially damaging to this government's policies. Talk to Judith Levitt. You'll have a common language with her.'

'Because she's Jewish?'

'No. Certainly not. It's only that she happens to be Scotland's Number One constitutional lawyer, and a member of my Cabinet. She can explain things to you better than I.'

The Rabbi let Montrose's suggestion go unanswered. To fill the silence, Montrose reached for his coffee. He drained the remaining contents in one gulp. His face flushed with the alcohol. A twisted network of red and violet capillaries mapped the skin of his nose and cheeks. 'But why this morning, Rabbi?' asked Montrose.

'Because I was woken up by a dream.' The truth sounded like madness.

---

[5]That is, living in the Land of Israel.

'A dream? Isn't that...religious fanaticism?'

'It would be, if I were a fanatic. But I'm not. Don't you see, Mr Prime Minister? We need to leave to survive. If we stay here, we'll be — how did you put it, sir? — "gobbled up by the big boys", just as surely as that little independent brewery was.'

'That was different. That was business.'

'You're quite right, Prime Minister. It was different. I'm talking historical revelation. It is written—' Montrose began to show his impatience. Slap, hammer, slap. '...enshrined, in the Jewish Constitution, if you will, received by Moses on Mt Sinai and handed down from his generation to this. If a Jew dreams a verse from the Bible, he or she is obligated to act on it, in other words, to do as the verse commands.'[6]

Montrose's jutting chin now betrayed more than just his age. 'This verse you dreamt, what did it say?'

'I regret, Prime Minister, that I am not at liberty to reveal the text to you, or to anyone for that matter. That remains between me and the MAKER OF DREAMS.'[7]

'In other words, Rabbi, the content of your radio talk was not your own idea?'

'I can't say that I think of the HEAVENLY KING OF KINGS as a hostile foreign power — if that's what you are suggesting.'

'The point is, Chief Rabbi, I want you to retract your call.'

Brew cupped his lower jaw and beard. 'No, Mr Montrose, with all due respect, I cannot do that.'

'Call it a clarification, then.'

'What is there to clarify? The Jewish community can no longer stay here.' Brew closed his eyes, as he spoke to himself in an undertone, 'Now what was it the wife told me not to forget, that wasn't written on her shopping list?'

Montrose's mallet abruptly ceased. 'Then at least I want your undertaking that you will not pursue this issue any further.' The Prime Minister waited for the Rabbi's answer.

Brew Moray rose, causing Montrose to look up. 'I can't.'

'You realise the consequences for Scotland if world opinion believes we're running some sort of anti-Semitic regime here—'

'I can't.'

Montrose's eyes flashed. But the rage in them quickly dissipated, only to be followed by a glare more sinister and intimidating than anger. The old man rose. 'Then there is no more to be said about the matter. One more moment of your valuable time, Rabbi, while I—' he flicked on the intercom, 'Mrs Jamieson, please have Mr Gunn available to chauffeur the good rabbi back to his car, and would you arrange for Mr Kenneth Keller to see me as soon as possible. We have urgent party business to discuss.'

'Yes, Prime Minister, and the ambassador is here; he's hopping mad—' The woman's voice sounded harassed.

'Tell him not now, Jamieson. I'll see him presently. Ask him to be patient—' His finger angrily released the talk button.

Montrose concluded the meeting in a mood of avuncular grandeur. Extending four thick, stubby fingers and a short, erect thumb, he said, 'Rabbi Moray, let me shake your hand in friendship, and wish you and your clan well.' Brew held out his hand. Montrose's vice-grip eclipsed the Rabbi's whole hand. He jerked down, once, hard, and held on. Brew looked straight into the old man's narrowed, squinting eyes. There was no mistaking the

---

[6]The Talmud says, "Rabbi Yohanan said: 'If on rising in the morning, a biblical verse comes to one's lips — this is a small prophecy.'" Tractate *Berachot* 55b.

[7]The Talmud elucidates: 'Raba said: "Although I [God] hide my face from them [the people of Israel], I shall speak to them [individually] in a dream."' Talmud, Tractate *Hagigah* 5b.

cold blue menace. When the handshake was over, the Rabbi openly rubbed his sore right hand and muttered, 'Whom the LORD loves, HE crushes with pain.'[8]

'Is it some sort of Jewish tradition, Rabbi, to rub your hand after you people shake?'

'Aye, a very old tradition, but one not usually practised much these days,' answered the Rabbi. Montrose pressed the buzzer for his butler.

'That's it,' remembered Brew, 'one box of *matzos*, the bread of affliction.' Awkwardly, with his left hand, he removed a folded paper from his inside jacket pocket, and shook it open by a corner. His wife's shopping list. On the back was his radio talk.

* * *

In the heart of Argyllshire lies Loch Awe, a large body of water somewhat inaccessible, even to this day. At the lake's northern extreme is a spit of land, where the outline of a castle's foundations can still clearly be seen.

Dunhoorn Castle, a ruined keep dating from the sixteenth and seventeenth centuries, was removed stone by stone from this site in the year Two thousand and four. The stones were brought to the Holy Land, as a gift to the Israeli people. In Jerusalem the castle ruins were reconstructed, restored to their original height and roofed over. The interior was fully modernised. Popularly known as the "Scottish Castle", the edifice was situated on a rise of barren, rocky land next to St Andrew's Scottish Church, between the defunct Turkish railway station and the Old City walls.

In Two thousand and seven, a few short weeks after declaring full independence from Great Britain, the newly formed Scottish government took over the entire top floor of the castle for its embassy in Israel. The first ambassador was a Jew, Donald Muriel. E.T.

---

[8]The Talmud records that "Rav Huna says, 'Whom the Holy One, blessed be He, loves, He crushes with painful sufferings.'" Tractate *Berachot* 5a.

Chapter III

Fear

[Monday evening, July 27, 2009]
Brew Moray pressed his shopping list between thumb and forefinger, hard. Behind him the double doors opened.

A thin, desolate-faced man sideswiped the Chief Rabbi in the doorway. He had one blue and one brown eye. The PM's bodyguards and a harried secretary followed a step behind him. She apologised, 'I couldn't stop him, Prime Minister! He barged right by me.'

'Mr Ambassador—' Montrose greeted him, 'A great pleasure to see you—'

Left momentarily unattended, Brew looked back. The doors were shut. The secretary was exchanging a significant glance with the butler. Sensing the touch of the Rabbi's eye on her, she broke off to see him out. As he walked with her, he tried to slip the shopping list back into his inside jacket pocket with one hand. 'Here, sir,' she said noticing his difficulty, 'let me help you. I'm Mrs Jamieson, the PM's receptionist.' They stopped and she held his jacket open for him. 'Thank you, you're very kind,' he said.

The Prime Minister's chauffeur was waiting for them in the reception room. Mrs Jamieson said, 'Sir...Mr Gunn will run you back to your car.' There was a skittishness in her voice. Brew hardly heard the chauffeur's 'Right, sir, after me, please.'

Brew came home late — with the shopping. The house was empty. He cancelled his students' meeting in Glasgow, hitched up the trailer, and left the plastic food bags in the car. As soon as Deborah came in from her appointment at the fertility clinic, he announced they were going camping.

'Brew Moray? Have you left your senses?' She felt somehow crippled, as if something were missing. He gave her no kiss, no hug. He always asked her about her treatment.

For an extended moment, Brew held her in his gaze before he said, 'No, our Debs. The opposite. The fog's lifting. It's all becoming clear, too clear.'

Brew drove vaguely north and west. Again and again he told his story. He was compelled not to let go of a single detail. 'I remember now, that's exactly what he said—' and reconstructing every exchange, every word, he made them holy. But above all, his narrative dwelt on 'the dark flare in Montrose's eyes' and 'the grip of his handshake'. At the end of each retelling, he took his right hand from the wheel, studied it, trying to re-live the physical pain which, from the ache in his tone, he seemed to regret was no longer with him. 'I wish,' he said accusingly, 'I could cut off this hand.'

'Don't say such things, Brew,' said Deborah fearfully. 'You're a better man than he is—'

'Please, Debs, don't patronise me.' His anger directed at her was for himself.

'And anyway he didn't hurt you that badly. He could have broken your hand.'

'Exactly. And I couldn't have stopped him.'

'Where are we going, Brew?' She hadn't asked before.

'I don't know. Except, for the time being, in a different direction.'

Deborah stared out the window. Daylight was still high in the north. All afternoon low banks of flying cloud had swept over the land, dragging behind them fast-racing shadows. In between the misty rains, the crests of weatherworn mountains rose to full majesty against patches of icy blue sky. Black swarms of midges left their dead on the windscreen. Waves of low-growing yellow scrub, coniferous bush and wild flowers vied for ascendancy along the banks of burns and rivers. Sheep and longhaired cattle dotted the steep-sided mountain meadows that reached down like green fingers into the glens.

Deborah stared out, but was looking inward, thinking. The man she had married was habitually a man of cycles — prayer three times a day, the Sabbath once a week, the festivals and fasts in their seasons and, sometimes, a television football match on Sundays. He did not easily tolerate surprises. He enjoyed a life of predictability: regular meals, sufficient sleep, familiar people, a schedule of activities, routine work times. His dynamism derived from complete control. Had there been children in his life, in their lives together, things would have been very different.

In the late afternoon Brew stopped the car and trailer at a lay-by for their first rest and food since setting out. After eating, Deborah fell asleep.

She slept until a clunking and jerking woke her. It was still light out, but growing dusky. All around them loomed the solid black outlines of mountain shapes. Groggy, she looked at her watch — ten past ten — then at Brew.

'We've run out of petrol,' he said.

'Where are we?' asked Deborah, alarmed.

'Don't know. Somewhere in the Highlands. West Highlands.'

'There's nothing out there. What do we do now?'

'Walk.'

'To where—?' Her voice cracked.

'Does it make any difference?'

'Why can't we just set up camp here, right here?' asked Deborah. 'Or sleep in the car tonight? It's not too cold in summer.'

'We could, but I'm a fugitive. Out here on the open road, the police might pick us up for illegal camping, or loitering. '

'Brew, I've never heard you talk like this before. A fugitive? You haven't done anything criminal.'

'Then why am I running?'

'Ask yourself—'

'Debs, that's what I've been doing all afternoon. And I can't find an answer I can grasp. I know this is hard for you. Try to understand. I've got to find a place where my prayers will speak to me. I feel we're near. Does that make any sense?'

'No.'

Taking only Deborah's handbag and a small rucksack, Brew and Deborah left the car, and began trekking. The road hugged the contours of a long loch. Everywhere, sheep glowed in the last glimmers of daylight. The sounds of night insects and lowing cows wove themselves into the dusk. A quarter moon hung low behind a row of hydroelectric pylons dangling wires like giant marionettes.

There was no traffic on the road. The loch narrowed into the muffled surge of a fast-rushing river. An hour after dark, they came to a solitary, brooding mansion. Peeling from neglect, the sign said, Tom— Hotel. From inside, dogs barked. An angry shout from a high window sent them away.

For the first time in his sheltered life Brew felt the flicker of fear.

* * *

Chapter IV

The Frasers

[Monday night-Tuesday morning, July 27-28, 2009]
'How much further can we walk?' asked Deborah, aching and shivering with the night cold. A misty drizzle started to fall.

'There—' he answered her, 'there's a sign, over there on that driveway.' The postbox read "Fraser".

The stone house at the bottom of the way was dark. A high wall at the back enclosed the farmyard, barn and storehouses. The front garden was open; a gravel path lined with whitewashed stones led to the house. Brew motioned Deborah to stay behind him, as he stepped up to the door. He raised a hand to the door-knocker, but held back. A fresh spasm of anxiety made him look about. He spotted an inscription chiselled into the lintel. In the moonlight, he had difficulty reading:

A. FRASER, 1889
On the seventh day HE
rested and was refreshed. (Ex. 31.17)

Taking heart from the quotation, Brew Moray knocked. A dog's rapid bark answered immediately, and went on until an orange light came through the window. Footfalls accompanied a man's voice shouting 'Puppy, quiet, there'. From behind the door, he asked, 'Who is it? At this hour of the night?'

'We're lost; our car ran out of petrol. Can you help us?' answered Brew.

A woman's voice called out. The man behind the door answered, 'I dinnae ken; see to the children.' He threw the bolt and turned the key. The door opened a crack. The man, square and squat in long underwear and hastily thrown-on trousers, held a crooked stick. His curious eyes thoroughly searched Brew and Deborah.

'Mr Fraser?' said Brew Moray. 'My wife and I, we're lost. We are sorry to bother you so late, but can you help us?'

From behind, Fraser's wife asked, 'Who are they, Fraser?'

'Strangers.' He asked them: 'Where d'you come from?'

'Edinburgh,' said the little man with a slight shiver.

'Don't sound too sure about that. You don't look like anglers. Run out of petrol, ya say?'

'Yes.' Brew wondered if he shouldn't have said 'Aye'.

'How d'ya get sa lost in the ferst place?'

Before Brew could say, the woman piped up, 'Fraser, can you no see, these folk are in need of somethin' warmin'. They're steamin' cold and scared. You can ask yer questions inside. Come in,' she said, 'and sit down.'

'Mother,' he objected, but the offer was made and he could not withdraw it.

There was only a paraffin lantern inside. The woman sat her guests down on the settee and energetically prodded the dying hearth while throwing on some kindling. 'Back to your beds,' shouted Fraser to the children's three ghostly outlines. He chased them back upstairs with a swing of the lantern. The woman of the house disappeared into kitchen 'to pu' on a kettle for some tea'. In the gloom of the livening fire, Brew and Deborah looked around the room. Deborah sensed that they were being watched. The unsure firelight barely reached to the top of the stairs. A girl with long hair was resting her chin on the banister. Her eyes, catching the orange from the crackling flame, glowed like fireflies. 'Elen,' said her father, coming back dressed, 'back to bed. Tomorrow—'

Mrs Fraser served them aromatic tea. Brew pulled a face at the first taste, but Deborah asked, 'How did you know I don't drink regular tea?'

'My honey-sweetened horehound tea — remedies colds and coughs even before you catch them. Drink up, now. The men don't like it, but in our family, it's the women that brew the tea.'

'And the trouble.' Fraser's remark drew no feminine fire.

Tea was sipped for some moments in awkward silence. All four tried not to be seen looking at each other over their cups. The Rabbi kept his cap on; Deborah self-consciously stared at her long dress. At last Fraser asked, 'Where'd'you say yer motor was, Mr—?'

'Moray. The car's two, maybe three hours walk down the main road.'

'We'll help you look for it in the morning.'

'We don't actually have a guestroom,' apologised Mrs Fraser. 'House is too small for that, or may be we've got too many young ones about. But the gerl can sleep in the loft tonight, and you can have her room. I'll just organise the bed for two.'

'Oh, no,' said Deborah, 'we couldn't. Let us take the loft. I'm sure it's comfortable. Please, we don't want to put you out.'

'You're not' came the girl's voice from the top of the stairs.

'Elen—' said her father, exasperated.

'I've made my bed,' she carried on without notice. 'And, anyway, I like sleeping in the loft in summer.'

'Now that's what I call good Christian hospitality—' chirped Mrs Fraser. Both Brew and Deborah hid behind a drink of tea, as the little woman continued, 'Now, I say we all go to bed and tomorrow we talk. Toilet and washroom are at the back of the house.'

'How can we thank you?' asked Brew.

'Tomorrow,' returned Fraser, resigned.

When Brew and Deborah came down in the morning, a large cooked breakfast of savoury smelling sausage and fried eggs was on the table. From a shelf over the deep sink a portable radio wired to a bundle of batteries blared news and music from a local station. The plaid-shirted Fraser and two sons were too busy tucking in to take notice of anything but their plates. The brothers were identical twins, thin-faced, square-shouldered, fourteen or fifteen years old. Their sister, a year or two younger with lively pecan-brown eyes, freckles and glowing red hair, immediately stopped her work and looked up with a welcoming tilt. At the spattering stove Mrs Fraser put an arm around the girl's shoulder, and asked how the couple had slept.

'Very well, thank you,' said Deborah, trying not to breathe. The cooking vapours unsettled her.

'El,' her father said mildly between chews, 'your mouth's open an' there's nae words in't.' Her brothers' grins smarted.

The girl had forgotten to stop looking. Seeing the blood come to her face, Deborah's shaded eyes showed her kindness. And the young girl inwardly welcomed the strange woman's sympathy.

Their hostess said, 'Go out and wash up. Breakfast is ready.'

Outside, Deborah said to Brew, 'We have to tell them.'

'Why?' he asked. 'We don't have to tell them what they haven't asked us.'

While Deborah washed her hands and face, the Rabbi said a curtailed morning service.

Back in the house, Fraser said, 'Sit down, folks. Make yersels at home. Plenty to go around. By the way, this is the wife Becky, our boys Ross and Crom, and daughter Elen — with one "l". My name's Alan — also one "l".'

'But I call him Fraser, and everybody calls me Mother,' said Becky.

The Rabbi touched his cap, and tipped his head. 'Brewster Moray, and this is Deborah, my wife.'

Fraser repeated the name thoughtfully, 'Moray... Brewster,' as though he recognised but could not immediately place it. Neither Brew nor Deborah volunteered more.

'Breakfast anyone?' invited Becky, proudly eyeing her table's bounty.

The pair of them looked at each other. Deborah said, 'Thank you, really, but I'm sorry, we can't eat anything warm or cooked for now; and no meat.'

Becky frowned in disappointment. 'No meat? Why not?' She looked at the full skillet on her stove. 'A person cannae live without protein.'

Deborah went on, 'We brought our own pots and pans and crockery, but it's all in the trailer with the car. Perhaps after breakfast Mr Fraser will take us. We have money.'

'We don't want yer money,' said Alan. 'I'll finish ma breakfast, an' we'll be away.'

'Father, can I come, too?' asked Elen.

'Is that all right, Mother, if El comes along?' The twins grazed their sister with looks of glumness and jealousy. She paid them no attention. Deborah's compassionate smile, though, did not go unnoticed.

Becky wasn't listening. 'At least a cup of roast dandelion root coffee?' she asked, holding a pot under the Morays' noses.

Brew looked doubtful, and said, 'Sounds... interesting, but no thank you.'

Deborah kept a straight face. 'Oh, never mind him. He's an orthodox coffee drinker, but I'll try a cup, please.'

Bouncing along the road in the Fraser's ancient Range Rover, Alan explained, 'The Frasers are crofters, sheep men, and proud of being "Wee Frees".[9] Most of the population from around Glen Garry, here, migrated to Canada 'bout two hundred year ago, but Frasers stayed.' After that, little was said until Elen, sitting in the back seat with Deborah, came out with 'Why's he wearin' that black hat under his cap?'

Instinctively, the Rabbi pushed his cap down. But it was too late. He twisted around, looked her in the eye, and said, 'Because we're Jewish.'

Alan's foot slipped and the Rover jolted.

'Do you know what Jewish is?' asked Deborah.

'Nooo,' answered Elen, 'not exactly.'

Alan slammed on the brakes and burst out with, 'Jews— Now I get it. You dinnae want to leave bonny Scotland. You're running away from that Chief fella I heard on the radio yesterday mornin', the madman who says all the Jews have ta leave Scotland now, before it's too late. You heard him, too, right, Elen?' The girl was lost, gawping at Deborah. Excited and driven by charity, Alan went on impetuously, 'Stop as long as you will. Scotland's your country. And a Fraser's house is your home for as long as you like. I mean it. Don't I, El?'

The girl, her rich red hair wind-blown and tousled, winked at Deborah, 'He means it.'

---

[9]The Church of Scotland Free, a break-away grouping of the Presbyterian Church.

They found the Morays' car and trailer. After Alan poured in petrol from a jerrycan, the Morays followed Fraser and Elen home. Over the last mile, Fraser raced ahead, ran in and told Mother the good news.

In the privacy of their own car, Brew maintained, 'But the Frasers are good, trusting people; we're welcome with them— I say we stay, if they let us.'

Deborah argued, 'They're a family, not well off. Perhaps not destitute, but life's not easy, the way they try to save electricity with lanterns and radios on batteries.'

'That's the way country folk live these days.'

'Brew, GOOD LORD, you're Chief Rabbi of Scotland, you can't just drop out.'

'Watch me.'

'And what about our chances for a child of our own? I'm in the middle of my cycle. I can't just stop—'

He glanced into her watery eyes, and said softly, 'We'll have another chance at the IVF. I know it. I see it.'

There was no arguing with Brew Moray when he said, 'I know it. I see it.'

* * *

Chapter V

The Fast

[Wednesday-Thursday, July 29-30, 2009]
Brew Moray said, 'From sundown tonight until sundown tomorrow, we fast; no food or drink may pass our lips. It is the saddest day of the year — the ninth day of the Hebrew month of Ab — and we are officially in mourning.' He said no more. The Frasers looked puzzled, but were too polite to ask questions.

Before the sunset, Brew and Deborah removed their shoes and ate a meal of hard-boiled eggs, red lentils and home-baked bread dipped in ash from the fireplace. They drank only water. From dusk, they sat on low stools, heads bowed; the Rabbi chanted mournfully.[10] Both cried.

Later in the evening, Alan asked, 'Brew, what's all this about? You got us feelin' low, too.'

From his low place, Brew explained, 'On this night, more than three thousand years ago, our forefathers and mothers cried out at the prospect of living as a free people in their own land.[11] And because Israel "wept without cause," today became a day of national tragedy.[12] On this same day the First and Second Temples in Jerusalem were destroyed. And there were other calamities. After the destruction of the Second Temple, a year later — to the day — the Romans razed Jerusalem to the ground and scattered her inhabitants around the world. On this day in Twelve-ninety, King Edward I signed the edict that compelled his Jewish subjects to leave England. Two hundred and two years later, also on the ninth day of Ab, Queen Isabella and King Ferdinand expelled the Jews from Spain after a thousand golden years. And today, ninety-five years ago, the First World War broke out.'

'I don't get it,' said Alan, looking down at Brew. 'I mean, I don't mean to be disrespectful, but why cry over a load of broken old stones, and a collection of coincidences that have built up over the centuries?' All were listening.

Brew stroked his untrimmed beard.[13] 'There's no need to apologise when asking a difficult question. It needs to be asked and to be answered. Many Jews ask the same question, and most Jews these days scoff at the idea of a day of national mourning. "What for?" they ask. "Aren't there more important, more immediate things to be sad about: the environment, people dying in the streets from disease and starvation, the constant threat of war and natural disaster?"'

'That's what I mean,' said Alan, coming down on one knee. 'How can you folks just pick out a day and say, let's mourn? I mean, turn it on and turn it off?'

'The answer is simple. If we Jews don't cry for Jerusalem — at least some of us — who will? But it's more than that. We set aside this day to ask ourselves, "How?" *How* did

---

[10]The Book of Lamentations is traditionally recited on the eve of the ninth of Ab.

[11]Rabbi Moray refers to Numbers 14.1: "The whole community raised their voice, and broke into a loud cry, and the people wept that night." This verse describes the Israelites' balking at the frightening report that the spies brought back to them of their Promised Land. That night of lamentation, according to rabbinical tradition, was the night of the ninth of Ab.

[12]Because Israel "wept without cause, [this day was] set aside for weeping throughout the generations to come." Talmud, Tractate *Ta'anit* 29a.

[13]As a sign of mourning in the nine days preceding the ninth day of Ab, it is customary not to cut the hair or pare the nails.

all our sorrows come about? Then, when we realise that we brought our sorrows on ourselves, we cry. We don't cry for broken stones; we cry for the Jerusalem that was, and that we turned our backs on. I suppose, we're really crying for the broken stones within us all. We're not just mourning the past; we're mourning the future, the future that our past has mapped out for us. But at the close of the day, there always comes an end to our fasting and mourning. This, we also know.'

'It seems we all have something to mourn, even if we don't fast,' said Becky.

The Rabbi stayed awake all night, crying without tears. Deborah slept in short spells on the hard floor. Whenever she woke up, she wept silently until she fell back to sleep.

At daybreak Brew stood to say prayers, but without his fringed white cloth and his little black boxes.[14] Afterwards, he sat, hunching over more and more with each passing hour.

In the brilliant afternoon Brew turned deathly grey. Beads of sweat gathered on his brow, his eyelids fluttered and he started to reel. Deborah caught him in her arms as he fell off his stool. 'Brew?' she said, 'What's wrong? What is it?'

He took her hand. She tightened her fingers around his. 'I've just had a premonition,' he said with dry eyes. 'I saw a man lying in a heap on the ground.'

'We must go back, now. Please, Brew,' she sobbed, 'now, today.' Her whole being shuddered.

'Deborah. Try not to cry,' he said, wiping the tears from her cheeks. 'We've got to stay. There's something here for us, both of us. I know it. We only have to find it. It all seems mad, I know, but there's a time for madness—'

Deborah set her face like marble and said nothing.

At the end of the fast, after taking only a few bites of her first meal in twenty-six hours, Deborah stood up at the table. All eyes embraced her. 'My goodness,' she said, as a growing smile eclipsed her face, 'I almost forgot. Brew, it's your birthday today!'[15]

Everyone but Mother laughed. She was put out because she had not been told in advance. As soon as supper was over, Mother, Elen, and Deborah collaborated to bake Brew a 'kosher' cake.

When the cake came out of the oven, Mother proudly asked Brew, 'Eh, how many candles?'

He paused. 'This year? Forty sorrows.'

Alan chuckled, 'Some day for a birthday. But it's like we sheep men say: the lambs grow older, even on foul days. Right, Mother?'

* * *

While in the Highlands, Rabbi Brew Moray passed his fortieth birthday. Jewish wisdom teaches: "At forty years one attains insight" (Ethics of the Fathers 5.24). The name Moray begins with the Hebrew letter "mem", whose "gematria" or numerical equivalent is forty.

The number forty is not a mystical number like seven, or a spiritual number like three, nor the perfect number, one. Forty is a natural number: the number of weeks from conception to birth. In the Hebrew Bible it is no coincidence that Noah's flood lasted forty days, that Moses stayed on the mountain forty nights, that the Israelite ex-slaves wandered in the wilderness forty years. Nature and history turned forty into a traditional period of development and ripening. With the culmination of any forty-long cycle of preparation, the task, the mission, the trial begins. E. T.

---

[14] The *tallit* (fringed prayer garment) and the *tefillin* (phylacteries) are not worn on the ninth of Ab, yet another sign of mourning.

[15] According to Jewish prophecies the Messiah will be born on the ninth of Ab.

Chapter VI

Manny Moray

[Thursday-Friday, July 30-31, 2009]
Anna Moray allowed herself a lie-in. The day was miserably overcast. It was also the ninth of Ab. The twist in her empty stomach made no sense. She felt no tears, either real or imagined, for Jerusalem, or the ruined Temple. How could she? She'd never seen the place.

She'd begun fasting only late in life, more out of sense of solidarity with her son, the Rabbi, than for any other reason. Since she could neither bathe nor breakfast this morning, she'd reckoned that the only thing an hour's extra sleep would delay was the dog's usual morning walk. As it was the day would be long enough.

For many of the same motives as Anna, her husband Manny also fasted. He'd gone to the synagogue. He had not kissed Anna "good morning" when he woke up. Physical contact was not in keeping with the day of mourning. But unlike Anna, he'd fasted all his life on this day, because that's what his father from the "Old Country" had done. Yet Immanuel Moray had always worked in his younger days. Work was allowed, and he had had little patience to sit in synagogue all day long listening to old men pining.

But now that he was retired, and his son was not only a rabbi, but the first Chief Rabbi of Scotland, he felt that he had little choice but to go public. His face would be missed if he were not in synagogue. His first-born Neville could take care of the business.

Against the chill, Anna wrapped herself in her dressing gown. As she brushed out her grey hair, her free hand opened the bedroom door to let in the dog. He was not there; he always pawed at the door, anxious to go outside. She appreciated her old schnauzer's friskiness first thing. It made her feel younger. The cold air in the bedroom diverted her concern from the dog. Anna pulled down the sash window. It being so dull outside, she drew open the curtains to let in more light. She glanced into the front garden. Her throat constricted, muffling her first shriek.

Anna stopped half way down the stairs. Screaming through cupped hands, 'It's Manny! It's Manny, out in the garden! Aggie!' Mrs Christmas came running through from the lounge, red duster in hand. When she saw Anna on the stairs, the duster dropped to the floor.

The old dog, so very disciplined, had been scratching and whimpering at the front door for an hour. Now he came scooting back to the bottom of the stairs, frantically bounding and wagging his short tail.

Manny Moray was no longer a man, just a faceless lump under a rumpled mac on the garden path. Anna fell on him as though she wanted to join him.

After calling emergency, Mrs Christmas came outside. She held Anna's convulsing shoulders and let her sob out her initial shock. After some long moments, as gently as she could, the ageing housekeeper pulled Anna away.

The old schnauzer, paws straight out in front, remained lying flat on the grass, a respectful yard from the body. The wail of sirens was in the air. Immanuel Moray died later on, during what turned into a brilliant summer afternoon.

The funeral was the next day.[16]

In her many years in service with the Moray family, Aggie Christmas had been to many Jewish funerals. But never had she seen so many mourners crowded around the pit. The whole community, it seemed, turned out for Manny. She thought that she knew every Jew in Scotland, but there were strangers, new faces she'd not seen before.

Part of the family and yet not, the housekeeper was able to stand back without notice or comment. She was uneasy for the widow's sake. She openly shielded her eyes and turned her head away from the graveside. She was looking for the Chief Rabbi, hoping that he would turn up. His wife Deborah was also not to be seen.

As she searched for Brew Moray, she used her eyes to keep Ford Christmas at a safe distance. She did not want to see him too closely. She had mercifully forgotten the finer details of his rugged face. Her broad memory picture of him contained only his height and handsome British army uniform. She watched him with Neville, shaking hands, gravely talking. He'd placed a black paper skullcap on his head for the occasion.

'Mrs Dougal-Christmas?'

She jumped. 'Did no one ever teach you, young lady, not to creep up on people when they're no' looking?'

There was no apology — only a second asking: 'Mrs Agnes Dougal-Christmas?' The inquisitor was like no breed of Jew she'd ever seen before. The woman was short, dark-skinned with a bush of kinky-wavy hair that was the gold-orange of an Indian summer sun. Her eyes were hidden behind fashionable, bubble-lens sunglasses. She had an accent, too.

'Yes— I'm she,' said the housekeeper, making a point of correctness. 'Do I know you?'

'That's not important for now. I'm looking for Rabbi Moray. You wouldn't have heard—'

'No, I wouldn't. What is it with me? Everybody's asking me that question today. Is there an "Information" sign stuck to ma back?' She peeked over her shoulder as if there were. When she turned around again, the dark woman was gone.

'Coming home without Manny—' Anna held back the end of the thought. She stopped in the garden and stared up. The old stone manse, their home for forty-five years, now stood before her a cold and lifeless monument. The two huge bays on either side of the entrance revealed a dining room and a salon as static as shop window displays. She remembered. Manny had impulsively bought the house for her and his growing family of three young children. She hadn't thought about that day for years: how Manny came home, papers in hand, so proud; and how angry she'd been with him for not consulting with her. In his defence he said he'd bought the place, 'because it was safe behind a high stone wall, and because a house on Canaan Lane had to be good for *Yidden*'.[17] The day that Anna first saw her new home, the afternoon sun was streaming in through the big bay windows.

The dog came out of nowhere to be by her side. Yet the animal did not acknowledge her presence. Instead, half-sitting, half-lying, he guarded the spot where he last saw his master. Anna knelt down to stroke his greying, wire-haired head and neck. His sharp ears

---

[16]My correspondents give three reasons for the haste of Jewish funerals: 1) swift recognition of the finality of death; 2) to keep the Biblical injunction of returning the body and soul to their sources as quickly as possible (see Eccles. 12.7); and 3) out of respect for the living to whom God gave noses.

[17]*Yidden* (singular, *Yid*), Yiddish for Jews. Properly pronounced *yeed* and *yeedden*.

flopped dolefully, and Anna said to him, 'Creatures understand so much more than we folk. I shouldn't be surprised if you knew exactly where our Brew is.'

Lagging back behind the widow, the tall man impatiently rolled his eyes and mumbled impatiently. 'Nev,' hissed the woman next to him, her face puffed with grief. 'Sophie,' he said impatiently, 'she's stalling.' Anna stared up at her bickering children. 'Mother,' said Neville, coming forward to offer her a hand up, 'it's time we went in; you've got to go in sometime.' Ignoring her son, Anna turned to his tearful sister, 'Sophie, where are our grandchildren?'

'They're at home, Mummy, with Jake. We haven't told them yet. C'mon, Mummy, come inside.' Sophie bent down to help her mother up.

Anna said, 'Let's all go in.'

Neville lingered behind with the black and tan schnauzer a while longer. '"Let's go in,"' he repeated, and scratching the animal's head, he muttered, 'Isn't that what I said?'

* * *

Chapter VII

The Shepherd

[From Monday, August 3, 2009]

'Mumps—' Fraser murmured for the third time. 'All right, Mother, you haven't said a word since we started home. What's gnawin' ya?'

In the rear seat of the Range Rover, Becky stroked Elen's fevered head on her lap. 'You know perfectly well, Fraser,' she said in a blistering tone.

Alan imagined the narrow-eyed look on Mother's face, but wasn't giving in. 'If I knew perfectly well, I wouldn't be askin'.'

'The incubation period— The doctor said, "two to three weeks". *They* could no' 've infected her. That's what you were sayin', in so many words, that all their fastin' and incantations last week sickened her, but they cannae 've—'

Shrugging, Alan mumbled, 'Seems the ride home from Fort Augustus gets bumpier every time we drive it.' After another half mile of Mother's fuming silence, he said, 'Right then, I admit it. I thought wrong. But in my book, it's nae what a person thinks, it's what he says and does that counts. I did tell them they could stop with us for as long as they like, and I meant it.'

She let a few minutes pass before offering a morsel of peace. 'Any good recipes in that paper?' While Becky and Elen waited to see the doctor, Fraser had bought a few needed supplies in town, and a newspaper to pass the time.

'Wouldn't know, Mother. Dinnae get that far yet.'

'Any news?'

'Depends on what you call news.'

Becky decided to be angry with him a while longer. 'I don't know why you waste our hard-earned money on foolish papers in the ferst place.' Becky looked down at Elen. Her rough fingertips feather-touched the painful swelling in the neck just below the ear lobe. In her sleep the child's intelligent brow wrinkled a little, and so prompted Becky to wallow in her oldest, most heartfelt refrain: 'I ask you, what kind of future can our Elen possibly expect on an isolated sheep farm?'

Alan found Brew in the barn, curled over a large book. His mouth lipped the words he read as though he were counting to himself. Fraser interrupted, 'Chief Rabbi—'

Brew looked up without any sign of surprise, as if he'd expected Alan. The crofter placed the open newspaper on the Rabbi's book. His picture was at the bottom of the front page under the title "Chief Rabbi Still Missing". Brew read; his face crumpled. The long story-caption concluded, "The Chief Rabbi's absence from his own father's funeral last week continues to draw comment in the Jewish community". 'I'd appreciate it if you didn't mention this just yet to Deborah. I'd like to tell her in my own way.' Alan nodded his agreement. 'So now that you know who I am, Mr Fraser, what are you going to do?'

'Right now? Nothing. Just ask questions.'

'I only take hard questions,' said Brew with a ripening twinkle, 'and then only if they're indiscreet.'

Alan cast his expression in cold marble.

Brew bowed his head to the crofter. 'Alan, you and Becky, you've opened your home, and your hearts to us. We've felt less at home in Jewish households. But when you want us to leave, say so. It's plain to see your life is hard here—'

'That's not what I'm askin'. There's something I cannae understand,' he began as he sat down. 'Ferst, you tell your people to leave Scotland, and then you, yerself, run off to the Highlands— It dinnae make sense.'

'Alan, when a Jew has a dream, he must—' and Brew told his story — everything — only keeping to himself the verse he dreamt and the Prime Minister's handshake. He ended, 'But for me, it's not enough just to have a dream. There has to be something more, a sign, maybe even a miracle. Am I putting myself across?'

'I believe you are,' said Alan, drawing closer. 'But you won't find signs and miracles in books. Nature, man. Nature's the place for wonders. Out in the meadows, in the sun and the rain, you'll learn to see and hear and feel. There's miracles enough, big ones and wee ones, happening all the time, but if a man hasn't got the good sense to get out there, then it's as if they never happened.' The crofter gave Brew no choice. He would learn to shepherd sheep, and Alan was going to teach him. 'As of tomorrow, Brew Moray, there's no more sittin' around readin' books in broad daylight for you. You're sweatin' for your keep.'

Brew closed his book.

'By the way, what's in that book that's so absorbin'?'

'Everything.'

'Like nature.'

'Like nature.'

Alan showed the newspaper to Becky. She looked at the picture. 'Have you shown it to him?'

'Yes, just now,' said Alan.

'What did he say?'

'That we're to call him "Brew", and the little woman's not to know—'

'Is that all?'

'We talked—' Alan summarised their conversation, finishing with, 'So what do you say, Mother? Mum's the word?'

'It's like you said in the car, Fraser, it all depends on what you call news.'

Early the next morning Alan brought the Rabbi his own crooked stick. Together with Alan, Ross and Crom and the sheepdog Puppy, Brew set out to graze the sheep. The flock behaved in sheepy ways, bleating all the time for no humanly fathomable reason, eating grass at one end, dropping it out at the other. Whenever a silly creature took it into its head to strike out alone, the dog — barking, circling, nudging — was there to cut it off and bring it back.

At first Puppy resented Brew. With each command he gave, the dog cocked his head at Alan, before charging into the flock. But when he came back to his master's side, tongue hanging out, it was Brew who knelt down to give him a solid pat on the side, and say 'well done, Puppy'.

Over the coming long summer days, Brew learned the countryside. He roamed the higher and lower meadows, trailed the banks of the River Garry, and wandered the old roads and tracks. Everywhere they went, Alan Fraser named the one-time owners of ruined croft houses along the way, and there were many.

After a fortnight the Rabbi was on his own. He took 'his' flock only to the greenest pastures, though these were furthest from 'home'. Even on the wettest, windiest days he made the trek. The changeable Highland weathers toned his cheeks and lightened his wild-growing hair and beard. His hands hardened. Colds and chaps and bruises toughened him. Whenever anyone remarked on his rugged appearance, his response was 'Work is a splendid means of warming oneself.'[18]

At times Brew imagined himself spending the rest of his life in the Highlands with nowhere he had to go, and no one he had to see. He carried no burden, except for a knapsack of food and water. The simple rhythm of a shepherd's day seemed aimless, yet so in tune with nature. Out in the open he often doubted the need for regular prayer to divide his days. The whole day was a prayer.[19]

But Brew did pray. In the morning the twins routinely fell in to watch. At a short distance they stood to attention and goggled at the swaying Rabbi's 'twiddling and untwiddling of the little black boxes.'[20] Sometimes, Alan also watched. And sometimes, he could not help thinking to himself, god-fearin' folk that we are, too, when it comes to prayin', we pray *for*... He *prays*.

* * *

---

[18]Talmud, Tractate *Gittin*, 67b.
[19]The observant Jew recites three prayer services a day, in the morning, afternoon and evening.
[20]See Ex. 13.9,16; Deut. 6.4-9, 11.13-21.

Chapter VIII

Seven Days of Mourning

[Thursday, August 6, 2009]

Anna mindlessly wiped a crumb off the kitchen table. 'Aggie, I'll never sleep again,' she said.

'Of course, you will. Later, I'll give Dr Ross a call.'

'For what? More pills? A person's got to wake up sometime. It's not just Manny. It's Brew. And Deborah, too. What's happened to them? Not a word from them...to anybody. People don't just disappear.'

'Drink your tea, Mrs Anna.' Aggie glanced at the kitchen clock: five thirty-seven, a.m. 'At least,' she said, '*Shivah's* almost over; it's the last morning. You can get up before lunch.'[21]

Anna couldn't hold back a thin smile, 'You know our rules better than we do.'

'Mrs Anna, if you'd baked as many cakes and scones and served as many teas as I have this week, you'd know the rules, too. Believe you me. When it's over, we'll take the dog for a walk together. That'll cheer us up.'

'Aggie, you're the greatest. You know, Brew once told me, he said, "There's going to be a special heaven for you."'

'He always was a good boy, your wee Brew. Maybe a bit dreamy, but a real angel, just like his Mum. And clever...like his Dad.' The old housekeeper reminisced. 'That littlest one of yours, did he ever tease me when he was small. You know, Brew was the reason why I decided to keep my married name, even if Ford Christmas was a low-life *shtarker*. Aye, it's true, because wee Brew used to say to me, "We're Jewish, but we have Christmas everyday."' Tears came to Anna's eyes.

'Now, now, c'mon, none of that.' Mrs Christmas went around the table to massage Anna's shoulders. 'I can feel Rabbi Brew here with us, Mrs Anna. I can. Something very important must be keeping him away, but his spirit's with us, with you. Can you no' feel it? I can.'

'But, Avigdor—' said Anna. She always stressed the second syllable, a habit the doctor had never been able to correct. But under the circumstances, he let it go. 'I don't read poetry,' she said apologetically, 'I'm sorry, I haven't the patience for it.'

'Read these. They're short. I'm prescribing them. Medicine. The best I know. Emily Dickinson. How many years have I known you, Anna? And your family?' She winced. 'Sorry, indelicate question. Look, love, you take this book' — he pressed it caringly

---

[21]The seven-day mourning period — called in Hebrew *shivah* from the number "seven" — begins immediately after a Jewish funeral. 'What is the measure of mourning? Three days for weeping, seven for lamenting, and thirty for abstaining from a haircut and pressed clothes. Beyond that, the Holy One says: "Ye are more compassionate toward the departed than I am."' Talmud, Tractate *Moed Katan*, 27a.

between her hands — 'it's only thin. There's more comfort in those lines than in any bottle. Take it from an old GP who knows. I'll drop by again next week to see how you're getting on.'

Mrs Christmas saw Dr Ross to the door and again thanked him for coming at such short notice. The air of cheerful well-being the chubby little physician brought into the house was gone as soon as he left. No sooner had Aggie closed the door than the chimes went. Most people during the mourning period hadn't knocked or rung, but quietly came straight in. Aggie opened thinking, what now? 'Och, you again,' she said.

In the morning light, Aggie's gaze fixed on her frizzy, copper-coloured hair. Dark glasses shielded her eyes. 'Is the Rabbi in?' she asked.

'Everybody in Scotland knows he's not in — to his widowed mother's great sorrow. Could I ask who's calling?' With all that had gone on during the week, Aggie realised that she'd not mentioned her first encounter with the unknown woman to anyone.

'Would you mind calling the Rabbi's brother or sister to the door for a moment? I'd like a word, if I may.'

She spoke an odd, hybrid English like nothing Aggie had ever heard before. She looked at the woman's strangeness for some clue to her accent, but finding none, said only, 'They're all still sitting their mourning period. They shouldn't get up for anyone.'

'I understand. The *shivah* — seven days.'

She didn't look Jewish, thought Aggie, but anybody can know things about Jews and their customs. 'No you cannot see them, not if you're going to upset them, no. Rabbi Moray isn't here,' concluded Aggie.

'And no one knows where he is?'

'Nobody, including you, young lady, otherwise you wouldn't be here, pestering us. Who are you, anyway?'

She was not easily intimidated. 'Who was the last person to see the Rabbi before he disappeared?'

'His wife, but she's gone, too. You wouldn't be from the police?' asked Aggie, more perplexed than ever.

'Speaking of whom, has anyone called the police to report a missing person?'

'If they have, I don't know. *Why* am I talking to you? Now won't you go? Before *I* call the police?'

'Aggie, who is it?' It was Sophie's voice.

Turning away from the caller, Mrs Christmas answered, 'Nobody, it's nobody.' Turning back again, the doorway was empty. 'Hmpf,' grumped the housekeeper as she slowly closed the door.

At the first opportunity, as soon as Anna went out of the room, Mrs Christmas informed Neville and Sophie of her two encounters with the 'black woman'. The three agreed not to tell Anna. Neville proposed phoning the police. 'Somebody ought to be searching for them.' But Sophie opposed the idea, saying, 'No, let's wait. There must be a perfectly good explanation, and after what Brew said on the radio, we might be stirring the coals for all of us.'

Just as Mrs Christmas was leaving, an excited voice broke into the sitting room, 'Did you hear? Did you hear? It's dreadful. And still no word from the Chief Rabbi?'

'Mr Sinclair!' exclaimed Sophie, startled.

'What is it? What's happened?' asked Neville.

'Where's your dear mother?' the old man came back. His shoulders seemed more hunched than usual, his red-rimmed eyes more bleary, his grizzly stubble longer. Mr Sinclair was one of those men born old, and kind with it.

'Upstairs,' Sophie shot back, embarrassed to have to say so.

'Good. Better that she shouldn't hear.' He eyed Aggie Christmas wavering in the doorway, but went on, 'It was awful, our *shul*, in the night. Did you no' hear, then?' asked Mr Sinclair.

'How should we have?' asked Neville. 'We haven't heard any news at all this week. And Dr Ross didn't mention anything this morning—'

'Him—' pooh-poohed the old man. 'Blood-suckers never tell you anything.' Again he asked, 'You don't know? Nobody called?'

'For Heaven's sakes, tell us, Mr Sinclair,' hissed Sophie.

The old man's face quivered with hurt. 'They've desecrated the synagogue.'

'No!' said Sophie and Neville in a single breath.

'Oh, yes. Spray paint. Scrawled, nasty, mean, like under bridges. A blue St Andrew's cross painted over a dripping red Star of David. Very big, right on the side of the building for everybody to see. And underneath, they sploshed, *HEEBS OUT! SCOTLAND FOR THE BRAVE!*'

At that moment Anna came back in. Sensing something wrong, she asked, 'What's happened?'

The three swallowed deeply, uncomfortably. Anna read their consternation. And Aggie's pillar-of-salt expression contributed to her dismay. Anna asked again, 'What happened? Something happened. Is it Brew?'

'No, Mama, nothing like that,' said Sophie, pulling the hair out of her face. 'C'mon, we shouldn't be standing.' For support she looked to Mr Sinclair, as the synagogue's beadle and one of the few Jews in Edinburgh who lived a religious life.

Instead of sitting, Anna stared at the little man, who always wore a black skullcap on his head. 'You've said something. You weren't planning to come again this week. You told me so yourself. So why—?'

'Please, Anna, it's nothing to concern you. You've got enough troubles. Why don't we all sit down? Right? We sit,' he said, trying unsuccessfully to hide his agitation.

As they sat, Mrs Christmas came forward to take orders for coffee and tea. The dog drifted in with her, taking up his spot by the fireplace. Mr Sinclair took the opportunity to further escape Anna's questions: 'So Aggie, how're you keeping?'

She answered, '*Azoy*, as we say in this household.' Her Scottish-pronounced Yiddish brought a smile to Mr Sinclair's thick lips. While these two bantered words, Neville taunted his sister under his breath, 'So the great Rabbi Moray wants to be a Jewish John Knox—'

Sophie spoke up, 'Neville, you'd not say that if you knew what kind of man John Knox really was.'

'And you wouldn't say *that* if you knew what kind of man Brew really is.'

'Neville— Sophie—' Anna's plea brought an uneasy silence to the room.

Neville held his mother locked in a frozen, emotionless gaze before blurting out, 'They've desecrated the synagogue.'

'And the people driving by, they hoot and whistle and jeer,' added Mr Sinclair not to be done out of the news he'd brought.

'It's all Brew's doing,' said Neville grimly. In shock everyone stared at him. 'It had to be said,' he defended himself.

There was nothing more to say. No one, not even the dog moved—

Without warning, the bay window exploded in a rain of glass. Before any human reacted, the dog was up and yelping. Anna fainted. Sophie shrieked. Mrs Christmas cringed, her fingers latticed over her mouth. Neville leapt to his feet, his eyes whipping in all directions. Mr Sinclair ducked and turned away, covering his head with his arms, seemingly expecting more. The curtains billowed and flapped in the wind.

The brick, lobbed over the high stone wall, had barely missed Anna's head.

'That's it. Now we call the police,' gritted Neville.

The seven days of mourning were over.

Anna woke up with the very real sound of glass shattering in her ears. She switched on the reading light, alerting the dog. Since Manny's death, he'd taken to sleeping by her bedside. His browed eyes looked up in sympathy.

She lay in bed afraid to turn off the light. All around her, inside her, all she felt was loneliness. The vast emptiness of life without Manny was unravelling her like a ball of string. She picked up Emily Dickinson, read one verse, then another. The words distracted her, relieved her. But only for a short while. And the darkness was back. Could nothing dispel the darkness in her?

The dog let out a sorrowful little whimper. Anna turned to him. His moist eyes seemed full of *human* understanding. 'Snappy, I thought I'd never say this to anyone — but I'm glad, glad that Manny wasn't here to see it.'

* * *

Chapter IX

Tsippi

[From Thursday, August 6, 2009]
The demands of an isolated crofter's home had left Deborah no time for self-pity. People and animals had to be fed. The cow milked. Eggs collected. Dishes, clothes, linens washed, by hand. Floors cleaned and brass polished. The work was hard, but satisfying. It made Deborah feel younger, stronger, more self-assured than at any other time in her married life. By the end of the day, a healthy tiredness had crept into every bone and muscle. At nights in bed there was so much she and Brew wanted to tell each other, but in minutes they were asleep.

Becky's interest in the finer points of the Jewish dietary laws and Sabbath observance was almost insatiable. At times, Mother made the Rabbi's wife feel like the proselytiser she was not. The two women worked closely together, scrubbing and koshering the Fraser kitchen, cooking traditional Jewish fare, and preparing the Sabbath on Fridays. No sacrifice was too much. From Friday evening to Saturday evening, there was no radio. The boys made long faces at going without their local station for a whole day, and Alan missed the weather forecasts.

Mother Fraser's curious behaviour could not simply be dismissed as Highland hospitality. Nor, apparently, was she driven by Christian charity: She made a point of not mentioning the Gospels or church or even using expressions like "the GOOD LORD".

And above all, Becky loved her children with warmth and goodness, but Deborah never saw her hug or kiss them. And in her sensitivity, Mother did not so much manipulate, as encourage contact between Deborah and her only daughter, in bed with the mumps.

'Deborah, why do you wear a wig all the time, and long skirts?' asked Elen, still looking flushed but feeling better. She was sitting up in bed, propped up against her pillows.

'You're supposed to be going to sleep, young lady.'

'Why?'

'Because I'm a woman, and a married woman.' Deborah sat on the bed.

'Am I a woman?'

'Hmm, let me see. Well, maybe not yet. But you're a very pretty young girl. And some day, you'll make a nice young man very happy.'

'You're trying to change the subject. I know you. What about my question?'

'Some of us, not all, mind you, believe we're happier when we dress modestly.'

'What's modestly?'

'I suppose it amounts to keeping life simple and decent, like you do here in the Highlands—' As she explained, Deborah could not help feeling that she was the object of a conspiracy — innocent, warm-hearted, well-meaning, but still a plot.

Elen stared deeply into Deborah's velvet eyes, and said, 'It sounds like a strange thing to say, but I feel I know you from another time, another place, or maybe in some other life when I was your child. Is it wrong to think such strange thoughts?'

Deborah slid closer to the child. 'I'd say, you're getting much better,' she said trying hard not to let her emotions run away with her. 'It's a very nice thing to say, one of the nicest things anyone has ever said to me, and I'll remember and cherish it.'

'Tell me about yoursel', please. What was it like when you were growin' up?'

'There's nothing much to tell. I'm from Edinburgh. An only child. I come from an average, middle-class family, we lived in an average house, I was an average girl. I got married, and lead a fairly average life, help my husband with his work, letters, calls, things like that. Only Brew and I—' She did not finish.

'Only Brew an' you, what?' asked Elen.

'Oh, nothing, dear, really. I shouldn't—'

'You shouldn't what?'

'Brew, Brew is the only thing special about me.'

'You know what I think?' said Elen leaning forward, 'I think you'd be special, even without him.'

'You know, you say the loveliest things. Here I am supposed be helping you get better, and *you* make *me* feel so good. Can I give you my own special name?'

'Sure.'

'From now on Elen, I'm calling you Tsippi.'

'Tsippi?' repeated the girl, a little unsure. Then she said it again, as if tasting a new flavour on her tongue, 'Tsippi— It sounds so pretty, just like a little chirping bird.'

'She likes you, does our little Elen,' observed Becky in a quiet moment of the day. 'You get on well with children.'

Deborah's cheeks reddened. 'I like her, too, very much. You have such a treasure in her.'

'You're telling me. And clever— I don't know where she gets it from. That child runs rings round the rest of this family.' Becky stopped her spinning for a moment, coming right out with it— 'Isn't it high time you and your husband had bairns of your own? Not that I'm wantin' to meddle, but you're good folk, an' the world always needs more good folk.'

Deborah dropped her hands crossed with wool. The corners of her eyes glistened. 'I don't believe that I'll ever have children of my own. We're trying everything medical, but it's not working, not so far.' Becky's apologetic frown indicated understanding, and a desire to retreat. 'Please,' said Deborah, 'it's good for me to talk to somebody who isn't a doctor. And I'm not sure Brew understands, either. He wants children because Judaism demands that we teach our children.[22] But I want a child to love.' Deborah wiped an eye. 'I'm blethering—'

'It's all right, love.'

'Whenever I can,' said Deborah looking up, 'I try to let other children be my own, to love children who are not my own. But it's not the same as having your own.' She stared into space. 'Sometimes, I have terrible, sick thoughts. Like it's a punishment. For something I did. I feel so guilty. Why me? Why us? See, I wear ruby earrings. They're meant to help. Brew got rabbis in Israel to stuff notes in the cracks of the Western Wall in Jerusalem, and send me blue threads that have been wrapped around Rachel's Tomb. I've had the blessings of old rabbis with white beards. These are the ways in our circles — I know it all sounds like hocus-pocus, superstition, and maybe it is — but when you're desperate, you try anything.'[23]

---

[22]Deut. 6.7.

[23]Throughout the ancient Middle East the ruby was considered a charm against bleeding. To this day Jewish lore in Orthodox circles encourages infertile women to wear a ruby to halt the cycle of

'We pray.'

'And so do I, and Brew prays. We give charity and pray. So far nothing has helped.'

'If you had a child, what would call it?' asked Becky.

'If it were a girl, Tsipporah, Tsippi for short. It means "little birdie". And a boy, well, I think I'd let Brew choose his name—

The crofter's wife smiled approvingly.

'Becky— You can't imagine what it's like. I sometimes try to justify things to myself, to find an answer I can live with. So when I'm feeling more charitable, I say to myself that the hands of the unborn rock the world. What I mean is, none of us know whose kids are born to ruin and whose are born to redeem; every child comes along only when this old world is ready for it, and I have to believe that the world just isn't ready for ours yet.'

'I've been thinking, too...a lot lately,' announced Becky in an introspective voice. 'And I think I have an idea. And I think now's the time. I believe you've been *brought* here for something. Listen—'

* * *

---

menstrual bleeding. However, the wearing of a ruby or any of the other practices Deborah mentions cannot succeed without *emunah shlemah*, that is, "complete faith".

Chapter X

Secrets

As soon as the Sabbath was over, Brew Moray came out with: 'Alan, Becky, we're leaving tomorrow.'

Alan swallowed, 'That's sudden.' He looked at Becky.

The twins grinned at each other, savouring the thought of going back to sausage and eggs for breakfast.

'Go on, then, Fraser,' prompted Mother.

'You two can't leave without takin' somethin',' he said worryingly.

'Taking something—?' asked Brew. 'We've taken so much already. We can never repay you, never.'

'Eh, may be you can,' said Alan, 'You said, you came here looking for signs and miracles, remember—?'

'True. And I've seen many,' answered Brew.

Becky took up her husband's drift, 'What Alan's trying to say is that, well, we want you to take Elen back to Edinburgh with you.'

'What?' exclaimed the Rabbi. 'I mean— It's out of the question!' He stared at Deborah. She looked over Elen's red head, not daring to meet the child's eyes darting from one grown-up to the next.

Alan spoke up, 'Brew, just listen a minute. Mother and I've talked this thing over for weeks now. And Elen agrees, too, don't you, El?'

The girl flashed a sly look in Deborah's direction.

'This is a conspiracy, against me,' said Brew turning from face to face. 'Parents don't just give away a child. It's not right.'

Alan was stern. 'Nobody's giving away anybody. Elen's a loan. Of course, Mother an' I'll miss our little El, but we got two more left to help run the place.' The boys turned sullen.

'HEAVEN forbid,' moaned the Rabbi. 'She's too young to go away.'

'She's twelve, Brew,' fired back Deborah. 'How old were you the first time your parents schlepped you off to your Uncle Max in Manchester?'

'That was different. He's family.'

Fraser carried on. 'Brew, what we're saying is, ferst, every day parents give up their children. They send them to kindergarten, summer camps, school, away to boardin' schools. Right?'

'Right, Alan,' conceded the Rabbi, 'but it's not the same—'

'Fact is,' began Becky, 'you can see for yoursel', there's no future for our Elen up here. She's got a good head on her shoulders — LORD only knows where she gets it from — and she deserves a good education, a fair start in life.'

'And if you haven't noticed, Brew,' carried on Alan, 'folk are leavin' the Highlands. There's no work up here. The North Sea oil's played out. Tourism's dropped off to practically nothin'. No more foreign anglers come here. You've seen the pylons, the broken wires — England dinnae buy our electricity any more. We're not starvin', but it's going to be years before Scotland recovers. Don't get us wrong. We're loyal, we're Highlanders, and proud Protestant folk, and those are the very things that make us sensible and sober.'

'Point taken,' said the Rabbi. 'Next.'

Becky continued. 'What we're askin' you and Deborah, take care of our Elen, see to it that she has schoolin'. We'll pay you what we can, but we know it probably won't be enough. But she's a good gerl, no trouble, and a willin' pair of hands. You've seen that for yourselves. And she'll come home in summers, and maybe over Christmas, oh, you know what I mean—'

The Rabbi's eyes glinted at her new found sensitivity. 'But that's the obstacle,' he said solemnly. 'We're Jewish. I'm a rabbi, a Chief Rabbi. Deborah is a rabbi's wife—'

'Brew!' frowned Deborah, 'I thought—'

'It's all right, Debs. They know exactly who we are—' he confirmed. 'It's been in the papers, but not on the local radio station. We were only trying to shield you from needless worry—' The Frasers nodded affirmatively, but were inwardly surprised that Brew had not let on until then. Before Deborah could say more, he went on, 'We live an Orthodox Jewish life at home. The child would feel restricted.'

'No I wouldn't,' said Elen with big eyes. 'Deborah says you live the way you do, because you're happy that way. So if you're happy, I'm happy.'

'But we Jews are leaving Scotland, maybe not tomorrow, or the next day, but sometime soon.'

'You still believe that—?' Alan's voice fluted with slight indignation.

'That's why we came here in the first place, looking for proof of my dream.'

'Well, sometimes you come looking for one thing and you find another. Elen's the answer to your other dream, a child,' said Alan.

The boys shared a snicker, but dried up immediately under their father's glower.

'For Deborah's sake,' urged Becky, 'say "yes".'

'I have to think about it. It can't be so simple, nothing in this world is,' objected the Rabbi, but with diminishing resistance.

Alan exploited his advantage. 'Your ancestors put their baby boy Moses in the Nile to save him.'

And Deborah argued, 'I know we can't compare the two things, but before the Holocaust, Jewish parents put their little ones on ships to Britain, knowing they would most likely never see them again. And they threw crying babies off the trains rather than let them be taken to the death camps. I know the two things not in the same league, but the Frasers are doing what they think is best for their only daughter. And I think it's a wonderful idea.'

Again, Becky had her say: 'Rabbi, never have Alan and I met a woman with a larger, more loving heart than your Deborah. She's got so much to give. And our Elen loves her in a very special way, like an older sister. We see it in her eyes. If I may say so, Brew and Deborah, to us, you're family. We wouldn't let our Elen go to just anybody—'

Brew turned to Deborah with mock rebuke, 'You knew about this. I didn't have a chance, did I?'

'You should talk, Brew Moray. You've been keeping your secrets, too,' answered Deborah, her face glowing.

'Well—' said the Rabbi, 'at least I know a good thing when I see it, and that smile on your face, our Debs, is the best thing I've seen in a long time.'

* * *

Brew and Deborah Moray remained in the Highlands exactly forty days and forty nights. E.T.

Chapter XI

Sabbath Morning

[Saturday morning, September 12, 2009]
Everyone stopped and stared at the side of the building. The scrawled hate had been painted over bright red — to match the brickwork.

Two men, though, paid the scar no attention. The heavier suit surveyed the whole prospect with a cold, dry eye. The concrete-capped, redbrick wall around the synagogue was discoloured, crumbling. It had been years since the rusting iron fence running along the top of the wall had seen a coat of black paint. The twin square columns of the outer gate were topped with matching ornamental lampposts. The white globes that once crowned the lampposts had been smashed by vandals long ago. The building itself looked solid — a nondescript, redbrick cube, punctuated only by six black windows and a small, plain entrance. Almost nothing identified the structure as a place of worship; it was easily passed by without notice. The big man remarked sparely, 'Salisbury Road synagogue, so this is it.'

Two uniformed policeman, patrolling the pavement in front of the building, acknowledged their superiors with a respectful nod.

Passing between the lampposts, the taller, younger suit prepared to enter an alien world. He tapped the crown of his grey hat. 'You keep your hat on, sir,' he suggested, adding, 'in these churches, the folk pray with their toppers on.'

'Been studying comparative religions, have we?' ridiculed the older man. His meaty chin tipped up, as he glared at the chiselled inscription over the entrance. 'Why can't they write in a language we can all read?'

'It's Hebrew, sir. Most of them don't know what it means, either,' explained the junior, now deeply conscious of the tingle of unbelonging that ran down the back of his long neck.

At the entrance two congregational guards wearing ill-fitting skullcaps were checking handbags and asking questions. The two suits flashed their IDs. One of the guards was too dismayed by the officers to do anything but step aside. The other said, 'Gentlemen, no writing or tape-recording allowed during the Sabbath service.'

'Official police business' was the brusque response of the bullish officer. The younger man, as he went through, informed the guards, 'We'll be at the back.'

The strangers climbed up three flights of steep, narrow stairs to the sanctuary. The heavy man puffed. His partner slipped in first. The synagogue was cave-quiet, everybody standing, reading prayerfully to themselves. It was surprisingly bright inside, flooded with light from chandeliers and twelve stained glass windows, six on either side. Every seat was taken. Over their shoulders, most of the men wore a fringed, white prayer-cloth embroidered with blue or black stripes. Hatted women and bareheaded girls sat apart from the men along the walls in raised rows, theatre style.

The big man whispered, 'Do you see *him*?'

Neville Moray finished reading and sat. The congregation began to look ragged, half up, half down. Leaning across to his neighbour, Neville asked, 'What do you say, brother-in-law? Beautiful morning for a storm in a tea cup, eh, Jake?'

'It's no joke—' said Jake. The dimple-faced two-year old on Jake Banks' knee looked up at his father who went on, 'You see those two characters at the back?'

Neville snatched a quick look. He half heard Jake saying, 'Jon Brodie...says...big bruiser...a detective.'

'How does he know?' asked Neville, after a second glance.

'Jon was at the door, checking. Right? Says he's seen him in court a few times. Nasty piece of work.' The toddler on Jake's lap wriggled impatiently. His father's prayer book slipped and fell shut. The gold inscription embossed on the blue buckram cover was faded, but still could be read.

Presented by
Anna and Immanuel Moray
to Jacob Banks
on the happy occasion of his marriage
to their beloved daughter Sophie
June 9, 1998/15 Tammuz 5758

'Place is packed—' remarked Neville, as he stood again for the oral repetition of the silent prayer.

'Looks like the Celtics' terraces with all this Glasgow crowd here today,' agreed Jake. His 'little striker' was squirming to run loose in the aisle. 'Word of the Rabbi's restoration sure got around fast. He only called Soph yesterday afternoon to announce his return.'

'Me, too,' said Neville, 'just minutes before the Sabbath came in. That reminds me of this beautiful joke—?'

The worshippers remained standing. The Ark was opened, the congregation sang triumphantly, and Mr Sinclair in his beadle's top hat removed the Torah Scroll. The hub of activity moved to the raised platform at the centre of the sanctuary.

As the Scroll was unfurled for reading, Deborah whispered into Tsippi's ear, 'Our lot here must seem so strange to you.' A circle of men huddled around the open scroll, which one of them began to read aloud.

'Touch chaotic' was Tsippi's remark.

'I'm impressed: That's a fine, big word coming from someone so young.' Deborah gave Tsippi a peck on the temple.

'I am twelve,' said Tsippi. 'And actually, it's not so different from our Assembly Hall, sort of austere.'

'Austere—' echoed Deborah, before she went on, 'Anyway, now we're reading the Scroll of the Law, like I told you—' After letting Tsippi listen for a while, Deborah said, 'You know that nice lady I was talking to earlier—'

'Which nice lady?' whispered back the redhead.

'Ms Landis, the teacher—' Deborah politely half-turned her head in that direction, but found herself, instead, captivated by a burnished face under a thatch of persimmon-coloured hair. She'd not noticed her before, sitting in the far back row.

'Oh, aye, that one,' nodded Tsippi, 'the one with the funny hat on that looks like the old Queen of England.'

'Yes, dear, well— She's going to help me enrol you into a good school. She's famous, our Ms Landis — remind me to tell you all about her. She was my English teacher.'

Deborah was next to Anna Moray and Sophie Banks. The little girl on Sophie's lap slept. Every time the Rabbi's wife spoke to Tsippi, her mother and sister-in-law exchanged sidelong glances.

The two detectives located him. He sat in the front row near the dais flanked by two others in top hats.

After the reading, the heavy parchment Scroll was held high above the congregation, lowered, rolled up and dressed again in its embroidered velvet mantel, silver breastplate and bells. Next came the word of the prophets read to a different chant. At last the men filed off the central platform with the Torah Scroll, and led the little parade through the aisles. Men and boys reached over one another to touch the Law with the corners of their fringed prayer shawls.

The two police detectives strained to catch their first sight of his face.

But when the Scroll came to the front, Brew Moray pulled his prayer-cloth over his head like a hood. He took the Torah on his shoulder, half-burying his face in the Scroll as if it were a soft pillow. And with his prayerbook in front of his eyes, the Chief Rabbi intoned the service's first words in English: 'May the supreme KING of kings preserve our Premier, Angus Montrose, in life, guard him and deliver him from all sorrow. May HE put the spirit of wisdom and understanding into his heart and into the hearts of all his counsellors, that they may uphold the peace of the nation, advance the welfare of its people, and deal kindly and truly with all Israel...and let us say, Amen.' The congregation repeated, 'Amen.'

The heavy-set detective curled his lip and raised his left eyebrow. His partner kept a straight face.

Mr Sinclair opened the Ark and, taking the Torah Scroll from the Rabbi, returned it to its space between two other Scrolls in the niche. By the time the Ark doors were closed and the curtains drawn shut, the last coughs, shuffles and whispers had dissolved into a heavy silence.

Brew Moray, wrapped in the voluminous folds of his prayer-cloth, mounted the two steps to the pulpit in front of the Ark. He lifted his face to the congregation. His beard had grown long and full. All eyes fixed on the Chief Rabbi.

* * *

Chapter XII

The Turtle

[Saturday morning, September 12, 2009]
Taking notes from his inner breast pocket, the Rabbi pressed himself as far forward as the edge of the pulpit allowed.

'Let me begin my remarks this morning by thanking all of those among you who have expressed your sympathies on the loss of our beloved father, Immanuel Moray, may his memory be for a blessing. Your words are a comfort.

'His sudden death was not only a blow to our dear mother and all our family, but also to many in this and the larger community. It's hard for a son to speak about a father without making both souls blush. I am sure his can hear mine.'

A faint, boyish smile tugged at the Rabbi's lips.

'So I will only say he was a working man, a considerate man, a lucky man, a generous man. He loved to tell stories, and to laugh at his own stories. That pure, infectious laughter he's passed on to our brother Neville. He was a builder of furniture, lasting works that so many of us enjoy sitting on, eating off and working at. His creative qualities he has left to our sister Sophie, the mother of his grandchildren. But above all, he was a dreamer of dreams, and that legacy I have inherited from him. May his memory be blessed, and may our mother, his wife Anna, be comforted.

'Many of you have also asked where I and my dear wife, Deborah, have been this last more than a month. At the risk of sounding flippant, I shall only say that our car ran out of petrol. And we were completely lost. It seems we had to get lost...for us to find ourselves.

'Earlier, I mentioned "words of comfort". Words. Word — a thing spoken. As a man who earns his living by the word, until quite recently, I've always thought that words were rather important. But now I know better. Words are more than important. Words are crucial. Words are all we have. Words of comfort, for example, are our only cushion against loss and death; words of righteousness, our only weapon against injustice; words of conciliation and prayer, our only hope for future understanding and peace.

'But think, isn't it strange, as the Twentieth-century philosopher Martin Buber pointed out, that the voice of HEAVEN came to Earth in the mouth of Moses, a self-confessed stutterer?[24] Wouldn't it have been better for the world's most precious words to have been brought down from HEAVEN by someone with a silver tongue or a golden voice? I think not. Smooth words are cunning, misleading.

'By giving our teacher Moses a stammering speech, the Torah reminds us that, for all their importance to human life, words are rather dull instruments, crude approximations, the imperfect grunts of language.

'And yet, our sacred Law is sometimes called the Word. Our weekly Portion says that the Law "is in your mouth and in your heart *to complete it*".[25] To complete it— What does

---

[24]*Moses* by Martin Buber; also see Deut. 4.10.
[25]Deut. 30.14.

that mean? It means that there is something more, beyond words. But I'm racing ahead of myself—'

The Rabbi's fringed prayer-cloth slipped off his shoulders. He broke off speaking to fold it back, and to draw fresh breath.

'Now, more than ever, I am sorely aware of the power of words. A single syllable can save a soul, or snuff out a life. With one word, it is possible to call up vast, hate-filled armies, or build a lasting peace. Words can found new nations, and words can bring down ancient empires. It took only four hundred and sixty-nine words to complete the entire universe,[26] as it is written, "Everyone who teaches his son the Book of Genesis is lifted beyond the text as though he himself had a hand in the Creation of the World."[27]

'Yes, words have a terrible power. And the most awesome power of words is their power of prophecy. I do not mean a simple forecasting of the future; I mean making events happen. Our Sages say, "Whatever HE is to do at the End, HE has done in part today."[28] And all that HE does, HE does through the medium of words. An awesome idea, awesome. Our freedom of action, expressed in our choice of words, is what affects the course of the world. I tell you, openly and candidly, I fear the sound of my own voice; more than that, I fear the meaning of the words I am about to say to you, but they must be said.

'Words hurt. I am aware that some of you, perhaps many, even most of you, have said that I spoke rashly, recklessly and imprudently, thus precipitating an unnecessary crisis.'

Whispered comments rustled through the rows. Some of the more emotional women dabbed their eyes. Jake hissed into Neville's ear, 'The only thing worse than anti-Semitism is a Jewish leader who condemns it, in public. I can imagine what our guests at the back must be thinking.' Neville turned to check the strangers, joined now by a few more, journalists, he reckoned.

'From the moment I spoke on the radio, our lives were changed. But why? They were only words. Nothing beyond words, puffs of breath. Did we do anything? No. Yet, those five minutes made us all Jews again: targets of distrust, prejudice and hatred. Our homes have been stoned, our cemeteries desecrated and our House of Worship, here, splattered with ugly slogans, against us all. All because of words.

'Who will promise us that the next brick that comes flying through a window will not hit someone on the head? Or a fist or club or bullet will not stop someone's heart? Must we suffer for being what we are? For being here? For saying what we say? For doing what we do? For believing what we believe? Must our bones be broken for the dreams we dream?

The Rabbi paused again to signal a change in direction.

'You all have your troubles— You— And you—'

A long finger stabbed in one direction, then another.

'You have back problems. You are worried about an operation. Your job is insecure. Your child's marks in school are dropping. You have a son on drugs. Your daughter isn't married yet. You have a parent confined to a wheelchair; a brother or sister ill with cancer; a grandparent in a home for the aged. You don't know how to tell your husband or wife that you are having an affair. The list of our problems is as long as the days of our lives. And then you turn on the radio— So even if you didn't have any problems before, you've got one now: You're a Jew; we're all Jews again. Before I spoke out, we could always shove our Jewishness in a drawer, under the knickers, where it belongs.'

Guilty smirks brushed over the faces of the more literal minded.

---

[26]By his count of the Hebrew words, Rabbi Moray comes to the end of Gen. 2.3 which completes Creation with the Seventh Day, the day of rest, the Sabbath.

[27]*Seder Arakim*, quoted in *Torah Sh'lemah* ("The Complete Torah") by Rabbi Menachem Kasher.

[28]*Tanna deVei Eliahu.*

'But should I have not said anything? Most of us, including my family and me , have lived freely and happily in Scotland for generations. Scotland is the only country that we've known and loved. We work here, educate our children here, take advantage of the opportunities to live where we please, and to worship in our own way. So why do I call on us as a community to leave? What gives me the right?'

At the rear eyes met and ears pricked up.

'Independent Scotland has become a desert for Jews. Admittedly, a lush, green desert, but still a desert. Last week's Portion of the Law reminded us of what was done for the people of Israel in the wilderness: "And I have walked you forty years in the desert, during which your clothes did not wear out on you and your shoes did not become tattered on your feet. But neither bread did you eat nor wine or strong liquor did you drink—"[29] And so it is with us in Scotland. We have wanted for nothing material during our long overnight stay here, but our spirit — from being away too long — has become depleted, deprived of the bread and wine of our true homeland—

'When I began I mentioned that sometimes a person has to get lost in order to find himself. A paradox. Let me explain. Let my words speak now to your eyes in the language of an image which I saw during my absence.'

Here came a deep lull as the Rabbi silently surveyed the congregation. His eyes closed to see—

'One day I wandered far from home with only a flock of sheep, a dog and a crooked stick for company. We were following a disused track, when the clouds turned black, and eclipsed the day. Sheet lightning flashed across the sky, followed instantly by frightening, long rolls of thunder. The heavens unleashed rivers of rain. I was soaked through and through. The whetted edge of the wind numbed my hands, and seared my face with sharp pricks of precipitation.

'I looked around for cover; there was none. The trees had been cut down long ago. Not even a bush was anywhere to be seen. Torrent after torrent of rain fell. The noise of it deafened me. And then hail came down, pummelling me. I was reduced to helpless tears. Faintness was beginning to consume me. The sheep and the dog started to lead the shepherd — up the road's shoulder to higher ground. The flock stopped and I crouched down on my haunches and waited with the animals for the weather to pass. I watched the waters gather along the track below and fill it like a canal.

'Turning my back to the rain and the road, I wrapped my arms around my knees. I saw I was on a little knoll. I looked around me. Close by I made out the remains of a fireplace and then the low, ruined foundations of a long-gone crofter's cottage.

'My eyes next settled on the manhole cover beside the ruin. It covered the septic tank. Almost imperceptibly at first, the cover started to lift off. I could not take my eyes away. It was being pushed up by a rusty old drum. The manhole cover finally tipped over and rolled to one side. From out of the hole below, the barrel rose and rose. Until it, too, fell over and rolled aside. At last a huge, old turtle emerged and clambered out of the hole. Its shell was flattened and deformed. The poor animal, driven out by the rising water, began to move, slowly and laboriously, heading down to the roadside. There, the beast crawled straight into a hole and sank down into the mud until only its snout and eyes remained visible—'

With pained slowness Brew Moray drew his hands over his face and beard. The congregation shifted expectantly. At the rear his pause was just long enough for a truncated exchange of whispered communication between the two detectives. The Rabbi's face lifted, he steadied his gaze, and his eyes opened, round and white, flashing with prophecy—

'We— We Scottish Jews are that turtle. We live in a black hole, under a manhole cover, with a rusty old drum of too many lost years on our backs. And our shells are deformed, but in

---

[29]Deut. 29.4.

the darkness we can see neither our own nor our neighbours' deformities. We carry on living like this even now. Then it begins to rain, and when it rains, we must finally move. If not, we drown. While we still have the strength to come up, we, too, must rise, and push aside all that holds us down. And perhaps, our destination is only a mudhole, but it's *our* mudhole where we can be free to breathe.'

As he pulled in the breath of air that would rally him for his final push, the Rabbi rolled his eyes heavenward.

'Now. Listen again to the words, the words of our Portion of the Law this very morning: "I call today on heaven and earth as witnesses! Life and death do I set before you, the blessing and the curse. And you must choose life for your sake and your children's sake, that you will live!"'[30]

* * *

The name Moray, when written in Hebrew, means "teacher". E.T.

---

[30]Deut. 30.19.

Chapter XIII

Leasing-making

[Saturday noon, September 12, 2009]

Eyes blinked as though coming from dark into light.

The Rabbi humbly bowed first to one side, then the other. He carefully refolded his notes along the original creases, and descended the two steps from the dais. The beadle, Mr Sinclair, in his top hat sprang to his feet and vigorously shook the Rabbi's hand. The congregational president in his high hat remained seated.

'Our President does not approve' was Neville's unsmiling comment to Jake. His brother-in-law wrapped a protective hand around his boy's small neck and shoulder before reacting: 'Davidson's bloody right not to approve. Your little brother hasn't done the Jews of Scotland any favours this morning. What kind of rabbi is it who speaks from his gut instead of his head?'

A quick-march hymn, paced even faster than usual, concluded the additional morning service. The journalists rushed out. No one heard Mr Sinclair's hoarsely shouted announcement of coming events, so loud was the buzz of talk. A few well-intentioned old men came forward to take the Chief Rabbi's hand, and wish him a peaceful Sabbath and 'long life' in sympathy for his recent loss. No one commented directly on his homily.

As Deborah, Tsippi, Anna and Sophie made their way to Brew's side, the Rabbi's wife noticed the copper-haired woman hovering. It appeared she was waiting to have a private word with the Rabbi. After hugs and modest kisses, Brew said, 'Go on downstairs, you lot. I'll be along in a minute.' He watched them exit. Downstairs in the community hall, the congregation would sanctify the Sabbath wine as they did every week.

To secure a private moment, Brew Moray assumed a vacant stare to fend off even the most persistent of his flock. He let his unblinking eyes, so shining, quick and intelligent, roam the shul so familiar to him from earliest boyhood. Rays of Sabbath sun filtered through the coloured window panels that looked so small and dingy from the outside. As he looked about with a warm sense of satisfaction and peace, his peripheral glance caught the approach of a diminutive figure. She wore shaded glasses, and her hair had the colour of soft burnished bronze. But before he could turn to her, his attention was diverted by a gruff 'Are you Brewster Moray, Chief Rabbi of Scotland?'

'Gentlemen, gentlemen,' Brew answered rabbinically, palms out, 'as a wise man once said, if you have to ask a man's name, you must either be a lawyer or a policeman.' The two strangers shared a quizzical, sidelong glance. Brew grabbed the lost second to look again for the woman, but she was gone.

'I'm Detective Sgt Keith MacKenzie and this is my colleague Detective Paul Dalziel of the Edinburgh City Police, Serious Crimes Division,' recited the paunchy face as he flashed his policeman's identity card and badge. 'We'll have to ask you to come with us to—'

'You're not Jewish,' interrupted the Rabbi.

'Course I'm not Jewish,' said MacKenzie, sharpishly.

'Of course you're not,' echoed Brew in a sadder tone.

'So why'd you ask?'

'For the same reason as you asked me my name: confirmation.'

'Confirmation of what?'

'Confirmation that you're not Jewish. You see, if you were Jewish, you might be the Messiah.[31] Now, I know you're not...Jewish.'

'Reverend, you may think this is a laughing matter—' said MacKenzie, as he fumbled to unbutton his belly-bloated jacket. 'Brewster Moray, we're arresting you on the charge of leasing-making as defined in the Constitution under—' he read from the paper he produced '—under Article Five, Sections Nine (b) and Eleven (a), Sub-sections (i) and (iii), respectively.'

Brew gazed from one to the other. Two stony expressions met his disbelief. 'We advise that you say nothing at this time, and come along peaceably with us,' said Dalziel, softening his facial features despite the dry tone.

'We'll take that copy of today's sermon in evidence, Reverend,' ordered MacKenzie. The Rabbi reached under the folds of his fringed prayer shawl. MacKenzie snatched the document before it was given. Brew felt the sting in his empty hand—[32]

'Gentlemen, I'm an advocate, Jonathan Brodie,' called out the grandfatherly figure hurrying up the aisle. 'What's the charge, Detective?'

'Leasing-making—'

'I see.' Brodie's jaw slackened, his eyelids dropped gravely. 'That's a warrant to arrest? May I?' MacKenzie handed him the writ. The lawyer read.

Brew clasped the stiff, embroidered collar of his prayer-cloth around his neck and throat. Brodie straightened up. 'Jon,' said the Rabbi, 'have I missed something here? I'm rather sure I haven't made or broken any leases lately.'

'No, Rabbi,' said the white-haired advocate, 'this has unfortunately nothing to do with leases. It's an old Scottish law the Estates have resurrected. It refers to untrue or subversive statements that may prejudice relations between the state and its citizens. It's tantamount to seditious libel in English law, or possibly, even treason.'

'In other words, these gentlemen are—'

Brodie's 'I'm afraid so' was ominous.

MacKenzie asked, 'If Mr—'

'Brodie, Jonathan, LL.M. Edin. I believe we've met before—'

'Mr Brodie, if you have no objections—'

'I have plenty, Detective MacKenzie, plenty—'

Brew's head, imploding with a sudden out-rush of blood, blanked out. He saw a spinning, colourful top from his childhood stop, reverse itself, and begin spinning again in the opposite direction. In less than a heartbeat his dizziness passed off, unnoticed by the others around him. He asked, 'Since when is truth a crime in Scotland? Jon — these men? They have the right to detain me?'

'I'm afraid so, Rabbi. You'll have to go with them,' confirmed the lawyer. 'They'll not be able to hold you on this charge, I'm convinced.' He placed a hand on the Rabbi's shoulder.

'Jon, how did you know to come up when you did?' asked the Rabbi, as if recovering some detached, floating memory.

---

[31]Potentially, any Jewish woman can be the mother of the Messiah, and at any time any Jewish male child can grow up to become the Anointed One (cf. Isaiah Ch. 11).

[32]The document remains in evidence among the papers of Brew Moray's police record. Now badly faded, it is the Rabbi's crude drawing of the turtle, a rough diagram of the crofter's house and the line the beast took from the septic tank to the mudhole in the road. It contains no writing, which could be compared to the original manuscript.

'An unusual woman—' said Brodie, distantly, 'with dark specs. For a second she lifted them, her specs — she had the most transparent eyes I think I've ever seen. Never met her before, but she knew my name. She intimated that you might be needing my services; I came straight away.'

'She was dark-skinned with orangy hair?' asked the Rabbi.

'Why, yes, she was,' confirmed Brodie.

Jake and Neville came striding in, deflecting all eyes up the centre aisle. They led the Moray women.

'Brew, what's going on? Are you all right?' called out Deborah even before she reached her husband's side.

Not wanting to alarm her, Brew said lightly, 'It seems these two gentlemen are requesting the pleasure of my company.'

'You mean, you're being arrested?' said Jake. Brew pressed his lips together.

'There must be some mistake,' protested Deborah, then turning to the advocate, 'Mr Brodie—'

The younger policeman apologised, cutting off Brodie, 'I'm sorry, madam, your husband's...eh...serious crime case.'

'Brew is a crime?' swallowed Deborah.

'No, missus,' MacKenzie corrected her, 'not "a crime" — *a*ccused — accused of a serious crime—'

The congregation were slowly ebbing back into the synagogue.

To the detectives, Brodie said, 'I shall, of course, accompany my client.'

'Your perfect right,' agreed Dalziel. 'Radio car's out front.'

'Gentlemen,' said the Rabbi, 'no cars on the Sabbath, no riding. If you wish to arrest me today, I will have to walk.'

'Hike back to the station? That's no' a good idea, Reverend,' said MacKenzie. Flummoxed, he appraised his over-large belly. 'This was supposed to be my day off.'

'And mine,' said Brew, catching a glimpse of his worried mother and sister, holding one another. 'Why don't you gentlemen both join us at home for Sabbath lunch? Cholent, traditional Jewish stew. We could pass an altogether peaceful afternoon as we wait for the day to conclude this evening.'

The two detectives stepped aside to confer. Dalziel reached for his pocket transceiver, but before he could say anything, Brodie cautioned him, 'Not in a synagogue, on the Sabbath.' Abashed, he looked to his partner for guidance. 'Outside, then,' nodded MacKenzie.

The sanctuary had completely refilled. A potent undercurrent of rumour, disbelief, and shock swept through congregation.

'They're arresting the Chief Rabbi—?'

'Arresting our rabbi?'

'What for?'

'Treason.'

'Treason?'

Returning, Dalziel wedged his way through the tightly knit crowd around the Rabbi. 'Headquarters say we're to bring him in — on foot,' he reported.

MacKenzie: 'For chrissakes. Now?'

Dalziel: 'That's what they said. Now.'

'We're going with you, Brew,' announced Deborah.

'Me, too?' asked Tsippi.

'Yes, you, too, dear,' replied Deborah.

Anna Moray hit a defiant note, 'Brewster, you're not going to prison without *me*.'

Neville said in a mocking aside, 'Of course he isn't, Mother. But these days, it's only one *man* to a cell.'

'Neville, I heard that,' said the old woman, her eyes moistening. 'Just like your father, always making me laugh when I should be crying.' Brew bent over to give his mother a reassuring peck on her forehead.

'We're also with you,' said Sophie, forgetting the little girl hanging on to her hand.

'What about the kids?' asked Jake, his arms full with their son. 'Soph, we can't both go. Somebody has to take them home.' The boy clung to his father's neck.

'Then you go home.' Sophie accused him as if he were deserting her.

Jake defended himself, 'You know I don't like crowds.' Backing off, he bumped into Neville, and mumbled, 'The kids—' Neville had nothing to say. His hands were in his pockets and his face, glum and stony, was set in his brother's direction. Jake tried again, speaking low, for Neville's ears only. 'If you want to disassociate yourself, come with us. I'm driving home with the kids.'

Neville was elsewhere, thinking aloud, 'Holy shit— Not good, Brew, not good at all.' He did not move. So Jake left him.

'We're all with you, Chief Rabbi,' somebody shouted.

'We're all coming,' called out another, feminine voice.

'You're not alone,' proclaimed a third.

From the edge of the crowd, a thin-haired old woman came up the aisle pushing a wheelchair, clearing people aside like a snowplough. She stopped near the Rabbi, and began furiously signing, hand and mouth, to the man in the wheelchair. 'What's Pearl saying, Izzy?' impatiently asked Neville.

More signing. Isidore Sofer in his wheelchair waved for silence. It went quiet, then he spoke. 'She's saying— "Rabbi, good on you!"'

* * *

From earliest times Scots law made no distinction between treason and leasing-making.

In his Chronicles (§135), John of Fordun (d. 1384) recorded, "In August, Thirteen twenty, Robert, king of Scotland, held his Parliament at Scone. There, Roger of Mowbray was convicted of high treason by leasing-making against the king. When he had been released from the trammels of the flesh, his body was taken down, whereupon it was condemned to be drawn by horses, hanged on the gallows, and beheaded. But the king had ruth, and was stirred with pity; so he yielded him up to God's judgement, and commanded that the body of the deceased be handed over for burial by the church without further shame."

The statutory offence of "leasing-making" first appears in Scots law in James I's Act of Fourteen twenty-four, though as the above demonstrates the expression was used at least a century before. In Fifteen eighty-four under James VI, the law was re-enacted in terms that "no one should, publicly or privately, in sermons, declarations, or familiar conferences, utter false or slanderous speeches against the king, his progenitors, or the council, under penalty of being punished as leasing-makers."

In Scotland's Constitution, ratified in the first Estates in Twenty o-eight, there is no provision for the death penalty for any offence. However, to deter the crime of leasing-making, defined as "the prevention of incitement to undermine national security, and/or the forcible subversion of constitutional order", the punishment for treasonous activity was fixed at the maximum penalty the law allowed: life imprisonment without parole and forfeiture of all goods and property to the state. E.T.

Chapter XIV

"Incident at Dean Bridge"

[Saturday afternoon, September 12, 2009]
With little talk the congregation funnelled though the synagogue gate into Salisbury Road. Men, women and children two or three abreast turned into Clerk Street, then walked down Nicolson, South Bridge, and on to North Bridge.

The Chief Rabbi of Scotland flanked by the two detectives, headed the march. His fringed prayer shawl blew from his head and shoulders like a white-feathered wing. His wife and Tsippi came next, and behind them, his mother and sister, arm in arm. The column was a hundred families long. Young people took turns helping Pearl push Izzy Sofer's wheelchair. Neville, eyes to the ground, brought up the rear, alone.

At the General Post Office the parade wheeled into All Scots Avenue. The older generations still called it Princes Street. As though taking a Sabbath stroll under the warm afternoon sun, some grandparents and parents nostalgically recalled the many former splendours of Edinburgh's broad high street. How the shopping was before so many of the English-owned chains pulled out, how the traffic would get backed up, and the clogged pavements at midday when the office workers came out for pub lunches. Elderly fingers pointed to the Scott Monument. Two years earlier its Gothic spire had been blasted by lightning, and never rebuilt. More recently as an economy measure, the city fathers voted to turn off the floodlights that illuminated the seated statue of Sir Walter Scott after dark. Parents looked wistfully at the slope below. Princes Street Gardens, once the city's pride and joy, was now untended and overgrown. Old men relived fond memories of childhood train spotting along the once busy railway tracks leading into Waverley Station; today the mainline platforms stood idle for long periods between the infrequent trains. Deborah said to Tsippi, 'In summer there used to be so many visitors, a person couldn't move in Edinburgh. The city swarmed. We'd get so fed up with them, but now the tourists don't come to Scotland any more—' She broke off, her voice dropping as if it hurt to finish. And Brew, seeing Edinburgh Castle for the first time since his return, twinged at the memory of his father's weekly ritual. Every Sunday he would watch Manny wind and set his ancient pocket watch to the one o'clock firing of the Time Gun. The Time Gun had fallen silent, when the Castle in part reverted to a prison.

Across the way Saturday shoppers stopped to gawk. Fingers pointed out the Chief Rabbi. Whisperers began spreading prejudice and hate.

Detective Sgt MacKenzie, sensing the volatility across the road, called for backup.

Police protection on horseback and motorcycles quickly arrived. Reporters and photographers, tapping into the police frequency, also came to dog the line. MacKenzie and Dalziel waved them back, but like ravenous scavengers the photographers on scooters swooped in, plucking shots.

Spontaneous whistles and shouted slurs emboldened the crowd. The marchers closed ranks. Instinctively, their pace quickened.

Dalziel could not keep his eyes off Brew Moray. He did not sweat. There were no signs of apprehension about him. On the contrary, he exuded a kindly, serene strength that Dalziel had never seen in any other man. The detective asked him, 'Rabbi, aren't you worried?'

Brew saw where the question was coming from, and said, 'I'm not thinking about now. I'm looking to a future when things will be better and brighter. That's why I'm walking faster. To get there sooner.'

The increased police and media presence only served to energise the cheers and catcalls. The marchers tried hard not to look. Then at the Mound corner, in a sound like a siren blast, someone yelled out at the top of his voice: **'JEEEW PUUUKE!'** The mob ignited. Legs kicked out, fists punched the air. Distorted lips hurled filth and invective, jeered and taunted, whistled and booed, spat and laughed. In minutes raucous, blaring voices forged themselves into a single, grotesque chant: **'JEW, GO HOME— JEW, GO PACK— JEW, GO HOME— JEW, GO BACK—'**

Tsippi looked up at Deborah and asked in all innocence, 'Why does Jesus make them hate us so much?'

'I don't know, dear,' Deborah answered, shaking her head, 'but if he can't stop them from hating, then nothing can.'

Once the march was past Edinburgh Castle, the abuse petered out. MacKenzie and Dalziel, their ties loosened, breathed more easily. The afternoon had grown unseasonably hot.

At the west end of All Scots Avenue, the file with its protective escort nervously banked round into Queensferry Street. Only long, narrow Dean Bridge spanning the Water of Leith lay between the marchers and Police Headquarters.

The police halted traffic at both ends of the bridge. There was no time to stop and enjoy the vistas, or the wooded banks sweeping down into the ravine far below.

As Rabbi Moray at the head of the march reached the far end of the bridge, the first shrill whistle sounded. Then came another, and another. Like a long train the column, stretching from one end of the bridge to the other, braked. Curious, the marchers peered over the wall. Emerging from behind trees and bushes, a young rabble of tattooed arms and faces, studded black leather jackets and knee-high motorcycle boots coalesced along the paths of the north slope. As one, they took a tentative, yet bold step forward. It was a challenge. Their faces looked up with twisted grins. In response to some unseen, unheard signal, there followed a sudden charge up the slope. The marchers froze. To the accompaniment of inhuman, blood chilling shrieks and howls, the skinheads hurled a volley of rotten tomatoes, raw eggs, stones and bricks on to the bridge. For a split second, the sky became a darkened arch, an avalanche descending. All around the dull clatter of pelting missiles rattled on the tarmac. And along the thin line backs doubled over and hands covered screaming heads.

Deep within the Rabbi, a fuse tripped. Self-control and discipline, basic living systems acquired and built up over decades, crashed. Thousands of hours of Torah learning, wiped out. Long, arduous lessons of Talmud study and debate, aborted. All in less than no time.

Eyes widened. Muscle fibres coiled. Senses heightened. Nerve bundles galvanised. Sweat boiled out.

In a swift, graceful move, Brew Moray snapped, turned and charged back on to the bridge. His hair streamed out, his beard bent back. Deborah's call never reached him. In the screaming confusion, both detectives were completely stalled by the prisoner's unexpected dash.

As he ran, the Rabbi spread open to the wind his fringed garment on outstretched arms. The four stringed corners snapped like jibing sails. He flew along the broken line like a fluttering wing, encouraging, exhorting, 'Keep going!' Keep marching! Don't stop! Don't panic! Don't look back!'

At the middle of the bridge, wild-eyed, he flung his prayer-cape over the side into the valley below. It dropped heavily, as dead as a flag shot from the mast, and the Rabbi cried out his wrath, **'STOOOOOOOOOOP!'** Then, again, faintly, 'Please, stop them.'

A single round of police fire into the air dispersed the onslaught. As the baying pack fled, the atmosphere hung heavy with the dying rings of their last derisive yelps.

Brew's white prayer-cloth disappeared under the bridge.

* * *

At the time all media reports and official government statements alluded to the events following the arrest of the Chief Rabbi as "the incident at Dean Bridge". E.T.

Chapter XV

'Poor Scotland'

[Saturday afternoon, September 12, 2009]
MacKenzie reacted first. With a heavyweight boxer's agility, he wheeled round, leaving Dalziel to chase along behind him. Even though Brew had stopped, MacKenzie pounced, wrestling him to the ground. Without waiting for Dalziel to catch up, MacKenzie dragged the Rabbi to his feet, and handcuffed him to his own wrist. With the prisoner in tow, he heaved, 'GOOD LORD's...not... handing out any more pilot licences today.' To a nearby police outrider, who tittered a bit too loudly at the remark, MacKenzie ordered, 'Button it, Sonny Jim, and see to the cuts and bruises.'

For an instant Brew floated in blackness. From deep within came a dim, distant voice saying, 'The Philistines are upon thee.'[33] And the rage in him evaporated as quickly as it had built up.

The walk back along the bridge was like a slow, shimmering mirage. Every stride he'd dashed only seconds before now played back — decompressed and dragged out by a thousand times.

Screaming babies clutched at their mothers' shivering breasts. Toddlers wailed, their eyes stinging with fright and older children, scared out of their minds, wrestled wildly with their parents like innocent, little creatures tethered in a blaze. Adolescents swore blackly at the backs of the fleeing pack, while old men and women smarted with anger and frustration. From several directions wailing ambulances arrived to evacuate the more seriously injured.

Ahead of him Brew saw a baby's dummy fall out of a tiny mouth. The infant started to cry. Without breaking step, Brew scooped up the rubber nipple in his free hand. MacKenzie jerked him back like a dog on a leash. Stretching his arm, the Rabbi defiantly reached the dummy back to the mother. Her droopy sad eyes smiled with uncomfortable gratitude, as the tall, pony-tailed man by her side tenderly stroked the new baby's plump, moist cheeks.

The women of his family did not wait for Brew to be brought back to the head of the march, but came running down the line.

'Brew, what have they done to you?' stammered Deborah.

He shook his head like a shame-faced child. His suit was soiled and creased.

Sophie said, 'You're not hurt, Brew, are you?'

Silence was the answer.

'Are you all right?' asked his mother.

Brew's eyes lifted. 'No, Mother, I'm not all right.' He said it evenly, without irony.

'Okay, okay, ladies,' interrupted MacKenzie, 'the parson's gonna live. Excitement's over. Let's keep the show moving.'

---

[33] Judges 16.20.

Back at the head of the column, Brew first hummed the tune without opening his lips. As his humming gathered momentum, he added the words. Gradually, he let his song grow louder, stronger, more haunting. He sang out,

> *Kol HaOlam Kulo*
> *Gesher Tsar Me'od...*
> All the world,
> the whole world,
> is a very narrow bridge;
> but the main thing is
> not to be afraid,
> not to be afraid at all.[34]

His song spread, lifting spirits. Those who did not know the words, hummed the melody. Over and over again.

Dalziel communicated shrugging bafflement to MacKenzie. 'Let them sing' was MacKenzie's reply, 'for all the good it'll do him.'

At the end of the hour-long march, the procession was mobbed by reporters and photographers on the lawn of Police Headquarters. The Rabbi was hustled inside. And the march broke up.

Before joining his client, Mr Brodie quickly reassured the Moray family. 'They have no cause to detain him,' he told them.

'I want to be with him,' said Deborah.

Brodie held her in his gaze. 'There's nothing you can do for him, Mrs Moray. They won't let you near him — not while he's in custody. This could take some time.'

'We'll wait.'

'Please go home, dear,' Brodie advised sympathetically. 'Let your family take you. Please.' He lifted a hand to steer her away.

Deborah took a dodging step back.

Brodie let his arm fall. The old man looked tired. 'Please yourself, then, but I'm sure the Rabbi would feel better knowing that you and the girl are safely at home. She can answer the phone for you.'

Deborah insisted on staying awhile. 'We'll rest,' she said looking about, 'over there on that bench under the tree.' Deborah and Tsippi sat down together.

Anna and Sophie also urged the Rabbi's wife to come away. Dry-eyed, she said she'd be all right. But as soon as they all went, Deborah had a quiet cry. Tsippi slipped a hand under her fingers and held tight.

Between sobs Deborah said, 'I'm sorry. Grown-ups... aren't...supposed to cry...in front of children.' She dried her tears.

'It's all right. Ma Mum cries a lot, too. She does it on the sly, when she thinks no one's looking.'

'I'm scared, Tsippi. I've kept it all bottled up. Maybe I shouldn't try to explain it, but, but have you ever had a close call, a near-accident?'

The girl's understanding brown eyes motioned Deborah to go on.

'Then you wake up in the middle of the night...and you can't go back to sleep again...because it keeps turning over and over in your mind: what might have happened, what could have happened. That's how I feel now: like I just woke up—'

---

[34]From a mystical Hassidic work, *Likutei Moharan* II, 48, by Rabbi Nachman ben Simchah of
   Bratslav (1772-1811). See also Chapter 28, fn. 64.

Inside Police Headquarters Brodie excused himself from the windowless room where the Rabbi was being held. He went to talk to the desk sergeant. Mackenzie followed him out. Brew sat inertly, handcuffed to a chair. Dalziel was seated across the table, ready to record any statement. A row of photographs of stern-looking former Chief Constables looked down on them. Brew counted fourteen.

From early childhood he'd always automatically counted things — marbles, jigsaw puzzle pieces, buttons, steps — anything that could be numbered, he counted. When he was bored in school, counting kept him occupied; he'd count the ink spots on his desk, or the words on a page in a book. He quickly learned to figure out how old people were from their date of birth, or name their birth year if he overheard how old they were. The habit stuck. He caught people out, lying about their ages, or discovered that the prayer books were disappearing off the synagogue shelves at an average rate of eleven a year—

Breaking his taciturnity, Dalziel volunteered, 'In case you were wondering, Rabbi Moray, we haven't charged you yet. But I'm afraid it's only a matter of time.'

'How long do you think I have to stay here?' asked the prisoner.

'A while.'

'Overnight?'

'Finding a sheriff on a Saturday may take a while. And it's possible—'

'Then what?' asked Brew.

'I don't know, exactly. First the desk sergeant, then Sheriff Court.'

'When? Today—? Tomorrow—?'

'You know, Rabbi, you ask too many questions.'

Brew looked up. No clock on the wall. 'Then can you tell me something simple, please: what's the time?'

Dalziel looked at his watch. He thought before answering. 'If you're asking if the Sabbath is over, the answer's no.'

Brew did not ask a second time, but reflected aloud as he examined himself, rumpled and sullied, 'I see you know something about our traditions. Good.'

'It's ours, as well.'

'So it is,' agreed the Rabbi, 'so it is. But have you ever asked yourself how we Jews know that the Sabbath is on a Saturday, and not some other day? After all, that first Sabbath Day happened a very long time ago. We might have lost track of the days.'

Dalziel took refuge in police-speak, 'Anything you say, sir, may be taken down and used in evidence against you.'

'You're quite right, Detective; I've said enough for one day.'

'That you have,' agreed Dalziel.

'But I'll say one thing more, then I'll be quiet. My father of blessed memory always warned me that the first step of any journey is always the hardest. "But," he used say, "if you get over that one without falling flat on your *tuches*, you'll go far, my son."' Brew Moray mimicked his father's voice.

Dalziel almost yielded to mild amusement, but bit his lip to wrestle a smile into a frown. 'This is no light matter, sir. You, and your lot, you're already standing mighty deep in it.'

'Poor Scotland.'

* * *

In my research of the extensive press coverage subsequent to Rabbi Brew Moray's arrest, I slowly became aware of a curious pattern in the visuals. I say "slowly", because the phenomenon I was detecting is not one of those things that immediately presents itself, but rather something that subliminally creeps into the subconscious. Only after long study of the documentation on the computer screen, did the "something" dawn on me that made me verbalise, albeit internally, that I was, indeed, seeing a discernible pattern. Once having "twigged" (an apt colloquialism from the Rabbi's time that I gladly resurrect in this context), I again reviewed the entire corpus of material I had electronically collected, this time paying strict attention to the illustrations only. My observation was wholly correct, and I believe I am the first to state it:

Every published image taken of Chief Rabbi Brew Moray during the march, both stills and videos, was without exception in some way unclear. In particular, the close-up images, the portraits, were either blurred from movement, out of focus, or in deep shadow. That is to say, no one managed to achieve a good likeness of the man, which is phenomenal, given the already advanced photographic systems of his day.

It would appear, though the idea is difficult to credit, that the holiness of the Sabbath and its prohibition against all creative labour inexplicably manifested itself on that day. E.T.

End Part One

PART TWO: AUTUMN EVENING

Chapter XVI

Edinburgh Castle

[Saturday-Sunday, September 12-13, 2009]
Chief Rabbi Brew Moray was charged with leasing-making and fingerprinted. His watch, house keys and belt were removed. Though the police threw his jacket over his head, he sensed the news photographers' flashing cameras through the fabric. Brew was bundled into a prison van. From inside he yelled out, 'Jon, where are they taking me?' The advocate called back. Amid the commotion, it sounded like 'Edinburgh Castle—'

Faceless officers led the handcuffed prisoner down. At the bottom of the steep, stone steps, a string of naked bulbs bathed the sloping, rock-hewn passage in a sickly yellow light. The underground air was cool, damp, heavy.

The officers delivered Brew to Cell Number Sixteen at end of the passage. No one said a word. One officer unlocked and pulled open the modernised solid steel door, while another shoved the prisoner down three steps into a large vaulted chamber. Behind him, the weighty door squealed shut with a final, muffled click.

For the second time in his life, Brew was fearful. This, he imagined, is what it must be like to be swallowed alive, whole. A cold shudder shook him. He gulped air. Blinked. The walls were stone. The floor was stone. A vault of stone.

Brew took stock: A metal bed pallet hung chained to the wall. No mattress, no blankets. A rusty folding chair, a card table. There was drinking water in a stainless steel jug on the table. A black plastic pail without a handle stood in the far corner.

He started to shiver. Chilled. Tired. Anxious. If he called out, who would hear him? Aloud he called out the verse that woke him. It seemed so long ago.

The single strip light on the ceiling buzzed and flickered. He felt the first faint tremors behind his eyes. He lay down on the hard bed, hoping to escape into sleep—

Headache woke him. Brew lay on his back, fully dressed. He turned on his side to the cold, damp wall. There was no escape from the strip lamp's flickering blue light. He rubbed his temples to release the throbbing. His empty stomach roiled with nausea. He yawned deeply, pulling in great gulps of stale air.

Brew got up to vomit into the black bucket. Seeing that the bucket stood in the middle of a sunken square (the squatter's brown-stained glaze was finely cracked like an old teacup) drove his sickness deeper into him. The Rabbi bent down closer not to miss, and saw his head's dark shape reflected on the surface of the water in the bucket. He sharply depressed his tongue with two fingers. His throat retched, but nothing came up. The bucket, he realised, covered the latrine hole; the water in the bucket was for flushing. He dragged the pail away. A biting outhouse stench snaked up his nose. The foulness set off paroxysms of gagging. He vomited in explosive spasms. The pure bile that came up set his mouth and throat on fire. He felt dizzy and weak. Breathing in short gasps, he heaved again, but nothing more came out.

Brew tipped some water down the latrine, replugged the hole with the bucket, and stumbled back to bed, exhausted. His headache subsided almost as quickly as it had come on. As usual, the relief he enjoyed swept away even the memory of his suffering. He instinctively looked at his wrist. No watch. Police had taken it. He tried to calculate how much time could have elapsed. Was it day or night? There was no window in his cell—

Brew woke up, stiff and shivering with cold. He covered his eyes with an arm to shut out the ceiling light, now flashing on and off at longer intervals. The throbbing in his head was entirely gone. His stomach was empty, but settled. The last thing he remembered before he must have fallen asleep was looking at his wrist. In the back of his mind, still fuddled with drowsiness, he felt vaguely grateful to be awake.

A scraping sound roused him to full consciousness. It took him a moment to trace its source. On the top step. A blue plastic tray had been pushed through a flap at the bottom of the cell door that he hadn't noticed before. No cutlery. The odour of breakfast pork sausage and porridge instantly permeated the vault. His throat constricted.[35]

Brew got up, went to the door. The disagreeable food was plunked in the middle of the tray. He tried to push the tray back, but the flap was locked in reverse. 'Please,' he said to the door, 'I can't eat this; take it away.' And louder, 'Take it away.' The tray stayed. His empty stomach heaved bringing up a bitter taste. He retreated to the opposite corner of his cell to escape the irritating smell. From there, he watched and waited.

After an indeterminate time, a dull knocking penetrated the door. The flap opened, a signal to return the tray. Brew went to the door and pushed the tray, untouched, back through.

'You've not taken your breakfast.' The voice coming through the flap, the first Brew had heard, was creaky, unsympathetic. 'You don't like our five-star fare, Number Sixteen?'

'I can't eat it.'

'That's not very sociable of you, Number Sixteen, rejecting our hospitality.'

'I take a special diet.'

'A special diet—?' said the voice with pitiless sarcasm. 'Our best cooked Sunday breakfast, not good enough for your sort—?'

Brew ignored the slur. 'I must see someone— My lawyer—'

'You just got here, man. Show some social grace. Be a little people-friendly. Like I said, it's Sunday. Shops are shut.' The thick voice cackled with mordant glee.

'Please, don't go away,' pleaded Brew. 'It's cold. The light flashes. No blankets, no mattress—'

'Who d'ya think I am? Five-star housekeeping?' He laughed at his own humour, then turned brutally serious, 'And if an inmate don't take his food when it's hot, he takes it cold.' The tray came back.

Brew stared at the top step. A taste of stomach acid welled up into his mouth. He swallowed it back. There was no other way. He looked over at the latrine hole. Taking a

---

[35]For observant Jews, the mere smell of pork is upsetting. Foods, with the exception of fruits and vegetables, are either "kosher" or "unkosher", that is, fit or unfit to be eaten. What constitutes the fitness or unfitness of a particular food or combination of foods is governed by the Jewish dietary laws, which originate in the Pentateuch. These laws, as refined in the Talmud, are too detailed and extensive to be treated adequately in a footnote. Suffice it to say, that first and second laws of "kashrut" — forbidding the eating of living flesh and blood (Gen. 9.4; Lev. 7.26-77, 17.10-14) and the cooking of the young in its mother's milk (Ex. 23.19, 34.26; Deut. 14.21), respectively — demonstrate the early reverence for both human and animal life embodied in these precepts.

deep breath, he snatched up the tray. It was all over in a single frenzied minute. The tray, scraped clean, was back at the flap.

The Rabbi tried to wash his hands, but the water in the pail was ice-cold and would not cut the pork fat. He held up his greasy fingers, palms to his face like mirrors. The smell of his hands was repulsive.

The creaky voice was right, he thought. He had never been a "people person". Because he was a rabbi, people would say that he was 'a good man, a nice person, a caring human being', but he knew better. He was selfish, stingy with his time and space, unable to imagine other peoples' pains and sorrows or genuinely share in their joys and successes. In many ways he was closed, preferring the sacred texts to human contact. Outwardly, he said and did the right things, but secretly he craved the life of a hermit. He worked hard at being there for others, but the truth was that he could never make himself over into the naturally warm, loving, compassionate soul that Deborah was. Smelling his fingers, he had no illusions about himself. He cried bitter tears.

Out of the depths of self-pity, Brew heard a voice screaming quietly, Remember— He splashed drinking water from the stainless pitcher over his hands three times, and repeated the blessing for ritual washing. He shook off the excess water.

Without the morning sun to point the way east,[36] the Rabbi faced the door, the only opening. He kissed the embroidered collar of his invisible prayer shawl and enveloped himself in its folds. Taking up a transparent phylactery box,[37] he wound its unseen strap like a bandage around his left arm seven times. As he said the blessings, he saw in his mind's eye the Fraser twins gawking, and smiled. The mime continued. He bound the second sacred black box between his eyes, then completed winding the imaginary strap around his left hand and fingers to form the beginning and end of the ALMIGHTY NAME. Brew closed his eyes, to feel the straps bite into skin and muscle. He could not hold back his tears, but these were tears of joy. When the prisoner of Cell Number Sixteen had let his emotion run its course, a wry, little smile flitted across his face. How fitting, he thought, to be in a penitentiary in the penitential month of Elul.[38] Brew smiled.

On his first dawnless morning in Edinburgh Castle, the Rabbi prayed, and while he prayed he was no prisoner, he was a free man.

*

'Brew— In custody? Jonathan— What can I do?' Her hand gripped the receiver so hard, it shook.

'Deborah, it's Sunday morning. There's no one to talk to.'

'Jonathan— You're his lawyer; you've got to help him. Where is he?' She was growing more distraught.

'Like I said, remanded in protective custody, pending a preliminary hearing. The duty Sergeant at Police Headquarters couldn't or wouldn't tell me where they were taking him,' Jonathan Brodie lied, thinking, poor woman's beside herself.

'How can they hold him like that?'

'It's standard procedure. Not to worry, we'll sort it out—'

---

[36]Jews in the west pray towards the east. But in fact, all Jewish prayer is directed towards Jerusalem. As one Hassidic rabbi put it, "Just as light reaches the eye from all directions, so too, is it with prayer coming to Jerusalem, the eye of the universe."

[37]See Chapter 1, fn. 1.

[38]The Hebrew month of Elul immediately precedes the High Holy Days — *Rosh Hashanah*, the Jewish New Year and *Yom Kippur*, the Day of Atonement. Beginning in Elul, the Jewish people are expected take an annual inventory of their collective soul. At the New Year tradition teaches that God's final reckoning for each individual is written down in the Book of Life, and on the Day of Atonement the Book is sealed for the coming year.

'Can they do that? Before the hearing?'

'Yes and no—' he said, then decided he had to admit, 'Apparently, the police are treating the Chief Rabbi's case seriously, as a threat to national security.' He droned on, 'In such cases, Scottish law provides that the accused be brought before the Sheriff Court not later than the first lawful day after being taken into custody, but, again, today is Sunday. I'm sorry, Deborah, there's nothing I can do. We have to wait until tomorrow morning. The law entitles the accused to have an advocate present during the procedure. I'm sure I can convince the Sheriff to release him. HEAVEN only knows — the Chief Rabbi of Scotland is no subversive! Do you want me and Ethel to come round?'

'Thank you. No. It won't be—' She was calming down. 'I mean, Sophie and Nev are coming over later. And I've got Tsippi. The phone hasn't stopped ringing—'

'Good they're coming. But I recommend you say as little as possible to anybody, and listen, dear, don't discuss Brew's case over the phone.'

'You think somebody's listening?' Her voice cracked.

A mistake. He shouldn't have said that. 'No, but you can never be sure. Look, as soon as I find out anything, I'll let you know. Not to worry.' The advocate tried to sound cheerfully professional.

'It's— It's— I know he's not eating, I know it. He can't eat anything they give him. You know it's not kosher. Jonathan, can't you—? Could you call Judith? Maybe she can—'

That would be backing his half-sister into a corner. Justice Minister, Scot, Jew in that order, Judith Levitt was too consummate a politician to jeopardise her public image, or even risk a private slap on the hand. Not for a Chief Rabbi, an alleged traitor to his country. If she tried pulling strings and the papers got hold of the story, it could backfire in the face of every Jew in Scotland, not least Brew Moray's. Montrose would be furious, the judiciary up in self-righteous arms, the public enraged, and a fair trial would become well nigh impossible. 'I'll talk to her, I promise you—'

The doorbell rang. 'Now who could that be?' she asked, flustered. 'Must go, Jonathan, must go. Call me back, please, the moment you hear something— And thank you, thank you—'

* * *

At the time of Brew Moray's arrest, Police Headquarters was equipped with only a few unbarred detention cells suitable for drunk-and-disorderlies. The lock-up at St Leonards Police Station was rated "low-security". Saughton Prison, though a high-security facility, was reserved for felons. For those who violently resisted Scottish independence, the government of the day allocated preferential accommodation.

The squat, forbidding excrescence of Edinburgh Castle was originally built to keep enemies out, not prisoners in. However, early on and from time to time in its long history, the Castle Rock with its stone-carved labyrinth of passages and chambers proved an ideal place of incarceration.

In the Seventeenth Century the first Marquis of Argyll gave his name to Argyll's Tower. There he slept his last night behind some of Scotland's sturdiest walls — ten to fifteen feet thick — before he was hanged on a charge of treason for his religious convictions. And in his turn the Marquis' son, the ninth Earl of Argyll, was also convicted of treason. Unlike his father, though, he was confined to a low-class vaulted cell in the dungeon. Of a wily disposition, he escaped disguised as a page, but eventually was recaptured and dispatched, too.

In St. Ives, his last but one novel, Robert Louis Stevenson plotted and executed a fictional escape from Edinburgh Castle. His daring French hero, the Viscount Anne de

Keroual de Saint Yves, and his Bonapartist comrades freed themselves from the dungeon on a fog-blind night. With the aid of a knotted rope the men climbed down the Castle Rock's craggy southern face. Of the factual prisoners from that era, all that remains are some graffiti inelegantly chiselled in the stone lintel over the prison quarter's main entrance.

During First World War the Red Clydesider[39] leader David Kirkwood was briefly locked up in one of the Castle's subterranean vaults. In the Second World War apartments within the Castle were converted into a military prison.

Thereafter, the Castle's prison operation was suspended until Twenty o-seven, when the double-storeyed passages under the Great Hall and the Queen Anne Barracks were again pressed into dungeon duty. The historic pinewood doors of the cells leading off the rough stoned passages were replaced with solid, state-of-the-art steel "slammers". The barred window-openings facing the green Pentland Hills south of the city were sealed up, and narrow air shafts installed. Ironically, it took Scottish independence to return the Castle's vaults to their original dark, damp, airless state of prison chambers. E.T.

---

[39]In the George Square demonstration for a 40-hour week on "Bloody Friday", January 31, 1919, the "Red Clydeside" movement reached its pinnacle, nearly turning Glasgow into a "Scottish Petrograd". Though primarily a labour movement, its leaders, one of whom was David Kirkwood, did not hesitate to invoke revolutionary notions such as a future "Scottish parliament".

Chapter XVII

God of Scotland

[Sunday morning, September 13, 2009]

The doorbell rang insistently. Deborah replaced the phone in its power unit. Worried sick about Brew, she gave no thought to the hour, that it was too early for Neville or Sophie to come. She also wasn't thinking about Tsippi in the kitchen. She just opened the door without asking who it was—

Caught off guard, she felt the blood rushing to her face. Angus Montrose's twenty-one inch television image had not prepared Deborah for the bear of a man who faced her.

'Mrs Moray—' he half asked, half stated.

She nodded, as if not quite sure.

'Good morning,' he went on. 'You'll pardon the unannounced nature of this call. I hope the hour is not too early, that I'm not intruding—' Instead of saying something, she stared at the Prime Minister's two hulking bodyguards.

'May I come in, Mrs Moray—? It's a raw morning — for all of us—'

Deborah stepped aside. He crossed over the threshold. 'The lounge is the first door on the left.' The words came out clipped, but without rancour. Her poise surprised her. The two security men followed him in, but remained outside in the hall. Before she closed the door, Deborah looked out. His official black Mercedes with dark tinted windows was parked on the street outside their South Lauder Road home. She wondered — quite absurdly — if any of their nosy neighbours had seen the Prime Minister of Scotland coming into her house. She shut the door.

As she walked down the hall, Deborah felt the security men's eyes follow her. She touched her wig to be sure it was in place.

Why had he come? To intimidate her? To question her? It had to do with Brew, obviously. Should she cooperate with him? Appease him? Defy him? Wasn't he, after all, responsible...for everything—?

Anxiety gave way to a grey, uneasy hope. Perhaps Montrose was a godsend. She could appeal to him. Here was the one man in Scotland who had the power to help Brew. If either Nev or Sophie should show up before he was finished— No, she prayed, their meeting must not be interrupted. She turned off the phone and went go in—

Montrose, holding his bulky, black case by his side, was standing in the lounge curiously looking around. The room's contents were totally unexpected, so much so that for the first moment he doubted the reality of where he was, as though he'd accidentally walked onto a movie set. Books, books, books — mostly huge, old volumes in sets — everywhere. Crammed in vertically and horizontally, they lined the walls from floor to ceiling. Among the shelves, there was one reserved for family and wedding photos, and a single glass case containing fancy silver cups and candlesticks and other mysterious objects that Montrose had never seen before. The Rabbi's simple wooden lectern and study table stood in the far corner. Nearer Montrose, at the entertaining end, the library was tastefully furnished with two inviting easy chairs, a plush velvet-covered sofa and a low coffee table. The cosy, learned atmosphere of the room filled his lungs. It was not so much a library, he concluded, as a home sanctuary — so different from the emptiness of most Scottish sitting rooms with only their televisions and computerised music centres.

Montrose jabbed his free hand at Deborah. She stared at it, and imagined Brew's slim fingers clamped in its grip. 'Religious Jewish women don't shake men's hands,' she explained, then smiling awkwardly added, 'except their husbands'.' His cheek twitched, as he let the rejected hand fall.

Deborah motioned him to sit down in one of the chairs. She perched herself on the edge of the settee. Just then Tsippi came in through the dining room from the kitchen. She had not seen the bodyguards. The happy expression on her face turned to awe. Deborah kept her eye on him as she said as naturally as she could, 'Tsippi, darling, this is Mr Montrose.' The youngster looked at Deborah, unsure of what to say or do. 'Would you please put on the kettle for our distinguished guest, dear?' The girl obeyed without a word.

Montrose said, 'Good-looking child, Mrs Moray. Yours—?' He had not intended to begin with small talk, so his words came out with disarming charm and sincerity. In the asking he vaguely remembered reading that the Moray couple was childless.

'We're very fortunate to have her. But at twelve, she's no child.'

'Yes, quite.'

'You don't know much about young folk, do you, Mr Montrose?'

'No, no, not on a personal level. And I'm afraid it's been some time since I was twelve—' He cut short his reflection. 'This call — to say the very least — is highly irregular and possibly unprecedented. I could have sent a representative, but I wanted to come personally. I am here on behalf of the Scottish government to express my deep, heart-felt regrets concerning yesterday's deplorable incident.'

Deborah was direct. 'I'm sorry, but why are you apologising to *me*? Shouldn't you be talking to my husband? When can I see him? Where are you holding him?'

'Mrs Moray, please understand, *I'm* not holding anyone. The law must take its course.'

'But you do know where he is—'

'My dear Mrs Moray, it is not for the Prime Minister to know the whereabouts of every suspect held on remand. Believe me, if I knew where the Rabbi was, I would tell you. But I don't.'

'My husband's no ordinary criminal. You can find out. You can help—'

'He's perfectly safe — of that I'm sure.' He popped open the outsized briefcase balanced on his knees. He tapped a note into his electronic organiser. 'Here, I've reminded myself to investigate. You're not to worry. No harm will come to your husband, I promise. Now, there's something important you can do for him—'

'I'm listening—'

Montrose instantly picked up on the coolness in her voice. He had to win her trust. 'As you know, I've spoken personally to the Rabbi— We had what the diplomats call a frank and open exchange of views. I like him. He's straight.' He pulled out some newspapers and other documents from his case. Snapping it shut, he easily swung it down to the floor. As he looked up, Tsippi was coming in with a cosy-covered teapot, two cups and biscuits on a tray.

'Thank you, dear,' said Deborah, 'On the coffee table, here, next to our visitor, that's lovely. Now, please, go upstairs—' Tsippi looked at the Scottish leader defiantly, so that only he saw. Her look slightly rattled him, but his pleasant 'Thank you, young lady' kept his expression neutral. Deborah poured the tea.

Montrose's speech quickened. 'I want you to understand the background, the gravity of the situation. Here in today's *Sunday Times*, the editorial, I quote: "It seems axiomatic that no sooner is a new frontier declared, than nascent nationalism turns a distrusting eye on the minorities trapped within its borders. The arrest yesterday of Scotland's Chief Rabbi on the transparently trumped-up charge of "leasing-making" — high treason, a life sentence —

is the latest addition to the long, grim and growing list of excesses committed by the Montrose regime. Here, in this island, on England's very doorstep, in the twenty-first century, we are not only being treated to the ugly spectre of riotous anti-Semitism in the streets but, more frighteningly, to the obscene irony that the leading victim of the violence was the one person to be arrested. Should the Moray prosecution proceed, whatever the verdict, Scotland will be found Guilty.'"[40]

'True—' agreed Deborah, 'and I hardly ever read the papers—'

'You know as well as I do — it's a complete distortion of the facts, a tissue of lies. Brewster Moray was arrested *before* the incident.' Without waiting, he picked up two other papers and read out the banner headlines, '"Clans Cry 'Kike!'"' and "Judas March!" That's the local gutter press,'[41] he said angrily, swatting the papers down with a sharp crack. 'Don't you see, if it were only Scotland's *reputation* on the line — do you think I would be appealing to you, here, now? No, it's so much more. The very future of our nation is at stake.'

Montrose put the newspapers aside, and then shuffled more documents. 'Listen.' He solemnly began to read, "His Majesty's Government views yesterday's arrest of the Chief Rabbi of Scotland with profound concern—" Blah, blah...now here it is. "His Majesty's Government hereby gives notice that it will aid and abet in every way, morally and materially, the small Jewish minority's express desire to exit the Scottish *experiment*. Signed, John Blakemore."'

Deborah sat unmoved. Her impassive face, her silence frustrated Montrose into sarcasm. 'Am I boring you? The Prime Minister of Westminster is using an isolated rock-throwing incident as a stick to beat us over the head — you, me, all of Scotland. It's political and diplomatic blackmail—' He stopped before he let himself be carried away by his own rhetoric.

Deborah folded her hands on her lap. 'I really don't understand the first thing about politics. All I know is yesterday, it was not us who shouted the obscenities, or threw the stones or hurt anyone. People were injured. They could have been killed. Have you forgotten? It was only yesterday.'

Montrose spoke glibly, 'Internal security reports confirm that, regrettable as it was, yesterday's violence was entirely spontaneous. In no way does what happened on Dean Bridge reflect the mood of the vast majority of the Scottish people.'

'I want to believe you, but making us march through the streets on our Sabbath day—'

'That march was a— It should never have been allowed to happen. The police personnel responsible have been severely reprimanded. There'll be an official inquiry. Heads will roll.'

'But the reality is what the paper said: Brew — the Chief Rabbi — is the only one sitting in prison today. Not the skinheads and not the police.' Her face muscles slackened.

His inner voice begged her, no tears. 'I will do all that is in my power, I assure you, to see that nothing like what happened yesterday ever happens again as long as I am Prime Minister.'

Deborah held back her impulse to cry. 'Mr Montrose, you don't take buses, do you?' She, too, could parry.

'No, not any more. What's your point?' His rashness betrayed him; he'd asked and now he'd have to listen.

'Just this. Last Wednesday I was on the Number Eighteen bus with the girl.' Deborah raised her eyes to indicate Tsippi upstairs. 'We were all by ourselves up top. Then, two young men came up. One tried to start with me, "Hey, pretty lassie—" I ignored him, stared straight ahead. The other was pouring a can of McEwans down his throat. Then what happened next, I can't explain it, it all happened so fast. They had words, vicious, horrible, like savages. One boxed the other straight in the face, the beer can flew up, and there was

[40]Editorial, *The Sunday Times*, September 13, 2009.
[41]The *Glasgow Sunday Globe* and *The Liberator*, also from September 13, 2009

blood everywhere. I rang the bell, the driver stopped the bus and we got off the bus and walked the rest of the way home.'

'I'm sorry to say that kind of petty violence is a legacy left to us as a result of English rule—'

'You really don't understand.'

'I think you've made your point. Now if we could—'

'No, I haven't finished—'

'What would you have us do, Mrs Moray?' he asked caustically. 'Table a bill against drinking beer and swearing in front of children, and another against illicit chatting up?

'Yes—' she said defiantly.

'And how do you propose that we enforce such laws?'

'*You* can't. You can't enforce laws that go against human nature. That's the point—' Deborah's tone stayed level. 'And if you understand that, then you must also accept that there is no law, no court, no power on this earth that can change our nature or our desire to leave Scotland.'

'You're turning this whole thing on its head. Let me start again. Neither I nor my government are coercing anybody to do anything.' In the absence of his hammer, Montrose started to tap his fist into his open hand. 'Now then, do I have your word that what I'm about to say is strictly confidential, and for nobody's ears except the Rabbi's?'

Deborah quailed, which Montrose took for an affirmative nod.

'I ask you, Mrs Moray, to convey to your husband what we believe is a reasonable and equitable solution to this whole, unfortunate situation. We propose to drop the leasing-making charge for a far lesser one, then free your husband on the condition...that you and he and his immediate family are on the next plane out of Turnhouse Airport. I appeal to you, personally, Mrs Moray, to bring him to his senses before it's too late—'

'How can I speak to him if you won't even tell me where he is?' parried the Rabbi's wife, despite the chill running through her.

Shaking with frustration, Montrose said, 'Apparently, I'm not making myself clear—'

Before he could finish, Deborah echoed his words, 'Oh, quite clear, but apparently, you do not know my husband. If you did, you'd know that he could never accept your conditions.'

The old politician's face went white. 'I see I'm wasting my time here—'

'No. Not if I can make *you* understand. Brew lives by an ancient code of law that is designed to make a man incorruptible. He is a rabbi, a rabbi with a mission. And as his wife I could not possibly do what you ask. I know that he can never agree to what you're suggesting, any more than you would have agreed to be Prime Minister of only Mull or Skye, instead of all of Scotland.'

'Then speak to his advocate—'

'What? Speak to Mr Brodie behind Brew's back—?' She was horrified at the thought.

Realising from the expression on Deborah's face that he'd made a fundamental mistake in approaching her, Montrose brought himself under control. He dropped his voice in the tough-talking manner of a politician bringing all his power to bear. 'There's something very important here for you to remember, Mrs Moray. Whatever happens, the very next day after the trial, win or lose, the world will forget the Chief Rabbi's name. That's not a promise, it's a fact.'

Abruptly lifting his briefcase, Montrose clicked it open, shoved his papers in and shut it. He rose without a word. He gave the Rabbi's study a last glance. As he did so, for a disquieting moment, he felt in the minority, surrounded by a powerful culture of books he could never understand.

Tsippi returned. She immediately sensed the uncomfortable stiffness permeating the atmosphere. Deborah jumped up. Tsippi moved to her side.

Montrose said disdainfully. 'Yes, a nice looking child. I envy people who have children, don't you, Mrs Moray?'

Hot blood slammed to Deborah's face. Her mouth opened and shut, but she said nothing.

'Now, as I believe I've already said, it's a raw morning.' The meeting was over. Montrose saw himself out. The front door closed with a soft double click.

Deborah and Tsippi stood rooted, looking at the tray. The tea had not been touched.

Montrose ordered his driver straight back to New Parliament House.

Alone in his office, he stared vacantly. He'd lost his temper. "Angry" Montrose. That's what the English press used to call him in his younger days—

The scrambled situation called for clear-headed thinking.

Why did he believe her? That Moray wouldn't budge. Moray, the incorruptible, as stubborn as an Old Testament prophet.

To seek the advice of his cabinet risked leaks and more bad press.

At least, he comforted himself, the negotiations had been going well, and he and his handpicked negotiating team of military experts were masterfully playing off one bidder against the other.

Montrose unlocked his top drawer. He took out two red envelopes marked "STRICTLY CONFIDENTIAL — PM ONLY", and reviewed their contents. Both from heads of state in the Middle East. Both were urgent. Requests that he meet with their ambassadors at the earliest possible opportunity.

Our military will have arms, he swore to himself.

He poured himself a whisky, looked at the glass.

Moray! Rabbi bloody Brewster Moray! He tried to force his concentration back on track. Everything had been going as planned, until *he* opened his mouth.

Montrose drank.

There had to be a way around the Moray minefield.

His glass empty, he poured another, gulped it down.

His mind came into sharp focus.

The *Times* was right: whatever the outcome of a trial, Scotland would be found guilty.

Yes, there was a way.

He picked up the red phone, pressed a program button, listened to the reassuring burble—

'Like some incorruptible Old Testament prophet—' he repeated aloud to himself. As he waited for an answer, he lapsed into thought: no, not in Scotland — there are no prophets. No. In Scotland there is only Angus Montrose. And in Scotland, Angus Montrose...is god.

* * *

Blakemore's highly significant allusion to "the Scottish experiment" refers to the initial trial period which Scotland's long-standing devolution movement won from Westminster. However, as is well known, in the year Twenty o-seven, in a wily late-night parliamentary manoeuvre, Montrose and the Scottish National Party (SNP) converted limited home rule into independence. And so the United Kingdom was broken up — exactly three hundred years to the day after the Seventeen o-seven Act of Union. The deciding vote for independence was cast by the woman subsequently appointed Justice Minister, Mrs Judith Levitt. What the media at the time and, later, the history books failed to point out — doubtless out of political correctness — was Mrs Levitt's religious persuasion. E.T.

Chapter XVIII

'A Crisis Too Soon'

[Sunday morning, September 13, 2009]
The door chime startled Neville in mid-sip. 'Damn.' He spilt tea over the front page of the *Sunday Free Scotsman.*

His first thought — the police — hit him in the gut. A delay would worry Deborah. He'd phoned her earlier. They'd arranged that he'd pop in at noontime. Then he talked to Sophie and his mother. Anna Moray invited him for late lunch at half past one. Perfect.

Neville shambled down the long hall of his Old Town flat. A glimpse of his Sunday morning stubble in the wall mirror made him wish he'd shaved.

The bell chimed again. Neville asked, 'Who is it?'

'You don't know me—' It was a woman's voice. She had an accent. He checked the peephole, unlatched and opened the door.

'Thanks,' she said.

'Who are you?' asked Neville.

'And a good morning to you, too—'

'I've seen you before. The funeral— You're the woman Mrs Christmas saw—'

'Well, am I coming in or not?'

Neville stared. She peeled away her dark glasses. Even in the dingy hallway, her eyes gleamed. Feline amber pierced by sharp black points. The darkness of her face contrasted exotically with the persimmon frizz of her hair. She had a slightly flat nose.

The small woman swept past him. She wore a short, well-tailored raincoat, belted at the waist. Neville, two or three steps behind, ran a man's eye down the shapely back to her strongly muscled calves and neat ankles. Rubbing his chin, he avoided a second look at the mirror.

In the sitting room, she turned on the television, raising the volume. She pointedly surveyed the piles of old newspapers, sunken wing chair and unmatched, plush settee, parchment-shaded standard lamp, the jungle of potted plants on a footlocker in the window, ancient LPs, flocked wallpaper, dull oil paintings and an early Twentieth-century brass ceiling lamp. A room straight out of a Grassmarket antique shop.

'I'd have de-Nevved the place...if I'd heard you were coming.' He spoke over the television.

She crossed a finger over her lips, then making the sign of the two zeros, gave a directional nod. Neville took her to the door. His confusion turned to purple embarrassment when her eyes communicated he was to come in, too.

'They could be listening—' she whispered. The woman was serious. She checked the medicine cabinet inside and the shaver socket for tampering. 'Bath's not likely to be bugged, safest room in the house. We can talk here.'

'Who *are* you?' Neville asked again.

'Same as you, mate, a Red Sea pedestrian—'

'You, a *landsman*?[42] You sound...Antipodean.'

---

[42]Yiddish, literally a "countryman", here signifying "Jewish".

'You say it like it's some sort of fungal disease.'

He corrected himself. 'Australian.'

Neville Moray's cheek muscles rippled. A chaotic string of questions raced through his head. For her part, the woman considered his height, six-foot plus. His hair was tousled, receding. And his eyes, sunk deep in their sockets, had the look of a melancholy jester. In appearance alone, he was so different from his brother.

'Why all the cloak-and-dagger crap? What do you want?' he demanded.

'Your help. I can't explain it all here. Trust me.'

'Why should I?'

'Simple, mate.' She dropped her voice to a purr. 'If you were my enemy, you'd be dead.'

Stunned, Neville took a long second to recover. 'Why me?'

'Because you're Brew Moray's brother. Enough?'

'No.'

'Well try this. Your brother's in it, hot and deep.'

'We've all got our problems, he just makes his own.'

'His trouble is your trouble.' Her eyes grew tighter, tougher.

'You committed Jewish types are all the same. Your necks are permanently twisted from looking over your shoulders.

'Even paranoids have enemies. You forgot what happened yesterday?'

'No, I haven't. A bunch of screaming, bone-headed wallies ranting *Sieg Heil*. No more, no less.'

'What makes you so sure?'

'Now you look here, Miss whatever-you-call-yourself and whoever-you-represent, it's like this: I'm my brother's brother, not his keeper. I reject his crazy, off-the-wall views. I love Edinburgh, I belong in Scotland, my family's lived here for four generations, I won't leave. I support Israel, an' I got nothing against Aussie accents.'

She flushed the toilet, and whispered over the rush of water, 'You didn't answer my question, mate. What about your brother's arrest? The attack on your Mum's place? It's not just the screaming skinheads. These are not isolated incidents. There's more to it than that. A lot more. And you better believe it.' He waited for her to say something more. 'Are we gonna stand in the bog listening to me flush the toilet all day?' she asked.

He was drawn to her, but sensed she would be unreachable. Neville could not even look her in the face. He took refuge in nonsense, 'Standing here like this reminds me of an old, old joke. This kid...this kid, sitting on the can, during the Blitz — remember the Blitz? — this kid pulls the chain — you ever seen a potty chain? What did you say your name was—?'

'I didn't. Guriat.'

'Real native Aussie, Guri— Sure. Anyway, the kid pulls the chain, just when a German bomb hits, and—'

'You know something, mate, I can see it's not safe to talk in here. Let's take a drive. Your car.'

'I got a date at twelve—'

'That gives us plenty of time.' She put her hand to the doorknob.

'Don't you want to hear the end of this story—?'

She shaded her eyes again. 'Some other time, mate.' The corners of her mouth hinted at a smile for the first time since she came in. The two left the flat separately.

Guriat went down first to let Neville lock up. In the grey mist and drizzle, the street downstairs was deserted, and only one customer was buying Sunday bread in the bakery next to Neville's entrance. She waited on the corner of East Crosscauseway and St Leonard's Street, where Neville picked her up. Driving at a crawl, he ringed the Queen's Drive around Arthur's Seat several times. First she only made small talk — how green the parkland was, how wet the weather was in Scotland, and how dry it was where she came from. Neville kept his eyes on the road but, whenever he sensed her looking out of the side window, he stole furtive glances at different parts of her. He wanted to see her eyes again. 'You still haven't told me who you are—' he asked.

She was evasive. 'That attack yesterday...had an official hand in it.'

'Prove it.'

'Ask yourself how—'

Neville started up again. 'Conspiracy. Where Jews are concerned, everything that happens is a conspiracy.'

'Do you want to hear this?' she asked sharply. Neville shied back. She continued, 'How'd they know about the march yesterday? It wasn't planned or announced.'

'Zombie yobs like that can sniff out a brawl a mile away. They love it.'

'Wrong. They're fascist bullyboys — well organised and trained. They're equipped with Motorolas tuned to police frequencies—'

'So are the hot news photographers on motor scooters. So what?'

'OK, but here the ruling party's using skinhead racists — unofficially — as positive symbols of strength and defiance to edge popular thinking to the right, into the nationalist camp.'

'Every revolution only comes about with an element of extremism. Why should Scotland be different?'

'Unfortunately, it isn't. Tartan purity and the ever-present threat of the English bogeyman are the foundations of Montrose's master plan to keep Scotland independent. In the minds of many, Scottish Jews are now associated with England. Overnight, the community is seen as a fifth column, an enemy of independence. Mind you, not everything that happened yesterday was orchestrated. The abuse on All Scots Avenue was completely spontaneous. The government's tactic is working a treat, mate. Makes you think.'

Neville stopped the car, where the road overlooks the University's rabbit warren of student residences. 'Fancy a quick ramble to the top? View's worth it, even in mucky weather like this.' Guriat agreed. Trudging up the steep ravine, they made straight for the top of Arthur's Seat. The summit looked down on misty clouds. Piercing the haze, Edinburgh's monuments, church spires, tower blocks and the Castle towers reminded Guriat of the pillars of salt that grew out of the morning mists of the Dead Sea. Only the outcroppings here were dark and melancholy, instead of white.

Neville, also thoughtfully taking in the view, made his own associations. 'Seems my little brother's dreaming these days, about mountains,' he said to himself. Deborah had told him on the phone about Brew's vision.

Guriat faced him; her bubble glasses made her look like an inquisitive bug. 'What?'

'Nothing important—' answered Neville.

She began again. 'Why'd they take the Rabbi all the way across town? To Police Headquarters? When there aren't even any holding cells there?'

'How should I know?' Neville wondered if this jaunt was such a good idea. Mist and drizzle began giving way to rain. 'Hey, I never finished my story. So the bomb hits, the dust settles, and nobody can find little Johnny—'

Guriat badgered, 'Normally they take suspects to the lock-up at St Leonard's police station? Which is right around the corner from the synagogue? Right?'

'I don't know. But it seems you do,' he sniffed. 'But *how* do you know?'

'We know. *How* we know is the one question you can't ask. But *we* know.'

'Who's *we*?'

Guriat turned her head to the Castle. 'Your brother's in there.' Neville swallowed. His little brother, his childhood 'wee Brewsy' — inside? Being treated like a subversive? It was a sobering revelation. 'Let's go,' he said dully, 'It's getting grot up here.'

'You know something,' said Guriat when they were back in the car, 'you have what my mother used to call "a very trying character".' Neville's hurt showed. Guriat eased off, 'Actually, she was talking about me when she said it.'

'Okay, you win. Happy?' He took off his cap.

'No,' she said.

'Didn't think you'd be.' He offered her tissues. She took one, and wiped her face dry.

'It's no game, *this thing*—'

Neville glanced at his watch. 'It's getting late—' He started the car. The windscreen wipers had a job keeping the rain off. Past the former Commonwealth Swimming Pool, renamed Freedom Pool, he headed for the Grange Road. The way led by the redbrick synagogue building. Neville looked at Guriat. She was looking at him.

'So what's "*this thing*"—?' he asked.

'I can't tell you everything, mate. All I can say is Scottish Jewry is in real danger.'

Neville gave her one of his here-we-go-again looks, but said, 'Try me—'

'Okay—' Her voice went flat and factual. 'The scenario goes like this. When Scotland broke with the United Kingdom two years ago, a certain Middle Eastern regime became alarmed at the news. Their analysts anticipated what they called "Scotland's Jewish haemorrhage". The fact that there were only six thousand Jews here at the time, tops, cut no ice with *them*.'

'And fewer now,' said Neville, 'So—'

'So, certain fanatical Islamic pressures from within and without were brought to bear. There are forces that will stop at nothing to prevent Jews, especially western Jews, making *aliyah*.'[43]

'Holy shit! You're Israeli—?'

'I thought you understood that, mate.'

'Christ, no. I had no idea. But it's beginning to fit—'

Guriat went on, 'Like I was saying, this particular state, with the financial backing of certain international middlemen, opened up secret negotiations — directly with Montrose. They offered him a range of modern weapons systems on incredibly easy terms, plus two conditions.'

'Only two?' said Neville.

'One: Caithness—'

'Caithness—? What's there? Oil? Stone quarries?'

'No. Uranium. Top secret.'

'Uranium—?' Neville let it sink in. 'But how—?'

She screwed up her face.

'Right, don't ask,' said Neville. 'And the second condition? — don't tell me — involves us lot.'

'Two: that Scotland finds ways of discouraging the Jewish community from leaving.'

'Sounds off the wall to me,' said Neville with growing interest.

'Is it?' asked Guriat.

'You tell me.'

'Your Montrose decided to get greedy. He covertly let my government know—'

'Israel—' Neville said it because he needed to hear himself say it out loud — to understand, to fit things into place.

'As if Israeli intelligence didn't already know,' she said derisively, 'about his filthy deals.'

'Why?'

'In the hope of wangling something out of *us*, too.'

'Playing one off against the other. The clever old fart—'

---

[43]Hebrew word, literally meaning "going up or ascent". In the present context, it signifies immigration to the Land of Israel.

'Guns for Jews. Don't underestimate Montrose. He's a smart player. The man shrewdly leaks information to each side about the other, constantly upping the ante. And he manages to keep it all out of the media.'

'Cute.'

'And now your Scottish Prime Minister is seeking legislation to impose heavy taxes on potential emigrants, and stop people who do leave from taking their life savings with.'

'And most of us have been consistently loyal to Montrose and supported home rule and independence all the way. I voted for the man. He's no anti-Semite.'

'No, he's not, not in the classic sense. He's a pragmatist.'

'The way you tell it, he's winning—'

'He thought he was. Then came the Chief Rabbi...with his DIVINE intervention.' She squared her shoulders. 'In his own innocent, pious way your brother has touched off a crisis too soon. But believe me, it would have come anyway.'

'My *meshuggener* crazy brother— Look, I'm beginning to believe you, but I can't accept that all Scotland is against us. I've lived here too long. You understand my sentiments—'

'Let your sentiments be with Scotland, but your place is with us, mate. Will you help?'

Neville pulled the car over. 'Why are you stopping?' she asked, while he let out a nervous breath with a whistle. 'I need to think.' But what in fact made him too jittery to drive on was her glaring at him behind reflective glasses, waiting for his answer. Her mouth was set, very sexy. Her natural aroma made him want to reach out and caress the velvet darkness of her taut skin and, like in one of those ancient James Bond films, boldly tear off those damned glasses for another look into her eyes. Cap it, man, he told himself, there's no way; you're forgetting who you are, a fucking joke.

While Neville scratched his head thinking, she gave him his first assignment: To begin compiling a list of the names, addresses, contact numbers of all known Jewish people in Scotland. 'Work day and night, Neville Moray, but quietly without arousing suspicion.' Then she said, 'Now tell me about Ford Christmas—' He gave her a questioning look. 'Well, I like him. Sharp salesman. You know he and Aggie are divorced, have been for many years.'

She shook her head. 'No, what I need to know is, can the man be bought?'

Neville looked in the rear-view mirror, pulled out, then glanced at her. She was waiting for his answer. 'I don't know exactly what you're talking about, I mean...it's not murder?'

'Hell, no.'

'Then if I know Ford, he'll take the carrot. He always needs more money than he can earn.'

Nearing South Lauder Road, Neville spotted a familiar red Ford wagon speeding by in the opposite direction. 'That's Deborah...going like the clappers. Wonder what's up—'

'She didn't see you,' observed Guriat. 'She's going in the direction of Morningside, your mother's house. You'd better get the hell over there. Drop me here.'

'How will I find you again?' asked Neville, stopping the car.

'I'll find you.'

Neville turned the car around. He looked back. She was gone.

* * *

Chapter XIX

Reverend Roy Roscoe

[Monday evening, September 14, 2009]
By the third evening, Brew knew every bump and blemish of the grey walls, stone floor, and vaulted ceiling of his reduced world. To distract himself, he withdrew into the stores of his mind. He invented numerical exercises, recited weekly Torah readings from memory, and prayed. But when his mind tired, black thoughts crept in. He easily doubted himself, his ability to judge character, to read motive, to react, to survive. In less than seventy-two hours, the Rabbi had learned to distrust the good and see evil in everyone.

Brew had not expected the flap to open again, not after the evening meal.

'Pull up a pew, Rabbi.' It was a new voice.

Brew, who was sitting on his bed, got up and dragged his chair to the door.

'That's better, Rabbi. Now we can talk. Name's Roy Roscoe, prison chaplain. Good evening.'

Prison chaplain— Brew's train of thinking went...trick, trap, mean-spirited, negative, uncharitable, prison chaplain— He was in no mood for a divinity school discussion of Judaism. And he did not want to hear spoutings of pious goodwill. He said a flat 'Evening, Reverend.'

'I'd have come sooner, you being new here an' a colleague, but Sunday is Sunday—' He sounded genuine, not the fire and brimstone variety, but a kindlier, slightly older man, maybe fifty.

'I understand.'

'An' the wee one was operated on last week, so I wanted to be there with a prayer. It was only what the doctors call a "minor procedure", but an op's an op.' He spoke easily, openly and with a down-to-earth touch that Brew was not used to in his Christian counterparts.

'Is the boy OK?' asked the Rabbi. Without being able to see the man or his body language, Brew sought other means to test his mettle.

'Eh...Rabbi, how did you know the baby was a laddie?'

'From your speech, it's a person's signature. What time is it?'

'Early. After eight. How do you mean, "signature"?'

'You're a grandfather.'

'Aye—'

'Which makes you a father.'

'Stepfather—'

'But you had only one child, a daughter.'

'Aye—?'

'But secretly all your life you wanted a son. Your stepdaughter gave you a grandson. And you love him like he was your own.'

'I say, you're better than a crystal ball, Rabbi.'

'The Zohar tells us, "From a man's mouth you can tell who he is."[44] When a person talks, he puts certain words in italics, in bold, and others in small print.'

Both prisoner and chaplain lapsed into thoughtful silence. Brew asked again, 'Your grandson, he's OK?'

'Thank HEAVEN, the doctor's got both barrels firing now. Amazin' how fast the littlest tykes get over the biggest things.'

Until then, reading the telltale signs in Roscoe's voice had put the odds in Brew's favour. His informed guesses had been correct. But now Brew detected a pull in another direction, not so clear. He risked, 'It sounds to me, that your dearest one has passed on. I'm sorry.'

'GOOD LORD, Rabbi Moray, I'm feeling the chill. At this rate you'll have me starkers, as naked as the day I was born. You Jewish people certainly still have the gift of prophecy,'

'Reverend Roscoe, I am only one Jew. And as for "the gift of prophecy", if this is where it's got me, I'm not so sure it's a gift.' Brew let a little space of time pass. 'So tell me, why be a prison chaplain?'

'Eh, well, it's a long story, Rabbi. Let's see now, it all began on January Eleventh, Nineteen ninety-one, the eve of the Gulf War. I was a Staff Sergeant—'

Roy Roscoe developed an acute pain in his right side while stationed with the Royal Scots Regiment on the Saudi-Kuwait border. Army doctors performed an emergency appendectomy in the main field hospital behind the lines. Hours after his operation, Joint Military Command ordered all beds immediately cleared in order to make way for the casualties expected in the coming days.

Still groggy from the anaesthetic and in considerable pain, Roy was bundled onto a Hercules transport for evacuation to greater safety. He was the only passenger on board. The empty plane was routinely flying out to bring back supplies from RAF Akrotiri on Cyprus. Over the Sinai peninsula in the middle of the night, a red warning light and piercing beep snapped the on-board engineer out of his kip. The hydraulic pressure in the landing carriage system had fallen to a dangerously low level. The plane had to be set down as soon as possible. King Hussein's tacit support for Saddam Hussein's regime ruled out the use of Jordan's facilities, and Egypt was no place for a seriously ill soldier. It was too late to turn back and Cyprus was still too far.

'That left Israel—' said Roy, clearly revelling in his story. Israel was not an ally, nor an enemy, but neither was she neutral. The outbreak of Operation Desert Storm and Iraq's Scud rocket attacks on Israel were still a few days away. The pilot radioed his Mayday call to the tower at Ben-Gurion Airport near Tel Aviv. Immediately, the controller instructed him to switch to a military frequency. After a few hasty minutes of British explanation and Israeli checks with Central Command, the RAF Hercules was given permission to land. At zero-one-hundred hours on January Twelfth, Roy was deplaned at Sde Elon Air Force base in the Lower Galilee. The diplomatically sensitive incident was never reported. 'Like it never happened,' Roy said.

Israeli doctors took one look at the patient and insisted that he be placed under post-operative care without delay. Roy was rushed by ambulance to Poriya Hospital overlooking Tiberias. He arrived in shock; the incision had torn open. He drifted in and out of consciousness with a high fever for ten days. His recovery was slow.

For security reasons Roy's interactions were strictly limited to doctors and nurses. He was confined to a private room. The view from the solitary window was mostly sky and a tantalisingly small jigsaw piece of the Sea of Galilee. 'It was so peaceful, folks were kind,

---

[44]The Zohar, or Book of Splendour, is a central work of Jewish mysticism, commentary and ancient lore dating from the 13th century. The exact source of the Rabbi's quotation here eludes me.

and I liked the sound of the language,' said Roy, recalling his stay as though it were yesterday.

When he was well enough to travel after three and half weeks in hospital and three extra days in a Tel Aviv hotel waiting for British Embassy bureaucratic wrangling, the worst of the war was over. Staff Sgt Roy Roscoe was shipped home to Scotland. The army debriefed him with strict orders not to reveal where he'd "served" during the Gulf War.

'I was never the same after Israel. I saw it as a turn of the ALMIGHTY'S hand at the steering wheel of life. In answer to HIS call—' Roy decided to learn the Holy Tongue well enough to read the Bible in the original. With only the aid of a *Teach Yourself Hebrew* grammar, a *Ben-Yehuda Pocket Dictionary* and some Berlitz tapes, he embarked on what became a life-long task. After he left the army, he took menial jobs to earn money for his education. He was twenty-seven when he slowly started to 'climb the steps of the Presbyterian ladder'— first lay reader, then deacon and finally, after seven years, Roy Roscoe was ordained a minister in the Church of Scotland.

Roy interrupted himself. 'Oh, my. I don't usually blether on like this. Here I am supposed to be comforting you—'

'You are,' answered Brew, grateful for the diversion Roy brought him. 'Please, go on. I'd like to hear more. Your wife, she must have been very special.'

'Oh, aye, she was...to put up with the likes of me.' Roy met and married Lucy soon after he began his Church work. She was a widow, who had a little four-year old daughter. Lucy and Roy decided not have children, because 'Jemima had been born a mite defective. You see,' he explained, 'Jemima has a good heart, but a weak head. And the local Jimmy Macs were quick to take advantage of her...situation.' In spite of her parents' explanations, pleadings and warnings, it happened. 'Jemima was only sixteen. Before the baby was born, my dear Lucy went, dead of a broken heart.'

Like the Ancient Mariner, thought Brew, who had his tale to tell, Roy went on. 'I didn't think I could love a child of sin. But after one look at his tiny wee face, the puritan in me melted away.'

So it was decided. The three generations would be best off living together. The baby, thank HEAVEN, was perfectly normal, except that one testicle had not descended. 'Nothing to worry about. As the doc said, "it's just a little snip of an operation we do when the baby gets a little older."'

Roy said that he was fond of telling his Murrayfield congregation, 'Little mouths convert disposable income into disposable nappies'. So to supplement his growing family's income, Reverend Roscoe gladly inherited the prison chaplain sideline from Reverend Wilkins, 'my old friend and predecessor at Murrayfield Church who suddenly died last year. So there you have it, Rabbi, the life and times of Reverend Roy Roscoe.'

Brew, his spirits lifted, calculated aloud. 'Let's see— the little lad's two, Jemima is eighteen, and Reverend Roscoe, you're forty-nine. Right?'

'Spot on, but how did know?'

'You told me.' Brew sounded pleased with himself.

'All right, then, let me think— I can convert our ages into Hebrew.' After a moment of reckoning, Roy came up with the conversions— 'Two is Beis, eighteen is Chai and forty-nine is Met.'

The Rabbi warmly congratulated the minister. But Roy had not rendered their ages as the numbers Brew expected, but as Hebrew letters combined into meaningful words. The words said that the baby had a "beis" or a home, that the girl had "chai" for life, but "met" meant that Roy would fall and die.[45] Hearing a second voice outside his door brought Brew back from his reverie.

'Good HEAVENS,' said Roy to the voice in amazement, 'is it already after eleven?'

'Who was that?' asked Brew.

'Officer Milne, on his rounds, come to tell me I have to go soon.'

'After eleven, I ought to be tucked up in bed. When will you come again?' Brew asked.

'Next Monday.' Then, off-handedly, Roy said, 'Ooo, by the way, Rabbi, what do they call it? Now what's that quaint phrase they use in Sheriff Court? Oh aye. "Pleading the diet"[46], that's it,' he answered his own question.

So that's his game, Brew concluded, engage my trust, and when I'm least expecting it, draw me out and snare me. 'That's right,' the Rabbi warily confirmed, '"pleading the diet".'

Chief Rabbi Brew Moray's morning court appearance had lasted only twenty minutes. During the hearing, he'd been intimately involved, yet strangely detached — because he never took his eyes off Deborah.

Sheriff Richard E. Calhoun in traditional wig, black robes and white collar sat on the bench. He put on his glasses and read out the charges. The procurator fiscal[47] then fired questions in short bursts at the suspect, prompting him to answer the charges. At this stage Jonathan Brodie had no right to object. Brew parroted, 'I refuse to answer questions on the advice of my advocate.' Calhoun cautioned the accused, 'Refusal to answer the state's questions at this stage can adversely prejudice your trial.' The Rabbi remained silent. Bail was denied, and the statutory remand period, the seven-day 'lie down' in custody was imposed. Brodie's plea for a temporary release during the Jewish New Year holiday in five days time was summarily dismissed.

The pang of seeing Deborah in court, but not being allowed to exchange even a single word, hurt more than the Sheriff's ruling.

Roy's voice came back. 'The papers say you entered a plea of "Not Guilty".'

'"Not Guilty", yes.' If this is some sort of trap, thought Brew, then why did Roscoe do most of the talking? Had he been recording their conversation? The incident at lunchtime rushed back into Brew's mind.

'On reflection,' said the Rabbi, thinking, let him record, 'there was only one good thing about this morning.'

'Which was—'

'The Sheriff agreed to allow kosher food to be brought to me once a day—' Brew had not touched any food for over two days — nothing since the slice of sponge cake he'd eaten on the Sabbath morning. Mr Sinclair was permitted to bring a kosher tray to the Castle gates, and a prison officer would deliver it to the Rabbi.

'Reverend Roscoe, who is the officer with the creaky voice?'

'Why do you ask?'

Brew decided to go on. 'The officer who brought in the kosher tray in called out "strip search!" I froze—' Brew had stared blankly as the creaky voice first tossed everything from

---

[45]Hebrew has two ways of expressing numbers: as cardinal numbers — achat (one), shtayim (two), shalosh (three), etc., or as represented by single or combined letters of the alphabet — aleph (one), bet or beis (two), gimel (three), etc. Thus "beis" means "house" and equals 2, "chet-yod", pronounced "chai", spells "life" and equals 18, while "mem-tet", pronounced "met", is the word for "fall" or "destruction" and equals 49. Numbers written as letters often form words, words which when spoken may reveal character, or even prophecy.

[46]Scots legal term, meaning to plead in court.

[47]Prosecutor.

the bed onto the floor. He then emptied the water from the pitcher and the bucket on the mattress and blankets, which had arrived only that morning. He rattled off the rules for inmates in solitary: no cigarettes, no papers, no books, no writing materials. Next, he ordered the prisoner to strip off his clothes. In a daze Brew did as he was told. Slapping on a latex glove, the officer shouted, 'Bend over,' and shoved his finger up. Brew jumped straight, sick with hurt and humiliation. His tormentor smirked, 'Lucky for you, you're clean,' and without taking the glove off, picked up the tray of food Mr Sinclair had brought, removed the plastic wrappings and stabbed with his gloved finger into each portion on the plate. Looking up, the creaky voice sneered at Brew naked and shivering. 'Sorry, sir,' he wheedled like a sour waiter, 'not enough seasoning for sir? What? No kosher salt—' He spat on the food. The spittle was brown, the colour and smell of stale tobacco. 'Now it's fit to eat. But dress for dinner first.' He threw prison pyjamas in Brew's face, and left chortling. Minutes later the prison food came in through the flap as usual.

Roy gave a nervy, embarrassed cough. 'Forgive me for saying this, Rabbi Moray, but I can't help it. Wicked men like him could only get born in a moment when the ALMIGHTY wasn't looking. That half-burnt face of his alone is enough to give a fella the willies. Murdo Duncan is his name. Chief prison officer. Scum always rises to the top. I'm ashamed to be a part of the human race, knowing the likes of him is one us— Tell me, can I get you something. You didn't eat?'

'I— I scraped away the little bits I thought I could manage to one side, and closed my eyes—'

* * *

Chapter XX

'Happy New Year'

[Sunday evening, September 20, 2009]

'Happy New Year, Soph.'[48]

Sophie suppressed a shriek. Welts like red patches on an inner tube covered her brother's face.

Neville reeled across the threshold. He smelled of sweat, and spoke in fear, 'I think it's what they call a warning—'

Sophie screamed, 'Jake! Jake!' Upstairs, Jake reluctantly dropped his Sunday paper on the kitchen table and pushed his bulk up from the chair.

Neville held on to the end of the banister to keep from falling over. Sophie helped support him. His breathing was rough. He was trembling. Her fingertips hovered over a fiery bruise on Neville's left temple. 'What have they done to you?'

Neville rasped, 'Don't think anything's broken.'

Again, Sophie called her husband.

'Jesus Almighty Christ!' puffed Jake as he stomped down the carpeted steps. 'Here, let me.' Jake wrapped Neville's free arm around his neck. 'What the hell kind of lamppost did you walk into, old son?'

'The kind that kicks—' slurred Neville.

Sophie slammed the front door shut. 'Let's get him upstairs, into the kitchen. I'll sponge him down.'

'Good man to have in my corner, our Sophie,' said Jake, snickering, as he eased Neville onto a chair.

Planting her knuckles on her ample hips, Sophie glowered, 'Men! Can't you lot ever cut out the cracks? Nev, you could have been killed.'

'Maybe we should get you over to the Infirmary, old son,' said Jake in contrition. 'Shouldn't this be reported to the police? Paper reports nasty incidents all over the shop. It's a bloody epidemic.'

Neville shook his head, 'I'll be all right. No hospitals. No cops, no cops.' Neville pushed something invisible with his bruised hand, as if to keep it at bay. 'I'll be all right in the morning.'

Sophie set a bowl on the table, spilling warm water over the edge. 'None of us will be all right in the morning, least of all you, Neville.' A hint of hysteria raised her voice to a fluty falsetto.

Two little voices called out, 'Mummy, Daddy— Is Uncle Nev here? Can we come kiss him good night?'

Sophie squawked, 'Benny, Naomi, you kids are supposed to be asleep.' To Jake, under her breath, 'Go in, please. I don't want them to see him like this. They'll have nightmares.'

---

[48]The Jewish New Year, or Rosh Hashanah, is celebrated over two days. The holiday is a time of reflection and hope, solemn prayers and festive meals. Rosh Hashanah symbolically bridges the year past to the year coming.

'Thanks, Soph,' said her brother.

'You belt up. I've had just about as much as I can stand in one evening.' Sophie dipped the cloth in the bowl. 'I'm sorry, I shouldn't have snapped.'

'Mummy— Daddy—'

'Go—' hissed Sophie.

Jake rushed off. 'Daddy's coming.'

Sophie twisted out the water from the cloth, and steadied her brother's head. 'It may sting a bit,' she said. At times like this she wished she'd stayed in Jerusalem—

From early childhood, Sophie had secretly dreamed of living in golden Jerusalem. With each passing year, her 'homing instinct' as she liked to call it, grew stronger. The alternative was deadly. To stay at home in dreary Edinburgh, 'hanging about like an old coat in a closet' for the rest of her life.

Also from very early on, Sophie was determined to become a nurse. As a child she loved to play 'sister'. When older, the girl her teachers called 'that young Miss Moray' did volunteer work at the Astley Ainslie Hospital. She liked cheering up the patients. At eighteen with school behind her, Sophie accepted that she was no academic, and so would never be the doctor her father wanted her to be. Anyway, she'd argue, medicine's impersonal, while nursing's relating. She would be a nurse, a carer and a comforter.

To combine her two lifelong dreams, Sophie applied to train in Jerusalem. She'd worked hard to fulfil the requirements, to complete innumerable forms, and line up references. The letter from the nursing school arrived on a dark day in March. She opened it. Acceptance! Relief and excitement fused through her. But also, for the first time in her life, Sophie felt the slight acidity of fright. Everything would be new and strange, and she had no relatives or friends in Jerusalem.

The day came to go. Anna Moray cried and hugged her baby like they'd never see each other again. Aggie Christmas held Sophie with barely controlled emotion. Manny, who disapproved of his only daughter going out to Israel, sent her off with a dry peck on the cheek. Neville gave her a brotherly handshake, unusually without a joke. Brew sent an electronic goodbye message on the day; he was away at the rabbinical seminary in Manchester.

And though she wouldn't have thought it, leaving Edinburgh was not easy. It was the city of her birth, the only place she'd ever lived. Pulling out of Waverley Station, alone on the train to London and the airport, Sophie helplessly shed tears for her hometown.

In Israel Sophie discovered she had a knack for Hebrew; her Scottish lilt gave her pronunciation a natural boost. Common sense and a fun-loving smile soon rewarded her with a circle of friends. While in training at Jerusalem's Hadassah Medical Center, the young student nurse from Scotland came into daily contact with hope and suffering, life and death. The key to it all, she concluded, seemed to be a common fate bound up in an ancient heritage. To satisfy her yearning to learn more about Judaism, Sophie attended night classes at a religious academy for girls in the Bayit Vegan neighbourhood.

At the beginning of her second year, Anna Moray mentioned in a letter that the son of a friend of a friend from Glasgow was planning to visit Israel. He'd finished reading bio-chemistry at Glasgow University, her mother wrote, and had been accepted to do an M.Sc. in immunology at Edinburgh University, so they'd have plenty in common. Would she show him around Jerusalem?

Jake Banks was big, blocky, confident, chummy. Even in the recession-ridden mid-Nineteen nineties, he knew how to have a good time. He loved Scotland and premier league football. From every pore he oozed Glasgow's reputation for rough edges, sentimentality and, above all, generosity. The student from 'home' dominated Sophie's time, but she didn't mind. She was falling in love.

The following year, Jake finished his Masters. Their letters and flights crisscrossed the Mediterranean, until Jake Banks proposed.

Sophie did not complete her nursing course. She gave up her career, her Jerusalem and much of her Jewish practice for Jake. She returned to Scotland, and the couple were joined under the marriage canopy at Edinburgh Synagogue on June Ninth, Nineteen ninety-eight.

After their wedding, Jake started studying accountancy part-time, because he decided he liked money better than science. He turned out to be good at making money in accounting and business, and still better, after he discovered the stock market.

As the flush of first love faded into the dirty socks of marriage, Sophie's longing for Jerusalem re-emerged, warmed by the flames of fond memories. From time to time she'd bring up her dream of living again in the Holy City. Jake easily fobbed her off. He needed to be in an English-speaking country for business reasons. Starting over and contending with Levantine commercial practices was not a sound formula for a successful career. The Middle East with all its tensions and conflicts was economically unstable, he argued.

In reality, they both knew that Jake was afraid. But Sophie loved her husband too much to confront him head on. Their unspoken truce had its merits: comfort, security, a good home, a stable marriage and family ties. Jake would have preferred to stay in Glasgow — football was *his* religion and the Celtics were *his* idols — but he sensed that living in Edinburgh was a vital compromise for his wife's sake.

The children came late, only after Jake was well established in business. Naomi was born first. She was two when Benjamin arrived on the eve of Scottish independence. With two tots to raise, Sophie gave up her dream of Jerusalem. Scotland would always be 'home'—

Neville flinched with every dab of Sophie's warm cloth. Worriedly looking at her brother, she repeated, 'Nev, I said, you're stopping here tonight. I don't want you waking up alone in the morning. You don't know what trauma can do to you.'

Jake came back into the kitchen. Seeing his brother-in-law cleaned up a little, he said, 'You Morays are cut from hard wood.' He gave Sophie a playful little kiss.

'Jake, please—' said Sophie. 'Go warm up the bed; you've got to be at work in the morning. I can organise the spare room for Nev, and clear up in here.' Jake left, muttering something about women. Sophie commented, 'That's for you, Nev, so you shouldn't think marriage is only a bed of roses. I'll make us some tea, and sort out your room for tonight.'

When Sophie came in again, Neville was shaking his throbbing head from side to side. 'I don't know anything any more, Soph. Nothing.' He stared into his milky tea. 'This thing is getting too big. It's wrecking our lives.'

Sophie had no answers. She stood in the middle of her kitchen. It was a good kitchen, if she said so herself. It was big, the biggest in the building. Kitchens in Georgian New Town flats were originally built small — intended for the cook, not the mistress of the house. But by taking over the larder and adjoining scullery, Sophie had hers expanded into a spacious, and yet cosy room. She enjoyed looking out on the Firth of Forth through the large, bright window over the stainless steel double sink. But best of all, the kitchen was her little green jungle. Sophie's beloved collection of forty-seven different furry-leafed African violets in foil-rimmed ceramic pots grew flamboyantly on shelves, counter tops, the refrigerator, and the spice rack, everywhere. Her kitchen, she thought, surveying it, would be the only place she'd miss, if—

'I don't know anything, any more,' Neville said again, as he picked up a spoon to stir his tea. 'I don't even know why I'm stirring this tea. Any word about Brew?'

'Nothing new, really.' Sophie sat down.

'Good. At least that,' said Neville. 'Has Deborah got over the Montrose visit? I never saw her so jittery as last Sunday.'

'It must have been harrowing for her, and tomorrow in court — again — won't be much better. At least Jon Brodie says she'll get to talk to Brew this time.'

'What about Mother? How's she?'

'As long as she's got the dog and Mrs Christmas, she'll be fine. She's always asking after you, Nev. Why don't you ever ring her?'

Neville sipped some tea. 'I wished I could just change stations and tune this life out.'

'Stop feeling sorry for yourself.'

Neville always thought his sister's slightly chubby face was particularly attractive when she was being assertive. Lucky Jake, lucky kids. 'Soph, tell me that I'm crazy for even thinking of wanting to stay here—'

'Don't you see, Nev? It's what Brew's saying: That *in Scotland* we're like wheels spinning in mud. We think we're stuck, but we can get out — with a little push.' Sophie stood up again, and looked down on her older brother's sweaty clumps of hair and his torn suit jacket.

Neville took a small Manila envelope out of an inside pocket, and slapped it on the table. 'Soph, do you know how many names I've got in here? Two hundred and bloody five. There's got to be more Jews in Edinburgh. I need to figure out how to do this crazy job.' He told her about his meeting with the Israeli agent. Neither knew what to say when he finished talking. Sophie stuck a little finger into the black soil of one of her potted plants. It came out damp and earthy. She'd been over-watering her 'babies' of late.

Neville started again. 'It's like Jake says, the papers are full of it. Every day another incident — death threats, beatings, dog crap pushed through letter boxes — too many hurt, and two dead.'

'Old men, from heart attacks,' Sophie said.

'OK, old men, but dead before their time. Now it's "ZOG"[49] this, and "ZOG" that, everywhere you go, on doors, walls. Why is it every time I see "Bastard", "Scum" or "Fucking" with "Yid" or "ZOG" tacked on, I get this knife-in-the-gut feeling?'

'It's not only us. The Asian and Black communities are feeling the heat, too,' said Sophie.

'Don't I know it. They blame us. A Bangladeshi, a good worker who's been with us for years, got bashed last week. Told me it was my fault, and quit the factory.' Neville turned his teacup around in its saucer. 'The anti-Semites know more about who the Jews are and where they live and work than we do. And every time something else happens, the media shout it from the rooftops, naming names and streets, giving everything but the house number.'

'Jon Brodie tells me that the police *do* catch a few of these thugs,' said Sophie, 'but some of the sheriffs are dismissing their crimes as "youthful misdemeanour", and giving them ridiculously light sentences. He says the courts are being pressured to be lenient. The government doesn't want the country to get a bad name.' Sophie sat again.

'You want to know what happened to me this evening, Soph?' Neville asked at last. Sophie kept quiet, let him talk. 'I'll tell you anyway. Put us both out of our misery. I'm being watched. Didn't dare go to synagogue...for *yontef*.[50] Had to give up driving — too easy to follow a car. To get here I hopped on and off three buses. I got off in Dean Street, opposite the church. I thought, right, that's bound to have shaken off any tail. Here I was

---

[49]Zionist Occupation Government.

[50]Yiddish from Hebrew, literally meaning a "good day", but designating any Jewish holiday, in this case the New Year holiday.

walking along in my own little bubble, an' over the road, a couple of total wallies, tattooed skinhead types, I mean the scene that makes cavemen look civilised, are slapping paint on a wall. I stop to gawp at that crap they're writing. And there comes this kind of empty second. Where everybody's sizing up the situation—

'The rest is slow motion, like one of those wildlife things you see on telly. The running. The tackle. The crumpling to the ground— I keep seeing it. Holy shit! Like it's not happening to me, but to some other poor sod—'

'Oh, my—' Sophie swallowed.

'They're on me like wild animals, kicking and punching the living crap out of me. I hear more than I feel. Somehow, there's no pain, only hurt. You know what the difference is?'

Sophie shook her head, no. Her eyes were stinging.

'I didn't get angry, Soph. I didn't hit back. I...didn't...hit...back,' Neville gagged. 'I couldn't look, I was so scared. I wanted to scream. I couldn't. I couldn't even scream.' Neville cupped his face in both hands. 'That's hurt.'

'Please, Nev, don't.'

'I was curled up on the ground. Taking it—'

'Nev—'

'I'm so ashamed. Where's the man in me? All I see is the worm,' he whimpered.

'Nev, don't hurt yourself any more. Please.'

'After it was over, I ran all the way here. Like a wee schoolboy. Thinking about it makes me sick.'

'Don't. If you'd've resisted, they might have killed you.' Sophie's teary eyes reddened. She took both his hands in hers, and pressed them to her burning face.

'You know, Soph,' said Neville, 'I don't know if Jake ever says it, but *I* think you're great.'

'That sounds like a miraculous recovery— Or maybe you're more hurt than I thought.'

'Now who's cracking jokes?' said Neville.

They wiped away their tears. Neville held up the envelope, and said, 'The bulk of the community live in Glasgow, but the cops have got my number. Anybody I meet with could also be marked. Maybe I shouldn't even be here.'

Sophie lifted an eyebrow. 'So you know what *I* say. I say *I* go across to Glasgow on a little shopping trip — looking for Jews. I'll go through on the train, get lost among the shoppers in the centre. I'd be ever so careful. Then I tootle off to as many synagogues, schools, old folks homes and whatever else—'

'OK, so you find a bod or two. Then what? "Hello, rabbi, we're going on exodus; give me your names, or else."'

'C'mon, be serious. I'll just say that we're raising money for Brew's legal defence. And we're wanting to blanket the entire community for funds, you know, a personal mailing campaign.'

'Soph, you're a genius.'

'One person will lead to another. I'll start a database on my computer.'

'And I'll double check people's names in the automated telecom listings to make sure their details are current.'

'That's it, think of ourselves as census takers.'

Neville turned pensive. 'I still don't know exactly why we're doing this. What *she* wants with all those names— I don't even know where to find the bloody woman.'

'What's her name again?'

'Guriat.'

'I saw her briefly, skulking around synagogue both days of the New Year,' said Sophie. 'Like Lilith in the night. You fancy her—'

'Don't, Soph.'

'Why not?' she smiled. 'Right, I shouldn't pry. It's late. Fancy a good, hot soak before bed?'

'That's the most relaxing offer I've had all day.'

On the way to his bath, Neville said, 'Good night, Soph, and thanks.'

Sophie stopped. 'I was just thinking, they weren't trying to rob you. Or they might have found that envelope—'

'That's what was so weird: They weren't actually hitting me *that* hard. They weren't trying to kill me, that's for sure. One of them had a short stick full of rusty nails, he kept waving it about. But he didn't use it. They were trying to scare me, a warning—'

'Did they say anything?'

'No, nothing. No threats, no curses. Not a word.'

'Did you see their faces?'

'No. Like I said, I was scared. The whole thing was over in seconds.'

'Nothing?'

'Except at the end. That's why it made some sort of sense.'

'Sense?' asked Sophie, her whole face tensing.

'Yes. A dark car drove up, slow. Stopped. For only a second. One of them shot the driver a look. The car screamed off, and the yobs beat it, too.'

'So—?' asked Sophie.

'I saw him.'

'Who?'

'The bastard, driving. You don't forget a face like that, Soph.'

'Who was he?

'Same copper that arrested Brew. The big filth.'

* * *

Chapter XXI

Gareth Gunn

[Monday, September 21, 2009]
Montrose's cabinet filed out. Only Justice Minister Judith Levitt looked back at the Prime Minister who remained behind, alone, to consider his next move. As he sat, thinking, he abstractedly gathered and squared his papers on the gleaming cabinet table. Finished, he looked around the empty seats of his government, Scotland's government, the first in three hundred years. He made up his mind. But as Montrose readied to go, he saw himself reflected in the mirror of the tabletop, and wavered. He cursed the lustrous blur, '*Damn him*. He's left me no choice.'

Fresh from the cabinet meeting, Angus Montrose walked in. 'Gareth.'
The chauffeur was half-leaning, half-sitting on the receptionist's desk. His peaked cap nested in his lap. At the sound of his name, Gunn let both feet drop to the carpet.
'You asked to see me, sir,' said the black-uniformed driver. He picked up his fallen cap from the floor.
'Yes, Gareth, you and I have business. Mrs Jamieson, we're not to be disturbed.'
'No, sir.' Her cheeks were burning.
Gareth Gunn followed Montrose through. The driver waited for the old man to get settled first before seating himself. Montrose pushed two squat glasses and a new bottle across his desk. 'Perhaps you'd like to join me in a drink?' Their eyes locked.
Gunn took off his leather gloves and poured both glasses full. 'What's the occasion, sir?' he asked, sliding one glass back and looking up. His grey-green eyes, catching the glare from the window, shut to a slit. Montrose swivelled round, and without getting up closed the heavy curtains. 'Better?'
'Much,' said Gunn.
Montrose said, 'Mrs Jamieson is *my* assistant—'
Gunn smiled, showing his bad teeth. Montrose was always reminded of snaggletoothed stones in country churchyards whenever he saw Gunn smile. The old man always thought Gunn handsome, until he opened his mouth. At their very first meeting, Montrose wanted to ask him why he never saw a dentist. Now, after nearly thirty years, it was too late to ask.
Montrose had taken to Gunn straight away, from the day the eighteen-year old sauntered into the Glasgow SNP[51] offices looking for a job. His working class pedigree was a refreshing change from the university-trained politicos and shrewd businessmen who had shared Montrose's crowded life, since the party elevated him to Glasgow district chairman.
After Gunn finished telling his brief but eventful life story, Montrose asked, 'But what can you do for our cause?'
'Drive.'

---

[51]Scottish National Party

'Done,' said Montrose with a look that said, young man, I like your style. They shook hands.

Over the years, Montrose allowed himself to grow close to his chauffeur, despite their differences in age and position. Gareth Gunn did much more than drive. Early on, sensing that Montrose's ambition left him no time for the ladies, Gunn made sure to keep his boss vicariously entertained with his own bedtime stories. In the confines of the official car, the two men could freely talk about many things.

Gunn was also an attentive and trusted listener. On long drives, Montrose liked to open up. He poured out smut on his political enemies, and enjoyed gloating over his latest in-fighting successes. Gunn instinctively steered clear of commenting on political matters at first. However, his job left him plenty of free time to read papers and chat up secretaries. His titbits of intelligence, dropped tactfully into Montrose's lap, often proved intriguing, and sometimes useful. And so Gunn gradually established himself in an informal advisory role.

'Mrs Jamieson—?' asked Montrose again.

Gunn's eyes glinted. 'Married women are always a challenge. They want it, and they don't want it. Isn't that right, sir?'

'Not Mrs Jamieson.' The old man's face iced over.

No one was more sensitive to the temperature changes in Montrose's mood than Gunn. 'Just a little toe in the pond; no intentions of putting my head under.'

'Good, good.' Montrose relaxed.

Even while serving as an MP at Westminster, Montrose still sat in the front seat with Gunn. But once elevated to Prime Minister, decorum dictated that Scotland's leader sit in the rear. In the past two years the driver and his passenger rarely saw each other except indirectly, as masks reflected in the rear-view mirror. Here, face-to-face, Gunn noticed the crevices, the filmy, red-rimmed eyes, the flap of skin under the chin. Montrose had aged.

'How long have we been together, Gareth?'

'You know as well as I do, sir, twenty-eight years.'

'A long overdue toast, then, to togetherness.' They raised their glasses and drank. 'I'm seventy-three. Tell me, Gareth, what do you see?'

'An older man.'

'I call that a good answer. Tactful—' This time Montrose poured the round. Lapsing into silence, he idly picked up the copperhead hammer, turned and twiddled it. The preliminaries were nearly over. 'It's not often I invite you to drink with me in my office, is it?'

'Only once before, if memory serves.' Gunn held his glass high, examining it like a jeweller inspecting a precious stone.

'Memory serves.' Montrose's hammer struck the cup of his hand with a smack.

Gunn emptied his glass unbidden, and immediately filled it again. As he put the bottle down, he looked Montrose straight in the eye.

The old man, laying his hammer aside, stared back. Then he, too, drank in one swallow.

Gunn pushed the bottle away from him. Montrose was on his own. He reached out without a murmur. Clutching his squat glass and the bottle, he joined them lip to lip, and poured. The fluid jerked out in three gushes. Montrose came to the point. 'We've got a problem, a disposal problem,' he said, then drank away the words in a single gulp.

Gunn instantaneously sensed his new position. 'Figured it was something along the Holloway line,' he said coldly. 'From all I hear, the cooler climate of Nova Scotia agrees with Frank.' Gunn smiled, his teeth showed.

The old man worked the knot of his tie. The last time he'd drunk with his chauffeur was at his Westminster office. Gunn, at Montrose's instigation, launched the rumour campaign that exploded in the "Holloway Affair". The messy police investigation that ensued scandalised Scottish Affairs Minister Frank Holloway. Rather than face a sensational trial, Holloway cut and ran to Canada. Nothing was ever traced to Montrose.

Gunn took the bottle by the neck, and poured again. He drew his forefinger around the rim of his glass. 'It's the Jew—'

'The Jew—' repeated Montrose, softly.

'The *Jew*—' Gunn crushed the word between his teeth the way a man puts his foot on a cigarette butt, grinding it into the ground.

The furrows on the old man's forehead deepened. 'Why the hot punch? You can't have met too many of the Chosen People.'

'Didn't need to meet too many. One was enough.'

'How so?'

'That lot — they'd peg their own mothers for a golf.'[52] Gunn waited.

'Go on, this interests me,' encouraged Montrose.

'Bastard screwed me, royally. I was a kid, sixteen.' As he spoke, Gunn did not look at Montrose; his finger circled his glass. 'Ever since there was Yids, somebody's been trying to get rid of them. Must be a damn good reason.' Gunn unbuttoned his jacket. 'You've got this problem—'

'No,' Montrose said, 'you tell me first— I mean, I don't think we've ever talked about this before. You say you don't like Jews— Because other folk don't like them? Historically?'

'Maybe—'

'Who was this..."bastard"? You've been holding out on me...all these years.'

'Just some maggoty blood sucker— Don't really like Catholics, either. So what—'

'This is not just "don't like". I hear hate. Why?'

'A man doesn't always need a reason—'

'Maybe not. Did you know him? This Jew—?'

'No. Not really. But so what. The little worm sold ma Mam's watch.' Gunn stiffened. 'She give it me, straight off her wrist, before she died. Told me to keep it away from my old man. "*He* is never to have it," she said.'

'I hear you.' Montrose assumed his most inviting expression, as he leaned forward on crossed forearms.

Gunn's flow accelerated. '*He* gave it to her...for her twenty-fifth birthday...a year after they got married. It...was the only thing nice he ever gave her...in the seventeen years they had together. I'd see her face in front of me whenever I looked at it.

'After Mam was gone, I got out of his house. The watch was the only thing I took. It was mine. But my old man had me charged for theft. Can you believe it? Ma own father? Sheriff let me keep the watch, but decided I'd be better off not living at home. That was my year in Borstal. After they let me out, I had nothing, but a tenner and Mam's watch. I pretended I was going home, but I didn't. Outside the gates, I stood there on the street, thinking what to do, where to go. On a whim, I blew the ten quid on a train ticket to Glasgow Central. I remember thinking, bloody big town for a Stirling lad. From the platform I went straight downstairs, kind of dopey, hoping something would turn up. Down on Argyle Street with the trains rumbling overhead, I felt scared. I looked around, and I saw this pawn, a wee shop like a mouse hole in a wall. I looked in the window, at all the shiny bits an' pieces. And I remembered seein' this film on telly, *The Glenn Miller Story*, where James Stewart's always hawking his trombone for a few crummy dollars when he's out of work, then he buys it back again whenever he's got a gig.

'So I went in. There was this little Jew behind the counter, black cap, stubbly chin and bulging blue eyes, all watery. He gives me a green ticket and twenty quid on the spot, no questions asked. Spoke Yiddishy, couldn't even speak English right. Told me, if I didn't

---

[52]Slang for a Scottish pound note. See Appendix 2.

redeem my ticket, he could sell the *vatch* after six weeks, without notifying me, 'cause only things over fifty quid's worth need notifying.

'After that I lived rough for a fortnight, until I picked up some work, humping furniture and clearing up at a upholsterer's. The minute I got paid at the end of the month, I went to redeem Mam's watch.' Gun wiped his forehead with his sleeve. 'I ran down to Central as fast as my legs would go. No bus. Just ran. I had the ticket in my hand. The Jew remembered. He just looked at me. I could see it. He didn't have to say it. Mam's watch was gone.' Gunn shook. 'I wanted to blow up the shitty little— To hurt him so bad. He sold it, Angus, he sold it—'

Montrose could not remember Gunn calling him "Angus" ever before. Not even on one of their early binges.

'Sure, he offered me money, they always do that. I wouldn't take it. But you know the worst—' Gunn pulled out his wallet, and opened it. 'I stood there...shaking—' He drew out a green chit, tattered, folded, brown around the edges. 'The worst was I did nothing, said nothing. Just tore and ran, so the fucker wouldn't see me...crying.' Gunn let the paper drop. 'Here's ma Mam's watch—'

The silence was shattered by Mrs Jamieson poking her head in. Montrose looked up. 'I thought I left instructions that we weren't to be disturbed.'

'Yes, I'm sorry, Prime Minister, but you've been so long. And Mrs Levitt's been waiting...to see you. She'd like a word, sir.'

'Mrs Levitt—?' said Montrose, recovering. 'Please ask her to be patient. We won't be much longer.'

Montrose bowed his head. His huge hands wiped his baldness from temples to crown to the back of his neck. As his fingers joined together prayerlike under his chin, he raised his face. 'Yes, like Holloway— But forever—'

'And ever. Amen,' quoted Gunn. 'Of course, we're talking serious rainy day savings. Sir—'

'Tomorrow, I will leave a briefcase on the back seat of the car. Lock it in the boot. If more funding is required, leave the case on the back seat with a note inside of how much—' Montrose began nervously playing with his hammer.

'It'll take time to arrange.'

'Time. There's to be no trial. It must be done before November second.'

'Jeez, tight. In the Castle—?'

'In the Castle. And something clear-cut, open and shut. No poison, no accident. Something the media will swallow, and not chew over. Men like *him* don't commit suicide.'

Gunn started to rim his glass round again. 'Let me get this straight. Unofficial execution. Maybe the act of a madman. In the open, plain to see, plenty of witnesses. Hmm, another prisoner— Maybe—'

In one swoop, Montrose lifted and drained his glass. 'If there were any other way— Hell knows I've tried.'

'We're talking premier league, here,' said Gunn.

'I know. And if anything, but anything goes wrong...Gareth Gunn is alone. I will deny, deny, deny.' Montrose's lower jaw slackened, hardly moving. 'And you and I, we don't talk about this again, ever. When it happens, the government will react with all the appropriate noises.' The voice Montrose heard — his own — sounded distant to him, as if it came out of another Montrose.

Gunn got up and put on his cap. 'This conversation never took place. Right?'

Montrose could not repeat the word, "right", not even in the closet of his own mind. 'After this is over, I fill the case one more time, yours to keep. Consider it your inheritance, from me to you, Gareth.'

Gunn reached for his glass, 'To Scotland,' and tipped it down his throat. 'Good whisky, sir. Don't bother to get up. I think I know the way out.' He set his empty glass next to Montrose's.

Even before Gunn closed the door behind him, Montrose was already resetting his mental stage for his Justice Minister. The butler announced her, 'Mrs Judith Levitt to see you, sir.'

'Thank you, Hamish.'

Large-built, erect, elegantly dressed, the lady marched straight in. 'Judith,' he said expansively. He stood up for her.

'I'll come directly to the point, Angus. We've known each other far too long for it to be otherwise.'

'Sit down, please, Judith,' he offered, waving her to the chair Gunn had vacated.

'I'll only be getting up again. The thing is, you know, Jonathan Brodie who is legal counsel acting for Rabbi Moray...he is my half-brother.'

'Your brother—? The man defending Moray, no, I didn't know.'

'No, half-brother. But unlike him — something else you don't know — by Jewish law, I'm *not* Jewish. Our father's second wife, my late mother, was Scottish, Presbyterian.[53] My late husband, Charles Levitt, was Jewish. It's all rather complicated.'

'Judith, my dear, I know what you're thinking—'

'No, Angus, you don't. Whatever the papers are insinuating, and despite what people may think, Moray means nothing to me...as a Jew.'

Montrose sat. 'So what's your point? Do sit down—'

'My point is that I am Minister of Justice. And Moray is a Scot, but he is a Scot who will not see justice in Scotland.' Montrose puffed up to speak. 'Angus, please. Let me finish. In effect, the pre-trial media circus is making it impossible to fairly try the man. And the opposition's line in the Estates yesterday was a dirty, contrived, point-scoring exercise, guaranteed to inflame public passion. Not only has the Rabbi been condemned before his trial, but by now, like it or not, every Jew in Scotland is tainted — ironically, including some of us, who are rejected by the Jewish people.'

'Not proven,' returned Montrose, indignantly.

Levitt shot back, 'Also considered a verdict in Scotland,[54] and one just as damning as guilty. Why didn't you let me raise the Moray affair in the Cabinet meeting this morning? You just scuppered the whole issue without giving any reason. Do you think I didn't see our colleagues sneaking looks at me — wondering where I stand? I'm sorry, very sorry, Angus. I'm handing in my letter of resignation.' She laid the letter on his desk, next to the two empty glasses. 'Angus, I'm left no other choice.'

Head down, studying his name on the envelope, Montrose said, 'We always have other choices. Always.'

* * *

---

[53] Only children born of a Jewish mother are considered Jews, according to the strict Orthodox interpretation of Jewish law. A child born of a Jewish father and a non-Jewish mother is not recognised as a Jew. The law stems from a statement in the Talmud, Tractate *Kiddushin*, 68b, "Your son by an Israelite woman is called your son, but your son by a foreign woman is not called your son."

[54] Scots law provides for three possible verdicts: guilty, not guilty, and not proven. The "not proven" verdict results when there is insufficient evidence to warrant a conviction, despite grave suspicion attaching to the accused.

Chapter XXII

Lessons

[Monday night, September 21, 2009]

Reverend Roscoe opened his folding chair. He brushed off the seat, then circled around it in the habitual way that an old dog does before hunkering down. The prison authorities did not let the chaplain enter inmates' cells without an officer in attendance. He'd long ago accepted the one major shortcoming of his pastoral visits: the solid steel door that separated him from his lost sheep. He knocked. 'Rabbi Moray? Roy Roscoe. Are you there?'

On his side of the door, Brew sat on the top step. A daydream flew him back to the cool, green chasm of his desert mountain. He saw himself sitting, and learning the holy books. He looked up at the stone sepulchre that ruled the secret place in eternal silence. The inscription ran before his eyes, but he still could not make out the swimming letters. Next, his mind jumped to the events of his morning in court. And now Roy channelled Brew's thoughts in another direction. 'Are you there?' he asks. If his question turned on 'there', where else could he be? But if 'you' were the crucial element, the answer was debatable. The body and the mind are separable. You, the mind, can be any place...in the past or future, free and carefree, while you, the body, sits locked up...here, now and maybe forever.

Roy knocked again, 'Rabbi? Are you all right?'

Brew bent down, and spoke into the flap. 'Fine, and you, Reverend?'

'All cylinders firing.'

'And the young lad—?'

'Ooo, back to bawlin' his head off whenever he's hungry, which seems all the time.' Roy let a moment of awkward silence pass before feeling compelled to say something. 'Apropos of nothing, did I ever tell you about the time I stayed up all night with a beautiful lassie? No, of course not. So pretty, and young— Poor thing was in hospital, very ill, cancer. She was only ten, but such a bright spark. She knew— And she wasn't afraid. She says to me, "Tomorrow, I'll be with Jesus, in heaven; and I'll be well again." Such an innocent she was. I sat with her all night. We lost her before the sun came up. I left the hospital angry, so angry. I shook both fists at HEAVEN, and I shouted at the top of my voice, I shouted, "YOU bastard, YOU!" And then I thought about it a moment, and chuckled out loud. And I said to HIM, "And YOUR son's a bastard, too."'

That story always worked with his parishioners. The Rabbi was not amused. Roy tried again, 'This Sunday's sermon's going to be on prophecy. It's something you said last week' — he tapped his temple — 'that got me thinking.'

'And what conclusions did you come to, Reverend?'

'Well, it goes something like this. Old-time prophecy's just got stopped at a red light. That's all. It's only a matter of time before the GOOD LORD changes the light to green, and folks can move on.'

'But what if prophecy's stuck not behind a red light, but an iron door?' asked the Rabbi, his voice sounding tired and morose.

Roy flicked an internal switch. 'I always like to begin my sermons with a funny story. HEAVEN only knows religion's serious enough without us lot going on like tired old miseries, sighing and sorrowing. How about this one for Sunday? A Scottish preacher, the likes of an Old Testament Prophet, famous for his spell-binding sermons, and one Sunday morning he was bellowing, "an' there was a-weepin' an' a-wailin' an' a-gnashin' of teeth throughout the land" and one of his parishioners, a little old lady in the pews, speaks up, "what if I havnae got any teeth?" And the preacher answers back, "Madam, teeth will be provided."'

This time Brew chuckled in spite of himself, 'Roy, if I weren't otherwise detained this Sunday, I'd want to hear that sermon.'

I know it's an old joke, Rabbi, but you've given me a great idea. You know, I preach in the prison chapel once a month. Maybe next time we could share the pulpit, you and I. What do you say?'

'I don't know,' Brew said, 'I'm no preacher, I'm a teacher, a rabbi—'

'So you tell them what the difference is, what it means to be a rabbi—'

'That's a thought—'

'You don't sound too sure, Rabbi,' said Roy. 'You can keep it very short. You know, my father was a publican. And he knew the secret of a good sermon, he did. Short an' sweet. He'd always say to me, "Son, watch their eyes. When they glaze over, put more top on the beer, an' call closing time."'

Again, Brew laughed. His laughing, however, came to a sudden end. 'The chief officer—Duncan. What if he—?'

Roy said simply, 'I will be there, with you.'

"...there, with you—" That morning Brew Moray had again been in Sheriff Court. The second hearing was shorter than the first. Again he'd not been allowed to speak to Deborah — despite the promises of Jon Brodie, his advocate. Worse, Sheriff Calhoun declared, 'The suspect is remanded in custody until his trial. And considering the sensitive nature and the magnitude of the alleged crimes, the accused shall be denied all visiting rights with the exception of legal counsel.' Trial was set to begin at ten o'clock on Monday, November second.

'Rabbi, could I ask you a favour—'

'"Ask, and it shall be given you—"'

And Roy continued, 'Seek, and ye shall find; knock, and it shall be opened unto you—'[55]

'Reverend—'

'Give me a Hebrew lesson or two. It isn't easy for a Murrayfield parson to find a good teacher.'

'That's all you're asking me—?'

'I can't afford to pay you much.'

'Away with you. Tell me another story or two, and that'll be all the payment I'll ever want.'

'Deal. Is there anything I can do for you? Anything I can get you?'

The Rabbi, without a moment's delay, said, 'As a matter of fact, there is something— Why don't we start our lessons with the Book of Jonah? It's short, and the Hebrew tells Jonah's story so powerfully, much better than any translation.'

Roy agreed. 'But you haven't told me what you want. I hope it's not the key to this door.'

Brew's answer was elusive. 'I've just made myself a resolution, and with your help, Reverend Roscoe, I'm going to keep it. But Monday night's too late. Can you come before?'

---

[55]Matt. 7.7.

'Will Sunday morning after church be all right?'

'Perfect. How will I ever be able to thank you?'

'Ooo, I'll think of some way that won't hurt too much,' said Roy with mock seriousness.

Roy Roscoe had a pure, refreshing impishness about him, one that the Rabbi had never before met among his Christian counterparts. 'You won't have any trouble getting in here on Sunday? I mean it's not your regular day,' Brew asked.

'Not to worry, Rabbi, not to worry— I can only come into a prisoner's cell in the presence of an officer, but if it is something I can pass through the flap, it's no problem. You still haven't told me what it is you want me to bring you.'

'Go to my wife Deborah, please, and tell her that I'm doing well, thanks to you, Reverend Roscoe—'

'Now, don't embarrass me, Rabbi—'

'I'm not. I'm flattering you.'

'Ooo, that's okay.'

Brew struggled to remain serious. 'Ask her for two prayer books for the Day of Atonement. One is for you. The Book of Jonah's in there, part of the afternoon service. Deborah will find it for you.'

'Day of Atonement—? I don't understand. Why not use the Bible?' asked Roy, perplexed.

'On the Day of Atonement, this coming Monday, we read the whole of Jonah aloud in the synagogue — all four chapters.'[56]

'Ah, of course, the Fast of Atonement — Yom Kippur — the most solemn day in the Jewish year. Why didn't you say so in the first place?' said Roy. 'May you be inscribed in the Book of Life.[57] Isn't that the blessing?'

'It is so. And may *we all* be inscribed in the Book of Life.' A twinge of guilt streaked through Brew for ever having doubted Reverend Roy Roscoe, or himself—

* * *

---

[56]It is, my sources inform me, something of a mystery why the Jewish Sages determined that the Book of Jonah should be read on the Day of Atonement. Many reasons are advanced by later commentators. Some say that the story was included to stress the insignificance of man in the universe: Throughout the book, Jonah is dwarfed, first by the powerful tempest, then by the great fish and finally, by his mammoth task of having to subdue the great city of Nineveh, "three days' walk across". However, others interpret the Book of Jonah to be about pride and defiance in the face of God: The Prophet tries to hide in a ship, to run away to Tarshish and then die at the bottom of the sea. Here the message is one of directions: No matter how far down the wrong path a person may go, it is never too late to turn back, and to repent.

There is no more enigmatic book in the Bible than Jonah. With its "no-end" ending, it's a very "modern short story" that asks more questions than it answers. Perhaps the Sages ordained the reading of Jonah on Yom Kippur because they felt that fasters could use the diversion of a good story on what is always a very long day.

[57]See Chapter 10, fn. 3.

Chapter XXIII

Two Meetings

[Sunday evening, September 27, 2009]
The weapon in Guriat Gaoni's shoulder bag had an oddball feel to it. Israel Military Industries had secretly designed and built the polymer KTL especially for defence. With the bullets removed, the entirely non-metal automatic was small and safe to carry through airport security checks. Agents called it the "belly barrel", because of the dual-purpose sound chamber under the gun-barrel. The device made harmless "para-blanks" explode with a deafening crack, while, conversely, silencing live rounds. Before leaving her room at the Howard Inn, Guriat had carefully reloaded the clip with fresh ammunition in the standard order: Two non-lethal para-blanks — 'the two good ones,' she called them — followed by eight deadly, hollow-point rounds. In all but the rarest cases, it had been proven that the first two explosive shots, fired in quick succession, temporarily disorient targets, driving them to take cover or retreat. But if a target persisted, the third and following rounds would kill.

She waited inconspicuously at a bus stop. It gave her an unimpeded view of the church. Dreary street lighting scattered over the rain-slick tarmac. The Indian shop on the near corner was still open. She heard shreds of music coming from the "Cross Keys" pub at the far end of the road. Traffic was normal.

The time was right. She stepped forward. For once she was not wearing dark glasses. On a rainy night in a tough inner Edinburgh neighbourhood, shades might have attracted somebody's unwelcome attention.

She casually dragged a finger across the bonnets of the parked cars. All but one, a silver-grey Merc 320D, were cold; she made a mental note of its registration number.

Over the road, she headed straight for the church. The notice board read,

MURRAYFIELD PARISH CHURCH
Rev Roy Roscoe, BD, Minister
Pray for Peace

Evening Prayer was over, and ten minutes had elapsed since the last worshipper left. The entrance door stood half open. Guriat mounted the steps and slipped inside without a sound. Only the vestibule was lit. Guided by the weak glow, she entered into the main church. A wide aisle cut down the middle of the low-raftered, unadorned sanctuary. Her eyes swept across the silent pews. Inside the shoulder bag, her thumb flipped off the KTL's safety. She started moving towards the altar in measured steps. Her gun hand tensed. A grey figure sat at the end of the first row. He was slumped to one side. 'Reverend Roy Roscoe—?'

His head jolted. Guriat stopped dead, ready to draw. 'Didn't hear you coming,' he said. 'Must have dozed off.'

'Roy Roscoe?'

'That's me. And there's nothing to be afraid of here, young lady.' It was *his* voice, matching the one she'd recorded from the telephone and listened to several times before setting out. 'We're alone. And I'm bound to say, from what I can see, you're a very pretty lass.'

Guriat exhaled. 'And you're not at all what I expected. More, dapper—' His white hairline crossed the crown of his head. Tufts of black hair grew out of his ears. His blue eyes picked up glints of dim light as he spoke. 'Charming the whiskers off the cat, that's my province. Do sit down.' She sat on the other side of the aisle. 'So, what can one nosy, old mendicant do for an angel like yourself?'

'A great deal,' she said.

'Is that all?' answered Roy. 'So when do we get started?'

The sensor built into her wristwatch remained on default. If Roy Roscoe were wired, the device would have activated, transmitting a tiny electric warning pulse to her skin. 'Are you always this cheerful, Reverend Roscoe? Or is it only when you're in the presence of an "angel"?'

'GOOD LORD, no, not always. But I try. Cheerfulness goes with the calling.'

'Being a minister?'

'No, being a human being.' Roy adjusted his head and shoulders for more comfort and better eye contact. 'The way I see it, with all that dull matter out there in the universe, we spiritual beings have a responsibility to be cheerful. The universe doesn't need more dull matter to make it go around. We're here because we need each other.' Guriat considered his philosophy. Nothing in her training had prepared her for such an encounter. In her line, corruptible politicians and sleazy businessmen were the usual objects of her attentions. He went on, 'I do blether on, don't I? Next week's sermon. I don't even know your name.'

'Hulda.' It was harder to lie without protective glasses.

'Unusual name, that. Hulda—'

'Reverend—'

'Call me Roy. It's easier.'

'Roy—' Guriat's lips pressed shut. For the first time in her career, she was approaching a source with no front, no dextrous posing, and only one small deception, her name. Her intuition told her that routine field patterns were not going to work here. From the beginning, this operation had been different, without precedent. Scotland was a backwater. There were none of the usual surveillance and security teams in place, no pre-arranged safe houses, no chain-of-command setup, and certainly no assassination squads. Liaising with the embassy and communications with Tel Aviv had had to be kept to the absolute minimum. She had no fallback position. All ongoing operational decisions were hers. Instinct and experience were her only guides. 'Your duties— You're the chaplain at Saughton Prison and Edinburgh Castle.'

Roy picked up immediately, 'This has something to do with Rabbi Moray. You're some sort of government agent. No, of course not. Not unless Mr Montrose is bringing back exiles from Australia—' He looked her straight in eye, letting her know that he would recognise and appreciate the truth.

'I'm Israeli.'

'That's better, now we can talk. Aye— Hulda— A Hebrew name, a prophetess. *Shanah Tovah*. Is that right? A Good Year.'

'Yes, thank you.' Guriat sensed Roscoe's irresistible humanity. 'I want you to know, it wasn't easy for me to come here. I carry a lot of overweight when it comes to Christians, but that's another story—' She caught herself. As a professional intelligence gatherer, she couldn't help admiring how subtle he was at opening people up. She began again, 'I know you passed Rabbi Moray a prayer book for Yom Kippur — the Day of Atonement — and that he's teaching you Hebrew.'

'You've spoken to Mr Sinclair—'

'I'd rather not say.' She paused. 'Look, the Jews in Scotland don't know who their friends are. Their real friends. But they're beginning to find out who their enemies are.' Again, she hesitated. 'I'm taking a big chance coming here like this. Talking to you. Trusting you. But I'm asking you to take an even bigger chance. To trust me. All I can say is, if you help us, it could be dangerous for you, very dangerous.'

'Keep going. I hear you.'

'The thing is, I'll stop right now and go away. You never saw me, and we never spoke.'

'I'm still in listening mode—' Roy leaned forward into the aisle.

'I need information. I understand you intend to ask Rabbi Moray to give the sermon at your next Sunday morning service in the Castle.'

'Correct. I have proposed the idea to him, but at the moment the offer stands open.'

'Do you think you can get him to agree?'

'Well, I believe he's a wee bit reticent, actually. He's leery of that sadist, Duncan, and with good reason.'

'Duncan?'

'Aye. Murdo Duncan, chief prison officer. The kind who's in the job to hurt people.'

'Again, I reiterate, Roy — talking to me can be hazardous to your health.'

'You don't look like Lucifer.'

'Not unless Lucifer's a woman. But you know what they say about the Devil coming in many guises.'

'The same is also said of his opposite number. Look, I'm going to be serious for a moment. As a minister I've spent a lot of time thinking about the big questions, perhaps too much. And I haven't come to a single conclusion. Not one. With a record like that I should have chucked in the GOOD LORD'S work ages ago. The way I see it, the only reason I haven't is because it's HIS way of steering me into places where I may be of use to others. I've given up asking how and why. I just believe and do.'

Guriat leaned closer, and asked, 'When will that prayer service be?'

'My standard time is the Sunday closest to the fifteenth of the month...let's see...diary,' mumbled Roy as he fished around in the pocket of his jacket. Flipping pages backwards and forwards, Roy said, 'Here we are...Sunday morning, October the eleventh.'

'Hmm, tight,' said Guriat. 'Any chance for the Sunday after? That will allow for all the Jewish holidays to finish.'

'The eighteenth. Aye, I could re-jig the date this month, if the Prison Governor agrees. Not a bad sort, he is. Usually an appeal to Christian charity works with him.'

'Time?'

'We kick off at eleven sharp.'

'Where is the service held?'

'In St Margaret's Chapel. You wouldn't be thinking what I think you're thinking.' Her steady look said, no comment. Roy swallowed his Adam's apple, then stood up, 'I'm not afraid to stand up and say that I think independence has made Scotland poorer in every way. And what the hell, sometimes miracles need a little prod.' He sat. 'Any more questions?'

Guriat suppressed a strong urge to get up and hug Roy. 'Yes. Are the prisoners shackled or handcuffed during the service?'

'Both — and they're chained together. There aren't many of them, about fifteen. But, if Rabbi Moray were to give a sermon from the pulpit, I'd take his case to the Governor. No one will stand before my congregation, aye, before the LORD, bound hand and foot.' Roy gave a devilish grin. 'Next.'

'Officers—'

'Usually no more than two, one inside, one out. They don't like my sermons,' he chuckled. But like a pricked balloon, he quickly went flat, 'Armed, I'm afraid— I've not succeeded in keeping firearms out of prayer meetings.' And to Guriat's 'Aha—' Roy added, 'The chapel door is double-locked from inside and out during the service. No tourists allowed in, you can imagine—'

'But family members *are* allowed to participate—?'

'Rarely. It's been known to happen. But not without a special pass from the Governor. Young lady, you're stretching that man's charitable nature into sainthood, not to mention testing my powers of persuasion to their limits. Anybody admitted to prison services is thoroughly body-searched. And it's Duncan who does the deed.'

'Last question, again. What do you think the chances are Rabbi Moray will agree to speak? My best guess is it wouldn't help your argument if you let on about our little talk.'

'He did say that he'd like to hear me preach a lesson, and we'd both like to see each other face to face.' Roy ringed his finger around his collar. 'But, well, whether he'll agree to speak—'

'If we can get his wife in, he'll agree. It's crucial— I don't think there's going to be any trial— I believe his life is in danger.'

'What makes you think you can trust me?'

'Because you're not afraid.'

'Oh, I *am* afraid. But I'm more afraid if I don't do something. Scripture says, "Your own friend and your father's friend, forsake not."[58] It's as simple as that. But there I go, gasbagging again.'

Guriat couldn't resist any longer. She got up, and gave him a peck on his head like a hummingbird dipping into a blossom. Each waited for the other to say something. Roy went first. 'Far be it for me to ask you what you're planning, but have you thought about how you'll spirit the good Rabbi out of the Castle? It's impregnable, you know.'

'Angels have wings—'

'As a matter of fact, I was thinking quite the opposite.' Roy kneaded his chin. 'Rather more like the route taken by old King Zedekiah.[59] When it comes to getting a body out of a tight spot, there's nothing like the tips you pick up in the Hebrew Bible.' Guriat's naked eyes probed him. 'Here, sit down again, lass,' — he patted the place next to him — 'the telling'll take a bit of time.' She sat. Roy began, 'I don't suppose you'd have heard of Augustus Wright.' He knew she hadn't. 'Well, then—'

*

A whistle had crept into his creaky voice. 'What do you want me to say?' Talking worked his chinless jaw and thick lips. The angry red skin on the left cheek and temple glistened with sweat. His cold, sparrowlike eyes rolled like glazed marbles. 'You still haven't told me your name...or who you are—'

---

[58]Proverbs 27.10. Reverend Roscoe appears to interpret "father" spelled with a capital "F", as in Father in Heaven.

[59]Roscoe's reference is to the legend of King Zedekiah's escape from the Babylonian siege of Jerusalem through a cave under the walls of the city. The cave exists, however, the Bible makes no specific link between the cave and Zedekiah's flight. See Jer. 39.4 and II Kings 25.4.

Gareth Gunn lowered his gaze to the hands folded across the man's barrel-chest. The knuckles were blue and his nails chewed to the quick. A small, black mark like an ink blot bruised the back of his right hand. Gunn looked harder. It was a tattoo.

'Look, I'll go over it once more,' said Gunn. Patiently, he told the man opposite him that he would be a millionaire 'in hard currency, English pounds, sterling. Go on, open it,' said the driver, directing his eyes to the envelope on the table. The man looked at it. 'In here,' Gunn pointed, 'you'll find an account number and details of an off-shore bank, and ten thousand quid, cash — your retainer, tax-free. We've already deposited half a million in *your* account, man. Don't take my word for it. Get in touch with the bank. You get the other half million when the job's done.'

'Quibbles,' said the burnt face. 'The colour of your money—' He tapped the table with the edge of a beer mat.

'Laundered as white as bleached sand,' Gunn assured him.

'I'm thinking,' said the other.

'Look, man, if it's not you, we'll find some other player. We don't repeat an offer like this. It's a once in a lifetime opportunity.' Gunn sipped his ale like nothing mattered. At the bar the Sunday night regulars were quietly talking under a low-hanging cloud of tobacco smoke. The Lanarks' hit single *Flower of Scotland* played in background.

'Why not make it look like suicide?' he asked. 'Why do it openly, with witnesses?' His voice was whistling again.

'Because—' answered Gunn, 'Like I said, the cops and the media types will ask questions if the man's found dead. That makes it a mystery, a challenge. Right? They'll dig. They won't rest until they find out who was behind it. This isn't a murder. It's gotta be an execution. Right?'

The drinks were on Gunn. He wasn't counting. As soon as his guest finished a pint, an attentive barmaid took away the empty glass and replaced it with another round. After every drink, the back of his tattooed hand wiped away the froth. The burnt cheek seemed to grow rawer with each pint.

'I'm no head-banging schizo,' he protested drunkenly.

'Nobody's sayin' you are. Look—' said the driver, trying hard not to show his exasperation, '*I* know you're not mental. *You* know you're not mental. But we make it look that way. So you can plead diminished responsibility on the grounds of temporary insanity. And there's your family history to prove it. Your father, mental disease. What they overlooked when you were hired into the correction service.'

'Old man's dead and gone. He did drugs, he wasn't mental.'

'Who gave you that burn?'

'Accident— He dinnae mean to. Lost his fuckin' temper, that's all.'

Gunn whispered, 'No, man, you claim child abuse. Scarred you for life, inside and out. You cop ten years in the facility at Carstairs Junction. Guaranteed five-star treatment, and in three to five *we* see you're out for good behaviour. What could be easier?'

'Who's this "we"?'

'I don't know any more than you. The gods pay me to be a messenger. Likes of you and me, shit, man, we're just mortals. Right?'

'Maybe you're the sunshine you say you are. Maybe not. But you don't understand nothing 'bout me.' The man's black eyes narrowed to angry incisions. 'I wouldnae be saying this if I wasn't half pissed. On the inside I'm Screw Numero Uno. Mr It. Yes, sir. No, sir. Get it? Men crap themselves when they see me coming. And ya know something. I like it that way. And ya know why? Because outside I'm nothing. The wife bitches me night and day; brats screamin' like stuck pigs; the house, a fuckin' sewer pipe, a bleedin' midden. Jeez— Do you hear what I'm saying?'

'Loud and clear. But lordin' it over scum'll never bring you what *you* want.'

'And what do I want, Mr Know-it-all?'

'Respect.' The driver's quietly spoken word hit him like a kick in the gut. Gunn pursued his advantage: 'Money brings a man respect.'

He shook his head like a dazed fighter. 'And you take care of the missus and the weans while I'm away?'

'Didn't I say that?' said Gunn.

'And when I do it, I keep yelling, "The dreams, the dreams, the dreams told me."'

'That's all there's to it. We take care of the rest.'

The tattooed hand reached out, fingers spread. He took the brown envelope. 'This doesn't mean, yes. First, I've got some checking to do.'

'You do that, friend. Tomorrow,' said Gunn, 'I'll be on Middle Pier, Granton Marina, six in the evening. Got that? Meet me there. We've got details to work out.'

'And if I don't?'

'You keep the cash in the envelope — shut-up money; as for the funds in the offshore, they'll just have to go looking for another depositor.'

'What's to stop me from drawing out my money right now?'

'It's in trust,' said Gunn, like a chess master pronouncing "mate".

'You've thought of everything.' He balled his right hand into a fist. The tattoo stretched into a lizard's padded foot.

Gunn pulled out a crisp fifty-pound note, and left it on the table. 'Tip for the barmaid,' he said with blase satisfaction. He slid out of the booth, and disappeared through the smoke.

On the way to his Mercedes, Gunn sucked in a lungful of fresh, rain-washed air. He passed the Murrayfield Church without notice. All his thoughts focused on the man he left behind at the "Cross Keys" — chief prison officer Murdo Duncan.

* * *

Chapter XXIV

Angels Don't Bleed

[Monday, September 28, 2009]

Brew stopped his praying to look up. The harsh, flickering fluorescence dazzled him. He pleaded, 'What right have *I* to stand before *YOU*—?'

The Fast of Yom Kippur had begun the evening before at sundown.[60] Brew stood, and resolved to stay standing until the next evening. He wrapped his head and shoulders in his blanket, and took the prayerbook that Roy had smuggled to him in his hands. Herein was his whole world. He began to atone. The walls of his vault reverberated with every sound he made. Each time he turned a page, the noise sounded as if his whole congregation were with him in his cell.

No food or drink passed his lips.

Many times throughout the night and day dark instances of the past year intruded. By his stubbornness and defiance, he had brought shame and suffering on the very community he was charged to guard and shepherd. Because he had been afraid, he was not there to honour his dear father's memory, or to cry with his mother and family. And the dream that he dreamt might have cost Deborah the chance to conceive the child she so desperately wanted. Brew had never asked her to forgive him.[61] Tears burned his cheeks, and fell onto the pages of his prayerbook.

From his place in the service Brew knew it was well past noon. These hours were the longest of the day. He was feeling weak, light-headed.

'What right have *I*—?' he asked again, his head spinning. He began to float lighter than air. At last his soul was growing the wings of an angel, and taking flight. Here was the answer Brew prayed for.

The Rabbi laid his open prayerbook on the bed. Reciting '"We bend the knee,"' he dropped to his knees, '"and bow in worship—"' he arched over, touching his hands and face to the stone floor.

Each year, at this time when he was his lowest, Brew heard the voice of Rabbi Rozanski, his first teacher whom he loved. The old man needed help getting up so those around him were near enough to hear him ask, 'What right have *I* to stand before *YOU*—?' He was gone now, but his question haunted Brew.

As the Rabbi, fully prostrate, was honouring the memory of his teacher, the lock turned, and the cell door swung open. Before Brew knew what was happening, Murdo Duncan rolled him over with his foot and yelped, 'Inspection, Rabbi!' Duncan picked up the open prayerbook from the bed, and snapped it shut with a crack. 'What's this? You

---

[60]The Hebrew calendar day begins and ends at sunset.

[61]On the Day of Atonement, according to the Jewish code of law, one has the right only to ask for God's forgiveness for transgressions against Him. There is no Divine atonement for sins committed against one's fellow man or woman, unless a sincere attempt is first made to ask forgiveness directly from the injured party. Should forgiveness be denied, only then may the transgressor turn to God.

know the rules. No unauthorised books.' His voice deadened. 'Where'd you get it? Who brought in this crock o' shit?'

Brew, reflexes cutting in, scrabbled to replace the skullcap knocked off his head. Duncan pushed him down again, pinning him underfoot like a hunter claiming his prey. From where he lay Brew turned his face upward to his tormentor. The prison officer's foot pressed harder, but under the intense, unflinching glare of Brew's eyes, Duncan staggered. His weight shifted back. 'What you looking at, you little fart?'

'Put the book down,' said the Rabbi. 'It means nothing to you.'

'You piss-water-poor excuse for a prick. No manners today? No "please and thank you, sir"? Who gave you the fuckin' book? That meddling preacher, right? What does it say?' Duncan removed his foot.

Slowly, Brew pushed himself up on all fours, and without taking his gaze off the prayerbook, came to his feet. 'Give me the book,' he repeated, holding out his hand, 'before you commit an indignity you will regret.'

'Look who's talking,' said Duncan through clenched teeth. His burnt cheek quivered. The ceiling light flickered in Duncan's black eyes and gleamed back in tiny multiple reflections.

Brew saw the blind hate of a man who hated himself. He said softly, 'You are interrupting a Jew's prayers on the holiest day of the year. I ask you, please, return the book, and leave.'

'Do you think I give a flying fuck about Jew prayers or Jew books? Or any of you bible-banging bastards?' snarled Duncan. He opened the book, and peered at the writing. A nasty little smirk began to play around the corners of his mouth.

The Rabbi warned, 'For the last time, for your own sake—'

The officer's face went black. 'Are you threatening me, little man?'

'No. No threat,' responded the Rabbi.

'Then what?'

'I'm saying, be careful—'

Duncan's eyes flicked from the book to the prisoner and back again. He stiffened, then turned his back on Brew like a reckless lion tamer. He went over to the black bucket, and brutally kicked it, spilling the water over the floor.

The Rabbi turned white.

Duncan stood over the hole, and opened the book. Grimly, he started tearing. Ripping out whole sections. And crumpling the paper into balls, he dropped them down the opening. 'Holy shit,' he crowed, his creaking voice thick with irony. 'Where are your poxy prayers now?'

Every muscle in Brew Moray's body recoiled. 'Noooo—' he cried out as he lunged for the prayerbook. With both hands he clutched at it, pulling, tugging, desperately trying to wrench it loose from Duncan's grip. Brew wrestled free only one of its precious leaves before Duncan unholstered his weapon, and with one powerful swipe of it flung the Rabbi away like a bear throwing aside a baying dog.

Brew went sprawling. His head hit the sharp edge of the table, knocking over the water pitcher. The blow momentarily stunned him. He lay in a heap.

Seeing blood oozing out of the prisoner's head, Duncan went to his side. 'I should kill you now — for attacking an officer,' he said, grinding the barrel of his weapon against Brew's temple. Dropping the book, Duncan pulled the prisoner's beard to turn his head. 'You'll live.'

Brew made a last, desperate grab to save his prayerbook. In answer Duncan smashed him a cracking backhand to the cheek with his pistol. Brew's head lolled, his eyes rolled. Duncan said to himself, 'You lousy buggers don't give up, do you?' He went back to the hole. 'Look, Rabbi, ashes to ashes, dust to dust,' he tonelessly mimicked. When nothing was left but the hard blue cover, Duncan dropped it. It was too big to go down the hole. So he unzipped his fly, and carefully urinated on it. Brew wanted to stop him. He tried to move his head and body. He couldn't. When he finished, Duncan set the empty bucket back. 'The next time you piss or shit, you won't forget what's down here, eh, Rabbi? Or who put it there.'

Brew hurt. The prison guard contemplated him for a moment, letting his rubbery cheek and lips stretch into a mocking grin, 'Well, holy man? Seems HE'S let your side down, hard.'

Brew's blood was on fire with anger and vengeance. But the knowledge that he was powerless to fight back overcame his fury with shame. As he left Duncan's laugh jeered.

Panting heavily, Brew slowly drew himself up on his bed and sat to wait for the shivering and faintness to pass. His cheek was numb, his skull throbbed. There was a dull burning in his arm muscles. He passed out for a few minutes. Coming back, he touched the bloody gash on his head in a reflex action. He looked at the blood on his fingertips. He was only a man. Angels don't bleed.

A sudden, desperate urge came over him: to rinse away the blood before it congealed in his hair. But he had no water, and even if he had, the laws of the Atonement Day, he knew, did not permit washing beyond the first knuckle of the fingers. No, he shouldn't have resisted. *He* had destroyed the solemnity of the day. He sat. His soul filled with self-pity, remorse, futility.

Then he remembered! Brew slowly bent over his knees to look. There, under his bed by his heels lay a torn, crumpled leaf — the one page of his prayerbook he had managed to save. Reaching down, Brew picked it up. His hands were shaking. Slowly and gently, not to tear it any more,[62] he unravelled the fragment. The page was from the Closing Service — the final prayers of the day — read as the sun is setting and the Book of Life is being signed and sealed.

The Rabbi rose. In tears, he pressed the shard of paper to his lips and kissed it, and read the one prayer left to him over and over—

.

The turning of the lock on his cell door abruptly ended the day. Brew folded his precious page in half, and pushed it in a pocket. The door slowly swung outward. The figure framed in the opening was white-haired and wore a blue-black blazer. A large plastic carrier bag dangled from his hand. Brew stared at him as though he were seeing for the first time in his life.

As the sorry spectacle of Brew Moray sank in, the familiar voice said, 'Oh, LORD ALMIGHTY!' Dropping his bag on the bed, he rushed to collect Brew in his arms. The welt on his cheek was hot.

'Reverend Roscoe—?' The Rabbi embraced Roy, saying, 'Reverend, Roy, you shouldn't see me like this.' Brew escaped, backpedalled a step, and looked himself up and down like a father critically eyeing a filthy little boy. 'Effects of one Day of Atonement—' He said it lamely, as a bad joke.

Noticing the crusted blood in Brew's hair, Roy blurted, 'Your head, man. What happened to you? Are you all right—? I came to bring you food and drink — to break your fast — and this is how I find you—?' Suddenly, Brew became aware of feeling empty. The roof of his mouth was achingly dry from thirst and fasting.

Duncan, who had been standing outside, chose that moment to make his presence known. An awkward silence descended. Brew, careful not to catch the prison officer's eye,

---

[62]The laws of the Sabbath and the Day of Atonement, also called Sabbath of Sabbaths, prohibit all work. Included in the 39 categories of forbidden work is any form of tearing.

answered, 'I...I blacked out from the fast, and fell—' The facile lie, made so soon after Yom Kippur, stabbed his conscience.

Without looking back, Roy understood. 'I'm here on sufferance, with the Governor's permission. My escort,' he made eyes behind him, 'is a prison rule meant to protect me against inmate violence; isn't that right, Mr Duncan?' The chief officer did not rise. 'Rabbi,' observed Roy with concern. 'That's a nasty bump, it might need stitches. I'll call the doctor—'

With Duncan in his vault, Brew had no alternative. He compounded his first untruth with a second, 'I'm fine, really. I need water to clean myself up, that's all—'

'Are you sure? You might be concussed,' prodded Roy. Brew said no more, and Roy, comprehending, changed the subject. 'You must be famished; your fast has been over for more than two hours now.'

Brew again felt the tightness at the back of his mouth. 'Yes— A hot drink to start with—' Roy took a flask out of the bag and poured a cup of steaming black coffee. 'Drink this while I get some water.' Roy took the pitcher and went out. Brew drank in small sips. Feeling giddy, he sat down on the bed. In Roy's short absence, Murdo Duncan warned the Rabbi to keep quiet. Brew drank and said nothing. Roy returned with a pitcherful of fresh water, and bathed Brew's cuts and bruises with his own handkerchief under Duncan's watchful eyes.

'Thank you, Reverend, that feels much better. By the way, how did you know that I like my coffee black?' said Brew holding out his cup for more.

'A certain ministering angel—'

'Deborah? How is she? Have you seen her?'

'No, not exactly. But your wife prepared everything you have here, and Mr Sinclair brought it over to me. That's why I wasn't here any earlier. Speaking of your better half, I think I can arrange for *you* to see her.' Brew gave the Murrayfield minister a desperate look. Roy faced Duncan, who was glowering. 'Mr Duncan, I hardly think the Rabbi here'll be attempting anything. Do you mind giving us a bit of space?' The chaplain's unusual assertiveness briefly threw Duncan off-balance. He dropped back. Behind cold black eyes, Duncan heard his answer: the dreams, the dreams— Roy spoke into Brew's ear, 'If you're willing to give us a talk at our next prayer meeting, I think I can arrange for her to be there. I'll have a word with the Governor. He's a good man, very understanding.' Brew whispered barely above a breath to Roy, 'Yes, speak to him, please.'

Roy bowed his head. 'Then it's settled. Now, how about some sustenance. You must be starving, man.' Roy reached for the plastic bag.

'Roy, can you stay? Knowing Deborah, I'm sure there's plenty.'

'It's really not up to me,' answered Roy, turning to glance at Duncan, who stood in the shadow.

'Then perhaps,' said the Rabbi, 'the officer will also join us—'

* * *

Chapter XXV

Door to Door

[Sunday morning, October 18, 2009]

He was about to ring. But his finger hung over the doorbell as he gave himself a moment to look around. There was nothing in Edinburgh quite like Glasgow's Newton Burns Garden Suburb. It was like an architect's sketch of ruler-straight roads, manicured lawns, perfectly squared flowerbeds, sterile trees and shrubs, and rows of modern, clean-built bungalows. The comfortable clone before him was set apart only by its number. He rang. A cautious voice asked through the letter flap, 'Who's that?'

'Ms Cameron, Margaret Cameron?'

The door cracked open. 'Och, no, there must be some mistake. She lives across the road.'

The slender, blue-suited man put a finger to his Harris Tweed trilby, and angled his head away. Looking at the house number, he then compared it to the address in his electronic organiser. 'My mistake, ma'am. It's No 389 I'm wanting, not 398.' A shadow of embarrassment glided over his slightly unbalanced mouth.

'Margaret's hardly ever in at this time of day. Works horrible hours, Sundays, too—' offered the woman.

With demonstrative show, he looked at his diary again. 'Nine *pm*! It seems I've made one right royal hash of it this morning!'

'You're English—' said the woman in a neighbourly tone.

'Guilty as charged. But the ex-wife's Scots. Am I good for a reprieve?'

She blushed. 'I wasn't meaning to be personal. Eh, can I tell Margaret you were here, Mr—'

'Ford.'

The door opened wider. 'Ford?'

'Like the car.' He went on, 'No, there's no need to say anything to Ms Cameron. I'll call back this evening.' The woman looked down at his large case on her doorstep. He volunteered, 'I'm new to this. Cosmetics salesman. A man's got to make a bite somehow—'

Taking advantage of the dry moment he'd created, Ford assessed her. She was on the right side of middle age. She looked plain in her dressing gown, but the curves were all there, and in the right places. Her lips were full, her cheeks, creamy. The with-it, wire glasses she wore stated that she cared about appearances. Their thick lenses distorted her eyes.

He emerged from his lapse the cheerful salesman: 'An all-natural, fresh-smelling, environmentally friendly line, produced exclusively from our own wild-growing flowers, herbs and plants. Only purchasable through a representative in your own home. Door to door. Marketing with the personal touch.'

'I see—' Her expression brightened. He was polite, not too pushy. Seemed honest enough. If he was down on his luck, it happens. And if he was a bit of a lad, well, men will be men. She self-consciously pushed up her glasses. 'Mrs Gordon, Cecily. I do believe in quality and good value—'

'As much as I'd like to show you our line, Mrs Gordon, Cecily— My diary's rather full this morning. Saturdays and Sundays are my busiest days. I'm sure you can appreciate that. It's a truism, punctuality is the cornerstone of direct sales, and I really don't want to be late for my nine-thirty client. But here's my card—' he said, diffidently. 'Let's make an appointment for another time right now.' Ford opened out his digital pad again, and keyed in the month. 'Now, then, let's see...one evening—?' She agreed. He scrolled through the days. 'How about next Saturday evening? The twenty-fourth? At seven?'

Cecily, sensing the hopefulness in his voice, said, 'Saturdays are good. I have the house to myself.'

He spoke as he wrote, 'Cecily Gordon, 3-8-9—'

'No, 3-9-8,' she corrected.

'Tsk, coming apart at the seams, I am,' he said looking directly into his newest client's eyes, '398 Coldstream Guards Crescent. Got it. Telephone—?'

She gave him the number and he snapped the diary shut. 'It's a date, and no more cockups. Promise.' Ford amazed himself. How easy it was. 'Oh, by the way, you wouldn't happen to know Ms Cameron's work number.'

She was studying his card, 'Mr John Ford— Margaret's work number, oh, I'm sorry, no— Actually, we're really not that close neighbours at all. And it's like I said, she's almost never at home during civilised hours...unlike yours truly.'

Ford Christmas breathed out lightly as he thought, good. The chances, then, of the two women gossiping about him were slim. He had no intention of visiting the Cameron woman. He'd simply lifted the name from her post box moments before ringing the Gordons' bell. His rationale was an old door-to-door ploy: Any recommendation will outsell any sales pitch; what's good for your neighbour is good for you. It was a gamble and it worked, he was in without complications.

Cecily mistook his relieved expression for something else. 'Apropos of nothing, my husband's another one, like Margaret, always away. He's a sea ferry captain.'

* * *

- 98 -

Chapter XXVI

"Wright's Wrong"

[Sunday morning, October 18, 2009]
Guriat Gaoni drove in circles without stopping. The concentration etched on her face had cut Neville out of her thought loop for the last two hours. In actuality her thinking was not directed, but as aimless as her driving.

The week-long Sukkoth festival[63] had been no holiday. It came and went without let-up in her preparations. Operation Snatch, they'd warned her, was a solo mission, no piece of cake. Support from the Israel Embassy in Edinburgh would be severely limited; only the military attaché could be called on for behind-the-scenes intelligence gathering and logistical "backup". Her brief was to facilitate. In the field she'd have to work with whatever local assistance she could manage to recruit. The Scottish government and the world had to believe that the actions of the Jewish community were entirely home-grown and self-driven. She'd intended to recruit Rabbi Brew Moray, but circumstances dictated otherwise. Right now, Neville was all she had. The Rabbi's brother was annoying, but not stupid.

The circling came to an abrupt end when Guriat, like a homing pigeon certain of its direction, headed south. Arriving at the Fairmilehead Waterworks, she nudged the blue van onto a kerb, set the handbrake, cut the engine, turned out the lights. An Edinburgh Corporation vehicle parked by the filter beds, even at one on a misty morning, was not likely to attract attention. Reaching behind the driver's seat, she swung a worker's satchel into her lap and produced a flask. Guriat poured two cups of coffee. Neville's 'thanks' was the first word he said in what seemed an eternity of driving. She wanted to be sure that they weren't being followed. By the time the police surveillance team positioned outside Neville's flat realised that he had slipped out the back door of the East Crosscauseway bakery shop, it was too late. The coffee break lasted only five minutes. Pulling away, Guriat began Neville's background briefing—

When she finished, Neville asked incredulously, 'Eh? The tunnel under the Castle? That they built for vehicle access? Oh Jeez, I remember— You're not suggesting we go in for a bite of take-away—'

Standard operating procedure dictated that the tunnel network be inspected in advance. For one reason to validate Roy Roscoe's information, for another to check that the passage was clear and safe. But the risk of showing her hand, of being discovered was too great. From all the indications she had seen, she was convinced: "Wright's Wrong" was there, where Roscoe said it was. And the fact that it was a well-kept secret was proof of Roscoe's genuineness.

---

[63]The autumn cycle of Jewish festivals begins with the New Year (Rosh Hashanah), climaxes on the Day of Atonement (Yom Kippur), and winds down on Sukkoth (Feast of Tabernacles). The flimsily built booths, in which Jews eat and sleep outside their permanent homes for one week, are meant to remind them that their sojourn to the Promised Land continues, and that from time immemorial Jews in strange lands have "come only to stay a while..." (Gen. 47.4).

Given her limited resources, she had thoroughly investigated Roy Roscoe; he and his Gulf War story checked out in Israel. Yet one scenario kept creeping into her under-mind thinking — that the good reverend was an MI-Six plant to destabilise Scotland. If so, he was the best sleeper British intelligence had ever produced. If he were a mole, then her first lesson in Bedouin warfare — "my enemy's enemy is my friend" — admirably applied.

Guriat peered hard into the windscreen. The mist was deepening into drizzle. All traffic lights flashed yellow.

The tunnel project, she reminded Neville, was finished about twenty years ago, in nineteen ninety-one to be exact. But when the British Army-administered Castle reverted to Scottish control and became in part a prison, the 'subterranean vehicle access' was secured and guarded at both ends night and day.

'Do you know who Augustus Wright was?' she asked.

Neville yawned. 'The name escapes me.'

Guriat laid out the facts. 'The access tunnel was built by Augustus Wright Contractors, Ltd. In its day it was considered a minor engineering feat. The five-hundred-ten foot long curving vehicular passage was cut through the Castle rock to separate the tourist hordes from motorised traffic — delivery vans, VIPs, military jeeps and lorries. The tunnel leads from the Esplanade outside the Castle wall, passes directly under St Margaret's Chapel, and exits at Mill's Mount on the inside.'

Neville interjected in a low, uncertain tone, 'But even if we could get into the Castle through the tunnel, we'd never get out the same way—'

'Bang on, mate,' said Guriat, softly. Finally, her "partner" was waking up. 'Well, this Wright, he built something that wasn't in the contract. The man was a good Christian—'

'Don't tell me he put in a niche for the collection basket.'

The Israeli agent gritted her teeth. 'You don't seem to understand. Lives, yours included, depend on what I'm saying. Now—'

'I make lame jokes when I get nervous. Sorry. Anyway, "He was a good Christian—"'

Guriat did not react to Neville's apology. 'Wright was concerned from the beginning that the tunnel plans did not include any emergency escape route—'

'I said I'm sorry,' he cut in. 'There's something we have, I have to say—'

'I heard you the first time,' she answered. 'Now, can I go on—?'

Neville crumpled. The thumping beat of the windscreen wipers filled the moment of emptiness between them.

'Right—' She went on explaining. 'Wright was concerned that if both ends of the tunnel were cut off, say, by an earthquake or flooding, there would be no escape for those trapped inside. But the military refused to approve any additional expenditure for the Castle tunnel. Fact was, the building codes didn't require an emergency exit for a shallow tunnel less than half a mile long. So when Wright's application to go over budget was denied, he went ahead and built a bolt-hole at his own expense, in secret, without the authorities' knowledge or approval. He dubbed his little secret "Wright's Wrong".'

For a second she took her eyes off the road to gauge his reaction. She wore reflective sunglasses even at night. 'You're thinking, if this "Wright's Wrong" was such a well-kept secret, then how the hell does *she* know about it? It's like I said,' she answered herself, 'Wright was a committed Christian. He belonged to the Murrayfield Church from boyhood. And even though he eventually left the neighbourhood as a successful engineer and contractor, Murrayfield was his church. Every Sunday.

'He was also a bachelor, and by all accounts a maverick. Apparently, the only person he confided in was Reverend Wilkins, the Murrayfield minister. At the time the local gutter press hinted that their relationship went beyond friendship. Nothing was ever proven, but the link between the two may be considered a corroborating factor. Both Wilkins and

Wright are dead now. But before Wilkins died, he passed on the secret of "Wright's Wrong" to the present pastor.'

It was Neville's turn. 'And this inheritor of the secret never saw any need to reveal the information, because the tunnel wasn't used any more.' He reasoned, 'OK, but, how can *you* be sure that the escape route is still an ironclad secret? And your source — this present vicar — how do *you* know he's kosher, that he isn't setting a trap?'

Again, Neville Moray was asking too many "how" questions. Guriat's first impulse was to deny him. But then she decided that a review of her reasoning would be a last chance for a second call, a final double check that she had not missed out some minor, but vital detail. If there were something she hadn't seen— Well, Neville wasn't stupid.

Guriat began her story from the day after she first met Roy Roscoe. Her lead problem had been to locate Wright's office. The firm was not listed in the phone book. At the Companies Registrar Office, the Wright file was a dead end; the company had ceased to exist.

She next checked newspaper archives. The quaint, yellowed clipping files at *The Free Scotsman* came up a complete blank. But the former head archivist — a nice old chap, who still put in a few hours a week — happened to be there the day she dropped in, and he remembered the tunnel project. He sent her to the Edinburgh Collection at the Central Library. There the staff tracked down an article in *Radical Scotland*, and some PR material put out by the Historic Scotland office. The fact that there was no mention of any emergency exit proved nothing either way.

Guriat next went to the Edinburgh Corporation Planning and Engineering Office. After a few preliminary questions mostly about her Australian accent, the department manager apologised that his office held no blueprints of the project. All Castle records were housed in London with the British Army. Quite a chatterer, he admitted that personally he knew nothing about the tunnel except for its existence. But more importantly, the mention of Augustus Wright's name sparked a vague recollection. The firm was renamed after the old man's death — 'maybe something like A. W. Engineering, Ltd.' The phone book confirmed the new name.

At A. W. Engineering, wearing a pert two-piece suit and her most charming smile, Guriat spun a cover story about being an Australian academic doing post-doctoral engineering research at Heriot-Watt University. The director's reluctance forced her to show him the photocopies of the Army blueprints.

'Army blueprints?' asked Neville. 'I must've missed something. How did you get—?'

Before going to A. W. Engineering, she'd got word to the Israeli military attache at the Edinburgh Embassy. He, in turn, passed on her request to his counterpart in London. On the pretext of plans to build a similar structure through bedrock in Israel, an Israeli agent easily obtained copies of blueprints of the Castle tunnel from the Army Records Office. The plans from London arrived in Edinburgh via Tel Aviv in the diplomatic pouch.

'How—?' he asked again.

'Don't ask, mate, don't ask. I showed him the photocopies, and said, "All I want is to compare your company records with the Army's." The bastard charged me handsomely for the privilege, but it was worth it. The plans were exactly the same, line for line. No "Wright's Wrong."'

In her mind, confirmation by omission was an indication, not a proof. All the evidence was circumstantial.

Neville, she noticed, had grown nervously quiet. Her change of direction hadn't escaped him. They were headed straight for the city centre. The van's high beams knifed through the night. Drizzle was fast becoming steady rain. Guriat brought the van up Morningside Road, Bruntsfield Place, then into Lothian Road. From there she swung a sharp right into Castle Terrace, leading into Johnston Terrace. At first sight of the looming Rock, driver and passenger breathed in sharply. At the end of Johnston Terrace, Guriat stopped, looked both ways, cut her lights, dropped into first and slowly inched up the steep incline leading to the Castle Esplanade. She stopped the van opposite Outlook Tower.

Neville stared straight ahead. Floodlighting and glinting coils of razor wire running the length of Half Moon Battery outlined Edinburgh Castle. He said, 'Right. You've just answered my big question. But one little thing still niggles me. Let's assume it's like the good reverend says. But answer me this: How can you be sure that the prison authorities haven't discovered "Wright's Wrong" and plugged it up? I mean, you can't ask *them*!'

Guriat took off her glasses and looked him squarely in the eye for the first time. The cold, catlike amber around her pupils gleamed in the dark. Locked in her gaze, she watched Neville's eyes shrink to narrow slits. Like it or not, he was her partner. He deserved an answer. 'The Murrayfield minister — Roy Roscoe — he's a good man. He's also the prison chaplain. He knows. He knows exactly where the escape passage comes out in the Castle. It's on his patch. And I believe him when he says it hasn't been tampered with. He's taking a big risk for your brother, mate, maybe the biggest risk of us all.'

* * *

Chapter XXVII

'Mark of a Good Plan'

[Sunday morning, October 18, 2009]

Guriat focused beyond the windscreen. Edinburgh Castle lay straight ahead of them bathed in floodlights and rain. No one guarded the outermost walls, not even at night. Security was lax.

Her watch said three twenty-five, on time. 'Now, here's what's happening—' she began. When she finished sketching out the scheme that she and Roy had engineered, all Neville said was 'Crazy.'

'Mark of a good plan,' said Guriat. 'The real problem here isn't pulling the rabbi out of the hat; it's getting the act off the stage. There'll be swarms of cops.'

'Seriously, no guards in the car tunnel?' he asked trying to find something she'd missed.

'Like I said before, the tunnel was closed off years ago. Men are posted at either end, but nobody goes inside...normally. But just in case—' she said, pulling out her KTL automatic, 'we've got plenty of back-up.' She explained 'the two good ones', the non-lethal blanks, followed by the deadly silent rounds. Neville shook his head. 'You can't back out now, mate. Nobody's life was ever saved without *some risk*.'

'Terrific. Like the only difference between a cash withdrawal and a bank robbery is "some risk". And who said anything about backing out. Like the Good Book says, "Where you die, I die." Eh?'

The drumming rain on the van's roof was getting louder. She switched on the radio. The news at four confirmed it: a gale. It was the one variable she had not taken into account. 'And your damn Scottish weather isn't helping, either.'

'Mine—?'

Guriat hopped out of the van, and came back in through the rear doors. In the mirror, Neville watched her slip into a yellow waterproof suit, waders, gloves and helmet. 'Your turn.' Neville swallowed, and wiped a hand over his face. 'What did they use to say? In for a penny, in for a pound.' He came round, and suited up.

After unloading everything except the blue bag, Guriat drove the van to the bottom of the stairs on Johnston Terrace. Neville waited alone. In the wind-driven rain, he ran an eye over the equipment — a large satchel of tools and another with torches, a gas monitor, gas masks and the four "Elsa-J" breathing kits she'd mentioned. There were also two more complete suits with hard hats.

Guriat came back. Even through the rain, Neville could see the change in her. The contours of the cheeks and jaw were rigid, her lips hardened with concentration. Charged for action, everything about the woman's body-set was saying, let's do it. She transferred four light bulb-sized grenades from her pockets to the toolbag. A sickening feeling shot through him.

'That manhole cover there,' said Guriat pointing down, 'the "WW" — you see it? That's the key: "*W*right's *W*rong".' She came here the day after her meeting in the Murrayfield church. Roscoe believed that the escape passage must exit somewhere near Outlook Tower. She had a hunch. That there had to be something, some sign. And there was. Though traffic-worn, the "WW" on the manhole cover shone like neon lights. She then toured the Castle, especially in and around St Margaret's Chapel.

Guriat handed Neville a hooked rod. He pried off the cast iron lid with ease. He was stronger than she expected.

Guriat kneeled at the rim. 'Inside,' she cautioned him, 'no talking. Hand signals only. Voices carry.' She plunged a torchlight into the shaft. A metal ladder was set in the concrete wall. She climbed down, about ten feet. At the bottom her light disappeared into the sewer. In seconds she was back, and waved Neville to follow. He hurriedly handed down the bags and suits, before clambering in. He slid the iron cover back in place over his head.

In the glare of their torches, Guriat and Neville could see that the man-sized main sloped upward, paralleling the steep incline of Castlehill and the Esplanade. Thousands of stalactites of green algae hung eerily from the ceiling. On the walls huge roaches, responding to human disturbance, moved in a solid mass like a flow of brown sludge. Dead dogs and cats with fur still clinging to their bones were skewered on filters. Guriat's first footsteps had scattered waterlogged rats in all directions. Their mad squeals in the dark kept the system frighteningly alive.

The fresh flow of rainwater and moving air helped cut the biting stench of human waste and death. Guriat, using the gas monitor, checked for methane and hydrogen sulphide. The air was safe to breathe. She signalled Neville to take the tool satchel and, grabbing the bag with the two extra suits and emergency breathing kits, she shot ahead. The sound of her splashing feet bounced off the walls.

Fanning his light from side to side, Neville held back. He stopped for every dead rat, some as big as cats, lying on the ledges. Then summoning his courage, he stepped widely around as though the carcass might jump up and bite him.

After ten minutes, the sewer levelled off and narrowed to an egg-shaped passage built of Victorian brick. Progress slowed. Neville's six-foot-four frame was bent nearly double, and he waddled like a duck. He started thinking how the whole world is nothing but tubes — mines, canals, tunnels, pipes, ducts, conduits, chimneys, sewers — either to funnel it in, or to funnel it out.

Guriat came to a sudden stop. Her light pointed at a muck-covered grating. There was a faint glint. It was stainless steel, obviously not as old as the sewer pipe. It seemed to be an intake or air vent. The opening, however, was no more than a foot square. Neville found another, similar-sized opening on his side.

Crouched on all fours, Guriat checked the grating more closely. The "WW" symbol she'd hoped to find imbedded in the design of the grillwork was not there.

Neville flashed his light through the grating by his shoulder. The pipe on the other side was no larger than the size of the vent. He did the same on Guriat's side. The space behind her grating was large enough for a man to get through. He gave an approving nod.

Charged situations like this threw Guriat's mind into high gear, often dislodging curious bits of trivia or some half-forgotten memory. She recalled a magazine article she once read with lots of pictures of X-rays and little white arrows pointing to amorphous blotches all over. The research showed that the doctors concentrated on the middle of the frame, often overlooking vital information in the corners and along edges.

Guriat shone her light all around the grid. Nothing. She began to wipe away the slime, and discovered that the grating was framed by a square of ceramic tiles built into the brickwork. She was sweating, despite the clammy cold of the sewer.

Neville scooped up water to help wash away the sludge. *Traach!* she exclaimed in Hebrew to herself. The second "WW" was etched in one of the tiles. But the monogram lay on its side. Guriat thought hard. Wright was no fool. Whatever he did was done with a purpose—

Neville put his torch between his teeth, and rummaged in the tool satchel, coming up with a large cold chisel and a hammer.

Guriat waved a hand, no hammering — someone might hear.

Neville jammed the chisel between the grating and its tile frame and pushed. Nothing budged. Grimacing, he tried again. The chisel slipped. Falling on his back into the slime, he bit off a curse between his teeth. Guriat sprang to his side, and he grabbed her shoulder to steady himself. With her help, he came to his knees holding on to her a moment longer than needed. She shot him an icy glare. It was the first time he'd touched her: What did she think? To let the angry sickness in his gut settle, Neville stared blankly into the darkness through the grid. Trash it, he told himself. Guriat tapped her watch on the crystal. Aye, aye, *sir*, said Neville to himself, I'm thinking. We're in the right place...but we're doing something wrong. Wright built a system to get trapped people out — fast. People are inside the car tunnel...so they'd be coming from the other side. So if I were on the other side...desperate to get out...with no tools...I'd just...give...a kick. Neville firmly grasped the grille-square and yanked it straight back. The grating and the frame of tiles around it popped right out.

He looked to her for approval, but she just went through. On the other side, the sewer forked right and left. The duct to the right was the smaller of the two. Guriat looked for another sign. Nothing, no monogram over either passage.

Faced with this new quandary, she reasoned, this is no treasure hunt. There are no false clues, and Wright had no reason to throw the dogs off the scent. She told herself to think. Think. Backsearch...yes. Her first lecture as an agent cadet. Backsearch was a Mossad problem-solving technique borrowed from accounting. You work backwards, tracing every step, until you isolate the place where you went wrong. Think, she told herself. It was only one step back. The "lazy" WW...Outback brands...one thought led to the next...brands had meanings. Lazy...no. Lying down...no. Pointing...maybe. If the "Ws" are directional like arrows, they're saying, go right. That's it! *Traach!*

The right-hand passage was the narrowest yet. Guriat and Neville crawled on hands and knees. Soon, the tunnel opened up. It was another vertical shaft. Guriat turned off her light. There was no sound, the silence of the deaf.

They were close. Neville was relieved to stand up. Guriat put down the suits she'd lugged, and felt around the walls. She found a built-in ladder like the one that they had come down two hours ago, and climbed up. Her helmet banged against something. She froze...expecting alarms to go off, doors to open, guards to charge in...but nothing happened— It was incredible. No electronic security system had ever been installed. She gave her heart rate time to slow. Her head had hit bars. She felt them — a storm drain. From the dull sound her helmet made and the smell of fresher air, she could tell that void above was large. Her inner voice said, thank YOU.

Climbing back down, Guriat barely whispered to Neville, 'The tunnel.' She put her hands on his shoulders and turned him around to go back, alone.

* * *

Chapter XXVIII

Rabbi in the Chapel

[Sunday morning, October 18, 2009]

Brew Moray counted fifteen in front of him — twelve men and three women. The prisoners were handcuffed, shackled and chained together. Their eyes, not used to daylight, smarted as they emerged. They muttered and complained at getting soaked in the pouring rain. But Brew breathed in the smell of clean, fresh air, and said the blessing for life. Had it been warm and sunny, he thought, it would have been even harder to bear this small taste of freedom.

The few Sunday tourists undeterred by the cold, wet weather either pointed their fingers or averted their eyes. The visitors were kept well away from the prisoners as they hobbled across the grounds. Officer Milne covered the flank while Murdo Duncan followed behind.

Under so dreich and dreary a sky, St Margaret's Chapel looked as though it were chiselled out of a single, solid rock. Steel grates secured all five narrow windows. Below the eaves, stains of rain like long black teeth bit into the chapel walls.

Roy Roscoe pushed open the arched door. The prisoners waited outside while Milne went in for a routine security check. At his all clear, the line clanked forward. As the inmates entered, Roy handed them a hymnbook, saying, 'Great to see you, brother' and 'Good of you to come, sister.'

To the Rabbi, Roy quoted, '"The last shall be first."'

'Matthew—' said Brew.

'Chapter Nineteen, Verse Thirty,' confirmed Roy, as he placed a hymnbook from the table by the entrance in the Rabbi's cuffed hands.

Deborah started. Brew's beard had grown wild, and he was shuffling in chains. From her place, sitting alone near the entrance, Deborah's eyes reached out to him, her mouth formed his name.

The line quickly pulled Brew past her into the chapel. He ached to touch her. He hadn't felt anything soft and warm for thirty days. But contact between husband and wife was forbidden. Duncan saw to that.

For the next, short moment the bright inner space of the arched chapel absorbed Brew. At the front, the columned chancel arch he remembered from boyhood visits was still as ornate as ever. The apse behind the arch was curtained off. The Rabbi noticed the vase of white lilies, the wooden board with the morning's hymn numbers, the folding chair for Roy to sit on, the Bible on the lectern.

The prisoners seated themselves on the two rows along the walls. Duncan sent Milne outside. The two officers double-locked and bolted the chapel door, the only exit, from inside and out, and established radio contact.

Duncan positioned himself by the door, adopting a rigid stance, legs splayed. A thumb nervously ran over the hammer and grip of his weapon. His eyes darted from Deborah to Mrs Morton at the upright piano to Roy Roscoe who stood before the congregation.

Roy signalled to Mrs Morton to begin. She played the Forty-third Psalm and, despite her frail looks, belted out the words. Reverend Roscoe sang and swayed. At the end of the introit, he cheerfully greeted, 'Good morning, all. All, good morning.' The prisoners' response was sullen.

Roy prayed silently and at some length for the welfare of his congregation. His idea of a prison service was to make it last as long as possible. For these men and women, spending years in solitary confinement, every free minute was a good minute.

The Reverend came out of his prayer, and called for Hymn number Three Hundred and Sixty-six. The congregation rose to the clang of cuffs and chains. Pages rustled. Mrs Morton drummed out the opening bars, and led off, 'Sing to the LORD a joyful song—' At the finish of the hymn-singing, Roy motioned all to be seated, and bow their heads, as he intoned, 'Let us pray. The morning is YOURS. And we are YOURS—'

The Bible reading came next. 'Genesis Three, Twenty-four.' Roy took out a slip of paper from under his black robe and with a big smile, read in Hebrew, "'*VaYegaresh et Halvri*—'" Brew tensed. It was not right. Roy had changed the text from "the *man*" to "the *Hebrew*". But Roy's English translation "'And HE drove out the man—'" was correct. As his Bible reading droned on, a sudden, clear understanding seized Brew. It was a warning. "And HE *drove out* the He*brew*" meant that he, Brew, would be driven out.

'All rise,' Roy called out with an upward sweeping hand. 'Hymn number Eleven, "Before the world began, the Word was there—"' Reverend Roscoe sang and clapped. At the beginning of each new verse, he shouted, 'C'mon now, let's raise the roof!' 'Louder, folks, with soul!' 'And one more time for the LORD!' At the end, his eyes bulging with joy, he panted, 'Now that's what *I* call worship.'

'This morning, this morning,' said Roy calming himself, 'we are very privileged to have with us the Chief Rabbi of Scotland, Brewster Moray.' To the rear, the chaplain said, 'If you will, Mr Duncan, please release the Chief Rabbi for the duration of his lesson.'

Duncan moved forward, lips moist, neck muscles twitching. All eyes followed him coming forward. Hard rain splattering against the windows softened the silence. Duncan sank his blackbird's eyes into Roy. Detaching the key from the ring on his belt and handing it to Roy, the chief officer muttered, 'You unlock him, Reverend.' Duncan's eyes swung wildly. He wiped his gun hand dry on his shirt, as Roy bent down on one knee to release Brew's fetters. Then the handcuffs came off and with them the chain that joined Brew to the next man. Taking his key back, Duncan warned, 'If he says anything out of line, this meeting's over.' Arm in arm, the Reverend and the Rabbi walked as free men to the lectern in front of the chancel curtain.

As Duncan returned to the rear, Brew hugged Deborah with his eyes. He saw her love embracing him. She leaned forward, and put her hands on her lap. Brew noticed she had on white gloves. She never wore gloves.

'The time has come,' announced Roy, 'for me to pass the baton to my fellow runner.' Doing a runner — Brew lowered his eyes. 'No long introductions, people. All you need to know is this man is *my* teacher.' To Brew he said: 'Rabbi, thank you for agreeing to talk to us this morning. I believe the message you bring us will also bring you joy. And,' throwing his voice, 'Mrs Moray — she's sitting at the rear, folks — thank you, too, for coming out to join us on this auspicious morning—'

Duncan interrupted, 'Get on with it, Reverend.'

'The LORD'S work can't be hurried, Mr Duncan.' Roy sat down on the folding chair next to the lilies.

The Rabbi stood alone. His eyes lowered, then lifted — suspended like a conductor's baton poised to begin. 'A rabbi teaching in St Margaret's Chapel must, indeed, be a rare event. Reverend Roscoe, I thank you for allowing me to speak today...and for your fine choice of text this morning.'

'Inspired choice, I'd have thought,' said Roy gently, lips pursed but eyes alive.

Brew agreed, 'Inspired—' He resisted the temptation to look at Roy. 'This morning, I thought I'd do something radical, like the Bible, and start at the beginning. From Ecclesiastes Three, Eleven, "HE has made everything beautiful *in its time*", we learn that the HOLY ONE makes new beginnings all the time—'

A murmured comment escaped from a stringy-haired, jug-eared man sitting near the lectern.

'Go on, speak up,' said the Rabbi.

'I just said, around here it's *ends* that count.' The congregation laughed.

Brew's eyes lit up. 'You've got a point. The truth is there to be told.'

Heads nodded. A young, close-shorn woman spoke up, 'I have a question—' The jawbone worked under the skin at her temples. 'Maybe it's daft—'

'Ask it, anyway.

'What's a rabbi?'

'That's a question I, too, have often asked myself. Reb Nachman, an early Hassidic master,[64] taught that when Satan is having difficulty misleading the world, he appoints rabbis to help him in his work.'[65]

First Roy, then everyone except Duncan, laughed.

'The real question is not what is a rabbi, but who is a rabbi.' Brew's upturned palms juggled invisible ideas. 'I believe, first and foremost, a rabbi must be a *mensch*, a human being. That's why we say, how can a rabbi who hasn't stumbled and fallen flat on his face once in a while teach others how to get up and begin again—?' Brew averted his eyes to the pianist in the far back corner.

Mrs Morton liked coming with 'Reverend Roy' to play for the 'in-crowd' as she called them. But this morning was different. She was fidgety, and without her playing to distract her, she thought she might explode. She knew what she had do, but not why. She'd practised a hundred times at home. All she could do now was sit primly, splice her fingers together in her lap, and wait for Roy's signal.

Deborah, too, had to wait — for Mrs Morton. Meanwhile, frightening questions intruded: Will the plan work? What if it doesn't? Will people be hurt? Has something been overlooked? Or miscalculated? And above all, would she have the strength and courage to play her role? Waves of queasiness gripped and released her. Deborah was glad she wore her mother's gloves; she imagined no one would see her hands trembling. The most difficult part so far was controlling that curious perverseness in her to stare at Murdo Duncan's face.

Duncan was also somewhere else: He heard neither the Rabbi nor the pounding wind and rain. He shifted, loosened his tie. The creases of his hand sparkled with gluey sweat. The weight of his service pistol tugging at his belt never felt so heavy as now. He stepped closer to where Deborah sat, and folded his arms tightly over his chest, knuckles pressed hard against his ribs. Bird's eyes. Staring, black and gleaming. And screaming in his head:

The dreams. The Dreams. THE DREAMS.

With Deborah so close, and yet unable to say even a single private word to her or touch his fingertips to hers, Brew churned inside with regrets and frustration. To be *half* free— To talk *cheerfully* about new beginnings— And to know now that every minute might be the *last*— It's all me, me. What about Deborah? Roy? And the others trapped in here—? Oh, GOOD LORD, no— He dared not meet Deborah's eyes, for fear he might betray whatever madness Roy Roscoe was planning.

---

[64]Rabbi Nachman ben Simchah of Bratslav (1772-1811), Hassidic leader and great-grandson of the Ba'al Shem Tov, founder of the Hassidic movement.

[65]From Rabbi Nachman's book *Likkutei Moharan*, 1806.

Roy sat cross-legged, politely listening to Brew, and seemingly quite unconcerned.

'But Rabbi—' This time it was a bald, hound-faced man who asked, 'Why do you Jews keep yourselves to yourselves like you do?'

The Rabbi forced a slight smile—

* * *

Chapter XXIX

'One More Push'

[Sunday morning, October 18, 2009]

The Rabbi asked the hound-faced prisoner, 'What does "holy" mean?'

'But, Rabbi,' he protested, 'I asked first, why you people keep yourselves to yourselves?'

'So you did,' said Brew, 'but your question...it misses the point—' The Rabbi would have asked him, how can a city be holy? a book? a language? or a person? or a people? He would have gently explained that the Hebrew word translated as "holy", really means "standing apart". But "apart" in its most positive sense. The Jewish people, he would have liked to say, are like a man and woman who marry — *a part* of the community and yet *apart* from it— But Brew said nothing. The blaze in Duncan's eyes cut him off cold.

Roy jumped up to cover. 'Mrs Morton, the Twenty-third Psalm, please.'

On cue, the old pianist grabbed her chest and swooned. All faces turned to her, mouths gaping, eyes wide open—

Duncan exploded, *'THE DREAMS! THE DREAMS!'* And in one fluid move, he drew, aimed and squeezed the trigger. Deborah's lunge impacted at the instant he shot.

It was over in less than a fraction of eternity. Only Deborah's blood-curdling

'BREW...W...W!' hung in the air.

A moist stain quickly spread over Roy's gown.

Mrs Morton fainted.

The prisoners threw themselves to the floor.

Brew grabbed the lectern, knocking Roy's Bible to the floor.

Roy was reeling. Brew caught him, and eased him into the folding chair. Roy asked, 'Can ya hear the rain, Rabbi?'

Untangling herself from Duncan, Deborah scrambled to her feet. Duncan's hair was sticky with blood. His head had struck the corner of the table by the entrance.

One, two, then three of the prisoners peeked over their shoulders. The shaven-headed woman stood up first. She called out, 'The keys.' And someone else yelled, 'The gun, get the piece.'

Deborah rushed to the front of the chapel.

Roy tugged at the Rabbi's pyjama sleeve. Pulling Brew's ear close to his lips, he said, 'I'll live. You and Deborah must get away. The apse, behind the curtain.' Roy tightened his grip, 'Hurry, man!'

Swearing and screaming, the chained prisoners stumbled over each other to where Duncan lay. The first prisoner, the bald-headed man, wedged the table up against the door, while others to the cry of 'Get the keys!' wildly tore at the ring on Duncan's belt. The shaven woman, first to unlock herself, passed on the keys. Meanwhile, the jug-eared man went for the weapon still in Murdo Duncan's clenched fist. His dive toppled the two men chained to either side of him. Handcuffs and shackles tore at arms and legs. In the prisoners' desperation to free themselves, the key ring fell to the floor. The scramble to retrieve it tied arms and legs into a snarled knot. The chapel rang with dark, shouted curses.

Blows, driven by a frenzy of madness, broke arms and cracked jaws. Men and women bit and clawed to shrieks of pain and anger. A jug ear was torn off.

Outside, Officer Milne heard the shouts. His crackling voice came over Duncan's radio. A siren began to sound.

Brew bent over Roy. 'We're taking you with us.' Deborah's face said no.

Violent banging at the bolted door thundered over the sounds of the prisoners' fighting and the rain.

The minister rasped, 'Behind the curtain. Hurry. Move the altar, the rug. Deborah, you know what to do.' He looked at her. 'Go. This is your chance. Leave me. I'll live.'

'We can't leave him,' said Brew, pleading.

Deborah was uncompromising. 'He's right, Brew. They're breaking down the door, any minute now—' She pulled him.

Roy was going pale and beginning to shiver. Deborah hurriedly slipped off her coat, and draped it over him. Brew kissed his forehead. Roy almost shouted, 'Go! "If not now, when?"'[66] Then faintly, he said, 'Blessings on you all,' as his eyes closed.

The melee raged on. Outside, officers hammered at the chapel door.

'Now!' said Deborah, and the couple slipped behind the curtain without being seen.

The chapel door crashed in. A shot was fired.

Behind the curtain, a solid, cloth-covered altar table occupied the apse. A plain brass Crucifix stood alone in the middle of the table. Deborah put the Cross on the floor, and motioned Brew to the altar. Together, they moved the heavy wooden table to one side, and Deborah pulled the rug away. Underneath was a wooden trapdoor with the "WW" monogram carved next to a flush ringbolt.

Brew lifted the ring, and pulled. The hatch would not budge. The veins in his temples almost burst with his straining.

Animal instinct took over in Deborah. She grabbed Brew's wrist and shook him loose. There was a tortured look in his eyes as she took the ring in her white gloves and *turned* it. The latch tongue slipped back and the trapdoor lifted.

Deborah went down first. Brew pulled the rug back over the hatch as he let it down. It closed with a reassuring click. The darkness inside was dazzling. The air felt cold and dank.

At the bottom of the shaft was a narrow passage. Deborah stooped down, and feeling her way forward, crawled on all fours. She led the way. In minutes they reached the end of the passage and a second shaft. Deborah, then Brew, stood. Dripping water but not a ray of light came down.

Deborah felt around the walls, and soon found a ladder. She guided Brew's hand to one of the rungs. He slowly climbed up, counting eight rungs. At the top, the shaft was blocked. He felt something metallic, barred like a storm drain. It would be heavy, but he placed his shoulder against it, breathed in deeply and pushed up. The grating gave way. The scraping noise it made as he slid it aside took his breath away. 'Sssh,' hissed Deborah. He poked his head out. There was not so much as a crack of light showing, but the air was fresh and perfectly still like in a cave. Brew climbed out and, reaching back, gave Deborah a hand up. Together they worked the storm cover back into place. Looking around in the dark, no next move presented itself.

It was a barely audible 'psst'. Brew and Deborah looked around. A short flash of light like a beacon at sea came out of another drain hole. It gave them their only glimpse of the car tunnel. And slightly louder, the voice called, 'Over here. Walk in the gutter.'

Hand in hand, Brew and Deborah walked in the water along the gutter. They left no tracks. At the next storm drain they peered in through the bars. Large tears rolled freely down their cheeks. Three pairs of hands easily removed the old iron grating. Guriat did not

---

[66]Hillel. *Mishna, Pirkei Avot* — Ethics of the Fathers, 1.14.

have to tell them to hurry. Deborah went in first, then Brew. He worked the grating back into place before being swallowed up. Less than a quarter of an hour had elapsed from the time they left St Margaret's Chapel.

*

At the beginning of those same few minutes, Roy's head slumped, his eyelids rolling shut. After a moment, he came to. His breathing was rough. He pressed his hand to his chest. Bringing it out from underneath Deborah's warm coat, he saw the redness oozing between his fingers. Covered in blood, his hand hardly seemed a part of him.

The sounds of the brawl did not reach Roy. The hearing part of his world was shutting down. But what he saw, all in heightened colour, seemed to throb. The overturned vase of lilies swam before his eyes. His Bible on the floor by the lectern pumped up to twice its size. The chit of paper with the verse from Genesis that he'd so laboriously copied out in Hebrew floated next to the Bible—

The chapel door caved in. Two rain-soaked blue uniforms burst through. The siren's maddening wail and the pelting rain came in, too. Milne fired a warning shot. The chapel went dead quiet, but almost instantly, pandemonium resumed. Cursing. Shouting. Clubbing. Duncan's weapon in the hands of a prisoner. Another shot. Screams of agony—

Unnoticed, Roy laboriously rolled onto the floor. Searing pain in his chest tortured him, almost beyond bearing. He waited. The spasm passed off. Roy crawled forward, smearing a trail of blood on the cold, flagstone floor. As he slipped under the curtain into the apse, he went beyond the threshold, where there was no more feeling, no more pain.

Roy saw the Cross on the apse floor. He watched it drift in and out of focus — sharpen and blur, sharpen and blur. 'SWEET LORD, let me finish—' He then looked up at the displaced altar table with its white cloth fringed in gold. His eyes tried its weight. The tabletop was solid oak, an inch and a half in thickness, and the spiralled legs as heavy as marble pillars.

Roy dragged himself to the altar table and reached up with one hand to its edge. Pushing with the other from the floor, he raised himself, first to one knee, then both, and finally to his feet.

Supporting his dying weight on the altar, Rev Roy Roscoe, minister of the Church of Scotland, Murrayfield Parish, prayed, 'Oh, LORD, just one more push.'

His hands tightened around the ends of the altar. It was all going blank. He drew his last breath as he straightened his back. The altar lifted off, and seemingly hovered in air before dropping squarely in the centre of the rug. Roy Roscoe fell on top of it, smiling.

* * *

The police report states that the prison chaplain's body was found only after the embattled prison authorities restored order, and realised that the Rabbi and his wife were missing.

It took thirty minutes to examine, photograph and finally remove Roscoe's body. Only then was the altar table moved and the escape hatch discovered.

Several mysteries baffled investigators at the time. How could the Cross have got from the altar table to a standing position on the floor without any fingerprints on it? And again, why were there were no fingerprints on the ringbolt?

There were also larger questions concerning Roy Roscoe. How did he know about the existence of the escape route? How could a dying man replace the heavy altar that had obviously been moved in order to gain access to the trapdoor? And why would a Christian minister want to cover the escaped Rabbi's trail?

The police followed the escape route into the disused car tunnel. But once inside the tunnel, they could find no way out. By the time the other storm drains in the tunnel were checked, the waters had risen to a level that made the sewers impassable.

Detectives noted the mysterious "WW" monogram on the trapdoor, but no one linked the initials to Wright, as his given name was Augustus. So the meaning of the letters went unexplained.

An original copy of the tunnel blueprint without "Wright's Wrong" from A.W. Engineering, Ltd. is appended to the Moray file. E.T.

Chapter XXX

'The Job'

[Sunday morning, October 18, 2009]

Again Gareth Gunn eyed the digital clock on the dash. For him, time seemed to stand still. He took his left hand off the wheel, checked his wristwatch. His hand was trembling. As the bulletproof Mercedes swerved, horns blared.

Montrose lurched sideways on the back seat. Papers on his knees fell to the floor; his briefcase slid across the red leather seat. 'As my chauffeur, may I make a special appeal to you. This is a straight Scottish road, not the Monte Carlo circuit.'

'Sorry, sir. It won't happen again. Had a bad night. Very bad.'

'Filthy weather,' said Montrose, peering out into greyness. 'The radio, please. I'll be wanting to hear the news.'

'What time's it now, sir?'

'Nearly ten. Didn't you just look at your watch, man? The radio, please.'

'I—' Sharply, Gareth slammed on the brakes. He almost missed a country stop sign. The black car heaved forward, springing back on its suspension. The security vehicle behind them screeched to a stop. 'What the hell, Gareth! What's got you so wired up this morning?'

Gareth stared at the pulsating digital colon between the hour and the minutes. 'It's over now.'

'For Chrissakes, man, what are you yammering on about?'

'The job—'

* * *

Chapter XXXI

A Liquid Language

[Sunday morning, October 18, 2009]
Guriat flicked on a small beam, and put a finger to her lips. The light fell on them harshly, casting their misshapen shadows around the bottom of the shaft. Brew and Deborah stood as still as shop window mannequins.

Guriat handed each a yellow sewersuit and, using her light, motioned them to dress. Brew quickly slipped the rubberised suit over his prison pyjamas. Deborah bit her lip at the one-piece, dropped her skirt, and in moments she, too, was dressed like a sewer worker. Guriat handed each gloves, waders, a helmet, and the "Elsa-J" emergency breathing mask.

As Deborah put on her rubber gloves, she saw by the torchlight that her elegant white gloves were soiled and torn. When her mother died, Deborah had kept them for a keepsake. They were her mother's wedding gloves, and Deborah had worn them only once, when she married Brew. By the time Guriat told her that she had to wear gloves in order not to leave fingerprints, it was late on Friday afternoon, too late for her to buy new ones. The next day was the Sabbath, and the day after, Sunday. Deborah had no other gloves suitable for a church service.

Overhead, rusty hinges creaked. There was a powerful surge of electricity as the tunnel lighting came on. The shaft suddenly filled with stripes of light through the barred storm drain. Angry voices shouted orders. There were sounds of running.

Guriat snapped off the torch, dropped to her knees, and scuttled back into the escape passage. The Morays followed, Deborah first.

They moved through the dark passage on hands and knees, jerkily like kids' pull toys. Heat and sweat quickly built up inside their suits. At the end of "Wright's Wrong", the three slithered into the ancient brick-built sewer. The pungent vapours brought Brew back to the squat hole in his cell floor. Guriat turned on her torchlight, and swore inwardly. Tight eddies swirled around her waist like furious insects. The water in the sewer was rising fast. Miming like a in-flight attendant, Guriat demonstrated the use of "Elsa-J" mask. Deborah and Brew practised putting their masks on. Guriat then held up ten fingers, inhaled noisily through her mouth, and lipped 'minutes' — ten minutes of emergency air.

Guriat found the vent cover in its tile frame at the bottom of the sewer where she and Neville had left it. Working feverishly, she and the Rabbi fitted it back into place.

Guriat drove herself and the Morays forward. With every step she could feel the storm waters increasing in speed and volume. Her goal was no longer escape. It was staying alive.

Deborah concentrated on her mother's white gloves. So what. What did anything matter now? Her only regret was the thought of dying without having a baby of her own.

Brew prayed.

> Let me be delivered from them that hate me,
> and from the watery depths.
> Let not the flood waters spill over me.[67]

Guriat kept moving. Death was not going to overtake her in a sewer.

They stopped at the entrance to the concrete main, and gaped. The ledges were lost under the current. Water crashed off the sidewalls like a turbulent river testing its banks. There was a terrifying roar. Tumbling bottles, cans, pieces of broken wood and tangled plastic bags swept by.

Guriat plunged in first. The flow carried her along. She used her hands and feet to keep from smashing into the walls.

Brew and Deborah followed. She could not swim. Trying to get a foothold, Deborah thrashed in the current. Brew held her arm, pushing her ahead. The buoyancy of her suit kept her head out of the water. With the strong tow pulling her in the right direction, she did not feel Brew letting go and dropping back.

A young cat, haplessly swept into the sewer and wild with fear, had bit and clawed into Brew's shoulder to save itself. The Rabbi clubbed the animal with his hand. Screaming, the cat dug in deeper. Brew slammed his arm and shoulder against the concrete wall. The cat refused to die. He throttled it, and even in death the mouth clung on. Brew tore it away together with a chunk of his suit and flesh. The hole in his suit let in a rush of icy water.

The torrent in the main, fed by many intakes, rose minute by minute. Less than a foot of headroom remained. Guriat turned and beamed her light behind her. The Morays had fallen behind. Deborah struggled, but not in panic. The Rabbi floated lopsided in the water with one shoulder down, and one up. It was only a matter of minutes before the water would reach the ceiling.

Guriat held up her emergency breathing kit, and broke silence above the roar of the torrent, 'Ten minutes' air!' Deborah and Brew fumbled to fit the life-saving masks over their heads.

As Guriat put on her "Elsa-J", a protruding ring on the ceiling knocked the rubberised torch out of her hand. In the blackness, she hit the rushing surface with her fist, screaming a silent *no*. She would not be defeated, not like this.

With her mask on, the roaring flood sounded different...muted, almost singing...in its own liquid language. For an indeterminate beat of time, Guriat listened. The song lulled her. Then she opened her eyes and saw. Ahead. A point of light.

* * *

---

[67]Psalm 69.15-16.

Chapter XXXII

Pillars of Smoke

[Sunday noon, October 18, 2009]

Guriat had no alternative but to go on: Neville's light should not have been on—

After three and half hours of clinging to the shaft ladder in the dark, Neville could stand it no longer. Fast-rising storm waters at his feet and claps of thunder above had sent his imagination into overdrive. 'To hell with her,' he muttered. He turned on the nine-volt battery lamp. At any moment he expected to see their drowned bodies washing through.

The tool satchel. In it four grenades. Next to him. Could the vibrations of thunder and traffic set them off? Using rope from the satchel, Neville tied one end to the handgrips and the other to the ladder below the water level, then lowered the heavy bag to the floor of the shaft.

He turned off the light. Again darkness played on his nerves. Every time a wheel rolled over the dripping manhole cover, Neville's head recoiled deep into his shoulders. The wails of police sirens going off unleashed the bitter memories of the march. His throat constricted, sending a sick rush through his gut. It felt like them kicking him, like being beaten, again. Happy New Year. The face in the car, the bull-faced detective, zigzagged like lightening across the night of his mind. He felt his blood thumping. He shook. Light on. Off. On.

A sudden scraping of metal against metal instantly concentrated Neville's mind. A second before the lid lifted off, he soundlessly slipped underwater. To his astonishment, the lamp was in his hand as he went under, and he'd even turned it off. Through the dark, muddy waters he sensed rather saw the daylight coming in overhead. He heard muffled voices. Fright sent him all the way to the bottom of the shaft. The rush of water was strongest near the bottom; the force tore him from the ladder. A desperate grab found the toolbag. It held him like a sea anchor for a few precious seconds. His lungs felt as if a great weight had fallen on him. Neville kicked wildly. One foot found purchase against the sewer wall, and stretching his long body to its limit, he managed to hook the lamp in his hand around the lowest rung of the ladder. His face grimaced in pain, as his arm muscles contracted, reeling him in against the stream. He scrambled up the ladder, broke the surface, his chest in flames. The spent air in his lungs exploded from his mouth. He sucked in. Sewer air never smelled so sweet. His body heaved in jerks. Neville looked up. There was only the faintest ring of grey light seeping in around the manhole cover. It took his mind some seconds to absorb that *they* were gone and he was safe. The blood pumping in him calmed. Neville flicked on his lamp—

Seeing Guriat come into the shaft, Neville dropped down the ladder into the water to help her. He was grinning like a chimpanzee. She slapped her hand over his mouth before he could say anything. With her free hand, she pulled off her breathing mask. Nothing, no emotion showed in her eyes.

Deborah and Brew came through. Deborah was breathless, half-drowned. Brew gently took off her mask for her, then his own. He guided her hand to the ladder and gave her a grateful hug, despite the searing gash in his shoulder. Neville clapped, once. Guriat shot him a withering look. Her disapproval doubled when she saw that the tool satchel was missing. She gestured Neville for the bag. He rolled his eyes like some dumb beast, who desperately wanted to explain but could not. His hand found the rope underwater and drew up the satchel.

Guriat snatched the bag, and tipped out the water. She attached a plasticised clip-on ID card to everyone's lapel and one to her own. Next she pulled out a pair of scissors, and passing them to the Rabbi, made clipping gestures with her fingers under her chin. She read Brew's unwillingness. The gas mask she handed him underscored the scissors. The beard had to go. Like a little boy suffering his first haircut, he sheared it off. Guriat, then demonstrated the way to strap their masks on and to test for airtightness by pressing against the filter. As many times as she had worn a gas mask in training and once in combat conditions during Operation *Akrav*,[68] Guriat never got used to having her face confined, her breathing restricted. Air tasting of black rubber always made her feel like her face was a drain being sucked at by a rubber plunger. No time for dark memories. Pulling out four olive green cannisters from the satchel, Guriat hung them by their handles on the nearest rung., then passed around a pre-written note. Rubber snouts bobbed up and down in the lamplight as each one in turn read, 'Smoke grenades. Not hazardous with a gas mask fitted.'

Guriat took the first grenade in hand, and pulled the pin—

From the moment the sirens went off, the whole area from the Castle drawbridge and moat to the Esplanade and Lookout Tower had become a no-man's-land, the outer edge of a war zone. To ward off any curious bystanders, uniformed policemen guarded the yellow barrier ribbon.

'Bloody fine weather for a breakout,' said Police Constable Six-Ten.

'Eh, lookie. What the hell's comin' off here?' said PC Five-Eleven, pointing down.

'Maybe we got ourselves a sewer rat.'

'Or two.'

The manhole cover came off. A tall column of dense, mustard-coloured smoke shot out. Two Edinburgh Corporation sewer workers in bright yellow suits emerged from the smoke like graveyard phantoms. One was short, the other very tall. Working quickly, the two shoved the cover back over the hole shutting off the fumes.

'Wha' in Jesus' name?' choked PC Five-Eleven, holding a soaking sleeve over his nose and mouth.

'Hydrogen sulphide, Constable, sewer gas,' shouted the tall sewerman, sounding remote through his gas mask.

'You dinna say,' coughed PC Six-Ten, holding his throat with both hands.

'Noxious, highly combustible, sir,' said the worker.

Plain-clothed security men and other police armed with machine pistols rapidly descended from the Esplanade and Castle. Coughing and spluttering, they kept their distance. An older man in a bowler hat and mackintosh took one step forward. 'What's going on here, Constable?' he asked. Before either of the patrolmen could answer, Guriat took off her hard hat and unmasked. She held her face up for all to see. 'Fair sexed Corporation workers! What next!' drawled the mac. She winked.

As the power of the stench gradually dissipated, the official came closer. Neville fixed on the water globules blowing from the bowler's brim. 'Constable!' called the man in the bowler hat.

---

[68]Hebrew, meaning "scorpion".

'Ser?' answered the two policemen as one. But before they could decide between themselves who would speak, Neville cut in, still speaking through his gas mask. 'We ca' neutralise it, sir, your honour—' he said bending slightly from the neck in the direction of the manhole, 'the sewer smoke, gas— But we'll need to fetch up some more equipment, and our van—'

Ignoring him completely, the official set his gaze between the two constables, and asked, 'Have you searched them, and verified their identities with Sewage and Drainage? How do we know these two are not the fugitives?'

Answering for both, PC Six-Ten said, 'Course, Mr Commissioner, we checked. But anyway, he's too tall an' no beard; the lass is dark-skinned an' curly-haired, whilst the wife is said to be pale. We ha' their photos right here, ser.' He produced them for all to see.

The Police Commissioner's knot of security people tightened. Some rechecked their own photos and shook their heads in disappointment.

'Sir?' interrupted Neville. 'Van's just down the steps on Johnston Terrace—' He broke off. At that moment a squall of rain blew in. The Commissioner's mac flattened against his chest. He bowed his head into the storm, a hand pressing on his bowler hat. When the gust let up, he ordered the sewer workers, 'You two, be quick about it.'

Neville tried to read the name on the Commissioner's ID tag, but couldn't see it through his gas mask. Guilelessly, he asked, 'By the way, what's up?'

Guriat, who'd already taken a step away, went white with fury: hell, Neville, not now.

'It's 'em friggin' Jews 'at's got us all up here in this piss water,' moaned PC Six-Ten.

'Guard your tongue, Jimmy, or you'll never make sergeant,' the official cautioned him. 'You and you,' he commanded the two PCs, 'stay with that hole. If two go down, make sure only two come up. Got it? The rest of you, to your duties.' To Neville and Guriat, 'I said, on your way.'

As soon as the mac was out of earshot, Six-Ten spat, 'Jimmy!'

'Why'd you lie to the Commissioner?' asked Five-Eleven.

'About checkin'?'

Five-Eleven looked grim.

Six-Ten snivelled. 'Wha d'ya 'xpect, in front o' all that lot? "Sorry, ser. Forgot, what, with all this shit 'at's comin' down, an' all." Friggin' Commissioner can check himself, if he's wantin'.'

In the van Guriat simmered, 'Smart arse. You had to ask, what's going on.' It came out as if her mouth were full of tacks.

'But if I hadn't asked, it would have looked *more* odd.' Neville, still wearing his helmet and mask, lowered his eyes as if not seeing was not being seen.

'Oh, take that damn mask off a minute,' said Guriat. 'You know who that was?'

'No, so what?'

'The Police Commissioner, Thomas Butterstone.'

Neville muttered, '"Friggin' Jews" — good on him, tearing a strip off that copper.'

Guriat started the engine. The wipers couldn't keep up with the lashing rain. Visibility was down to a few yards. As they inched up the hill, she decided Neville had been right to ask, and slightly regretted her outburst. But she apologised for nothing. Instead, she quickly recapped the plan's next phase.

Guriat drove through the barrier ribbon, and backed up the van to the manhole. She and Neville masked and hatted up. The two policemen watched from a safe distance as Neville went around the back of the van and swung open the rear doors. The doors hung directly over the manhole, partially shielding it from view. Five-Eleven dashed across, inspected the back of the van, and seeing nothing suspicious, only a blue satchel stamped with an official "Edinburgh Corporation" seal in luminous white letters, waved the workers on. The tall worker cheerily shouted out to the retreating policeman, 'No need to lock up with you lot around, eh?' Meanwhile the little woman grabbed the blue bag.

The two constables, pinching their noses, backed away, as the sewer workers lifted the cover off the manhole and climbed in. The long-legged sewerman soon reemerged. Waving his arms, he warned the two policemen further back. After a short delay, there came column of thick, yellow, sulphurous smoke like the earlier one. As it cleared, the short worker climbed out clutching the blue satchel, and heaved it into the back of the van. The two masked workers then positioned themselves behind the van doors, one on either side, and peered down the manhole. A third pillar of smoke[69] shot straight up from the hole, immediately followed by the fourth and last cloud. 'Right,' shouted the lanky one, 'that's done it,' and from either side, he and the little woman slammed shut the van's rear doors.

Without removing her mask or helmet, she took the driver's side. The tall one by himself nudged the iron lid over the manhole. As he climbed into the passenger's seat, puffing, he could not resist calling out to the rain-sodden constables, 'Scotland needs more brave men like your good selves. Hope you catch the wee bastard.' The van drove off, leaving the two coppers still holding their noses.

'For you, sir.' A rain-soaked aide covered the speaker as he handed over the mobile phone. 'It's the PM.'

'Thank you,' said the Police Commissioner, stepping away. 'Prime Minister. Butterstone here—'

'Mr Commissioner— We've just heard the radio news. I'm out of town. Brief me. The Rabbi has escaped? Is that verified?'

'It is, sir, confirmed.'

'How?'

'We don't yet, sir. But the pair of them will be found within the Castle walls. The Governor assures me that that there is no escape from the Rock. A thorough and meticulous search is being conducted as we speak. No stone will be left unturned. You have my word, Prime Minister. We'll find them.'

'I want every man jack in the force on this. And not just inside the bloody Castle. All over the city. Understood?'

'Sir, you are aware we have a freak storm...serious flooding...widespread power cuts. Thousands of people stranded, homeless. There are dead and missing. I can't take policemen off vital emergency duties.'

'The ramifications of the escape are such that the entire police force — without exception — must be redirected to finding the fugitive.'

'Prime Minister, all leave is cancelled. But it would be criminal of me to order men assigned to the public welfare to abandon their duties at a time like this—'

'Corporation rescue services and the fire department can take care of the citizens.'

'For the sake of one prison escapee?'

'The man must be found, Mr Butterstone. He's a far greater threat to Scotland's security than any gale. Do it!'

'Sir, there have been casualties here—'

'I'll hear about it when we get back to town. The moment the fugitive's apprehended, I want to know—' There was a final nothing.

---

[69]Joel 3.3. See also Ex. 13.21.

The Commissioner switched off the phone, dropped it in his pocket. He looked over the city. To some unseen spot on the horizon, he said, 'Edinburgh will not forget this day, nor forgive you — sir.' He took off his hat, letting it fall to his side. He did not feel the rain falling on his bare head.

* * *

The first systematic weather records in Scotland date from Eighteen eighty. The Great Gale of Twenty o-nine remains the worst on record. In Edinburgh during the first seven hours alone, eighteen inches of rain and hail fell. Winds gusted to over ninety miles an hour, blowing off roofs and felling trees. Widespread flooding knocked out underground telephone and electricity lines. By late morning muddy waters, particularly in low-lying areas, turned roads into fast-running rivers.

The gale left some one thousand four hundred families homeless. Property damage amounted to one and a quarter million Scottish pounds. Three toddlers and ten pensioners drowned. One emergency repairman was electrocuted.

Miraculously, Edinburgh's combined drainage and sewer system, including some sections around the Castle dating from Victorian times, managed to handle the storm's unnatural volume of water without serious damage. E.T.

Chapter XXXIII

Autumn Leaves

[Sunday noon, October 18, 2009]

Guriat unmasked. 'Buccleuch Place,' she said between deep breaths. The others took off their gas masks and helmets.

The next moments hung. There was no sound in the van, only the rhythmic beat of the windscreen wipers. Their tiny universe seemed to float, as though suspended in a liquid matrix.

Outside, everything passed in a haze. Edinburgh was as it always was, but nothing seemed quite real or believable. Only Guriat looked back. They were not being followed. She watched the Castle Rock fade behind banks of mist and rain.

Brew steered the van onto the George IV Bridge. He drove by the Sheriff Court building as mindless of it as of a green light. Driving aggravated the bite-wound in his shoulder. He clamped his teeth against the pain.

Deborah looked into the rear-view mirror, and saw Brew's arid stare. She read in his glazed eyes her own thoughts. That it had all gone wrong, that Roy Roscoe was dead. She cried, without tears or sound. But Deborah could not control her trembling hands.

Sensing unease, Guriat turned around. Her eyes fell on the Rabbi's wife. Somehow she knew: Roy. Guriat tried to see his face. To remember his warm, spirited laughter. To feel his love. Woman to woman, Guriat awkwardly folded Deborah in her arms, letting her cry for him, and for her.

Coming to an almost complete stop, the van turned into Buccleuch Place. The wheels hit the cobbles of the short street with a rapid thumping. Seeing the empty shop at the top of the road turned Neville's head around. Once, everybody knew the "old Jewish shop". It was an Edinburgh landmark, a familiar haunt of the Moray brothers since boyhood. Landis's closed down years ago. Neville pictured the kosher haggis, the cold meats and the spaghetti of mince piled high in the refrigerated showcase. The oldest, Neville always went along with his mother to Landis's on Sunday morning. It was his "job" to help her carry the family's weekly meat supply to the car.

Except for Landis's on the corner, Buccleuch Place was solidly walled on either side with drab Old Town houses, all belonging to the university. It was Sunday, no lectures, and the library would not open until two. With no students about, the street was deserted.

Brew parked at the bottom of the road by The Meadows. As he turned off the ignition, a lightning bolt shot through his shoulder. His eyes closed tightly against the pain. Across the velvet blackness flashed the Mountain of the Salt Land. Then came the aura, like a flame-thrower, to liquefy and dispel the image.

Even before they came to a full stop, Guriat leapt from the rear of the van. She retrieved one of the large bin bags from the edge of the park. The previous day had ended in an unusually warm autumn evening. Before the storm, there had been heaps of crisp, rust and copper leaves neatly raked up alongside the Jawbone path and Middle Meadow Walk. Some of the leaves were stuffed in ballooning, black plastic bags. The job wasn't finished, so there was little chance they would be collected before Monday. That gave Guriat the idea to half-empty one of the bags and put the clothes in it. As she left, she couldn't resist kicking the piled leaves like a kid.

Back inside the van, Guriat untied the bag. It contained the four clear plastic sacks of clothes. She said, 'Here. These are dry, and plain, so you won't stand out. Change now. Hurry. We can't hang around here.' She parcelled them out.

As he took his, Brew looked at her. He remembered the lustrous amber of her hair from the day he was arrested. He identified her accent — Australian — but it was impure, skewed with some other, unrecognisable influence. Whoever she was, thought Brew, she was cunning. For a short moment, locked in the naked penetration of her glowing, golden eyes, he forgot his pain. In that same fraction of time, Guriat allowed herself her first close look at the man she'd saved. His black eyes showed tiredness. The cheeks, lined and sunken from prison, dug deeply into the scrubby remains of his beard. A glaze of sweat coated his forehead and temples. His lips were pale and waxy. But below the surface she sensed a depth of being she could only guess at. He was so different from Neville.

The men in the front, the women in the back struggled out of their sewer gear. Out of the corner of his eye, Neville caught a glimpse of the burnished skin of *her* shoulder and upper arm. A tingling shot through him like the hot thrill of a roller coaster ride. As he shifted his eyes not to be caught staring, Neville noticed the blood on his brother's sleeve. 'You're hurt,' he said.

Deborah looked up. 'Brew—'

He made little of it, saying it looked worse than it was, and that the pain came and went. Brew didn't say that he had to kill the cat.

Guriat asked Neville for the van's ignition keys. She unclasped the old house key from the set and gave it to Deborah. 'The key to your safe house — Landis's old shop. Use the back entrance in the mews between Buccleuch Place and the end of Meadow Lane.' Knowing nothing of Guriat's plan beyond the escape, Deborah held the key without moving. Guriat said, 'It was Neville's idea.' Brew gave his brother a vacant look, but said nothing as Guriat went on, 'Eve Landis gave me the key, no questions asked. The place is stocked with everything you'll need...food, air mattresses, blankets, cooking utensils— Rabbi, there's a first aid kit upstairs. Rub your arm with plenty of antiseptic cream for the time being. I'll bring antibiotics as soon as I can. Now, you've got to get going—'

As Brew painfully opened his door, Deborah asked Guriat, 'Is Tsippi all right?'

'The girl? Sure. She's in good hands with the Landis woman—' After bagging the clothes in the park, Guriat, as planned, had collected Tsippi from the Morningside Library just before evening closing time, and taken her to Eve Landis's.

As Deborah squeezed out from the rear through the driver's door, Brew motioned Neville to roll down his window. Smiling faintly, he said, 'Landis's...without the meat.' It was Brew's way of saying thanks. Neville understood, and gazing skyward, he said, 'Aye, well, complain to the MANAGEMENT.' Both brothers needed to laugh, to share a brief release.

As an afterthought, Brew asked Guriat, 'Is there any writing paper in the shop?'

'Paper—?' she answered impatiently. 'Paper, pens, sure, you'll get, along with the antibios.' A siren wailed past the top of the road. 'Now, get the hell out of sight.'

As Deborah took Brew by the hand, he said, 'You're shivering. No wonder, in this rain.'

A few steps on, Deborah answered with a slow smile, 'And you're hurt. A fine pair we are.'

At the mews door, Brew held Deborah's wet, round face in both hands. 'Debs, thanks to you, I *will* finish what I have pledged to do.'

Deborah turned the lock. 'I don't understand. Finish what?'

'Never mind for now. It's what you said that counts. That we're a fine pair. Alive, and together!'

'Brew Moray, I love you so much.' Behind the closed door they hugged, though he could hold her with only one arm. 'I know, Debs. I know you are worried about Tsippi, and us. But I promise you...it *will* all come right. I know it. I see it—'

Guriat climbed forward into the driver's seat with Neville next to her. As she inserted the key into the ignition, she took a parting look over the Meadows. No more heaps of autumn leaves. All blown away in the gale. She slipped on her silver-lensed sunglasses, turned the key, and calmly drove away.

Strangely, Neville felt no pride, no elation. He'd just come through an ordeal, saved his brother's life, and his own. He'd seen a side of himself that he'd never seen before, that he'd never known he had.

Sitting beside her, all he could feel was trapped. He wanted to tell her that whatever he'd done, he'd done for her, and for her alone. She hadn't said a word to him, as if he wasn't there, as if he wasn't a man. He wanted to hold her, to tell her: I'm here, I care for you, I— Instead, her quiet kept him quiet.

Bringing the van to a fast-braking stop in an empty car park, she simply said, 'Over there' — she pointed — 'in those supermarket rubbish skips.'

'Back to our usual working relationship—'

'Working's the only kind of relationship you and I will ever have, mate,' she said, not looking at him, even for a second. 'So don't make this any harder than it has to be.'

After disposing of the suits and tools in the dumpsters, they sat in the van as if taking a workers' tea break. 'Time,' she said, more clipped and stiff than ever. 'Parting of the ways. But don't go home and don't go to the factory. Both places are bound to be watched now. Also, no calls. To anybody. All public phones will be dial-tone monitored.'

'What's that mean?' asked Neville.

'It means the moment you dial any number — relatives, friends, associates — they've linked to you, alarms go off. Satellites and high-speed computers pinpoint the position of the caller in less than half a minute.'

'Cell phones, too?'

'Even faster. If the number belongs to a mobile or public phone, they dispatch a squad car to try and run down the caller.'

'So where does that leave me? What about the *gescheft*?'

'The business — you can forget it. It's gone.'

'Just like that. You know something, Miss—' Neville wanted to tell her that she was about as cold as a polar bear's turd, but it stuck in his gullet. She said, 'Hey, mate, let's get something straight. I didn't make the situation. If I haven't said it before, your brother owes you one. And so do I—'

'Thanks for the citation. I'll remember to wear it proudly.'

Guriat had seen it before — the aftershock following a mission. She began again, 'Look, Neville, I know this isn't easy for you. It's not easy for any of us. And I'd be less than candid if I didn't say that I think things are going to get worse, damn it, a lot worse.'

'Your honesty touches me.'

She let his sarcasm go. 'For now, you lie low, live rough, on the streets, B & Bs, bedsits, anywhere you don't have to show ID, use credit cards or give cheques. Disguise yourself. They'll be looking for you. And like I said, no telephone contact with anyone you've ever called before. And no cash card withdrawals — they can also home in on you the moment you stick plastic in the wall. Here's five hundred.' She handed him some money. 'I'll top it up next Sunday, a week from today. Botanic Gardens, the benches on the path south of the Palm House. Ten fifteen, a.m., sharp.'

'You think of everything,' said Neville. Getting out of the van, he came straight out with it. 'Tell me, are you so dangerous to be around that you can't let anyone get close to you?'

'Yes.'

* * *

On Wednesday, January eighth, Twenty-ten the following item appeared at the bottom of the City News page of the Free Scotsman:

Xmas "bonus" to Edinburgh city

Staff Reporter

The Edinburgh Municipal spokesman's office disclosed yesterday that officials found a "spare" maintenance van parked with the city's fleet. The discovery came during the Corporation's annual post-holiday audit. The source of the windfall vehicle remains a mystery. Police are investigating.

E.T.

End Part Two

PART THREE: WINTER NIGHT

Chapter XXXIV

'The *Right* Thing'

[Thursday morning, October 22, 2009]
The Moderator of the Church of Scotland, the Rt Rev Dr Ian Edward MacMulder, officiated. Roy's weeping daughter Jemima wrapped in a long, black, lacy gown, stood next to the Moderator holding her baby boy. The infant cried. MacMulder interrupted his eulogy time and again to chastise mother and baby with stern looks. It was unclear which disturbed his sensibilities more: Little Roy's wailing or the feeble-minded mother's inappropriately exposed cleavage. With each halt, Jemima self-consciously rocked and shushed the child, but he would not be consoled.

When Roy Roscoe's coffin was lowered into the ground, Jemima buckled. On her knees, clutching Roy to her breast, she leaned into the pit and sobbed, 'Father, don't leave us like this.' It was not the Moderator, but a nearby churchman and a small dark-skinned woman under a black hat and veil who raised the mother and child.

As the couple led Jemima away, trembling, little Roy stopped crying, and uncurled his balled-up fists to make ten fat little fingers. The baby's contented gurgling was no consolation to his mother. Jemima kept stopping and turning back 'for one last look'. With each turn, the breeze caught her mousy brown hair and slapped it around her eyes and temples.

The veiled woman said to the young parson, 'They're all alone in the world.' She had an Australian accent.

'You're not from here?' he asked. 'You're a relation of the deceased?'

Before answering, the veiled woman glanced at Jemima. She was too distracted to be listening. 'Let's just say,' she answered in a subdued whisper, 'he was the father I never had, and leave it at that.'

'I'm sorry.' The young man peered into her veil. 'It shouldn't have happened. Him dying like that.'

'Like what?' she asked.

'In church. Shot in the back.'

'Shot in the back?' she repeated thoughtfully.

'Of course *I* wasn't there,' he said in a hushed voice. 'I only know what I read.'

'What *do* you read?' she asked, rubbing Jemima's bare, goose-pimpled arm.

He reflected, then said, 'That he was shot in the back...when the Jewish priest got away.'

'You think the rabbi shot Rev Roscoe?' Her intonation expressed sincere interest.

'Who else but a Jewish person would bring a gun into a church?' he asked. Then thinking a moment, he said, 'That doesn't sound prejudiced, does it?'

She proffered no answer. Instead, she became abrupt, 'What about Roy's daughter, and the baby? They've got no family. Will the church help them? Will you?'

'I...I don't know.' He shook his head. 'I try to do the Christian thing—'

She brought her face close to his and raised her veil. Her eyes were concealed under mirror lenses. 'How about doing the *right* thing—' She turned away and disappeared into the crowd.

* * *

As a matter of record Rev Roy Roscoe's funeral cortege proceeded west from Murrayfield Parish Church to the Corstorphine Hill Cemetery. It was a long procession.

Roscoe's funeral was held up for four days by the aftermath of the gale that extended right up to the hour of his burial. At the sudden reappearance of blue skies, according to one source, one mourner whispered 'how inappropriate it was for the sun to shine on so sad an event'. Many who were gathered in the sunshine to hear the funeral service had never met Roy in life. They attended because, following the breakout, the Scottish media whipped up an outpouring of Scottish nationalism by casting Roscoe in the role of sacrificial lamb.

Also, the funeral was delayed by the inquest. The coroner ruled that 'imprisoned enemies of the state were unsuitable, unworthy and unfit witnesses to give evidence' as to the cause of the chaplain's death. Chief Officer Murdo Duncan, in a comatose state from a blow to the head, was unavailable to testify. Without clear forensic evidence and no admissible witnesses at the hearing, the coroner concluded 'death by misadventure' in the case of Rev Roy Roscoe.

Three prisoners, including the notorious shaven-headed Dr Tessa Tripp, died with Roscoe in St Margaret's Chapel or later of their wounds; the other twelve recovered from their various injuries.

Duncan never regained consciousness. Falling into a persistent vegetative state, he was kept alive on a life-support system for twelve years. His wife and children never received more than normal state benefits. E.T.

Chapter XXXV

Mad-dog King

[Thursday morning, October 22, 2009]
Kenneth Keller could not take his eyes off Montrose's copperhead hammer. It rose and fell in his palm with a flat slapping sound like an oar on the water. It made Keller want to scream, or run out of the Prime Minister's office without saying a word, or ask Montrose to stop. But none of these were workable alternatives. Instead, he meekly began, 'Sir, if I may say so, the exit tax is already proving very unpopular—'

Angus Montrose answered, 'The public forgets that fifty per cent of the levy is refunded on a person's return to the country.'

'Nevertheless, sir, the ordinary tourist's spending power abroad is effectively cut by an estimated twenty to thirty per cent, and for families—'

'The measure was designed to preserve the Treasury's hard currency. That, Mr Party Chairman Kenneth Keller, is the message you have to get across to the rank and file.'

Montrose's habit chipped away at Keller's nerve. He shuffled his papers, and started over again, 'The reason I asked to see you today, sir, is on account of— It's...this latest emigrant property forfeiture bill you proposed— It will turn the Scottish people against us.'

Putting the hammer down, Montrose leaned forward. 'Ken, we've worked together for a long time. Think a moment.'

'Sir—' Without the hammer, Keller could hear himself speak. 'I have thought long and hard about this bill.'

'And you're against tabling it.'

Keller nodded, once. His had become a voice without power. Party politics and distant elections now took a back seat to the pressing affairs of state. With Montrose successfully raised to the top on the seesaw of government, Keller's position as party chairman had dropped, almost to level of grass roots.

'Why are you against it—? Because it's unpopular?'

'No, sir.' Keller pressed his point, 'Because it will effectively turn Scotland into a nation of hostages.'

'A nation of hostages—' repeated Montrose. 'Rather harsh, don't you think, young man?'

Calling him 'young man' was a swipe Keller could duck and forget. But not the hammer habit— It unfailingly brought to mind his late father's wooden ruler, the sound of him rapping it monotonously on the edge of his desk. As a boy Keller loathed himself for his fear of the ruler. As an adult he could still feel its sting across his open palm. The only child of a mother who died giving birth to him, he was raised by his father. Kenneth Keller Sr was the stern headmaster of Aberdeen's Smeaton Academy for Boys. He required respect from all boys, including his own son. Young Kenneth was expected to call his father 'Sir' at all times. He carried the habit into adulthood. Kenneth Keller addressed Montrose with the same 'Sir' as he used to his father.

'Keller—?'

'Harsh? No, sir. It's only that the bill as proposed is tantamount to the payment of ransom money.'

'Ransom money? Is that what you call it?'

Keller had gone too far to stop now. 'If we want to discourage mass emigration, surely there are more positive measures we can take.'

'It's not mass emigration that the forfeiture bill is aimed at. On the contrary, the target here is a very limited segment of the population.'

'You mean the Jewish community.' Hearing himself say it, Keller sounded strange and distant, even to his own ears.

Montrose fanned his huge hand. 'I didn't say that. All I am saying is, we can't lay ourselves open to a charge of discrimination. And because *they* control and manipulate world opinion—'

Keller went pale. 'Sir, do you believe that?'

'Abroad, they've turned an escaped criminal into an winged angel. And made me the devil incarnate.'

Keller watched Montrose's cusped knuckles turn red, then white as his grip tightened around his hammer's wooden handle. 'Surely, sir,' he dared, 'your skin is thicker than newsprint. If I may remind you, your duty is to react to the needs of the people, not to words on a page—' Something was happening to him. Something he couldn't understand. He was defying a whole lifetime of paternal programming. He was defying himself.

'My duty, Mr Party Chairman, is to the nation, and its defence. Whosoever threatens the security of the state is my enemy, your enemy, our enemy. No more, no less.'

'Prime Minister, people are saying—'

Montrose restarted his habit. 'People are always saying—'

'Party members, then — openly, candidly — are saying that you haven't got your finger on the pulse, that you've lost touch with reality...since this rabbi affair began.'

'Are you one of those people? Kenneth? I've always thought of you as a man of deference.'

'I appeal to you. Listen to yourself. Listen to *what* you're saying. Scotland has no enemies, but if we keep going like this we'll have no friends, either.' Never before in his life had he spoken out like this.

'Mr Chairman,' said Montrose, inhaling, 'this afternoon I have a meeting. A fateful meeting. For us all. And quite honestly, I tell you, I don't know what I'll say, or can say.' He exhaled. 'And do you know why?'

'No?'

'Because that damned Chief Rabbi is on the loose.'

'Distance yourself from the whole episode, sir. It will ruin you.'

'I can't. It's gone too far.'

'You must. If you don't, you'll sink yourself, and our party with you.'

'I said, I can't, Keller. You don't know what's at stake here. What's going on.'

'Tell me, sir, what *is* going on? Something's happening—'

'What are you driving at, Keller?'

'Just this. The signs — the crazy weather, that old minister's death on the altar, the Chief Rabbi's...unexplained, if not miraculous escape. It's like we've entered into a vacuum, into a field of negative energy. It's like Scotland is spinning out of orbit.'

Montrose stepped up the drumming. 'Go on, Keller. You're beginning to interest me.'

'I'm not a churchgoer, or even a religious man, but I was raised on the Old Testament. As though it had been written by a Scotsman. Lately, there's been a phrase. That keeps banging away at me. That won't leave me be—'

'They preach at me—' said Montrose in a whispered undertone of sarcasm.

'"Remember Amalek,"'[70] and again, Keller repeated, slower, lower, more ominously, *"Remember Amalek"* — It wouldn't leave me till I looked it up. I opened my Bible, and I couldn't understand it. Still can't.' Montrose cocked an unbelieving eyebrow. 'Amalek was a mad-dog king who attacked Israel as they came out of Egypt. He hit from the rear, killing off the stragglers, the weakest and poorest. The Bible tells the Israelites to erase Amalek's memory, forever. But it also says, remember what Amalek did, and prophesies war with a new Amalek in every generation.' Keller summed up, 'Forgotten, yet remembered. Blotted out, but forever a cowardly, implacable enemy of the Jewish people throughout time. Makes no sense—'

Montrose's hammer sank harder, deeper into his palm. Yet the only sound Keller now heard was his voice echoing around his head. Makes no sense, he repeated to himself. It was like somebody else, somebody he didn't know, was speaking through his mouth. He murmured aloud, 'The Jews—'

'What about them?'

'In my whole life I've only come across the odd individual. Here and there. Never known any closely. Almost none in Aberdeen. And yet...and yet as a group, there's something irresistible about that lot. Irresistible and incomprehensible. Something no one can escape—'

The slap tapping decelerated, telegraphing another change in Montrose's mood. 'Mr Party Chairman,' he said impatiently, dismissively, 'now you're talking nonsense.'

'Am I? Maybe I am. But the fact that I have the courage to do so says something to me.'

Montrose blew cold. 'I think this meeting is over.'

'Prime Minister.' Keller rose to go. With his eyes Montrose escorted the party chairman to the door, where he stopped and turned. 'Please, whatever is driving you, leave it. For all our sakes. Leave it, before it's too late.'

The hammer stopped.

* * *

---

[70]Ex. 17.8-16; Deut. 25.17-19. Cf. 1Sam. 15.2f; 27.8f.

Chapter XXXVI

Oriental Splendours

[Thursday afternoon, October 22, 2009]
Tsippi could not stop staring at Eve Landis's huge porcelain pots (gold-rimmed and painted with bright red and green Indian elephants), teakwood stands and tables (intricately carved and inlaid with mother-of-pearl), huge tusks (finely sculpted into overcrowded river boats), glass domes and boxes built like miniature Shinto shrines (one encased an ivory horse on its back, and another contained a white elephant with a screaming monkey in its trunk and a lion biting its tail), puzzling balls within balls on spindly stands, spider-armed jade figurines, and on the walls everywhere, black-framed pictures and faded scrolls (depicting ancient, unreal mountains and gorges flanked by vertical rows of bamboo-style writing).

Deborah had hugged and kissed Tsippi. The young Highlander would be stopping at Auntie Eve's 'just for a night, maybe two', while Deborah went away to bring Brew home. A woman called Guriat collected her at the Morningside library. On the drive over, the small dark figure in shaded glasses said almost nothing, only that Tsippi would now be staying with Ms Landis 'for a while'.

The twelve-year old sat rigid on a high-backed chair at the dining room table in the formal, dustfree atmosphere that had been her home for the last five days.

'Aren't you hungry, dear?' asked Eve, who sat opposite. 'You eat like a bird.' Eve Landis's double chin flapped whenever she said anything. Her hair was bluish, two glazed grey-green eyes reflected highlights like Christmas tree baubles, and her nose and lips seemed to be taken from elsewhere and stuck on.

'How old are you, ma'am?' asked Tsippi.

'That's a very forward question, young lady, to ask somebody you hardly know,' said Eve, taken aback but trying not to show it.

Tsippi's black eyebrows pushed up at her flaming red hair. She fixed her gaze on a green vase in the far corner of the dining room. Finally, she said, 'You sound so young, but your skin's...well, ma'am—'

'Remember, call me Aunt Eve.'

'Yes, ma'am.'

'Don't you like me, Tsippi?' Without waiting for a reply, the schoolteacher said, 'I like you.'

Tsippi returned her attention directly to Eve, but couldn't think of what to say. So she looked at the food on the table. There was smoked salmon and cold cuts and chopped chicken liver. Tsippi decided now was the time. 'I dinnae really like meat, ma'am — I mean, Aunt Eve — not for afternoon tea, anyway.'

'Why ever not?'

'Because we live on a croft with sheep...'

Eve wasn't listening. 'But meat is very good for you.'

'...and sheep are better alive than dead. We can drink their milk, an' make cheese from it. Ma mother spins wool and knits it into jumpers and socks.' The girl pushed her plate away. 'We dinnae eat them, ever. Not even at Christmas.'

'But there's no mutton here.'

'I know.'

'You ate pork for breakfast, didn't you?'

'Aye, Father and the boys do. Mother and I, we cook it, but we don't eat it.'

'You know, dear, my father was a purveyor of fine meat. He always used to say, "Flesh is the only food fit for the human carnivore."' Eve smiled at the memory, but in the awkwardness that followed, she joined her young guest in surveying the oriental splendours of her dining room and lounge, through the arch.

Tsippi tried again, 'Where is Mr Landis?'

'My father? He passed on, dear.'

'I meant your husband.'

'Oh, I see.' Eve primly forked a bite into her mouth, as she debated with herself if now was the time to mention that she had never married. She decided another time, saying only, 'I'm not used to having company, especially nice little girls. But if you like it here, dear, you can stay as long as you like. I'm certainly not going anywhere.'

* * *

Chapter XXXVII

The Pearl

[Thursday afternoon, October 22, 2009]
Gareth Gunn was back to his normal driving duties. All-round he was feeling quite satisfied with himself. The Rabbi was not dead. There was no blood on his conscience. That the chaplain had died was an accident, nothing to do with him. Gunn suffered no remorse. And though the conspiracy was in ashes, he could not be blamed. *His* tracks were covered. Given the coroner's findings, whatever Duncan said or did now (should he ever come out of his coma) could easily be dismissed as the ravings of a certified madman. That left only Montrose who could link him to the chief prison officer. But the old bear was not given to suicide, political or otherwise. Best of all, the money Montrose had paid him could never be taken back.

The chauffeur let out the clutch and squirted out from the car park under New Parliament House. The PM's bodyguards in their car were already out of sight. For almost a year, Gunn had been driving the Scottish leader to these meetings that never appeared in his office diary. The anonymous silver-grey Mercedes travelled the short distance without fanfare, alone in the normal flow of Edinburgh traffic. Montrose sat hidden in the back seat behind smoke-tinted windows and pleated curtains.

Waiting for a traffic light, Gunn assessed his passenger's mood signs in the rear-view mirror. The old man's lips were grimly sealed. Adopting a nice-weather-for-the-time-of-year tone Gunn began, 'They haven't found him yet—?'

'If they had,' answered Montrose, 'you'd have heard about it before me.'

Gunn changed the subject. 'Which door d'you think it'll be today?' It was a game they played. The object was to predict from which of the mosque's three doors the ambassador would emerge.

'Gareth, on a day like today, a man cuts his losses.'

Montrose was on a short fuse. Gunn shut up. Instead, he contemplated the changes that had overtaken the grim, greystone slum behind Nicolson Street. The mosque had changed practically everything. Five times a day the muezzin's amplified call to prayer pierced the quiet of the neighbourhood. In retaliation the remaining churches sounded their bells louder and more frequently in a vain attempt to turn back the tide. But now most of the people in the neighbourhood walked around in long grey gowns and sandals. The men wore turbans or tarbooshes, and the women, black headdresses and veils. Elderly notables fumbled their worry beads in the streets.

Gunn could still remember the local cinema, friendly pubs and cheap digs around here. These were long gone, demolished to accommodate the central mosque. The Moslems proudly styled it "The Pearl of Edinburgh", or simply, "The Pearl". Glazed blue and green tiles covered the massive exterior. Horseshoe-shaped windows pierced the walls. A mosaic of flowing Arabic script tied a wide ribbon around the square building. The roof was a flattened dome crowned with a yawning crescent. At the eastern corner a spindly minaret reached for the sky. The entrance to "The Pearl" was from the west. Via the footbath in a foreshortened courtyard, believers approached three equally high and wide Moorish arches supported by blue and red veined marble pillars. Under each arch, like a sunken eye, was a single door. The three wooden doors were curiously unequal in size. The southernmost portal was the largest, highest and widest. The middle opening was smaller by a third, while the smallest appeared no more than half the size of the largest. Over each door was a different quotation from the Koran. These doors were the source of Gunn's little game.

And there was a second departure from the otherwise exact symmetry of The Pearl, which Gunn knew nothing of. On the outer wall at the back of the mosque, the outline of an arch could be perceived, but only in strong sunlight. The blueprint line corresponding to the *mihrab*, the prayer niche, was mistakenly punched through the wall for an emergency exit. When the ignorant Scottish builders realised their error, the hole was quickly resealed. Among the Moslem community, speculation and legends about the faint arch abounded. The devout claimed that the arch was built over a large chip of the Foundation Stone[71] brought from Jerusalem. The Sufis harboured another belief: that "The Pearl" was the *New Outer Mosque*.[72] As "proof" they claimed that some of the precious stones that once encrusted the sacred inner portals to the great synagogue at Medina[73] were imbedded within the nearly invisible arch. And when Jerusalem was retaken, the arch would miraculously open to reveal its treasure.

Nearly there, Gunn turned right at the familiar sign of "The Pit and Bull" on Nicolson Square. The pub was the last refuge of the neighbourhood's "drinking public". After a few pints, the talk inevitably came round to the invading 'Pakis and Turks', and from there to the mosque, the 'quer kirk: the only bog in Scotland tiled on the outside'.

Gunn parked in the reserved space outside the mosque. Montrose's bodyguards had set up police barriers on the pavement to divert foot traffic to the other side of the street. Passers-by paid little attention. Wealthy, visiting Moslem notables and important Arab dignitaries regularly frequented "The Pearl" at any hour.

A thin, balding man of medium height in a dark, pinstriped suit slipped out of the middle door. At the same time, two larger, heavier, pale-complexioned men, visibly uneasy in their loose-fitting galabiyah robes, exited from the smallest door.

Gunn had been guessing the ambassador would choose the middle door. Damn, he thought, if he'd made the wager he'd have been five pounds richer. He got out of the Mercedes.

The three men that came from the mosque formed a tight circle as Gunn opened Montrose's door. The two pale-skinned security men looked up and down the pavement, while the gentleman in the suit pronounced his standard greeting, 'You are a punctual man, *Re'is*[74] of the Scots.' His disconcerting eyes, one brown, the other blue, peered coldly into the car.

'Your Excellency, Mr Ambassador,' said Montrose. As usual for these visits he had covered his head with a black-banded Arab keffiyeh.

Just as Montrose was sliding out of the car, a tall, scruffy, bearded man in a sock cap and hooded parka rounded the corner. First one, then the second galabiyah stiffened. The ambassador was too intent on maintaining decorum to notice him. The unit of four men with Montrose concealed in the middle moved smartly from the car. Passing through the courtyard, the party disappeared through the smallest, the north door. The chauffeur stayed with the silver-grey Mercedes.

The scruff only caught a fleeting glimpse. He could not be sure. He sauntered closer, ignoring the barrier. 'Swish set of wheels you got there, old son.' Gunn shot him a poisonous look, as he lowered himself into the driver's seat and shut the door. Montrose going into the mosque— It bore

---

[71]The Foundation Stone or sacred omphalos, regarded as the navel of the world by Jews and Moslems and considered the launching pad of the Prophet's night journey to Heaven, is enshrined under the Dome of the Rock. See the Koran, Sura 17.1.

[72]The original "Outer Mosque" is held to be Al-Aksa, built on the Temple Mount at Jerusalem.

[73]In 620 AD the Prophet conquered Medina. The Jews living in the city were either converted or exterminated, and the spoils included the jewel-encrusted doors of their synagogue.

[74]Arabic, "head" and by extension, "captain" or "leader".

thinking about, but somewhere else. To hang around here would make him conspicuous. A fugitive, Neville could not risk arousing suspicions. As he moved off, the Merc's registration plates attracted his attention. The number happened to end in his initials: NM.

* * *

Chapter XXXVIII

Iskandar al-Munar

[Thursday afternoon, October 22, 2009]

In the mosque's arabesque foyer the four men added their shoes to those already there. Bowing with a flourish, the ambassador doubled his greeting, 'In the name of the Merciful and Compassionate, welcome, Honoured Guest.' He was careful not to mention the Prime Minister's name in what was still a public area.

'Your Excellency—' repeated Montrose.

As a mark of respect Ambassador Iskandar al-Munar fell in half a pace behind the Prime Minister. Montrose's two bodyguards led the way inside. As usual on these occasions they had come ahead, slipped into Middle Eastern robes, and discreetly checked out the mosque. Except for its few servants, the Pearl was empty, closed to worshippers and visitors at this hour of the day.

Well inside, it was safe for Montrose to take off his headdress. With each visit he found it harder to resist the sensual appeal of the mosque's open inner space. There was peace in the shady coolness that refreshed the thirsty spirit like an oasis spring. Stockinged feet responded to the textures of the intricate patterns woven into the oriental rugs that blanketed every inch of the floor. The sweep of arches and columns in two files tracked his eye to the far wall. There, he held the empty *mihrab*, the prayer niche, in his view. His gazing eyes then climbed the steep wooden stairs to the *mimbar*, the canopied pulpit reserved for the preacher. From there his vision soared up to the colossal chandelier suspended from the highest point of the domed ceiling. Montrose hardly noticed the strident, nasal chanting any more. The chanter, a young boy, squatted before an open Koran on a low bookstand. Two old *ulama*, knowers of the faith, and the purple turbaned imam rocked in time to the boy's reading. Only one thing spoiled the atmosphere of the mosque for Montrose: the residue of sweat that hung heavy in the air.

Mr al-Munar ushered the Scottish leader into the usual place, a small library entered through a veil over the door. Here, their negotiations would not be disturbed. The robed bodyguards remained outside. Montrose seated himself opposite al-Munar on the higher of the two ottomans, another sign of deference to his rank. Between them, dividing them, was the traditional low-standing brass tray balanced on folding legs of inlaid mahogany. The round tray was hospitably laid with the traditional brass pot and miniature china cups. A tendril of steam coiled up from the spout of the pot.

'Coffee, Mr Prime Minister?'

'Please.' The rituals, coded words and repeated gestures had established themselves in a now-familiar pattern in these delicate and secret talks. Montrose had learned that any alteration in the routine, however small, carried significance.

Al-Munar poured the oily brown liquid into the two thimble-sized cups with a steady hand. He delicately passed one to Montrose. 'May Allah preserve you.'

'And yourself, Excellency.' Montrose toasted but did not drink. Strong, over-sweet and spiced with cardamom, the coffee was not to his taste. Yet, in the service of his country, he would always finish the first cup — the minimum Levantine etiquette required to satisfy the demands of hospitality.

'Your Scottish rain—' The diplomat's hollow cheek muscles quivered. Montrose was never quite sure if the man was complaining, stating a fact or making polite conversation. His highly refined English delivery obscured plain meaning. 'Your Scottish rain— All the rugs here were rolled up in case of...water damage. However, as you have seen all are back in place. Ah, but Allah is generous.'

'Too generous, sometimes,' said Montrose, 'at least, where rain in Scotland is concerned. Was there flooding here?'

'The Koran promises us: "The hour of Doom is sure to come".[75] It appears, *E'ham-du L'ill-ah* — Praise be to Allah that the hour was delayed. No, no flooding here. Our mosque was spared.'

Sometimes, the diplomatic small talk went on half an hour. It was a testing time. Montrose had made up his mind to go on the offensive. 'Mr al-Munar, tell me — the three doors. Why are they different sizes? It is a question I have often asked myself.'

The ambassador studied the cup between his thumb and forefinger, and then took an excruciatingly long sip. 'If you read Arabic, Mr Prime Minister, you would know. You would not have had to ask.'

'Why is it that whenever we enter or leave the mosque, we always go through the smallest door? Yet Your Excellency alone may come and go through any door.'

'The smallest portal is the only one through which honourable gentlemen may enter.'

'By "honourable gentlemen", Mr Ambassador, I understand you to mean...eh, unbelievers.'

'Not a formulation I like to use.'

'But it is used by others of your faith?' said Montrose, asking.

Al-Munar's two-coloured eyes flared. Having to allow "unbelievers" to pass for his tactful "honourable gentlemen" left him no choice but to answer Montrose's less than diplomatic question: 'The great south door is the Mecca Gate; to its left, a third in size, is the Medina Gate; and the smallest, by half, is the Gate to Jerusalem, *El-Kuds* — the Holy City. Jerusalem belongs to all three Peoples of the Book. Through the Jerusalem Gate all may enter—'

'I see,' said the Scot, cutting in. 'But why, then, is the Jerusalem door the smallest of the three?'

Iskandar al-Munar balked. But in the light of his answer, the justifiable logic of the second question could not be denied. The ambassador was being forced to elaborate, revealing more of himself than he wished to. '*El-Kuds*, Jerusalem is in the hands of the enemy. Please, understand — in the beginning Mohammed, the Servant of Allah, extended the hand of friendship and protection to them and their faith. No, actually, more. *His teachings* paid homage to *their teachings*. And yet, they rejected the Prophet, blessings on his name. Again and again, this nation have demonstrated their treacherous stubbornness. We have learned from history that their lasting perfidy will not die of itself. It must be destroyed...as the Prophet destroyed their tribes at Medina.'

Keller's 'mad-dog king' flashed into Montrose's mind. He felt an odd sensation at hearing someone speak so openly, with such vitriol of his hatred for a whole people. Surely, he told himself, *he* did not share al-Munar's twisted convictions. He asked, 'You mean the Jews—'

'Yes— Jews—' answered al-Munar. 'Yesterday, and today they are strong— We cannot yet defeat them in open war. But tomorrow, like the moon in its phases, they will

---

[75]Sura 22.6

become bloated, then thin and weak, until they finally disappear altogether. While Islam, always the Crescent, remains forever young. When Jerusalem falls into Moslem hands again, the Gates of the Pearl will be renamed. The southern Gate, the largest, will then become the Jerusalem Gate — open to all. And all will enter as true believers.' The ambassador drained his coffee; his face relaxed. 'And our reward— In the day Jerusalem is retaken the Arch of The Pearl will open and its mysteries will be revealed for all to see.'

Montrose blinked.

'You have not heard of the Arch?' asked the ambassador. When al-Munar finished briefly recounting its legend and promise, Montrose shook with a fine, involuntary tremor. At once the Arch seduced and intimidated him. He asked in disbelief, 'Here? In Edinburgh?'

Al-Munar's eyes glinted at the unexpected advantage Montrose's little outburst handed him. 'Yes. Here. The Pearl of Edinburgh is the New Outer Mosque. Today the Arch is hidden, dormant. But soon, very soon all the West will come to hear of it, to seek it out, and through its splendours find the True Faith.' The ambassador poured himself another cup of coffee.

Taking the hint, Montrose drained his first cup to the muddy bottom and clumsily set it down. Al-Munar poured him a second cup, knowing full well it would not be drunk.

Montrose straightened himself. 'Our philosopher John Malcolm Campbell had a saying. "The first and last rule of negotiations is to conclude them."'

Al-Munar, his disturbing eyes boring into the big man, counter-challenged with equal directness. 'My government...is...frankly concerned—'

Montrose was ready. 'There is no need for concern. None.' He parried, using the very points — the exit tax and the property forfeiture bill — that Keller had taken up with him. 'There is no doubt in my mind that the latter legislation will be passed into law before the end of this session of the Estates.'

The ambassador's response was considered. 'Your lists were long, very long, and we have filled them to the last bullet. You, personally, have approved the final status report of the independent inspectors. Scrupulous confidentiality has been maintained throughout the negotiating period. Even now as we speak, the materiel is being warehoused at the quayside. Eight ships flying flags of convenience have been chartered, and are waiting to be loaded. The first shipment could be in the Clyde in ten days' time. My government have kept to the bargain.'

'You are implying, Excellency, that I have not—' returned Montrose in a tone so smoothly diplomatic, it had a matte finish.

'This escape—' Al-Munar's expression displayed deep disappointment. 'My government will not release the arms until such time as it is entirely satisfied that the Scottish Jews will remain in Scotland. That is the linchpin of our bargain.'

'What difference does one man make?'

'I will answer you. The Prophet, peace upon his name, was one man.'

'I have assured you, Ambassador al-Munar — and your government, directly — that the Jewish community will not be allowed to emigrate.'

Al-Munar projected hurt surprise, as if betrayed by a friend. 'I am a messenger. No more.'

A humble reminder, reflected Montrose, that in negotiating directly with so lowly a servant of his nation, a maverick among states, he the Premier of Scotland had unbalanced the diplomatic process. But to hold talks, even secret talks, with any more senior official would surely have risked arousing unwanted media interest. The international community would then have been forced to react. And Scotland would not achieve her goal, a viable defence and security order— A bead of sweat formed on his temple. 'What are your government's demands?'

'Two points. One: Find and liquidate the Jewish leader.'

How naive he had been. When he had made his first overtures, the Jewish variable seemed of no great significance. Guns for souls. It appeared so simple, so cheap. But now the equation had become an insoluble, lop-sided tangle with him caught in the middle— 'The ambassador is perfectly aware that Scotland is a democracy rooted in justice. Here, we do not "liquidate" our enemies.'

'I do not wish—' The ambassador's unequal eyes closed to find the correct formula. 'Let me begin again. There is reason to believe that an attempt was made on the life of the Jew at the time of his escape. One had only to read between the lines to know that the operation was abortive, a miscarriage of planning and execution.' Al-Munar's carefully manicured phrasing almost made the botched murder attempt sound like a medical procedure.

The allegation called for a swift denial. 'Mr Ambassador, you have windmills in your head.' The uneasy silence that followed was filled by the boy-reader's insistent chanting of the Koran.

'Second point: That your secret diplomacy with the Zionist entity continue at its present level.'

Only Montrose heard the searing explosion in his skull. He knows nothing. Call his bluff— 'Israel has normal relations with Scotland, and maintains an Embassy in Edinburgh. Yes, my government talks to them. I talk to them.'

'About arms deals? With respect, please do not deny it. You will do yourself a disservice.'

'I don't deny that they, too, are a major arms exporter.'

The next came out in a low, ominous whisper, 'We...are... perfectly aware—'

'Aware of what, Mr Ambassador?' Spontaneously, Montrose started to slap his fist into his palm.

'Aware of the fact that the Zionists know every detail of *our* negotiations. They know you, personally, have secretly concluded a massive package deal with my government. They know that your scientists at the Dounreay nuclear reprocessing plant are converting uranium to fissionable weapons-grade material. They know of your duplicity, because I tell them. And still they continue to secretly negotiate with your officials. Why—?'

Montrose contemplated saying that the Israeli track was a smokescreen, a legitimate front to cover up his personal dealings with a pariah state. Instead, pushing his face forward, he resorted to bluster, 'Your Excellency Mr al-Munar, neither you, your government nor any government on this earth can dictate to me with whom I or my officials may or may not talk. And let me tell you something else — between us — personally, I'll talk to Satan Almighty, if I have to, to get what Scotland needs.'

'That's just it. Your people are talking to the Jewish devil.' Holy Jesus in Heaven, Montrose cursed inwardly. 'They play our game, because we are playing the nuclear card.' Al-Munar's thin lips stretched. 'Why do you think the Royal Navy is not seen off your coasts?'

'Why should they be? Scotland poses no threat to England. On the contrary—'

'Exactly. But if His Majesty's government got wind of the amount and sophistication of the armaments you are about to secure for your nation in exchange for refined uranium 235, Blakemore would seal off Scotland, hermetically, without a second thought. And obviously, before the weapons arrive. A complete aerial and naval blockade. Bad for business. Indeed, your clandestine dealings with a...a "loose-cannon" Islamic regime might be just the pretext he's been waiting for — to bully Scotland back into the fold, if necessary, by a justifiable use of the military option.'

'That's just the point. The Scottish people have the right, the duty to defend their nation's independence by any means—'

'No, Mr Prime Minister, that is not the point. The point is England doesn't know about *our* deal. Why not?'

'Because neither you nor I am telling them.'

'Wrong. Because the Zionist dogs aren't telling them.'

'They wouldn't. In principle, we might still procure weapons from them— They'd be shooting themselves in the foot—'

'Again, I say with humble apologies for my bluntness — wrong. You are missing the key element underpinning the whole scenario. The Zionists know they have no chance of winning your contract, now or in the future. Nor are they interested in your uranium. They have the bomb. No, the occupiers of Jerusalem will reveal nothing to England for one reason and one reason alone: the defence of Jewish lives. Israel is sworn to protect and save Jews under threat wherever they are. That is their abiding weakness, their historical Achilles' heel. Simply put, an English blockade is not in the Zionist interest as long as there are Jews in Scotland.'

The dawning came like a white flash. Montrose paled. He had ensnared himself on a sticky thread of his own making in an ancient and complex web of animosity that originated with a 'mad-dog king'. Was he, Angus Montrose, inheriting Amalek's mantle here, in the Pearl of Edinburgh? He tasted the dryness in his mouth as he said, 'Let me think—'

Al-Munar's bicolour eyes flashed. 'It is only the Zionists — no one else — who want more Jews on Arab lands and in Holy Jerusalem. In their war against the Arab nation, every man, woman and child is a reinforcement. But the reality of the situation is that every immigrant who is allowed to come is another obstacle to the world peace that we are all praying for. Surely, Mr Prime Minister, you must see that. My government calls for your answers.'

Montrose wiped his forehead. The sweat left a large stain on his white handkerchief. 'What have the Jews done to you?' he asked.

'No, Mr Montrose. The question is — what are the Jews doing to *you*?'

* * *

Chapter XXXIX

Snappy

[Thursday afternoon, October 22, 2009]

The old manse behind the wall on Canaan Lane was growing chilly. In the early days of winter by four in the afternoon, teatime, the sitting room was already quite gloomy. Still, it was too early in the season to light the gas fire.

Cup, spoon and saucer clattered in Anna Moray's hand as she came through. Hot tea, a woolly jumper and a cardigan were enough to see her through the late afternoon without heat. Two digestives were wedged under the Spode teacup — the broken-handled one that Manny had cemented back together. It had outlasted him.

The old wing chair faced the mantelpiece. Its velvet upholstery started out bright moss green. Now a little greyed, tired, wrinkled, lumpy, cosy, comforting, it was Manny's chair. Every afternoon her widow's day ended there.

Once settled with her cup and saucer cradled in her lap, Anna would helplessly be drawn through the bay window to the path outside. Her memories would complete the picture of Manny lying there cold and still. Next, the brick crashing through the glass came to mind. It was a sound that would never leave her. Her brooding thoughts then leapt to the news of Brew's breakout. She waited for the phone to ring, for him to walk through the door at any time now. It didn't happen, not even a hoped-for letter came. A few more motionless moments would pass and she'd snap out of it, nibble a biscuit, sip some tea.

With the deepening darkness, Anna switched on the table lamp by her side. The sixty watts hardly escaped the yellowed shade; the light barely reached the far corners of the room. Beneath the lamp stood their wedding photo in a tarnished silver frame. Over the years the colour print had faded: Manny's black tie and tails were grey, and Anna's flowing white wedding dress, a smoky blue.

The old woman reached down and stroked her dog's head between the ears. As usual she said, 'We're both getting on, aren't we, Snappy? Mustn't let it get us down, eh, boy?' At her feet the old schnauzer gave a little yowl, and then yawned, tongue out. His name started out as S 'n' P for salt and pepper, because of the wiry white hairs that salted his black and tan coat, even as a puppy. Aggie Christmas, though, always claimed the dog's name was SNP, as in Scottish National Party. 'No dirty politics in this house,' Manny used to rib her, so S 'n' P soon became Snap, then Snappy.

Snappy didn't "talk" much any more. Like Anna, part of him also died when Manny went. In his old age he was mostly content to lie stretched out, half asleep. True, that morning he had cornered a field mouse in the kitchen, but he let the rodent slip by and out the door. Though comical and half-hearted, his chase showed that he still had some of the old fire from his younger days. When he was in his prime, he had a baritone bark that was far deeper than his medium size indicated.

The letterbox flap rattled and the doorbell rang. 'Strange,' said Anna, thinking that there had been no afternoon deliveries for decades. 'Maybe it's Brew?' As she'd given Aggie an afternoon off to visit friends, she pushed herself up to see what had come. The old hound began to bark and hop around like a frisky young puppy. 'What's come over *you*? Act your age,' she chided her pet, while making her way to the front door. She flicked on the light in the vestibule. The dog bounced around her feet, whimpering and snapping. 'Get away, get away!' she said, sounding short-tempered. She stooped down and picked up the envelope. The beast bounded knee-high on all fours and yapped shrilly at the envelope. 'What on earth's got into you?'

The plain Manila envelope was thick. There was no name on it. She turned it over. No return address. She looked for a postmark. None. 'Odd.' She was about to put her little finger under the flap. Snappy growled, showing her his yellowed teeth. 'You poor old dog,' she soothed. 'Have I been neglecting you?' She put the envelope down on the hexagonal table in the hall, bent down and rubbed her friend's bearded chin between her hands. Gently, he took the end of her sleeve in his teeth, and tugged at it. 'What is it, Snappy? Tell me.' The animal wagged its stubby tail and swung its head, as though it had something important to show her. 'No, you don't want your walk, we've done that,' she reasoned, as though speaking for him. 'I see. You're wanting in. A drink of water? Is that it?' She petted him on the neck, straightened herself, picked up the letter, and said amiably, 'Lead on.' Snappy's encouraging "woof" had recaptured some of its youthful bass.

The old dog's gait was urgent, demanding. His tags jingled. He kept looking back over his shoulder to see that his mistress was with him. Instead of following, she went back into the dimly lit salon. 'We'll just leave this letter here,' she said, putting it down on the side table under the lamp. The dog jumped at it. Her half-drunk cup of tea spilled into its saucer and onto the table. 'No, Snappy,' cried Anna. 'Now, you're making a nuisance of yourself. We'll have to clean this mess up,' she muttered. 'And maybe we should call the vet.'

The dog followed her into the kitchen, and there he scratched at his water bowl. 'So that's it,' she said. 'We're thirsty, are we? And here I thought you were about to cash in your tags, or whatever they say.' The old woman smiled thinly at her joke. As she picked up his bowl to fill it at the sink, Snappy quietly padded out the door, then tore into a frantic run back to the lounge.

Anna's back was turned only a moment. 'Where are you?' She looked under the table. She heard the crash. 'What now?' blurted Anna. 'What in Heaven's name is going on with that dog of mine?' She followed the sounds to the salon.

In the lounge, Snappy had knocked over the side table. The envelope fell to the floor. Snappy pounced on it, first pawing at it, then ferociously clamping it between his jaws, grinding, mauling—

A dull, but powerful blast shook the house. Anna was thrown back on her feet. **'Snappy!'** she cried out, breaking into a run.

The lounge door swung skewed on one hinge. Inside the room, acrid smoke and dust swirled. Curtains, ripped and ragged, flapped outwardly in the day's greying light. Deep gashes in the wing chair's green upholstery haemorrhaged cotton stuffing. The silver picture frame was on the floor, empty. The Spode cup that Manny had repaired was nowhere.

But all Anna saw was animal fur and brains splattered over the doorpost in vicious dark red gobs.

'Snappeeeeee —' His name faded on her lips as she fainted to the floor.

* * *

Chapter XL

Jake Banks

[Friday morning, October 23, 2009]
Jake Banks yawned deeply, sickeningly. There was no air in the basement of National Police Headquarters. Unshowered, his hairy chest itched from sweat. His mouth was dry. The stickiness around his groin had turned to dried scale, pulling hair and skin. He swore to himself that if he were free tomorrow, he'd go to Easter Road Park. Rangers were playing Hibs.

Assuming an unfocused stare, Jake looked around himself for the hundredth time. The walls were stark, featureless, the seats cloned in moulded plastic of a uniform dull green. Two bearded officers wearing padded body armour and holding black submachine guns across their chests guarded the one door.

No one was allowed to talk. The sixteen suspects, all Edinburgh Jews, were respectable, middle-aged men known to Jake. There was only one woman: Sophie Moray-Banks, his wife. And two children, also his. Naomi and Benny were asleep. Sophie had insisted they come. There had been no one to leave them with. At four o'clock in the morning it was far too early to call on Mrs Allison next door.

Sophie's stiffness chilled Jake. She stared ahead, trancelike. She was concerned about her mother's phone being off the hook for hours. And angry with him for pooh-poohing it as nothing to worry about, and for not letting her go round. Then there were the hidden files in her computer—

Every ten or twelve minutes the door opened. Shoulders squared, eyes looked up. Another name was called from inside. All watched the designated person rise, teeter forward then vanish through the door. No one came back. Jake tried anticipating questions and rehearsing answers. It was no use; his mind refused to focus—

It had been a short night. With both hands Sophie had roughly shaken him from a deep sleep. He moaned. His penis, locked in the warm folds of a blonde-haired dream, released a spasmodic eruption. Jake sprang up. The hot trickle running between his thighs shamed him.

Doorbell ringing— Knocking— 'Police! Open up!'

Sophie was out of bed, throwing on her bathrobe. 'Jake, they'll break down the door if we don't get downstairs.' Awake and aware, he hit the light switch and heaved himself to the edge of the bed. Sophie threw him his dressing gown as she yelled, 'Coming—!' He wrapped himself up, fumbling with the belt. Breathing hard, he grabbed his watch and wallet from the bedside table and slipped them into a pocket.

The children huddled together in the hall were scared witless, and screaming as though the house were on fire. Sophie caught them in her arms. She concentrated her voice into an urgent whisper, 'Jake, for Heaven's sake, get the door!'

As he ran down, the sliminess lubricating his crotch made him self-aware. The fear of a body search terrified him.

The police conducted their raid in an orderly, apologetic style. Jake could see from Detective Paul Dalziel's disturbed expression that the whole affair was distasteful to him. But throughout the half hour that the raid lasted, the flat reverberated with sharp-edged voices crackling from police radios, drawers opening and closing, books and papers being rifled through.

With a sobbing, trembling child on each arm, Sophie sat rigidly as she watched her home and family being violated. Jake caught her glancing at her computer more than once. Though the name-and-address database she'd been working on was in an encrypted file in a hidden corner of her hard disk, he knew that any small-beer hacker could pick it open like a two-quid lock. When one of the policewomen idly neared the machine, Sophie squawked like an angry jay, 'Look all you want. You won't find them. They're not here.' The stratagem worked, distracting the woman away.

Jake skimmed the search warrant again. He got no further than the names Rabbi Brew Moray, Deborah Moray, Neville Moray— As he leaned back, the lump in his dressing gown pocket made itself felt. The guard standing over the family noticed. 'My watch and wallet, that's all,' Jake said.

'Slow, then.'

Jake eased his billfold out. The policeman was satisfied. Jake shuffled impatiently through his collection of plasticised cards. He slipped one out — his season football ticket, his proof of Scottish fidelity. Holding it up like a badge of honour, Jake said in his broadest Glaswegian accent, 'See, Constable, there must be a mistake. See, look, I'm a loyal Rangers supporter.' The PC was unmoved. Probably a bloody Hearts or Hibs man, thought Jake regretting his move. Sophie buried her face in her hands.

Dalziel announced, 'I'm sorry. You'll both have to get dressed. My orders are to detain you for further questioning.'

'What about the children?' pleaded Sophie, 'I'm not leaving without them.' Dalziel reluctantly agreed. A breakfast of jam sandwiches was prepared for the children before the family were taken away in a police wagon.

The vehicle floated noiselessly through the eerie pre-dawn streets. Blue and red strobes, filtered through the barred windows, dazzled Jake. Putting his hand to his brow, he wondered if their nosy neighbours had watched the police taking him away? If photographers and reporters would be waiting at the other end? If he would be charged? And if his business—?

'Sophie Moray-Banks.' Hearing his wife's name called out brought Jake back with a start. To cover his jumpiness he slipped a reassuring hand around the children. They were the last people in the outer room.

Inside, in the presence of a policewoman Detective Paul Dalziel asked her the routine questions, for the record. Sophie convincingly denied all knowledge of her missing family's whereabouts. After fifteen minutes Dalziel turned off the recorder, and said, 'Before you go, Mrs Banks, there's something you ought to know.'

Sophie's mind raced in all directions.

'Your mother—'

'Oh, my G—' She clapped her hand to her mouth.

'She's recovering in hospital from shock. She's a very lucky woman—' Briefly, Dalziel outlined the report he'd seen earlier. '...and, Mrs Moray, you understand, this is strictly confidential—' His whisper made it clear that he was relaying privileged information without authorisation.

'Thank you, Detective. Thank you.'

Sophie was the only person who left the way she came in, through the outer room. Jake saw the frenzied look on her face. All she said was 'It's mother—' She rushed off, taking the children, leaving him last to be called.

'Jacob Banks—' The voice that called Jake in was different, lower pitched.

Three men stood around the interrogation table. Two were in uniform. The big man wore a dull suit. Jake remembered him: Dalziel's superior, the detective who arrested Brew. 'Where is the young detective?' Jake asked of no one in particular.

'Sit down.' It was a command. 'I'm Detective Sergeant Keith MacKenzie. State your name, address and current employment.'

Jake began, 'You know who I am. Am being I charged?'

Grinding his finger into the "stop" button, MacKenzie switched off the tape recorder. 'This is *my* show. I ask, you answer. Now, let's start again — for the record.' He rewound the tape a second and pressed the "record" button. Jake spoke his name, address, and occupation, clearly. MacKenzie started. He fired his questions in short bursts. In between volleys, he stopped and stared at Jake in long, silent periods of thinking.

After half an hour, MacKenzie sent one of the uniforms out of the room. He slowly heaved himself up, walked around to Jake's side of the table and, with his over-hanging belly only inches away from Jake's face, he loosened his belt a notch. Seeing the cracked, curled leather raised a bitter squirt of bile to the back of Jake's throat. Then like a boxer dropping his robe before a fight, the detective let his jacket fall to the floor. As he flipped off the recorder, Jake saw greasy ovals of sweat under his arms. The remaining policemen now left, as if on cue. MacKenzie circled behind Jake. Clapping him on the shoulders, MacKenzie sighed, 'Jacob, Jacob—' He worked his fingers hard into the back of Jake's neck, and slowly lowered his big face down to Jake's ear. 'What is going to become of you lot? Jacob—?'

Jake said nothing. The man's stale beer-and-smoke breath sickened him.

'I understand Neville Moray, your brother-in-law, got into a nasty brawl last month—' Jake squirmed.

MacKenzie's thumb dug in. 'I'm not an complicated man— Jacob—?'

'No, sir.'

'Neither of us are looking for complications—'

'No—'

'You and me, we both want to get our business done here and go home. Right? We want to go home to our families—

Jake stammered, 'There is...something. But—'

'Tsk. No buts. We don't make deals.' MacKenzie sounded insulted, then disappointed, 'Jacob—'

'In that case, I want my advocate present.'

MacKenzie relaxed his massaging hands, smiled serenely and said for Jake's ear only, 'We don't make deals, but we do honour our word—' He switched on the tape.

Jacob Banks signed his statement, and went home.

The next day, Saturday, he watched his Glasgow Rangers lose one-nil to Hibernian in pouring rain.

* * *

Following the raids, the record shows that a number of Jews made discreet appeals to various Christian bodies for help. Induced by fear, the indignity of discrimination or the desire to remain in Scotland, some Jews embraced Christianity. All proselytes were welcomed, particularly the Jewish partners of mixed marriages. Their baptisms were performed in low-key ceremonies. The Church viewed each new convert as an important victory for Christ. E.T.

Chapter XLI

Only Fiction

[Friday night, October 23, 2009]
The door crashed in without warning. Two uniforms — fast moving blurs in bulletproof vests — threw the woman against the wall. Following them inside, two grey suits in jerky, birdlike dips and turns jabbed steely, short-barrelled guns in all directions.

'Eve Landis?' she was asked.

Eve barely nodded.

'Police.' Flashing IDs. 'Detective Sgt Keith MacKenzie. My partner, Detective Paul Dalziel.' Eve remembered them both, arresting the Chief Rabbi and from the march. Dalziel served the search warrant into her quivering hands. She glanced over the swimming print, down the page, to the signature at the bottom: Richard E. Calhoun, Sheriff. She'd once taught a Calhoun. Kathy.

The uniformed pair fanned out downstairs. The two detectives stormed up to the bedrooms. Unexpectedly left alone, Eve drew a deep, calming breath. She suddenly remembered. It was too late by the time her short legs brought her upstairs. Elen's room was already wide open. Eve rushed to the door. The girl was on her feet, icy still. Dalziel faced her. MacKenzie, eyebrows locked, was reading from a sheet of paper. Without a sound, Eve came forward and took Tsippi in her arms. Her thin body was rigid. Over Eve's shoulder, Tsippi's frozen gaze bored into the belly of the man who was reading *her* letter.

Downstairs, Eve heard breaking, crashing, shattering. She shut her eyes tightly, as if not seeing would cut out hearing. Every time another vessel was smashed, she flinched, tightening her grip on the child.

Eve could not form words. She wanted to beg them to stop it. No more. To beg them to tell her why they were doing this to her.

The no-neck detective read aloud, '"Dear Deborah—"'

Tsippi cut him off, saying that it was a homework assignment — to write a letter to a friend.

'You're lying.' A bubble of MacKenzie's spit hit the paper. 'Deborah? Deborah Moray?' Inflamed, Tsippi struggled to free herself from Eve's grip. 'This "homework" is not finished, not signed. Who are you? What's your name?' asked MacKenzie. Tsippi's lips twitched, but she said nothing.

'Her name is Elen,' said Eve, finding her voice. The detective sergeant turned on the old woman. He used questions like a stick, to beat her with. Who? When? Do you? Have you seen the Morays since Sunday? Has *she*? Does *she* know where they are? Who's hiding them? MacKenzie kept saying that he had information—

Eve's answers were yeses, noes, head shakings, and time and again — 'I told you, I don't know.'

'You people—' said MacKenzie in frustration. 'Maybe we should just take the girl — social services—'

Eve protested to Dalziel. That she was a Scot, a good citizen, a teacher of English at a respected school. As she spoke about her career, a picture of Kathy Calhoun unexpectedly formed in her mind. Bright, pretty girl. Probably why the name stuck. Had her father been a sheriff?

The younger detective took over. He seated Eve on the bed, with Tsippi next to her. His enquiries were delicate probes, seemingly inserted at random. He asked Eve about relationships, times, places, dates. He scribbled, checked answers against his notes, asked more questions.

He then asked MacKenzie to see the letter. After a glance at it, he spoke to Tsippi in a grownup way. She told him the truth about herself, which sounded so outlandish it had to be believed. As Tsippi and Dalziel quietly spoke, Eve's whole body shuddered uncontrollably. Her attention split between her interrogators and the clatter above her. Dull footsteps drummed on the ceiling. She heard old wardrobes knocked to the attic floor; suitcases, trunks, emptied of their contents and kicked about; precious Passover dishes, bowls, cutlery, pots and pans dumped from their wicker baskets.[76]

Eve Landis asked, who would compensate her for the damage? Replace the irreplaceable? Mend the irreparable? Were there no laws? No guarantees? No protection? No security?

MacKenzie answered that this was a security operation.

Dusty, sweaty, cap in hands, the two uniformed policemen came in. They reported finding no evidence to link either the child or the woman to the fugitives. The four police huddled in conversation.

Eve picked up Tsippi's letter — left on the bed — and silently began to read it. She closed her eyes and mumbled, 'A page out of Anne Frank's diary—'

MacKenzie broke away from his colleagues. 'A diary? Frank?'

Dalziel faced his superior: 'A book, he explained, from the last century. A young girl in Amsterdam...kept a diary...while hiding from the Nazis. A neighbour turned the family in. The Germans liquidated the girl.'

MacKenzie went livid: 'She crapping on us? Saying we're Nazis. Is that it?'

Dalziel placated MacKenzie: 'No, sir. She's an English teacher, and teachers like to talk about the books they read. Anyway, it's only fiction—'

Eve repeated, dreamily, 'Only fiction. That's right, young man, only fiction.' She grinned a crazy grin.

MacKenzie summed up the exercise: 'Waste of time, false lead, let's get the hell out of here.' Without so much as a look back, the four filed out. Moments later two cars drove off.

Eve and Tsippi sat together, frozen like cardboard cutouts. Eve began to laugh, hysterically. Her father's shop on Buccleuch Place. And the fools never asked. Frightened by the old woman's crazy chortling, Tsippi got up and went down. Everywhere: broken ivory, smashed vases— Sensing Eve behind her, Tsippi looked back over her shoulder. The old woman's face was strangely unfocused. She calmly bent down and picked up the search warrant. Her eyes flashed. She remembered: Kathy's father *was* a sheriff.

* * *

---

[76]For the Passover festival week, all routine kitchen and dining utensils and equipment are put away in observant homes. A complete and separate set of implements for eating and cooking is reserved exclusively for Passover, and only these may be used during the festival. Throughout the rest of the year the Passover implements, often fine family heirlooms, are stored safely away in cupboards, closets or attics.

The laws of Passover, which stem from the Biblical commandment (Ex. 12.15) to eat only unleavened bread (matzah) and rid the home of all leaven, are among the most complicated and difficult to strictly observe.

Three decades after Eve Landis's death, the then owner of her home unearthed a black plastic rubbish bag when digging up a flowerbed in the back garden. The bag was filled with colourful porcelain shards. Fired with curiosity, he dug up the entire back garden. He found twenty-nine bagfuls of china or ivory. Each bag contained a single piece, every one a collector's item, all shattered. Together with the broken contents was a descriptive label inside each bag. The "mystery finds" made the local news. The stories provocatively asked, 'Who buried them and when?' But the records show no follow-ups. No one bothered to look for answers. E.T.

Chapter XLII

'A Modern Exodus'

[Friday-Saturday, October 23-24, 2009]
Guriat slowly levelled her weapon in the direction of the noise. The staircase creaked again. 'Who's there—?' It was Brew Moray's voice.

'Rabbi—' breathed Guriat. 'I brought you paper.' The flickering light of the Sabbath candles on the table did not reach the dark corner where she was. The Rabbi, coming down the rickety stairs, said, 'I see you're the multi-directional model: as good at breaking in as you are at breaking out—' There was relaxed playfulness in Brew's voice.

Dropping the KTL back into her shoulder bag, Guriat answered in kind. 'I could hardly knock. Nobody's here, remember?' She came out of the shadows.

'Brew, who is it?' Deborah asked quietly from the top of the stairs.

'Our friend,' he said.

Guriat lifted her glasses like a visor. The amber of her eyes glinted. She asked Brew about the cat bite on his arm. He reported, 'Thankfully, no infection.' He was taking the antibiotics that she'd slipped through the letterbox earlier in the week.

Just then the first Sabbath candle went out. It left a sharp tang in the air. Guriat never forgot the very first time she smelled a wax candle's last gasp. 'Funny,' she said to Brew, 'how they never burn out at the same time.'

The Rabbi had only ever given thought to kindling the Sabbath candles, never to their going out. At a loss for words, he murmured, 'Oh, yes, *Gut Shabbes*.'

'*Shabbat Shalom*,' answered Guriat, always preferring the Hebrew to the Yiddish. The two moved closer. 'How did you know I was here?' she asked him in a whisper.

'I sensed a feline presence.' He spoke in a prescient tone.

'Why feline?' she asked defensively.

'The Talmud says, "Had the Torah not been given to us, we would have learned modesty from the cat."[77] It was the presence of modesty that brought me down—'

Guriat had let herself into the shop only minutes before the Rabbi came down. She had not made a sound. A thin layer of sawdust still remained spread over the backroom floor. At the front of the "Jewish" shop the white marble top on the refrigerated counter had been left as it was, scarred and chipped, its glass front, cracked like forked lightning. The needle on the weighing scales pointed off at a crazy angle below the zero. Three keys on the electric adding-machine were permanently depressed. The cash drawer in the till stood open as though the last sale had been rung up just minutes ago, instead of years.

Whenever Guriat thought about it, the idea amused her: generations of Edinburgh Jews brought up on kosher haggis. One thought led to the next: Eve Landis, only child, never married, the last of her line. Neville once mentioned that Eve could not bring herself to part with the shop where her father and her grandfather had worked all their lives.

Deborah said, 'Come upstairs.'

---

[77] R. Yohanan b. Nappaha, Talmud, Tractate *Eruvin*, 100b.

'Your writing paper—' said Guriat to the Rabbi.

'Oh, leave it there,' he answered. The package of paper lay on the chopping block, where she'd put it when she came in. It embarrassed her. She ought to have known better. It is forbidden to write on the Sabbath, so handling anything to do with writing was also forbidden.

But for the faint streetlight penetrating the dusty curtain, the upper floor would have been completely dark. Seating themselves on the two folding beds, Brew asked, 'May we finally know your name?'

'Guriat.'

'Guriat — interesting name — some modern Hebrew variation on a young lioness. You are here to help, but who exactly are you, Ms—?'

'Guriat,' she evaded.

Brew would not be put off. 'Guriat who?'

'Gaoni, but that's not for publication, Rabbi.'

'Not your original name. You took it when you made *aliyah*.'[78]

'Correct.'

'What was your father's name?'

'My father's name? He was a Murrie.'

'A Murrie?'

'Queenslander. Native Australian. Aboriginal.'

'Ah, an Aborigine. I see. And your mother.'

'My mother—?' said Guriat, stealing a moment to sort her thoughts. 'She was actually born in Glasgow. Her parents were from Germany — Holocaust survivors.' The English sounded wrong, she needed to say it in Hebrew: '*Nitzolei HaSho'ah*— Somehow, they ended up in Scotland after the War. But in the early Nineteen fifties the family left Glasgow and went out to Australia. My mother was three at the time.'

'What was their name?'

'Originally Stein, which they changed to Stone.' Perhaps Guriat should have minded the cross-examination, but she had come to accept the pedigree thing as part of being Jewish. 'My grandparents reacted to their Holocaust experience by changing their name and running as far away from their Jewishness as they could. It worked. Their one child, my mother, ran away even further and married young. She chose a man of colour—' Guriat did not finish.

'If it's too painful—' said Deborah, cautiously cutting in, 'you don't have to tell us.'

'Being Jewish carries a package. My name then was Hilda Unipon—' Guriat's story poured out. She was born and grew up in an Outback world of spinifex, musters, boab trees, gymkhanas, sweaty hatbands and long droughts. Her father worked on an isolated cattle station in the shadow of Mount Isa, Western Queensland. It was a lonely existence for a little girl. In school, from the earliest age, a mysterious, invisible barrier came between her and the other children. There were plenty of other half-castes, but she was different, as though she were handicapped.

Hilda's father adored his girl, and called her 'my little kitten'. He was good, kind. But as with so many of the Anangu, [79] he was perceived as weak and lazy. He hated competing for a living in a white world. He hated killing calves. Even for food. Whenever he killed a calf, he came home smelling of blood. Hilda hated that smell on her father. He was killed in a cattle muster when she was four.

---

[78]Hebrew, literally, "ascent"; "making *aliyah*" is the expression meaning "immigration to Israel".
[79]Anangu is the name the native Australian people prefer to call themselves.

Her mother was strong. Throughout life she called herself 'bloody-minded'. That was her way of saying 'to hell with where I come from, it's where I am that counts'. Hilda never knew if her mother really loved her father, or if she married him so that his black skin and curly hair would set her parents' teeth on edge. After all, their choice for her, a liberal, un-Jewish upbringing, denied her the right to choose for herself who she would be.

After Unipon's death, Hilda's mother remarried. Her stepfather was a white man. He drank. Her mother's second husband sickened, and by the time Hilda was an adolescent, he, too, was dead. Her mother did not marry a third time. As for Hilda, she was becoming a healthy, capable young woman. She could handle many chores around the station — cook, ride horses, brand cattle. And she was good in school.

Twice, when she was six and eight, Hilda's mother brought her to her grandparents in Sydney. Her mother did not stay. In private, they called each other Hermann and Selma, but to the outside world they were Henry and Sally Stone. They had funny accents. Both were gone by the time Hilda was nine.

They behaved oddly. Her grandmother silently lit two white candles, but only on Friday nights. Almost shamefully, her grandfather said words in a strange language over a silver cup of red wine. He gave little Hilda a sip to drink. It was sweet and good. Hilda understood nothing of these things at the time, and her grandparents told her not say anything about it to her mother.

Hilda's young mind held on to the memories. She never forgot the day she learned the truth about herself. It was a Saturday, her fifteenth birthday. She happened to hear a rabbi on the BBC World Service. He was speaking in honour of Jerusalem's Three-thousandth Anniversary. In his five-minute talk he mentioned lighting Sabbath candles and blessing the wine. It tripped her memory.

She mentioned the rabbi's radio talk to her mother. She pretended not to hear. So Hilda took a risk and asked why Grandma lit candles and Grandpa drank red wine on Friday night. All her mother said was 'Something they never did for me'. Then after a moment's thought, she told Hilda that *she* was Jewish. And everything made sense.

After that, Hilda Unipon began to claw her way back to her roots. She read and reread the few books she could lay her hands on. On Friday nights she secretly lit candles in her room. She would watch them, as other children watched television, spellbound. No matter how alike they seemed, they never went out together. The sharp smell and final gasp of curling smoke kept alive the memory of her grandparents.

It didn't take her long to make up her mind. She would leave Queensland and go to Israel.

Before leaving home, she armed herself with as much biographical information about her grandparents, especially her grandmother, as she could get her mother to remember.[80] At first her mother resisted, but Hilda's determination pried loose old memories; talking about her Jewish roots was a relief. By the time Hilda Unipon left Australia she had a notebook full of family names, a list of smaller and bigger towns in Poland and Germany and notes about places to go in Jerusalem and Tel Aviv to find out more. Her secret hope was to meet some long-lost relatives in Israel.

In her newly adopted country, she discovered that there were many Jews of dark skin, not Aboriginals, but enough like her so she felt at home. She began learning Hebrew while working as a volunteer on Kibbutz Sde Boker in the Negev.

'I love the desert. Sometimes I'd stay out all night, listening to sounds of nothingness under the starriest skies I ever saw. The jackals with glowing green eyes would walk around me, but I was never scared. The Bedouin became my friends. They still were

---

[80]A person's Jewishness is passed on through the mother's line, according to Jewish law, *Halachah*. See Chapter 21, fn. 2.

nomads then, wandering freely between the Negev and northern Sinai. There was one man, very special to me, a medical doctor and headman of his tribe. He spoke beautiful Hebrew, and gave me my new name. He called me the Little Lioness — Guriat. He showed me the desert, like nobody else could. And once, together, we climbed Jebel el Sabha, the Mountain of the Salt Land. There is a Bedouin legend about the mountain, which says that ALLAH brought the remains of Moses there from Mt Nebo on the night of his death, to be sure nobody found his tomb. Sometimes I was gone for days. The boys on the kibbutz went berserk—'

Although she was Jewish by birth, the rabbinical authorities in Beersheba, nevertheless, insisted on a formal conversion. It took her three years of religious study and practice to become legally recognised as a Jew. On adopting Israeli citizenship, Hilda Unipon proudly changed her name to Guriat Gaoni. She went into the army. Her earthy straight talking, common sense and cool nerve earned her the respect of her officers. But that same toughness and maturity scarred off friends. So she cultivated her exotic image, and kept herself to herself. Guriat distinguished herself as a soldier. She signed on for an extra six months to do the officers' course. She came through at the head of her class. She considered making the army her career. It was not to be. Her commander brought her name to the attention of the Mossad, Israel's intelligence community. Years later she learned that her initial "interview" was conducted under the guise of an innocuous manpower survey—

'It's getting late,' the Rabbi broke in, 'and what three know is no secret.'[81]

Guriat came back to the present with a jolt. 'You are good listeners...to get *me* to talk like that.' To change the subject, Guriat said, 'Rabbi, you're so different from your brother.'

'He is the son of our father, of blessed memory; I take after our mother's family.'[82]

'Your mother,' said Guriat remembering they had no radio, 'you can't have heard.' She briefed them. Brew's limp 'Where will it all end?' expressed his powerlessness. At the news of the morning raids the Rabbi predicted, 'There's worse to come.' After a short silence, he asked, 'Did Roy make it?' Deborah remembered Guriat's hug in the van, and bowed her head.

Guriat coolly reported the facts of the funeral, Jemima and little Roy.

'A good friend; his memory deserves better,' said Brew thoughtfully.

Outside a cat cried.

Deborah asked, 'How's Tsippi? When will we see her again?'

'I'm sorry, but frankly, I don't know. You've got to understand, Mrs Moray. Communication with her could jeopardise everything.'

'When will I see her?' asked Deborah again.

'Maybe before Hanukkah.'

'Not before the end of December!'[83] shuddered Deborah. The thought of being trapped in the shop for two whole months panicked her into miserable silence. In the darkness, Brew put his arm around his wife's shoulders.

Guriat repeated, 'I'm sorry. But picture a twelve-year old cooped up here—' The Israeli then remembered the package downstairs. 'Rabbi, I also brought you a *siddur* and a *Chumash*.'[84]

'That was thoughtful.'

'And I'll try and bring whatever I else can, for you both, to keep away the cabin fever.'

Deborah said cheering herself up, 'I can write to her, on the paper you brought. Is that all right?'

---

[81] Yiddish proverb.

[82] Moray's maternal grandfather, Ozias Loewy, was clearly descended from the priestly tribe of Levi. The Levites are charged with teaching the "Torah to Israel" (Deut. 33.10).

[83] In 2009 the first night of the eight-day Hanukkah festival was December 25.

[84] Hebrew, a *siddur* is a combined daily and Sabbath prayer book and a *Chumash* is the Five Books of Moses.

'So long as the letters are never sent—' said Guriat, with clear note of compassion.

'How's Neville, then?' asked Brew.

'Living rough.' The Israeli explained the circumstances that led to Neville's life on the streets.

Brew then asked about Sophie and her family.

'She's tops. You know, she's been secretly assembling a list of all Jews known to the community.'

'A list? asked Deborah. 'Isn't that dangerous? If it fell into the wrong hands?' Brew added, 'Good point.'

'"Squirrels that don't run up trees don't collect nuts." Old Aussie proverb. Not that we had any squirrels, or nuts where I come from.'

The Rabbi clapped his hands. 'Guriat Gaoni...you're not married?' His statement was a question.

'Brew Moray!' Deborah was scandalised.

'What's a rabbi for if he can't ask an attractive young woman if she's married or not?'

'No, Rabbi, I'm not.' Her answered betrayed no emotion.

'You're twenty-eight. It's getting late.'

'How did you know how old I am? I didn't tell you.'

'Ah, but you did. You were fifteen in nineteen ninety-six, Jerusalem's Three-thousandth Anniversary. Simple arithmetic.' Guriat remembered. 'You know, my brother Neville's also not married,' he pressed.

'I'm aware.' There was a slight tartness in her answer.

'Ah, it's like that.'

'Brew!' protested Deborah, elbowing him in the ribs.

'Oy! Marriage is one long joyous tragedy.'

Silence was Guriat's response. Inside, she was trying to work out why she didn't lash out at him for being so personal. Anybody else, and she would have.

'When he gets like this,' said Deborah, 'it's time we turn him off. This list, you mentioned. What's it for?'

'A modern exodus.'

'A modern exodus—,' repeated Brew. 'You have a plan—'

Guriat Gaoni spent the next long minutes outlining her mission. When she finished, a dreadful emptiness filled the room.

Deborah spoke first. 'It doesn't make sense. I don't understand. Why do we have to commit a crime? Why can't we just...just *charter* a ship and *go*?'

'If only it were that easy— But think a minute. Scotland doesn't want Jews leaving. Montrose is holding the entire community hostage. Not that anyone realises it—' Guriat explained.

'Incredible!' said Brew, as though he were witnessing a stellar explosion. 'Being held to ransom, and not even being aware of it. Who will believe it?'

'I'm afraid nobody,' said Guriat darkly. A distant twitter of birdsong, the first of the Sabbath morning, floated in on the icy air. It was still blackest night. 'I must leave, before it's light.'

The Rabbi suppressed a yawn. 'Ms Gaoni, Debs is right. Your rather radical solution to our problem begs questions, ethical and moral questions with many ramifications in Jewish Law.'

Guriat had not anticipated his Halachic scruples. 'It is not stealing. There'll be full compensation for any damages. Guaranteed. Hasn't Israel always paid her debts, in full?'

'Still,' said the Rabbi, almost out of hearing, 'I will have think about what you say.'

A second bird chirped. Differently from the first.

* * *

Chapter XLIII

Solemn Promise

'Debs, there is one thing I have to do,' announced Brew with all the gravity of a solemn promise, 'before I leave Scotland—'

As soon as the Sabbath was out, the Rabbi left. He refused to tell Deborah where he was going or for how long. 'Not to worry,' was all he said.

Deborah knew she could not stop him.

* * *

Chapter XLIV

'We Are a Cosmetics Revolution'

[Saturday evening, October 24, 2009]

'We are a cosmetics revolution,' began the salesman with a flourish.

Pots, jars and bottles in all sizes, shapes, colours — his entire range was spread across the Plexiglas coffee table. Stuck to each item was a green label lettered in gold:

HIGHLANDER
The Natural Way to Beauty

Made in Scotland
Min of Agriculture No 19745

A card tag was rubberbanded around each product. The handwriting on the tag declared the contents: cleansing lotions, moisturising creams, hair conditioners and deodorants. The presentation reminded Cecily Gordon of similar packaging encountered at roadside stands and farmers' shops. When asked, Ford Christmas explained that HIGHLANDER was a small, up-and-coming concern that kept costs down by buying up used glass vessels and refilling them with its own fine line of beauty care products.

For almost an hour Cecily listened, opened, smelled and sampled. She bought little. 'A drink, Mr Ford?' she asked, giving her glasses a push up her nose, 'I'm having one.'

'It's John, call me John. Now, then, what—' The whirring of the grandfather clock gearing up to strike delayed him. 'As I was saying, what are you offering?'

'We have a grand selection. Captain Hugh gets all his liquid goods duty-free.' She got up, and took two small glasses from the showcase sideboard. 'Come see what takes your fancy?'

'That old expression coming back?' was Christmas' response. She looked at him, not understanding. '"Take a fancy" — haven't heard it in years, and coming from a modern girl like you—'

'Me? A modern girl?'

Come to think of it, thought the salesman as he got up to join her, she did seem a bit Victorian in a room full of ultra-modern Castellioni furniture.

Cecily opened the cool-lit corner cupboard. Christmas ran an interested eye over the fine array of exotic labels. 'The Glen Ord.' Reaching in, he passed the bottle over to her. As he did so, he asked, his forehead rucking up with interest, 'Hugh? — your husband? — you mentioned he's a ferry captain?'

'Cap'n Hugh· Gordon. Yes. I'll have a gin — bottom shelf, please.' Her fingers touched his as she took the second bottle from him.

'No children?' he asked politely.

'No. You?' She poured the two drinks.

'A daughter, sixteen.'

'A nubile teenager.' She gave him his whiskey neat, and gestured him back to the uncomfortably deep-seated sofa. Again her little finger pushed at the bridge of her glasses — a high styled wire frame with thick oval lenses that magnified and distorted her moody blue eyes. 'Is she pretty?'

'Silly question to ask a father. Talented, too. Plays a mean harp.'

'Beautiful instrument. I have some harp concertos on tone button.' Eager to please, she jumped up. The Gordons' EMOH Sound Repro Unit (SRU) was the last word. Highly unlikely, thought Christmas, that it was bought anywhere in Scotland. With each keystroke the screen displayed a new menu. At last the microtone button (MTB) she was searching for came up, its contents listed on the screen. 'Shall we have the Mozart *Concerto for Flute and Harp* or Debussy's *Danse Sacré et Profane*?'

'The Debussy,' he said, just as the antique clock ticked and struck. An hour had passed.

'Let's just wait for Grandpa to finish,' she said.

Christmas counted inwardly as the clock chimed eight times. Stoutly, he resisted the urge to take a closer look at the inscription on the dial face. With Grandpa's last robust reverberations still resounding in his ear, Cecily jabbed the start button.

For Christmas, neither the whisky, the clock nor the music were enough relieve his qualms. The room's sterility with its cold, energy-saving lighting did not help, either.

Cecily came back to the sofa, and raised her glass to the opening bars. Christmas followed. 'To poetry in lotion,' she punned, dropping her eyes to the table. Then looking directly at the Englishman, she opened her shiny, red lips and tipped up her glass.

He laughed, punched the air with his glass in her direction, and sipped. 'Yes, to poetry in lotion. Well said. I'll pass it on to the management — if you haven't copyrighted it.'

'Feel free.' She swigged. 'Your daughter? She studies? The harp, I mean?'

'Matter of fact, yes.' He eyed her. 'London. She has all the makings of a great soloist.'

'Och, away with you.' The gin was taking hold. 'Must cost a bomb to keep a child studying away like that.'

'It does.' Christmas's angular Adam's apple rode up over his tie. 'Serious dosh.'

'Mind if I get a mite personal for a moment? John? Old Scottish habit.'

He waved his glass. 'Try me—'

Cecily wiped her innocent-looking pageboy cut back behind her ears. She wore small rubies through pierced lobes. 'Eh, how can a man—?'

'...who sells cosmetics door-to-door afford to put a child through a conservatory in London?'

'Aye, that's the one.'

'She's good, very good. And works hard. She has a full scholarship, but she'd never have got there but for the family my wife does for—' He cut himself off. 'Actually, we're divorced—'

'Divorced?' Cecily raised an eyebrow over the rim of her spectacles.

'That's another story.'

The captain's wife projected an understanding pout. 'You know, for an Englishman, you're very sweet. You're saying— Your ex's family—'

'Not her family. She works for them, done for them all her life. Been very handsome, they 'ave, from the beginning. Very musical folk, too. Their youngest boy, he's brilliant, born with a real ear for music. So they understood about talent and training, and the readies it costs to support a young musician.' Christmas stopped. 'I'm talking too much.'

'No, go on,' she said, 'can I get you a refill?'

'It's a very fine drop of nectar, that. Half. Otherwise, I won't be able to fill out your order form.' She gave him a mock look of disapproval, as she took his glass and got up. 'I thought we'd passed that stage.' She poured him a generous half. 'So, go on, John. You were saying about your wife's rich employers.'

'Ex-wife.' He went on. 'Without them our daughter would never have got started, never mind going all the way to London. Scraping together the money to keep a child in lessons and buy her her own harp kept us hard at it for years. Now she has a scholarship, but it won't last forever. What broke up our marriage was the wife's insisting we pay her family back every penny we borrowed from them — with interest. They didn't need it. They didn't miss it. They didn't want it.' She handed him his drink, and he slugged back an appreciative swallow.

'Your ex wasn't wanting to owe anybody anything in this life. Was that it?'

'Blessed with the full measure of Scots pride, she is. I could never understand it. Rich in business was her old guv. He'd say to her, "Pay it back when you can, dear." She was his *housekeeper*. I was always between jobs. He knew we didn't have much. And the lady of the house, she'd go even further, "One day our son and your daughter, they'll play a duet together. Here in Edinburgh, at the Usher Hall. Think how proud we'll all be. Imagine the CD. Everybody in Scotland'll have one."'

'Fine folk, by the sound of it.'

'The best,' agreed Christmas. 'But their boy gave up his music for religion. They are...Jewish— These days, what with everything, one can feel a touch sorry for that lot.'

Cecily's mood soured. 'None of that affects us. Not our business. Religion. Politics. You see this house, the room, the furniture. This is my world. Actually, it's Hugh's — his taste. Only thing that's mine is Grandpa over there. He belonged to my mother's mother. Now he's mine. Hugh hates him in here. Moans all the time, "that clock completely ruins the decor." He paid some interior designer thousands for this lot. And there's Grandpa sticking out like a sore thumb.'

'I like him, too,' said Christmas. 'Only thing I do like in this room is that clock.'

Cecily smiled invitingly. 'You mean that—'

The salesman considered a moment. 'The only thing other than you.'

'Do you really like me?' Her glasses slipped down her nose again. Again, she pushed them up. 'I loathe these, too. Stupid design. Make me look like a bloody school-leaver serving in a high street shop. Hugh, again. Always buying "the little lady-wife" things...things I don't need or want. The man's fifty-two. Can't get it up any more without the bluest, raunchiest pictures anybody ever saw. Make me sick, they do. See this face? Without these glasses' — she took them off — 'it's me. Real. Like the clock.'

'May I have a closer look?'

'Sure,' she said.

Christmas dislodged his long frame from the dent it made in the leather sofa and walked across the room to Grandpa.

Cecily Gordon's naked frown followed him.

Christmas studied the antique, taller than he was, from a respectful distance. The name "John Wright" and the Eskdale village "Langholm" were penned across the clock's faded dial.

'I'm only thirty-nine,' she said. He turned. She was fingering her short hair. 'Locked in this house week after week. If it wasn't for Grandpa's ticking and chiming I'd go bonkers. He's the only other presence in this house. Regular as clockwork.' She laughed a hollow laugh.

Christmas moved back around the table, glancing at his merchandise. 'Is there anything I can leave for you?' he asked, sitting down close to her.

Her hand slipped to her glass of gin. She drained it, then said, 'I thought you'd be the fun sort, John Ford. I just want a bit of company, that's all. Stay and talk to me.'

'With Grandpa watching?'

'He's seen it all before.' She held out her hands.

'Has he now?' He took her hands in his, but looked up at the loud-ticking clock. 'The old stick doesn't let another man forget he's around.'

'He does when you kiss me.'

'So Grandpa's a little more modern than he looks.' He drew her lips close to his, saying, 'And maybe like you, I'm a little more old-fashioned.' He sank his tongue into her mouth.

* * *

Scotland's most renowned harpist, Caroline "Carrie" Dougal (who dropped the name Christmas early in her career) never had the opportunity to perform with Brewster Moray. He gave up the violin for the rabbinate. However, Dougal's most popular recording ever became the Duet for Violin and Harp, written especially in her honour by the Israeli composer Elon Tokatly. Wherever she appeared, she always dedicated her performance of this music to the Moray family. Oddly, she did not once play this piece live in Scotland. E.T.

Chapter XLV

Aggie

[Sunday morning, October 25, 2009]
Everything about Agnes Dougal-Christmas was slightly pinched, small, sharp, birdlike. Once Aggie's hair was all dark; now fingers of grey reached up from the roots. Her little paisley-shaped eyes sparkled.

The housekeeper dropped by on her way home from church to see how Anna was 'keeping'. She surveyed the cramped dining room. After the bombing, the table and chairs were pushed up against the wall to make room for a moth-eaten settee hauled up from the basement. Manny's old CD player was in the corner. He'd liked music at meal times.

Anna began, 'The insurance assessor was around to inspect the bomb damage this morning—' The lounge was a blemish on the whole house, boarded up and closed off, a place to be avoided like a quarantine room. Anna Moray added, 'Odd of those folk to work on a Sunday—'

Aggie clasped her hands on her lap. 'It's these times we live in,' she said. 'Seems lately good sense has taken leave of the whole world.'

'And now,' Anna went on, 'just before you came in, not an hour after the man's gone, the company's claims agent calls up. She makes all the right noises, pleasant and understanding. Then comes this man's voice in the background. She excuses herself a moment, like she's got to go somewhere — urgent — you know. When she's back, she explains to me, all jumpy and uncomfortable sounding, that my policy only covers fire, water and theft. It's the state that compensates the victims of..."terror acts". She rings off without so much as a by-your-leave. And we've been with that company ever since we bought the place. Paid and paid, and not so much as a single claim, till now.' Anna Moray dropped her voice, 'Aggie, I don't know who's who or what's what any more. It's like living in a soap bubble. I'm an old woman, a widow. I don't want to have to think about when the bubble's bursting, but when I hear voices in the background—'

Aggie's eyes grew filmy with the hurt of fellow feeling.

'Aggie, I'm sorry. I have no right to ask you to share our troubles.'

'But Anna, darling, you and dear Manny always shared *our* problems. Maybe I don't understand, can't understand, but I can still share.'

Anna's gratitude welled up in her face. 'I feel so selfish these days. I never ask you how your Carrie is getting on.' Her hand automatically dropped down to pet the pet that was no longer at her feet. She withdrew it. 'I keep doing that.'

'Och, azoy. London suits her; it's so exciting and fun. And she says she's learning so much — fingering, technique — but what do I know about music?' Aggie lowered her eyes.

'Something wrong—?' asked Anna.

'I don't know. It's just that...well...Ford called on me last week. In person. Didn't come in. He looked...odd...nervous, but excited—'

'And—'

'He's up to something, something no good.' Aggie hesitated. Anna raised an eyebrow. 'I know it. Said he's got a "scheme" going. A scheme that will bring in money, money enough to buy our Carrie ten harps.' Aggie's gaze fell on her hands. 'Why I ever married him, the scoundrel. He's got himself mixed up in something dirty, I know it. And I don't want our daughter profitin' from his dirty deeds. It's wrong—'

Anna could think of nothing to say.

Aggie's face began to change. 'You worry about your troubles, I worry about mine. It's when our worries make us forget that we've all got troubles that we've really got something to worry about. Well, you know what I mean.' Anna laughed, then Aggie. 'Now that's better,' said the housekeeper, taking Anna's liver-speckled hand between hers. 'What do you say, I make us a nice spot of tea.'

'And while we drink it,' chirped Anna, 'we listen to some of Manny's music? Good idea?'

'Very good idea,' said Aggie.

'What will it be?'

'Oh, Mendelssohn. The violin concerto.' Aggie gently closed her eyes. 'It's so beautiful, it carries me away.'

* * *

Chapter XLVI

Scruffers

[Sunday morning, October 25, 2009]

There were more of them. Scruffers. Scruffs. Down-and-outs. The poor sod brigade.

How many times in his life had he passed an old duffer by? Had he gawped without being seen to gawp, then quickly moved on?

'C'mon, lady.' He babbled just like they babbled.

Empty shells that shifted from bench to bench. Lowlife always sat at one end or the other, never in the middle, even if there were a hundred empty benches around. Always at the end. In pairs and threesomes, the homeless kept their distance. Intimacy was with the bench, not with each other.

He glanced at his watch. 'Where the hell are you?'

He crossed his legs, and dared to look up at the world before him. Sunday morning couples. Babies in prams. Kids with lollies. Dogs on long leashes. The world hadn't changed. Not for them. At least not much.

All scruffs looked the same. Same build, same size, same age. Cracked, ruddy skin. Stiff, grey hair poking out from underneath caps and balaclavas. Rough stubble on jutting chins and sunken cheeks. Threadbare jackets. Holed grey trousers, and shoes two sizes too big, stuffed full of newspaper.

'You're bloody, bleedin' late, woman.'

Scruffers' faces never seemed to have eyes — only dark shadows and squints. It was nearly impossible to tell which way they were looking, never mind what they were seeing. He'd often heard them humming. Tuneless, gritty noises, coming out of tight-lipped mouths.

Teams of mowers, pruners and tenders kept the gardens looking as glossy as a postcard. Exotic plants inside their Victorian glasshouses were kept fed, watered, manicured and warm. While the scruffs sat out in the cold and damp.

'Maybe something happened to you?'

Now he knew what went on behind the squinting eyes of the faceless: replays of all the bad calls in life that had brought them to the bench. People weren't born on park benches.

'For chrissakes, don't leave me like this,' he moaned, like a man bereaved.

Humanity cast off from humanity. There were more of them these days. He'd become one, waiting. Consigned to the bench. A scruffer's bench.

Screwing his eyes shut as if in prayer, Neville cursed her aloud: 'Bitch!' The slats moved under him. He opened his eyes. She was sitting at the far end of *his* bench. She pretended to be reading the *Sunday Free Scotsman* magazine section. For once, she did not look incongruous in eye cheaters. It was a sunny day.

'You're late,' said Neville out the side of his mouth.

'Don't look, don't talk,' hissed Guriat. 'Just listen.' Doglike, Neville instantly shifted his eyes to his knees.

'I had to be sure you weren't being watched, mate.' After a week of living rough, Neville wasn't giving security much thought. She went on, 'Your brother's safe. Saw them last night. Your mum's shaken, but she'll live.' Neville had seen the headlines on the newsstands. She lowered her paper, and took an invigorating breath as if enjoying the Indian summer weather. 'Listen— You're on your own, man. Your sister, mother — stay away from them. Cops are covering them, day and night.

'I want you to speak for Brew. Keep to names on the list I'm giving you.' Neville nodded. 'Tell people what's happening. Make them understand this thing's not gonna blow over. That it's gone way beyond the Rabbi. Tell them quietly. Face to face. They have to believe you. Make them believe you. '

Neville started humming tunelessly through his nose.

'Then tell people to pass the word on. Selectively. No idle talk to children or neighbours. We haven't got a lot of time. The fuse is set and ticking.'

His humming gave way to a schoolboy's whistling, the sort where the breath passes discordantly over the tongue.

'Further instructions will be issued as necessary. For now, let people prepare themselves in their minds.'

Neville abruptly ceased his noise. 'For what?' It came out as a breath.

'For a long, sleepless night.'

Oh, Jeez, thought Neville.

She might have said more, but a breeze caught her magazine. She wrestled with it, until it was flattened on her lap.

A long night, he sneered inwardly. Have you heard the one about the day the sky fell in? No? It's going to be one helluva black night when it does. Ha, ha. Neville made a grudging sign of money with his fingers.

'Here, in the pages of this paper,' she said, raising it to cover her face again, 'you'll find a short list of people and addresses to see and a thousand pounds in cabers and reels.[85] I'm leaving it on the bench when I get up.' Neville kept his head down. 'I'm going now. Watch your back. We can't have *you* getting caught.'

'No. Wait. I saw him.' He looked up like an obedient hound.

'Dammit, mate, keep your head down,' she hissed from behind her paper. 'Saw who?'

'Montrose.'

She flipped a page. 'Where?'

'The Pearl.' Neville hardly parted his teeth.

'On Thursday, around one. Right?' She put her paper down on the bench.

'How'd *you* know?'

Guriat came to her feet.

Hardly turning his head, Neville's gaze reached up to her: 'Thinking about you was what kept me going this last week,' he whispered desperately.

She left as though he wasn't there.

* * *

---

[85]Slang names of Scottish money. See Appendix 2.

Chapter XLVII

"Our Ms Landis"

[Monday morning, October 26, 2009]
Precisely because of the raids, Eve Landis went to the Jane Urquhart College for Women on Monday morning, as usual, as she had done for the last twenty-seven years. Her first two periods of teaching kept her mind off the horrors of Friday night.

At the ten thirty break she routinely checked her pigeonhole for post and memos. There was one envelope. "E. Landis" was boldly written on it in blue ink. Eve instantly recognised Mrs Samuels' flowing hand. The note inside requested her presence in the headmistress' room at the lunch hour. No reason was given.

* * *

One of Eve Landis's former pupils at the Jane Urquhart College for Women, Kathy Calhoun was to write in her memoir, 'We all called her "our Ms Landis". The police raid on her home (splashed all over the papers at the time), and her subsequent removal from teaching came as a terrible shock. Until then, we girls never knew Ms Landis was a Jew.'

Calhoun grew up to become an internationally renowned film star. What the actress omits to say in her published life's story is that her father Sheriff Richard E. Calhoun signed the police search warrant, and that he was on the school's Board of Governors at the time of Ms Landis's summary dismissal. In her last film, the mature Calhoun poignantly played the tragic role of a prim-talking schoolteacher inspired by Ms Landis. E.T.

Chapter XLVIII

'Afraid...Like You'

[Tuesday evening, October 27, 2009]
The children goggled from the door. At Sophie's feet on the kitchen floor, a spinach of fuzzy leaves and broken purple petals, tangled roots and black earth spilled out of a shattered clay pot. Naomi mouthed, Mummy's African violet. Benny turned his small face to his father. Jake stood abjectly by his chair. His half-eaten supper of tomato paste over rice and a slice of grey turkey meat had been pushed away.

Sophie stepped back from the plant she'd dropped. 'Now see what I've done!' Jake protested, 'I'm sorry.' Naomi and Benny linked hands. 'You children, back to bed, now!' Her smouldering temper sent them scurrying. Sophie was still holding the miniature watering can. It no longer had a purpose. She shook it loose as if were a crawling thing. 'How could you?' she said. 'Have you any idea what they did to that poor woman? In front of the child. Have you? GOOD LORD! Why?'

'They wouldn't let me go. I had to tell them *something*. For chrissakes, I have a business to run...a...'

'Is that all there is? Money and football?'

'...a...family to support. They wouldn't let me *bloody* go.'

Sophie shrieked, 'Friday, the police smash up her whole house. An' now she's lost her job.' She moved closer to him. 'Because of *you*. And "your business to run."'

Jake looked up from the crusting mess of red, white and grey on his plate. 'I could be in jail now. For obstructing justice, or some such. Did you want to see me locked up?'

'It was scare tactics. Nobody was arrested Friday morning.'

'That we know now.'

'Still, you didn't have to offer them *any* information. You're telling me, you caved in. If you hadn't said anything, the police would have never known about that girl.'

'That detective would have found out. I said, I'm sorry, Soph. What do you want from me? I'm sorry...I should never have told you.'

'Stop saying, "I'm sorry."'

'But *why* did Eve Landis call you this morning?' he asked.

'She called me...this morning—' Her rage was spent, in its place came bitter sadness. 'Her voice on the phone, it was so...so small. She sounded as if she'd never be whole again. She said she had to see me. So I went round. They wrecked her place, Jake, all those lovely, precious things she had.'

'But she's all right. The kid's okay. Nobody got hurt. That's the main thing,' he whimpered in his defence.

'That's not the point! You don't understand what you've done, do you?' Jake shook his head. 'She was sacked yesterday, after twenty-seven years. The Board of Governors as much as said she brought shame on the school, because the police raided her, because of you.'

'But...but why did she call *you*?' he asked again.

'Because she wanted me to talk to Brew. She wanted me to tell him that he's destroying too many lives. To ask him to give himself up. Before more people's lives are ruined. Before more people are dead. She said to me, "You have children—"'

'What did you say?'

'I said, how can I talk to him? I don't know where Brew is.'

(But I do. I didn't give him away to the police. I know where he's hiding, and I will tell you.)

'But she wouldn't have asked you in the first place,' reasoned Jake, 'unless she thought *you* knew where he is.'

'I *am* his sister.' *(No, I don't want to hear it. I don't want to know where Brew is, I can't talk to him, I have the children to think of.)* Sophie said to Jake, 'Say something.'

'I was afraid.'

Sophie kneeled down, and slowly began to pull the soil together, into a heap under the broken plant. 'I ought to tell her...what you've done...to her. But I can't.'

Jake walked out.

Sophie stopped her mound making, and stood up. Snatching the miniature watering can, she threw it at her husband's plate. 'I can't— Because I'm afraid...like you—'

* * *

Chapter XLIX

Alec Ace

[Monday, November 16, 2009]

In the weeks after his park-bench meeting with Guriat, Neville lived in constant, low-grade fear. At every turn he looked over his shoulder. Any sudden noise or movement spooked him.

On a diet of white bread sandwiches and coffee from styrofoam cups, he grew gaunt, and seemingly taller. He carried a small case of newly bought clothes, and moved from one bed and breakfast accommodation to the next, never staying more than two or three days. He used false names.

Nights gave him no comfort, and little rest. Coming into stuffy, unfamiliar rooms, he fell exhausted, fully clothed on the bed. Sleep was never far from consciousness, or for long. She woke him in the night, then kept him lying awake for hours in the dark. Guriat. Her name consumed him. He convinced himself that if his inner voice called to her loud enough and long enough, she would hear him in her dreams. And she would answer him in his dreams. She didn't.

Neville went into the community to be his brother's voice. Some listened politely, others argued. Most conceded there was a threat, but that it was not very real, and certainly not near at hand.

Neville soon recognised that he was not engaged in a debate to be won or lost. All he could do was issue the storm warnings.

–No, no, Rabbi— Doctor— Professor— (they were all the same)

–This thing. It won't go away.

–That's not what the Chief Rabbi said. He's not telling *us* to leave Scotland. He's saying, *Scotland* is leaving us.

–The practicalities? *Teeth will be provided.* (Awkward silence.) So it's an old joke. *Teeth will be provided.*

–The dangers? Greater, if we stay.

At the end of every interview, Neville asked, 'Can you think of anybody else I could talk to?'

Rabbi Vivienne Falk mentioned 'an odd little man'. He came to her New Reform Synagogue in Glasgow once a year on the Day of Atonement. 'He comes alone,' she said, 'for three-four years now. At the end of the day I have no idea where he breaks his fast. He ducks out before I can talk to him. And no one knows who he is. But about a week later,' she added almost as an afterthought, 'during the Eight Days of Tabernacles, a generous cheque posted from the Isle of Gigha turns up on my desk. I assume it's him. I ought to call and thank him, I know, but we're so pushed here — I just never bother to look up his phone number. His name? The cheque says simply Mr A Ace.'

Twenty minutes on the ferry under a warm morning sun...how did Stevenson put it? "To travel is better than to arrive." A. Ace's address on Gigha was in the telephone book.

Neville found the cottage easily, thanks to the map of the island posted at the ferry landing. 'Lovely garden,' he remarked to the man whose large head hung between thick shoulders. He was deeply absorbed in weeding. The gardener scrambled to his feet, looked up, and answered, 'Hard work. Keeps me nose to the ground.' He mushed his Ss with a slight spittiness. His eyebrows were slanted at a worried angle, even though he smiled. An image of a no-neck snowman formed in Neville's mind, as he watched him brush the grit off his hands. 'Me, personally, I prefer to keep ma toes to the ground. Oh, never mind. Wasn't funny anyway. I'm Neville Moray. Mr. Ace—?' He nodded, 'Alec.' Neville hesitated. 'Eh, I couldn't call before coming. Rabbi Falk...in Glasgow...she pointed me in your direction. I don't quite know how to begin—' The little man offered an open hand: 'Moray's the name? Say no more.' He invited Neville in for a cup of tea, leaving his tools where they lay.

Ace worked comfortably in his untidy kitchen. He put saucers under the mugs, commenting, 'Special for company.' Without being asked, Ace launched into his story. Born and bred in Manchester, both parents passed on, and without brothers and sisters, he had no close family. He'd worked his whole life on the P & O Lines, a Purser's Assistant. Never more than an assistant. He'd retired young with a reasonable pension. 'I haven't got a lot here, but it's plenty for me.'

To fill in the empty hours on the job, Ace took up short-wave radio networking. As he sailed around the world, he kept in touch with other transceiver jockeys like himself. 'Radio people almost never meet; that's the way we like it. The beauty of the thing is being able to turn the radio off whenever you get fed up with the company.' Ace's hobby explained why the kitchen table was littered with bits of electronics, ends of molten solder, and pockmarked with burn holes.

'So why Gigha?' Neville asked, interestedly.

He came to Gigha in Twenty o-six to be near the sea. 'It's like being on a boat, only better — it doesn't move. But, seriously, it's pretty here, and peaceful. I like it. And folks aren't nosy.'

Again, Neville changed tack. Asked Ace about storms and wrecks. His face fell as he slurred, 'Twenty plus years, and I still see-it. The funny thing of it was, I was sailing home from a busman's holiday. Just out of Zeebrugge — it happened, in minutes — the boat, she began to list, turning turtle so fast, that an old hand, the likes of yours truly, grabs the rail, I mean, with both hands. Before I knew it, she was on her side, water sloshing in like Niagara Falls. What was a passageway one minute, the next was the deepest shaft I ever saw. I dangled there for dear life. All around me, folks screaming, yelling. I looked down. People were dropping in, sucked down like into one of those sci-fi wormholes. It's a thing I'll never get out of my head.'

'What was the name of the ship?' asked Neville.

'*Herald of Free Enterprise*. March Sixth, Nineteen eighty-seven. I swore, if I got out alive, I'd never go on another ferry.'

'But you worked for P & O after that?' said Neville.

'Work, yes. Cruise liners, yes. Car ferries, definitely not. In any case the *Herald* was a Townsend Thorenson vessel.'

'Don't you have to take a ferry to get off the island here?'

'Once a year. To go to Glasgow for Yom Kippur. I figure,' said Ace, lightening up, 'that the day before Yom Kippur HE's too busy to sink boats and, the day after, too fagged out.'

Neville laughed.

'No ring?' asked Ace straight out. 'Not married?'

'No,' said Neville, without the usual shame he felt. 'You, Alec— Ever been married—?'

'No, never. What woman would have wanted me?' he asked. 'In my job? No prospects, never at home, what did I have to offer a woman? And Jewish women. You know what it's like. They'd sooner step in hot dog turd, than look at me.' His whole face lifted. 'Funny, though, I could never see m'self with a *shiksa*.'[86] Neville's eyes hugged Alec like a long-lost brother. They were the same, only differently packaged.

Over a bachelors' late lunch of packaged onion soup, bread and cheese, the Rabbi's brother began to explain his mission. Alec listened without question. His response: 'Sure, you hear things, even here. But, look, I've got my cottage, my radio, and my life just the way I like it. Anyway, I'm a once-a-year Jew, or is it, I'm a Jew once a year? I'll think about it.'

'Then, maybe we'll see each other again. Oh, I almost forgot.' Neville pulled out a letter. 'This is for you, from my brother. It's been...very nice, Alec.'

'For me, too.'

'Hell, no, it's been far more than nice,' Neville declared, 'being here—'

'Don't try to say it, man. Let's just wrap things up as they are.' Still seated, Neville pulled a face. Alec stood. 'We've got another hour before the ferry goes back.' Ace reminisced, 'In better times there were two ferries a day in and out. Nowadays only two a week — the mail run. I'll see you down to the landing. I need to catch the post office on the way, before it closes.'

While Ace was buying stamps from the old woman behind the barred window, Neville detached himself, looked around. The nearest wall was taken up with a large notice board. Neville vaguely absorbed himself in the scribbled scraps of paper and file cards: mostly offers and a few requests. Ace was chatting. A blind corner of the small post office drew him in. It was a Rogues' Gallery of A4-size police posters. A heavy black border framed each sheet. The head-and-shoulders shots in three views were in colour. One of them was *him*. His picture, his name, his vital statistics, and in black letters, it said **WANTED**. Next to him: his brother, **WANTED**, his sister-in-law, **WANTED**.

His own face was his enemy. There was no escaping, not even on the tiniest island. All of Scotland was hunting him, them. It took all his strength to conquer the stricken feeling that gripped him, to prise his eyes away, and slowly walk out. The tinkle of the doorbell sounded like an alarm. Not to run, he told himself. He kept his head down, crossed the road and pressed his attention into a sporting shop window. He couldn't think. His ears buzzed.

'I turn around and you're gone,' said Ace, tapping Neville on the shoulder. Neville shrank, backing off. 'I think it's better we shouldn't be seen together. I can find my own way back to the ferry.'

'But why?' asked Alec, mystified and disappointed. 'You're shivering.'

'Am I? Look, if anybody asks, just tell them you were giving directions to a lost stranger.'

'I don't understand. What's happening?' The worried slope of Ace's eyebrows underlined his concern.

Again, Neville was evasive. 'Do people around here know you're Jewish?'

'No. I keep it under my hat, so to speak. For the *goyim* here, I'm English.'

'Best keep it that way.'

Neville hurried away. The sky had gone gloomy.

* * *

---

[86]A non-Jewish woman.

Chapter L

'Your Ticket's Your Receipt'

[Tuesday, November 17, 2009]

Guriat contemplated the sea-going ferries, dramatically photographed from every possible angle. More than anything else though, the faded colours and the unstuck corners curling off the wall struck her eye.

'Old poster pictures, all that's left of our once proud fleet,' said the agent, an older man with a fresh, eager face. He was alone. 'Help you, miss?'

'The Belfast ferry, mate,' she said.

''stralia—' The man mimicked the accent.

'Right in one,' she nodded.

He said dreamily, 'Been there. Once. The Antipodes—'

'Like it out there, did you?' she asked.

'Did I like it? That weather, those beaches, the healthy suntans. Should've stayed.'

'Why didn't you?'

'Inertia? Habit? Family? Daft, isn't it?' He looked beyond her. His thin fingers raked a thatch of light brown hair diagonally across his head. His eyes came back, showing a desire to talk. Guriat slightly lifted her sunglasses, an invitation for him to go on. 'Aye, maybe I should've stopped away. Instead, I end up here, staring at ferryboats on a wall. For years now Scotland's been selling off her fleet, ever since the North Sea oil started drying up. But after Independence the sell-off really took off. Sell off, took off— Funny, eh—? Services are right down, in every port, across the board.' Guriat cocked her head for him to explain. 'Scotland's shrinking. Folk are leaving the outlying regions, the islands. Demand for food, medicines and basic maintenance materials is right down. Ferry schedules are cut back. Fewer tourists come. As the island economies dry up, more folk leave. It's a vicious spiral. People come south to the big population centres where, surprise, surprise, there's no work. Where's it all going to end, I ask you?'

'You asking me, mate?' said Guriat sounding sympathetic.

The man sank into a darker mood. 'You know what I think? I think that our bright lights in Parliament House are pretty dim. The nationalists actually believed that expat Scots would come back here, flying in like homing pigeons the day after Independence. It didn't happen. Now, if the government rams through that property forfeiture bill—'

Guriat prompted him, 'Sounds like you ought to be in politics.'

'Thanks, but no thanks. If you want my opinion, that law'll turn this country into a prison. Anybody wanting out 'll have to hijack a plane, or something.'

Guriat stiffened.

'I said something wrong?' he asked.

'Nothing I wouldn't have said,' she answered, easily regaining her smile.

'Right. Cairnryan to Belfast. At least that ferry's still running. Date?'

'Monday, November thirtieth.'

'Let's see,' he said, consulting a schedule, 'yes, we have a sailing, yes, that morning. Six hundred hours.' He looked to her for confirmation, then asked, 'Single or return?'

'One way.'

'I'll need to see some ID, please.' She handed him an Australian passport; he tapped G-loria G-raham and the passport number into the computer. 'Car?'

'It'll be a hire car,' she replied.

'Oh, right then.' He pressed a key, the printer clattered. 'Just fill in the car licence number here.' He handed her the ticket. 'That'll be thirty-seven pounds Scots, please.'

She paid in cash. 'Your ticket's your receipt,' he said.

'Thanks, mate. Out of curiosity, do people really need to pre-book ferry crossings?'

'These days? Huh. Anybody who shows up forty-five minutes before departure is away.' He rang up the sale. As Guriat got up to leave, he asked in a hushed voice, 'Hope you're not offended by anything I might've said, you know, you being kind of dark complexioned, an' all. You're not...Jewish, are you?'

'Me?' Guriat laughed.

He stretched his neck. 'You know what I can't figure out?'

'No, what?'

'How the bloody Zionists did it?'

'Did what?'

'I mean, got their people to go back home. Why, even our wee lot here want to bugger off back to their Holy Land.'

'Tell me, when you were in Australia...' Guriat paused for effect, 'did people suggest you go back where you came from?'

'No.' His face turned white.

'There's your answer then. Think about it.' She turned smartly before he could recover. On the way out, she wondered what she would have said if his answer had been yes.

* * *

Chapter LI

'A Bold Move'

[Tuesday night, November 17, 2009]
Slowly sliding her finger under the flap, Guriat Gaoni opened the envelope and took out its contents. For a brief moment her mind went off the purpose of her visit—

It was an oversight, not a blunder. She and her superiors in Tel Aviv never once considered that the Scottish Chief Rabbi might object to their rescue plan on religious grounds. And neither could she nor her Mossad bosses have predicted Brew Moray's dream-inspired, ill-timed bombshell. It was unprecedented. In a five-minute radio broadcast, the Chief Rabbi effectively scotched months of painstaking planning and preparation—

The back room of the shop was cold and dark. Guriat stuck a penlight in her mouth like a cigarette. Her photo-document training had ingrained in her the need for keeping both hands free.

Brew Moray sat diagonally across from her. Guriat gave him a sidelong glance, no more. The uneven glow from her small torch cut his face in two, half lit, half hidden.

She held the Rabbi's ruling up to her naked eyes, thumbing its thickness — five full pages. His Hebrew script was square and even. For clarity's sake he'd taken the trouble to vowel point certain letters with dots and dashes. The document intimidated her—

Was it almost a year ago since she walked in to what she anticipated to be a routine meeting? The young field officer entered a room with detailed maps of Edinburgh and Glasgow pinned to the walls. Folders marked "Highly Confidential" were spread over the table. The presence of the Chief of the Mossad was totally unexpected. This was not going to be an ordinary session.

Wasting no time, her immediate superior, Rafael "Pete" Petrovski, briefed her. He completed his statement with 'The threat is like a noose around the neck of the entire Scottish Jewish community. Only they don't know it yet.' Amos Lev-Ari, commander of the "Morning Star" division charged with saving Jewish communities in danger, was solemn. 'The operation calls for a single field agent to go in and, working undercover, coordinate the removal of the entire community, before the Montrose government can turn Jews into pawns in a secret arms deal—'

With the penlight in her mouth, the saliva collected and she couldn't swallow it. She would have skipped the ruling's long introductory deliberations and flipped straight to the end. But she knew enough about rabbinical responsa to know that the tight reasoning throughout weighed as heavily as the conclusion. She began to read from the beginning—

Lev-Ari went on: 'As yet, their lives are not in any overt danger. But in this day and age, Israel is in a position not to wait for Jewish lives to be lost before we act. I remind you, Gaoni, this department is proud of its operations in Ethiopia, Russia, Sarajevo. We've spirited tens of thousands of Jews out of life-threatening situations.'

Petrovski said with confidence, 'We have the beginnings of a plan. You were selected from our ranks as the field officer best suited to the task. At this stage, if you're in, your input becomes vital. What do you say, Guri?' he asked, quickly adding, 'You'll work alone; it could be dangerous, very dangerous.' They were asking her to be a "jumper", somebody sent in to do the job, then get out quick—

Reading in the dark by a dancing ray of light taxed her concentration. From time to time she looked away. Each time, she found Brew's one light-pointed eye gazing at her—

'It's yes, Pete.' Petrovski's asking her was a formality. Her 'yes' was blind, like signing a release form before an emergency operation. The Mossad Chief and Lev-Ari, showing no sign of approval, gave Petrovski the nod to continue: 'You will travel to Scotland on an Australian passport in the name of Gloria Graham. There, you'll liaise directly with the head of Scottish Jewry, Chief Rabbi Brewster Moray. From all accounts, he's a good man, relatively young, highly active and intelligent. More importantly, reports indicate that he's genuinely respected by a wide spectrum of a typically splintered Diaspora community.'

Guriat asked about the man's 'personal status'.

'Married, no children,' answered Lev-Ari. He tapped a file. 'It's all here.' Alternating, Petrovski and Lev-Ari sketched out the personalities and the mission to her. 'The sticking point with this whole operation is a means of getting the people out. Scotland is no third world country. Air space is solidly covered by former British air defences and radar. You don't just drop Hercules C-130s in there without anyone knowing it. We think we've got the answer—'

The stairs creaked. For Guriat, it was a welcome distraction. The Rabbi's closely argued decision on the laws of theft were heavy going. Deborah came down looking pale and tired.

'Debs, you all right?' asked Brew.

'Couldn't sleep, that's all.' Her voice whined.

'She's reading it,' said Brew in a hushed voice.

'Good, isn't it?' Deborah said to Guriat.

The Israeli agent happily gave her mouth a rest from the penlight. 'You've read it?'

'No. But my husband told me exactly what's in it.'

Guriat believed her non-committal 'I see' hit the exact note she was aiming at. Respectful, but not approving. She felt bitchy, because she couldn't help seeing the woman as a liability. She felt sorry for Brew Moray—

When Lev-Ari came out with the palatable phrase 'commandeer a ship', Guriat's barely controlled interpretation was 'You mean...hijack? We've never done anything like that before.'

Pete got in excitedly, 'Your reaction, Guri — that's just it. They won't be expecting it. Nobody will. That's the beauty of it.'

Lev-Ari: 'It's also going to be your toughest challenge. You're going to have to improvise right down the line on this one. We'll give you all the backdrop support we can...before, during and after. But how you do it, Gaoni — the logistics — is your problem—'

Brew and Deborah lapsed into silence to let Guriat continue reading. She was beginning to appreciate the Rabbi's overall argument. The reasoning and logic were mathematically precise. The legalities brought to bear on the question left no loose ends. And what impressed her most was, that without sources, he was able to quote rabbinical authorities down through the ages and give the references, all from memory. Before she was finished, Guriat couldn't help herself saying, 'Rabbi, this is something, mate.'

'Glad you like it so far,' he said modestly, careful not to give away the concluding decision.

Deborah filled the kettle with water and placed it on the single hot plate. 'It's cold down here on a winter night,' she said. While they waited for the water to boil, Deborah asked Guriat, 'Tell me something, if you don't mind, please. Why you? Why a woman?'

'The simple answer is, it was my superiors' decision.'

'Right,' said Deborah with finality.

At that moment Guriat felt sorry for her. She was in a precarious position. She'd been married for ten years, to a rabbi, and no children. He could divorce her. Why didn't he?

As part of her preparation, Guriat had read the Morays' file, more than once. The Mossad's efficiency sometimes bordered on the excessive. It contained a copy of their complete medical records: years of trying to have a baby. Guriat couldn't help asking herself if he still bothered to sleep with her.

The Israeli deflected her cattiness, 'Why me? A woman's less suspicious. A man takes a big risk carrying a weapon; a woman's less liable to be checked. But there's something else, it goes a lot deeper. I call it, my theory. It's that most Israelis think they know everything. But what they don't know, and will never figure out, is the mentality of the small-community Jew. They can't understand that Jews living at margins have to learn to speak two languages — one for ourselves and one for the others.' Guriat let her ideas sink in as she went back to the last page—

Lev-Ari said grimly, 'Nothing must be left to chance, nothing. We have no safety net on this one.'

'Does this operation have a name yet?' she asked.

'Yes,' said Pete, '"Operation Snatch", from the Book of Psalms, "to snatch the afflicted"'[87]

Guriat read the last paragraph, twice, then took the penlight out of her mouth, and turned it off. The Rabbi's decision was binding. He had decreed. Guriat leaned back. It felt good after being hunched up so long. She allowed herself to drink from the cup Deborah had set before her. It was sugar-sweetened hot water. They'd run out of tea and coffee. Guriat's only words were 'Thank you'.

Brew licked the sweetness off his lips. 'I wonder how many of us will answer the call to leave. You know, when the HOLY ONE took HIS people out of slavery, HE was *stealing* Egyptian property. Oh, yes, HE stole Egypt's slaves right from under Pharaoh's nose. Then HE goes and makes a very strange promise to Moses, "...your sons and daughters will *save* Egypt."'[88]

'I don't quite get it, Rabbi. How does ripping off somebody save him?' asked Guriat.

'What it means is, when I shook Montrose's hand, I saw into his eyes. And what I saw was that bonny Scotland would be better off without *us*. Shame *they* don't see it that way.'

'Who's *they*?' she asked. 'The Scots or the Jews?'

'Both,' answered Brew.

Guriat replaced the responsa in its envelope. 'May I keep this?'

'You brought the paper. It's yours—'

The Mossad Chief reserved his one comment until the very last. He said, 'It is a bold move—'

* * *

Brew Moray's ruling is considered a classic work of rabbinical responsa.[89] *His courageous decision marks a turning point in Jewish legal thinking: A clear departure away from the abstract Messianic hopes of centuries, and a return to the absolute practicality of "...we will do and we will hearken" (Ex. 24:7). E.T.*

---

[87]Ps. 10.9.

[88]Ex. 3.21-22 and 12.36. Rabbi Moray's ironic use of the word "stealing" here is highly original and idiosyncratic. He contends that the Egyptian leadership, by enslaving the Israelites and robbing them of their labour and, thus, their lives, were the original thieves. God's encouraging the Egyptians to pay their freed slaves compensation was the "saving" rather than "spoiling of Egypt", as the fallacious English translation and resultant proverb would have it. See J.H. Hertz's *The Pentateuch and Haftorahs* (Soncino) pp. 217-18 for a detailed explanation of the Hebrew grammar and the moral and psychological justifications of compensation.

[89]See Appendix 1 for an abridged version of Rabbi Moray's responsa on theft in order to save life.

Chapter LII

Mr Sinclair

[Sunday morning, November 29, 2009]

'Don't turn around. Just walk. Straight ahead.'

The old man jumped. 'There you are.' Without looking back he did as he was told. As he left the sheltered entrance of the Portobello swimming pool for the promenade, he unfurled his black umbrella. It was drizzling.

'Nice day for a stroll, wouldn't you say, Mr Sinclair?' said the voice, catching up.

'Always with the jokes, young Neville, just like your dear old father. I miss him. Speaking of jokes' — the old man drew a finger across his upper lip — 'I hardly recognise you.'

'This growth? Covers about as much of me as a fig leaf. What I need is to cut a foot off my legs. That'd stump the bastards.'

'A foot off his legs, he says.' Sinclair forced a laugh.

'Here, if you'll give me the umbrella, it'll do us both some good.' The old man passed it over. Neville held it high in front of them against the wind and mist. Sinclair walked slowly, and Neville governed his stride accordingly. 'How's the missus keeping?' asked Neville.

'Good as can be expected, under the circumstances. We keep getting letters from the children; they're wanting us to fold our tents and move on. They're both threatening to come home and pack us up. Can you credit it?'

'Tell them to stay away,' said Neville. So many of his contemporaries had gone. Brew and Sophie had also left, though circumstances brought them back. He never even tried to break away. For him Edinburgh had been like a dog's collar — restrictive, but comfortable.

Neville passed the umbrella from one hand to the other, and switched sides with Sinclair. The drab winter weather had set in for the day. The promenade between Portobello and Joppa was deserted except for a few wind-blown figures walking their dogs. Nobody was in the sea.

'So, how'd things go yesterday morning?'

'"Who knows. Who knows the spirit of man, if it goes up to the high places—"' sighed Sinclair.

'"...and the spirit of the animal, if it goes down to earth..."'[90] said Neville, completing the quotation.

'So, young man, you remember.'

Neville remembered all right. Mr Sinclair had taught him his bar mitzvah. Afterwards, the synagogue warden asked Neville if he wanted to carry on 'to learn'. Neville, feeling his young adulthood, was flattered. Together they began learning the Book of Ecclesiastes. One Sunday, for some reason that he'd long forgotten, Neville had to bring his little brother

---

[90]Eccles. 3.21.

along. Brew, at ten, was already brilliant. Sinclair called him a 'talmid chochem'[91] and he continued to come. With Brew there, Neville was reduced to silence or making silly boyish remarks. Soon he stopped coming.

'Who knows,' repeated Sinclair. 'Only folk with a letter from Rabbi Moray were let in. Every letter[92] had a different Biblical quotation in it...with chapter and verse, mind you. That brother of yours, he always was a genius.'

'I don't tell everybody this, Mr Sinclair, but before I was born, I generously donated my brain cells to his egg.'

'Always the jokes. Very good. You're a generous lad, always were, right from the start. Sharing your lessons with your younger brother; together we made him Chief Rabbi, eh—'

The mist rolled down in cloudy waves. Neville motioned Sinclair to a bench. 'Don't mind if I do,' said the old man. They sat opposite the children's paddling pool at the edge of the Joppa salt works.

'I said it just like *she* told me,' reported the beadle, annoyingly chewing his gums. The times and rendezvous points came to congregational leaders from the Israeli agent as a follow-up to Neville's meetings. 'I slipped it into the announcements at the end of the service...as neat as a new pin, if I do say so myself.' The usual congregational announcements included a generous invitation for everyone — without exception — to meet for an 'old-fashioned beer and skittles evening'. The hour and the name and location of a country pub were repeated twice.

'Such a hush I never heard—' The old man chewed his teeth. 'Folk were stunned blind, as if they'd seen a miracle. Then somebody stands , like the reed in that pond down there, and yammers, '"What?! Tomorrow night?!"'

'Then what?' asked Neville as two young men appeared out of the mist headed to the pool. One cradled the sleek red hull of a large model sailing boat in his arms. The other one carried the radio control unit.

'Like I said, who knows.' Sinclair went on like a blow-by-blow commentator describing a scene of pandemonium. 'If you ask me, who's coming and who's not, I couldn't tell you. Who knows?'

The two enthusiasts first tested the boat's electronic helm on land. Satisfied that the rudder was working, they knelt down at the water's edge to launch their sleek craft. The wind swiftly drove the vessel on a broad reach to the middle of the pool. She tacked several times. For a while Mr Sinclair and Neville sat watching the miniature yacht go through her paces. The mist and drizzle were turning to needles of rain.

The old man broke the spell. 'After Shabbes,' he announced, 'I rang Frankelstein in Glasgow.'

'What? That *meshugger* Rebbe? The Hassid, [93] Felix Frankelstein? Crikey, man, what d'you say to him? His phone's probably tapped.'

---

[91]Literally, "a disciple of the wise". Here, it is a term of praise for a scholar, a learned Jew, particularly a young one.

[92]None of these warning letters is extant today. The implication, however farfetched it may seem, is that Rabbi Moray wrote personal letters to the head of every Jewish family in Scotland during his safe house stay. The Rabbi's letter notified Jews all over Scotland to go to synagogue on the Saturday morning of November 28. (The Sabbath was appropriately called, after the first word of the Hebrew Scriptural reading, *VaYetze* — "And he left...") The letters were apparently distributed by hand, at least some by Neville and presumably some by Sophia. To the credit of the Scottish Jewish community, none fell into the wrong hands. The assumed reason not one of them survived is that they were collected like entrance tickets at the synagogues and destroyed.

[93]Hassidism, a movement which established itself throughout Eastern Europe in the 18th century, stressed Jewish spiritualism and mysticism as opposed to legal "hair-splitting" and scholarship "for

'Oy! And Rabbi Falk?' asked Sinclair.

Neville rolled his eyes. 'Hers, too.'

'Now I understand,' said Sinclair. 'They both blethered on what wonderful talks they gave in synagogue. Frankelstein goes on about 'when Jacob left Beersheba, why the whole city was ruined without him.'[94] Vivienne Falk wasn't any better, just prettier sounding. She's on about Jacob's ladder.[95] Decided it's all alle—, alle—'

'Allegory,' prodded Neville.

'That's it, allegory. Instead of angels, it's us lot who's climbing up and down, to and from Zion. After that, I gave up with the phone.'

Just then a gust of wind knocked the sailing boat down. After an instant, it righted itself. The sails fluttered, then filled with air again. The red hull headed straight for the far bank. Her helm would not respond. 'Water must have got in the mechanism,' Neville supposed. The lad not holding the control box made a mad dash around the pool. Neville, quick to his feet, also chased the wind. The crippled boat dashed itself against the far bank.

Shaking his head, Neville slowly came back to Mr Sinclair. 'The boat's wrecked,' he said, adding, 'I really don't know why I did that.'

Sinclair was elsewhere. 'So, young Neville, do you remember how our chapter of Ecclesiastes ended?'

'You mean the last verse?'

The old caretaker's face crumpled a little. 'Aye, the very last verse, Chapter Three. You haven't forgotten—?'

'I'm not sure if I can remember,' answered Neville, thinking hard.

'Try—' He gave Neville a pat on the shoulder, and said again, 'Try. Remember what I used to teach you when you were little? We never know what we're made of till we try. Now—'

'The Preacher says— "I saw that there is nothing better than that a man should enjoy his work, that's his lot; because, who will bring him to see what will be after him?"'[96]

The old man's eyes shone large, 'You see, you do remember.'

* * *

its own sake". Hassidic rabbis, spoken of as "Rebbe", are revered for their learning and spiritual attainments. Within his community, the Rebbe's word is the law of kings. To outsiders, Hassidic Rebbes are often considered *meshugger*, in other words, "crazy" or "mad" in their zealous devotion to the ultra-Orthodox way of life.

[94]"Jacob left Beersheba..." (Gen. 28.10). The Jewish commentators remark that the reason this verse appears is to indicate that, "The departure of a righteous man from a city leaves its mark. When a righteous man is in the city, he is its lustre, its renown, its glory. Once he leaves, gone is its lustre, its renown, its glory" (Midrash Bereshit [Genesis] Rabbah 68.6).

[95]Gen. 28.10-15.

[96]Eccles. 3.22.

Chapter LIII

'To Sniff the Wind'

[Monday pre-dawn, November 30, 2009]
Capt Hugh Gordon was out on the bridge wing 'to sniff the wind'. A full moon and the icy pre-dawn air forecast the clear weather to hold. Proudly planting his hands on the *Duchess's* teak railing, the ferry captain thought, uneventful crossing.

Gordon's black, gimlet eyes and jet brows contrasted sharply with the whiteness of his moustache and pointed goatee. His dark blue, brass-buttoned uniform accentuated his bulging stomach and short legs.

Though vaguely conscious of the frequent double-thump of axles rumbling over the loading ramp, he did not question the heavy traffic coming aboard. His thoughts moved on quickly. The lights along the Cairnryan quayside conjured up a snapshot that he'd taken there of Cecily before they were married. A warm twinge of hardness permeated his groin. He saw her, young and lovely, alone at home, waiting for him.

With an hour to go before departure, the ship's master was needed in the wheelhouse. As he came in, the burly, overweight helmsman was saying, 'A queer lot of the buggers out early—' Gordon cut him off with a stern look, but realising the helmsman was right, he lied, 'Same thought crossed my mind.'

The watch officer, lips pressed to the intercom, was talking to the car deck. Without lifting his thin face, he rolled his eyes and said, almost painfully, 'It's chock-a-block this morning, foot passengers, too.'

Gordon couldn't figure it. In winter, on a weekday early morning crossing, roll-on, roll-off ferries barely reached thirty percent of full capacity. Over the last two years Caledonian Ferries had lost thousands in revenue. Yet, this morning the punters were out.

The hand-held radio crackled to life. Gordon took it, 'Bridge, Captain speaking.' It was the engine room mate Warboys reporting, 'Chief says we're all set to sail, sir.' Gordon asked about fuel. The *Duchess* had been oiled up, ninety tons, the day before, answered Warboys.

When Gordon hung up, the watch officer asked, 'Check fresh water? Maybe alert catering?'

'My thoughts, exactly. Pass the word to bring on more supplies. There's still time.' Gordon waved a hand. 'And get some sleep.' Relieved, the officer acknowledged, 'I can use it.'

The mate's departure left the Captain alone with his surly helmsman. Gordon raised a pair of binoculars, but did not bring them to his eyes. The picture of Cecily was back. A ship-to-shore teasy-talky chat with her tempted him, but not with the helmsman there and at that early hour — five forty-four by the ship's clock.

Jake Banks could not focus. He stood looking at his children fast asleep in Sophie's arms, but all he could think of was the litter around him. The forward lounge on C Deck was already a tip of cigarette stubs and ashes, beer cans, brown bottles, white-scummed glasses and plates of half-eaten food topped with crumpled serviettes. And the ferry had not even cast off. What would things be like after a few days at sea, he asked himself.

Stale smoke, over-heating and crowding suffocated him, while cold condensation oozing from the walls' oily whiteness made him shiver. The recliners were hard, plasticky and all occupied.

Jake was hungry and could not eat, he was tired and could not sleep. People pressed and jostled him from all sides. He could not get away from them, their questions, and their rumours. And he was sure he would be seasick.

Sophie, too, was exhausted and dozing. He brought his lips to her hand, then to her cheek. 'I'm going to check,' he said. Slowly rolling her head, she woke. 'I'm going to check,' he said again. 'Maybe they've tightened things up below, and I can get the car on. We paid for it, didn't we? Practically everything we have is still in the boot.'

'Don't stay away long, Jake, not too long.'

'I won't.' Jake looked at the children again. Benny's fisted little thumb was stuck in his mouth. Naomi cuddled her favourite button-faced Fred Bear. Jake's jaw trembled. He kissed Sophie's hand again. 'You're knocked out. Try to sleep a bit more.' He bent over his 'wee striker', then his 'little lassie', and kissed them on the hair of their sleeping heads.

'Jake—' Sophie wrenched open her bleary eyes; their redness projected a glazed, deadened look that expressed what she dared not.

Jake shrank back. People all around him. Jews. Cackling like fowl. Quickly, he took Sophie's head between his hands, and pulling her face to his, kissed her again. 'Stay right here,' he said, 'I love you, Soph.'

She said, 'You'd better go then. There's not much time.'

After a couple of pints to dull his senses, Neville went on a short inspection tour around C Deck. The sign on the door warning "Drivers' Club Room — Private" drew him in. Nude calendars and faded colour posters of Caledonian Company ferries, photographed from every possible angle, covered the walls. The bar was tucked away in the far corner. Tables and chairs, mostly empty, were scattered around on the once plush wall-to-wall carpeting. Neville, bending from the neck not to attract attention, quietly closed the door.

'Every week fuckin' less of us. What's the fucked-up economy coming to?' snarled one old-timer, disgustedly throwing down the paper he was reading. 'Count yer lucky stars that we got Ulster,' chimed in another through toothless gums. A younger man, dragging on a cigarette, complained, 'I wasn't born when "the troubles" begun. What was it? Forty years ago? Fifty?' Said the gums, 'What's it matter. You young folk don't even know what an Orangeman is any more.' Another, sitting alone, his ears full of grey hairs, cut in, 'Listen to the smart arse professor.' Toothless shot back: 'At least I dinnae fart through ma teeth like some.' The young driver, his cigarette wagging in his mouth, piped up, 'Eh, all right. If it weren't for the "Scottish option", where'd *we* be? Out drivin' wheelbarras 'stead of the artics — that's where.' Paper reader: 'But if ya ain't noticed, Johnny, truckin's dyin', the roads are for shit, an' ferries...call this service?' Smoker: 'The way Ah see it, Ulster's got a peace, autonomy, 'cause of Scotland, an' we got a run a week 'tween Cairnryan and Belfast. That's a damn sight better than nothin'. Only smart thing this government's done, soft-soapin' Northern Ireland into b'comin' Scotland's first pr'tectorate.' Hairy ears: 'An', hell, what'll be our second? England? Like Shetland didn't desert us for Norway.' Paper reader: 'Christ, you lot. How'd we get on t' this in the first place—?' Then noticing Neville, he asked, 'Can we help you, shorty. You a driver?'

Neville muttered, 'Sorry, my mistake,' and scuttled out.

'She's not here; I've looked everywhere.' Deborah's moist lips shone.

'Keep your voice down,' ordered Guriat. She gestured, as if to say, you don't know who's listening. A corner booth in the crowded lounge bar with its hubbub of music and voices became their temporary "op room". It was also the public area closest to the bridge.

Brew touched Deborah's quivering shoulder. His eyes asked, are you sure?

Deborah swallowed. 'Tsippi would have found me by now if she were here. We should have gone to Eve's, to collect her. We, we abandoned her,' she charged Guriat in a voice crackling with blame. The dark woman, her eyes permanently hidden behind shaded lenses, had flatly refused to make the detour to Landis's house.

'Come to think of it I haven't seen Eve, either?' said Neville, joining the circle.

'Nobody's seen her,' confirmed Deborah, her mouth contorted.

'Mother's here,' said Neville to Brew, 'in the passenger lounge, with Soph and the kids.'

'Thank HEAVEN,' said the Rabbi.

Changing the subject, Guriat observed, 'No-shows seem to be in majority.'

'Maybe they're the lucky ones,' hissed Deborah through clenched lips.

'Debs—' said the Rabbi, lowering his voice, 'After all we've gone through to be here tonight.'

The set of her jaw signalled that she was not about to recant. 'That woman kept her, I'm sure of it. I'm sure—'

Deborah broke down. Neville accompanied her out. Their mother would look after her.

The ship's horn startled Anna Moray. As the horn blast died away the car ramp closed, sending a cold metallic jolt through the decks. The hull juddered as the engines delivered a surge of power to the screws. The forward thrust overcame the ship's deadweight and, slowly, the red and green lights outside the windows moved backwards.

Anna promised Sophie to watch out for Jake. Sophie, relieved and so very tired, dropped off again. Nothing woke her sleeping children.

As the *Duchess of Galloway* slipped her berth, Anna saw hushed faces turning to each other. Shoulders shrugged. Long draughts of beer went down. The only sounds were watches buzzing the hour, babies crying, and old men muttering prayers. Outside on deck, she could see small clusters of passengers. Cairnryan's lights quickly receded into the frosty blackness of the pre-dawn.

Then there were the 'others' near her. Drinking and talking or playing the machines, they seemed at first sight quite at ease. But Anna soon caught the men darting glances at the outlandish side-curls, full beards and black hats of the Hassidim. Even more openly, the ladies wondered at the head-scarved Orthodox women with their broods of young, silky haired children in colourful skullcaps.

The *Duchess*, well on her way, cut a wide wake up Loch Ryan. She was past Milleur Point and into open sea when Neville came in with Deborah. Anna saw her distress and hugged her. Their whispering woke Sophie up. Before fully opening her eyes, she asked, 'Jake, is that you?'

The waiting was hard. Brew said to her, 'She didn't mean it. She's very upset.' Guriat's eye-masked face gave nothing away.

Brew wore an ordinary workingman's tweed cap and jacket. He sat facing wall. It was wrong of him to sit in a booth with his back to the people. But the risk of his being identified could jeopardise the whole operation. If only he could turn around and see them. Brew tried again. 'Are *they* staring at me?'

Guriat looked past the Rabbi.

Had it been only six hours ago that she'd driven up to the shop in a black cab to collect Brew and Deborah? Was it really forty-three days since the breakout? Should they have stopped at Eve Landis's South Grey Street home for the Scottish girl? Why didn't the old woman bring her, damn it?

The taxi left the city on the A702, southwest. One-hundred-thirty-one miles later, they were at the Galloway bridge-town of Newton Stewart. The "Thirty-nine Steps" pub on the Station Road was closed at half past one when Guriat cautiously pulled into the car park. It was the second time that night.[97] The number of cars from Edinburgh was disappointing. Family, property interests, business commitments, apathy, lethargy and, above all, fear kept people away. Many of those who were there she recognised in the moonlight: the Brodies, the Sinclairs, Dr Avigdor Ross, Mrs Judith Levitt and her husband, Sophie and Jake Banks and their kids, Neville driving Anna Moray in her old Rover—

Guriat patterned the next phase of Operation Snatch on Israeli army call-up methods. Quickly passing the word, she dispatched four cars from Newton Stewart to the other pre-arranged assembly points outside Ballantrae, Glenluce, Stranraer and Girvan. There, other communities would be waiting along dark side roads or in car parks behind quiet country pubs — places where fifty or sixty or even seventy cars would not be noticed. The message was to meet at the ferry landing at Cairnryan, before five.

Advocate Jonathan Brodie, when she came to his car, was the only one to ask about the Rabbi. Seeing his oily grin, Guriat sidestepped the question with 'Mr, Mrs Brodie. Nice looking pair of lambs. Yours?' As the older woman's eyes darted from one sleeping child to the other, an unsure twinge hovered around her lips. Guriat reassured her, 'Everyone's feeling a little like that at the moment.'

Ethel Brodie said, 'They're our grandchildren. Their parents stayed behind — to wrap things up—'

"'To wrap things up—"' Hearing those words in her mind brought Guriat back to the lounge bar. Neville was just coming back. A small, compact man whom she had not seen before was with him. Neville introduced him. 'This is Alec Ace from Gigha Island. Mr Ace spent his whole working life at sea. You said,' turning to Guriat, 'you wanted somebody who knows something about ships.' Ace tipped his eyebrows worriedly, as Neville went on with his introductions in a muted voice without names, 'My brother, and...our friend.' Ace bowed his round, close-cropped head. He spoke in short bursts, more slurred than Neville remembered. 'I was Assistant Purser, the family name was Axelrod, Ace is my name now, changed it by deed poll, I'm into short-wave radios—'

Guriat wasn't hearing him. The time was very near. She was deeply preoccupied with a thousand unknowns, above all, with the question: who was Hugh Gordon, Captain of the *Duchess of Galloway*?

* * *

The Duchess's *keel was laid down at the Werf Gusto Shipyards of Schiedam in Holland. She was launched on October Twenty-first, Nineteen eighty-two, and entered service on February Twenty-sixth, Nineteen eighty-three. The ferry was powered by two 8,000 bhp Werkspoor TM 420 eight-cylinder diesels, and her service speed ran to 19.3 knots. Christened the* Spyros Georgios II *by her first owners, the Greek Poseidon-Trident Lines, their newest ferry plied their oldest short-haul commission between Piraeus and the inner Cyclades, the so-called "barren route". After eight years in service, she was sold to the Ma'abarot-Yam Company of Ashdod in Israel. After a complete refit, the renamed* M-Y

---

[97]The narrative seems to suggest that the Israeli agent had driven down earlier the same evening to be sure the police were not waiting for them.

Zevulun *inaugurated the young company's popular Eilat — Sharm el-Sheikh excursion route. When Egyptian-Israeli relations soured in the wake of Egypt's Islamic takeover in the year Twenty o-five, the Israeli ferry was withdrawn. Two years later the ageing vessel found a buyer, the Cairnryan-based Caledonian Ferry Company Ltd., and was re-christened the* Duchess of Galloway IV.

A brass plaque at the head of the main companionway, though painted over, doubtlessly caught the eye of at least some of the passengers who came aboard on November Thirtieth. It was inscribed in Hebrew and English: 'M-Y Zevulun, *refitted, Israel Shipyards, Haifa, June Twenty-fourth, Nineteen ninety-one.' Around the edge of the oval plate was a verse from Uri Zvi Greenberg's poem* Ma'asei BiYerushalmi: 'A people whose sons sail the seas cannot die, for their way is ever through water and fire.' E.T.

Chapter LIV

Ferryjack

[Monday pre-dawn, November 30, 2009]
'Time to meet Captain Gordon.' Guriat unfastened the flap of her shoulder bag. 'One ditzy Australian tourist is about to check out driving a ferry boat.' She turned to Neville: 'Give me ten minutes.' He acknowledged with a deep swallow. His fingers in his jacket pocket nervously fumbled the roll of electrical tape like worry beads. The Israeli agent lowered her voice to Brew, 'If there's any special blessing for a situation like this, now's the time to say it.'

'It's not a blessing. It's a prayer.'

*

The salesman lit the dial of his wristwatch — five forty-four. Ford Christmas's nerve-driven internal alarm had not let him down. The woman next to him slept on, her breathing soft, even. To his parting touch, she was supple and giving. He slipped from between the sheets. In the darkness, he edged barefoot along the length of the bed. Every time the floorboards creaked, he stopped. With one hand extended like a blind man's cane, Christmas reached out for the satiny pink chair at the foot of the bed, where he'd thrown his clothes the evening before. The woman moaned; her limbs contracted, she turned then stretched. To be sure not to wake her, he waited a full minute, naked and rigid, before moving again. He dressed in a quiet hurry. Then sinking into the pink chair, he gave his nerves time to settle. One more deep breath. Ready. His long fingers felt around by the side of the chair, first finding the edge, then the handle of his salesman's case. Lighter than usual, the case swung easily to his knees. With thumbs on the locks, eyes fixed in the direction of Cecily's bedside phone, Christmas sat back, and waited.

*

Guriat quickly made her way up to the bridge. She hardly noticed the stinging cold, as she slipped under the nylon rope barrier signed "No Entry — Authorised Personnel Only". She tapped on the thick window of the wheelhouse door. The helmsman pointed Gordon's attention to his left. By the pale light from inside, Guriat's features appeared darkly exotic. Her lips formed a lost, innocent smile.

Without hesitation, Gordon unlocked the door. Placing himself in the opening, he said, 'Hugh Gordon, ship's master. And what can I do for you on a frosty morning like this?'

'My name's Gloria—' Gordon shifted his weight with uncertainty. She casually slipped off her designer glasses, swelled her chest and with the shadow of a tongue lick, she breathed, 'Gloria—'

'Gloria.' The white head remained discreetly level though the eyeballs yo-yoed up and down. 'Lovely name. Lost, are you? This is the bridge.'

'Oh, is that what you call it?' Guriat spoke thickly like an Outback sheep-dodger. 'I'm from Australia. Never been on a ferry before, I was just wondering...Skipper...now that I'm up here, could you show me how it all works? You know, how you drive a great big boat like this?'

'Australia. That's a mighty long way for a pretty young lass to come, now isn't it? I don't see why not.' Gordon stepped aside.

Guriat walked in, drawling, 'Thank you, Skipper—'

'Cap'n Gordon, Hugh.'

The man at the wheel turned his big head her way. 'Sir, isn't admitting passengers to the bridge—'

'—the master's privilege.' Gordon was more dismissive than derisory. The helmsman swallowed his tongue.

'This is *sooo* exciting, Captain. Wait till I write home,' bubbled the young Australian. 'Is that the *compass*?' She pointed to the separate console nearest her; the screen's light tinged her finger a phosphorescent green.

'As a matter of fact, miss, that's an Armour Brown gyro compass.'

'All right! Look at all these dials and levers. And you know what every one of them does, don't you, Cap'n Gordon?'

'Aye, dear. It's called "knowing the ropes".'

'You're really cute, Skipper, just like a koala bear.' She took a step closer, fondled the edge of the main control console. 'And I love the Scottish accent.' She pointed— 'Hey, what's that, over here?'

Gordon turned to see. 'That? That's the Decca navigation system, with a colour display anti-collision set — a beautiful piece of kit. See—'

'Decca? Like the old record company?'

The helmsman sniffed.

'Not exactly...Gloria. Our Decca gives us a fix, our position.'

'Like GPS?'

'Aye, we have GPS, too.'

'Hey, you see. I did geography in school. I'm not...not distracting you boys, am I?'

'Not at all,' said Gordon, puffing himself up. 'The pleasure's all mine. All part of the service. Maybe I can buy you a drink when we land. There's always a bit of down time after docking. I don't know the first thing about Australia — I mean, Down Under.'

'Unreal!' She ran her fingers down the strap of her shoulder bag. The gesture focused his attention on her salient curves. 'Hey, Cap, is that the ship-to-shore telephone?'

Gordon chuckled, 'No, no, that's GMDSS radio equipment. Over there, against the bulkhead, VHF transceivers. We don't call it ship-to-shore any more.'

'Can you call somebody, Cap? Your wife? Doesn't she worry about you? Aren't you thinking about her when you're out here alone like this?'

'What makes you think that I'm—'

' —that you're married? A nice, cuddly man like you, Skipper?'

The helmsman enjoyed a quiet smirk.

'Will you still have that drink with me?'

Guriat winked. 'What's a drink between mates? Of course, I will. Now, go on. Phone her.'

'Bit too early for the little lady.'

'Aw, c'mon. For me.'

'She'll be fast asleep.'

'Then maybe it's time to wake her—' Guriat took one step back, lifted the flap of her shoulder bag and coolly pulled out the KTL. She steadied the weapon in two hands, pointing the bulbous barrel at arm's length into Gordon's face.

'What the hell blazes is this? Who are you?'

The helmsman spun around.

'You. Hands where I can see them — on the wheel. Captain, we're taking over the ship.'

Gordon slowly raised his hands. His brass-buttoned coat rode up over his belt.

'Neville? You there? Door's open.'

Neville squinted through the window, then stepped in.

Gordon reached higher. 'What are you going to do with us? Who are you? This is piracy!

The woman asked, 'Is this thing on autopilot?'

'Aye, y' bloody black bitch,' answered the helmsman.

'Shut your face, Mr Ives,' growled Gordon. 'Tell them nothing.'

Guriat said sharply, 'Neville, cuff them. You, Captain, hands down, easy, to the front.' Neville tightly bound Gordon's crossed wrists with several turns of tape. Each pull from the roll gave off a sharp ratcheting noise. As he moved on to the helmsman, Guriat ordered him, 'You. Slowly ease your hands behind your back.'

Before Neville can tape him, Ives ducks, turns, and hammers his right elbow into Neville's ribs. Spinning round, he follows through with an upper cut. The blow misses, glancing off Neville's throat. Both men are knocked off-balance. Neville recovers first, throws himself at Ives, all arms and legs spread out like a net. With Neville clinging to him, Ives topples to the deck. The helmsman roars. Neville, red-faced, grimacing and puffing violently, leg scissors around Ives' thighs. He locks his arms wrist-in-hand below the sailor's shoulder blades, and gouges his chin into Ives' collarbone. Guriat's eyes dart between Gordon and the scuffle. Grunting like a muzzled dog and shadowboxing with his bound hands, Gordon urges his man on. Ives loosens an arm from Neville's clinch. In a sudden levering move helped by a desperate kick against the console, Ives rolls Neville over. Short, punishing jabs to Neville's back, below the kidney, echo a dull, hollow sound. Eyes clamped shut, Neville groans in agony. Guriat jerks her weapon at Gordon. 'Call him off. Now.' She drops her aim. 'Or I'll shoot him.' Gordon makes a move towards her. She raises the KTL, fires a ringing blank over his shoulder. Gordon calls out. Ives lands a cracking blow. Neville's clinch is broken, his breathing short, in low rasps. Exploiting the moment, Gordon, bellowing like a wounded animal, lunges for Guriat. She sidesteps, and he plunges to the deck. In the same blink of time a fire extinguisher crashes in through the door window opposite. Guriat whirls. A hand reaches in to turn the latch lock—

* * *

Chapter LV

First Light

The wheelhouse door swings open. Brew.

As Ives, his white shirt sweated through, reared up, Brew lifted the extinguisher, and quietly saying, 'For the children—' he brought it down across the seaman's bullish head. Ives collapsed like a tyre, shot through. The Rabbi rolled the dead weight off his brother. Guriat, keeping her KTL trained on Gordon, pinched Ives' jugular below the jaw. The blow was stunning, not fatal.

Neville was groggy and disoriented. His fingers, contracting like claws, dug into Brew's arm. 'Who taught you to put out fires?' he gasped, as Brew helped him sit up.

'Let's get this one up,' said Guriat. 'Captain's got a very important call to make.' From either side, the Rabbi and Guriat lifted Gordon to his feet. 'Who are you people? You'll pay for this. You'll never take over my ship.'

'We just did,' said the Israeli agent.

The Rabbi elaborated, 'To be more precise, sir, you are chartering your vessel to us. You'll be amply compensated, and in due time, with HIS help, your ship will be returned.'

'Who the hell are you? I've seen you, somewhere, before—'

'Brewster Moray, ex-Chief Rabbi of Scotland.'

The name took Gordon's breath away. 'This is my brother, Neville, and our colleague here prefers to remain anonymous.'

'You're...you're...the Jew.'

'Yes, Captain, the truth is there to be told. And in my profession being Jewish is something of an asset—'

'More like an occupational hazard,' groaned Neville, feeling sick.

'On my ship.' Gordon's voice croaked. 'Sweet Jesus.'

'Also one of ours,' said Brew, exchanging the wry Moray smile with his brother.

Guriat unhooked the VHF receiver. 'Now, Captain, you're going to talk to your wife.' She dialled the number she memorised.

'What have you done to her?'

'Nothing.'

'You won't get away with this. This is out-and-out piracy.'

The phone rang. Guriat put the receiver into his taped hands. 'It's your wife.'

Cecily woozily switched on the bedside light. Christmas calmly opened his case, as she fumbled for the phone, answering from her pillow, 'Hello, hello—'

'Cecily, is that you? Are you all right, Cuddles?'

There was no answer. Seeing Christmas in the chair at the foot of her bed, she leapt up like a sprung trap. His fisted hands rested on his case, balled around the grip of a short-barrelled revolver. 'Just tell your husband what you see,' he said.

'Hugh—' There was a long lapse. 'Hugh, there's a man here, in our bedroom, with a...a gun.'

Gordon lowered the phone. 'You, you Christ-hating bastards—' Gordon spoke again into the receiver, 'Cecily, stay calm. We'll get you out of this thing. I promise.'

Christmas got up. 'Let me speak to him.' Cecily handed the phone to him, and then shrank back.

'Captain Gordon—'

'You one of them?'

'...I don't want to see your wife hurt. I mean, she won't be in any fit condition to—'

'Shut up, Ford!' screamed Cecily.

Gordon heard. 'You been spiking her—?'

Christmas said with an ominous flatness, 'She lives if you cooperate—'

'Cecily!'

'If you don't, she dies. Either way I get paid.' He gave the phone back to Cecily. 'Hugh, Hugh. He was here when I woke up. He's got a gun. Do as they say, please, Hugh.'

Gordon staggered back, letting the receiver fall away from his ear. 'Whatever it takes, I will get home! And if I find out—' Guriat, poking her weapon in Gordon's ribs, cut him short, 'That's enough, Captain.'

The Rabbi understood. To Guriat, in a tone full of indignation and confusion, he said, 'I never agreed to this. I said, we don't take hostages.'

'We're not. The captain's wife is our insurance that nobody here gets hurt. As soon as the ship is in our hands, she goes free. Is that understood, Captain?' As Guriat snatched the phone out of his hands, Gordon swore, 'I'll get home! I'll get home! Christ, if it's the last thing I do.'

She held the receiver to her chest. 'Rabbi, we'll discuss this later. After we've secured the ship—'

'I forbid it.'

Guriat switched to Hebrew. She spoke in a hurried, harsh whisper, 'Rabbi, we're at war. Scotland was planning to sacrifice you and your whole community. We do what we have to—'

'But two wrongs don't make a right.'

'But sometimes they make sense.'

Guriat went back to the VHF, instructing Mrs Gordon to hand over the phone to her 'guest'.

'What next?' Neville asked, painfully getting up.

'Now that we have the good captain's undivided attention, we inform the crew and passengers that the ship is under new management.'

'You're enjoying this,' said Gordon. 'You won't get away with it.'

Ignoring him, Guriat slipped the KTL back into her handbag. Again, concealing her face behind sunglasses, she searched his pockets. Taking Gordon's keys, she asked, 'Which one opens the weapons locker?'

He pointed resentfully.

'Where?'

'In my cabin, forward, below the bridge.'

'Does anyone else have a key?'

'No.'

'For some reason, I believe you.' The Israeli ordered him to summon the ship's mates and senior staff to the bridge. She let Gordon break the news of the hijack to them. Citing the danger to his wife's life, he spoke of a 'checkmate situation'.

Guriat's follow-on began. 'All we want is the ship; no crew or passengers will be taken hostage. But any violence will be met with violence.' She kept their identities privileged information. The officers were given their instructions, and cautioned not to alarm the passengers. Guriat reminded them, 'Nobody's going to want to be responsible for anything happening to the lovely Mrs Gordon. Right, Captain?' The ship's mates filed out, taking the groaning helmsman with them. Staying in the shadows, Brew kept silent.

Guriat said, 'Time now to bring the *Duchess* to a slow and dignified stop. If you don't mind, sir.'

Slowly, Gordon drew back the two main control levers. The RPM indicator needles fell. At the same time the steady vibrations of cruising speed eased off.

Fifteen minutes later the fifty-three crew and catering staff under the first officer's command were away in the portside launch. The Rabbi came forward, his lips working. 'A prayer,' he explained, '...for their safety.'

Guriat handed Gordon a message. 'Public announcement.'

He started to read silently. Stopped. The note shook in his tape-bound hands. 'You won't get away with this. There will be consequences. Retaliation.' His vague threats left Guriat unmoved. 'Read,' she ordered.

Gordon flicked on the PA system. 'Attention all passengers. Attention all passengers. This is your captain, Hugh Gordon, speaking from the bridge.' He swallowed. 'The ship, the *Duchess of Galloway*, has been hijacked — I repeat, HIJACKED — and shortly will be changing course to an undisclosed destination. Do not, I repeat, do not panic. No one will be hurt, as long as everyone cooperates. The crew have been evacuated. My wife is in danger of her life on the mainland; she will die if there is any violence, threatened or actual. Only those passengers who wish to return to Scotland are immediately to assemble at the Emergency Muster Station on E Deck, starboard: that is, by the lifeboat, forward, the right side of the ship facing the bow. Proceed at once — again — AT ONCE. There, you will await my further instructions. I repeat: there is no cause for panic. Keep calm. Dress warmly. I now repeat this message from the beginning—' When he finished, Gordon raved, 'These terrorists will never see another sunset—'

The public address system was still on. Guriat slapped the microphone away. The feedback was ear piercing. Forgetting the tape, Gordon burned the skin of his wrists trying to cover his ears. Guriat chopped him across the cheek, saying, 'One more trick like that—' She ordered him to radio the Belfast harbour master. 'Inform them that you are having some minor engine trouble, and that you estimate a delay of forty-five to sixty minutes. And be careful how you say it.' She waved the open VHF line to Christmas under his nose as a warning.

When Gordon finished speaking, he said, 'You can't keep a thing like this secret, not for long.'

'Long enough,' answered the Israeli. 'Long enough—'

Gordon said, 'The authorities know our exact position. When they find out—'

'*When* is the operative word, but now—' Again she spoke to Christmas: 'Lioness to X-M. I'm ringing off now. If your phone does not ring again in fifteen minutes — mark — one-five minutes, you know what to do.' She hung up. 'Captain, you heard. If you and all the passengers are not in that boat and away in a quarter of hour, Mrs Gordon—'

The Rabbi's protest died in his throat. It was checkmate — all around.

Neville swallowed sickeningly. She *was* capable of murder. And yet, Guriat's frighteningly alien potential for destruction made her all the more beautiful, and irresistible.

Deborah sat motionless. Anna shrugged, and stared at Deborah; she could not understand her daughter-in-law's passion for a child who was not her own. The start of the captain's Tannoy announcement startled both women, and also woke up Sophie and the children.

Anna Moray said, 'The ship, it's stopped.' She was first to stand up. Instinctively, she backed away, closer to the wall. Deborah, then Sophie with Naomi and Benny in hand joined Anna. Soon Jews all over the ship were retreating, and so separating themselves from the "others", who were about to leave.

At first, none of the others moved. Shocked and bewildered, their eyes searched each other. The majority, the Jews standing apart, met all inquisitive looks with blank, uninformative faces. Deborah twitched, about to say something consoling to the ones nearest her, but Anna squeezed her wrist. When, in the next seconds, nothing happened either confirming the captain's announcement or saving them from it, questions surfaced like boiling bubbles.

'Hijack?
'Who?'
'Where are they?'
'What are they going to do to us?'
'What about our cars?'
'How do we know that was the captain?'

Woodenly, first one, then another, started to pick up coats and hats. More followed. The "others" made their way forward.

In the drivers' lounge, a short, fierce argument broke out: to resist or not. Some of the men grimly watched the door. At any moment they expected masked, armed hijackers to rush in. When nothing happened, the smoker snuffed out his cigarette. Grabbing his jacket, he said, 'Hell, lads, Ah 'm nae stayin' here. Let's see what this thing's all aboot. Comin'?' Nobody wanted to be left behind.

At the muster station, Captain Gordon hurried the passengers into the sixty-five-seat lifeboat. The words he stressed — 'hijack', 'unknown terrorists', 'no time', 'wife's life', 'life jackets' — floated up to the bridge wing. Next, Gordon counted them: 'sixty-five, sixty-six, sixty-seven. Is that everyone who's leaving?' There was a buzz of voices, then stillness. Gordon shouted up to the bridge, 'The boat's overloaded.'

Guriat answered, 'We can't spare the bigger lifeboats. It's perfectly calm out there and in another half hour, it'll be light.'

Gordon cupped his mouth. 'The leader. Let me speak to your leader. I appeal to you. We'll be swamped.' Voices swore, grumbled and begged.

The Rabbi called back, 'Hurry, Captain. You can put people into the crew's boat. But for now, go, before it's too late. For your wife's sake—' From the bridge Guriat and Brew heard the slow whirr of winches lowering away, and the sound of steel cables passing slowly through pulleys. The boat splashed heavily into the water.

There was also much movement on the decks below. In the last dark of night, ghostly shapes leaned over the sides to see the lifeboat off.

'You've set yourselves a course straight to hell,' raved Gordon, then lowering his tone to the men and women around him, he promised, 'I'll see them drown, every last one of them.'

The lifeboat's engine opened up, engaging the screw. Over its steady gurgle, Gordon called back, 'We're away. We're away. If he kills Ceci—' Her name retreated into the abyss.

Guriat went in and made the call.

*

Christmas answered. He was relieved. Putting the gun away in his sales case, he said, 'It wasn't loaded.' Then out of habit he looked at his watch. Already after seven. With hindsight, he realised that the hour had gone by without Grandpa Clock's chimes. His mistress, caught up in last evening's passion, had forgotten to give him his weekly wind.

Cecily uncovered herself. 'Take me with you. Please, Ford. I don't know what this was all about. I don't care. Just take me away.' As she spoke, she left her bed and put her arms around him.

'I can't.'

'He's so jealous. Insanely jealous. After this morning, whatever I say, he'll never believe me. He *heard* me shouting your name...I know it. He'll make my life hell.' Christmas felt Cecily's quick breathing through her short, frilly nightdress tied at the waist and curved around her firm, plump breasts.

'Cecily, you're too good for him. You're still young, attractive. You can leave him. His career is ruined. What's there to stay for?'

'I love you. I want to go with you.'

'You can't.'

'Why not?' She let him go, stood back, to read his face.

'I'm slime. Good enough answer for you? I'm out of here, and I'm gone. Free of Scotland, for good. Nothing you say or do can stop me.'

'Why, Ford? Why did you do it?'

'Money. A lot of money. Enough to buy a harp, ten harps.'

*

Captain Gordon, taking the Rabbi's suggestion, transferred five passengers, all drivers, to the crew's lifeboat. Then setting off together, the launches made for the lights of Portpatrick Harbour on the Rhinns of Galloway coast. On landing Gordon counted the passengers and crew — twice. One crewman was missing.

*

At the greying edge of night's end, the Rabbi gazed up at the heavens and said to himself, 'The stars and galaxies are shining like a zillion, happy, gleaming eyes.' Lowering his eyes, he could just make out the divide between sea and sky. The light accelerated, the new day came fast.

'Brew—'

'Nev—? I must sound like a nutter—'

'No, just counting to yourself, like you always used to when you were a kid.'

'Are you all right to be on your feet?' asked Brew.

'A little punch-drunk. Before you get carried away...thanks.'

'For what?'

'Putting out the fire,' said Neville.

'Isn't that what brothers are for? If you hadn't risked your life for me and Deborah, I'd still be in the Castle, perhaps dead.'

'So we're all square, eh?' Neville held out his hand. Brew took it, and pulling him close, the brothers embraced as they had never done before. 'Bloody hell, don't squeeze, brother,' said Neville, feeling his aching ribs and strung-out muscles. 'I'm going in.'

Inside the wheelhouse, her back was turned to him. Guriat was fingering the control panel as if to convince herself of its reality. With sudden awareness, she turned round with snake-strike speed. 'I didn't hear you coming in.' She slipped off her glasses, giving Neville a brief moment to picture her: the eyes full of fire. She was aglow, suffused with pride and satisfaction. And then rubbing her hands together, she said, 'Well, that was easy—' and turned away as though he didn't exist.

The blood drained from Neville's skull. Steadying himself against the doorjamb, he hoped his pain did not show.

* * *

Today, two lifeboat wrecks can still be seen beached just north of Portpatrick, down from the golf links. Both are shells, rusted through and plundered of anything worth taking long ago. However, a bit of the white paint remains under the gunwales around the bow of the boat further inshore. On close inspection four remaining, weather-scarred letters — O W A Y — can still be made out. E.T.

Chapter LVI

Runaway Home

[Monday pre-dawn, November 30, 2009]
Jake Banks was awake again. Trembling all over. Tangled, twisted sheets cold and damp with sweat. He moved to the other side of the bed, Soph's side. He pulled the covers over his head.

Why didn't he stay with them?

He saw the kids asleep in her arms. He heard the lies he told her. And he tasted the kisses, those last sweet kisses he gave them on their sleeping heads.

Was it last night?

He could feel the daylight. He turned his head away from it.

He began to blubber.

He buried his eyes in the crook of his arm.

The light would not let him run away.

* * *

Chapter LVII

Geography

[Monday morning, November 30, 2009]
Eve Landis put her teacup down. 'Elen, why do you look at me like that?'

She asked again, 'Why dinnae we go last night? Beer and skittles—'

'Why-didn't-we-go?' Eve corrected her. 'Because I didn't want to go, and you're too young to understand the madness of grown-ups.'

'Yes, Aunt.' After that, breakfast continued with an uneasy politeness, more palpable than usual. Patting her lips with the cloth serviette, Tsippi asked to be excused.

'Oh, yes, the time—' said Eve.

'I think I'd like to go to the public library after school.'

'That's beautiful, dear. Of course, you should go to the library. You're old enough, I won't worry. Have you money for the bus fare home?'

'No.'

'You go get ready for school, and I'll find you some change from my purse.'

Upstairs Tsippi took longer than usual. Eve waited for her at the bottom of the stairs. As she came down, Tsippi felt the old woman's eyes questioning the over-stuffed school bag on her back. 'It's sports today,' said the girl, answering the unspoken challenge.

'Of course. I forgot. Come on, then. Let's get a move on. We don't want you to be late. Oh, and here's money for the bus home.' Tsippi opened her purse, and the old woman dropped in a whole handful of change. 'That's because I was sharp with you earlier. Buy yourself something nice to eat.' Eve proudly watched Tsippi as she carefully tucked the purse into her knapsack. In the hall the spinster adjusted Tsippi's school tie and blue blazer, then fussed over each toggle and loop as she buttoned up the girl's woolly car coat. 'By the way, what are you going to study at the library this afternoon?'

'Geography. Maps for ma project.'

'*My* project. You must tell me all about it this evening over tea. I'll make something nice...with potatoes, you like potatoes. Maybe Aunt Eve can help you with your lesson. After all, a teacher is a teacher.'

In the car on the way to school Eve Landis babbled on. Tsippi kept tight-lipped.

* * *

Chapter LVIII

447-989

447-989. The number jumped into Brew's mind. It was his parents' first telephone number. 447-989.

The Rabbi's announcement over the ferry's Tannoy was short. 'This is Rabbi Moray speaking. *The ship is ours.*' He called Mr Alec Ace to the bridge, and then briefly introduced Guriat Gaoni as 'Israel's representative'. Her appeal began, 'Our initial, over-riding task is to prepare ourselves and our ship for the long voyage ahead.' She called on everyone 'ready to pitch in' to meet in the forward lounge on C Deck in five minutes.

Neville stayed on the bridge to wait for Ace.

On the way to the lounge, Guriat said to Brew, almost idly, '"For the children—" You could have killed that man—'

Brew replied simply, 'He was killing my brother.'

Guriat let it drop. 'Right. As long as this tub is in Scottish waters, the operation is in danger. The first hours are crucial. It is imperative we organise our defences.'

'Against what?' asked Brew, incredulously.

'Anything. Everything. Montrose. There's no doubt about it. His sick mind will blow when he hears about this. He's going to want to stop us. He's got a whole list of good reasons. And you, Rabbi, you're at the top of that list.'

'There'll be no attack,' he said as though voicing it made it so.

'You shook the man's hand,' Guriat reminded him. 'You saw the ice in his eyes.'

'Not even Montrose would attack an unarmed ship with hundreds of innocent men, women and children aboard. It would stir up an international outcry. This is the Twenty-first century.'

'What century ever stopped our enemies?' Her question impacted on the Rabbi with such force that he stopped short. Brew searched deeply into her eyes like no man had ever done before.

'You've brought weapons on board?'

'No way. I could have been caught, jeopardising the whole mission.'

'Outside help?'

'Not until we make it to English waters — at least an hour away. For now, we're on our own.'

'And, if we *are* attacked—'

'We've got nothing to defend ourselves with,' she admitted. 'But *they* don't know that.' The shadow of a smile played on her lips.

How different Brew was from Neville, she thought. When his eyes blazed, she could feel them drawing her into him. 'So how do you propose we defend ourselves?' he asked.

'It's called improvisation and deception.'

447-989. The digits, their rhythm, played like an old song. 447-989.

Alec Ace met them on the stairs, and asked why the ferry was 'dead in the water'. Guriat told him, 'Get us to English waters as fast as possible.'

In the wheelhouse, Ace studied the array of dials and levers on the main control console. His eyebrows sloped at an angle greater than usual.

'You sure you know what you're doing, Alec?' asked Neville.

'If you've seen one ship's bridge you've seen them all.'

'You sure?' asked Neville again. 'That dickheadshit' — he rubbed the bruise under his jawbone — 'kept his hand on this control over here.'

'A ship's just like a woman, old son; they all have the same bits and bobs. Not that I know that much about women. But I spent plenty of time on the bridge, watching—'

Neville bit his tongue as Ace talked to himself. 'Let's see. What next? Take a reading off the GPS satellite position finder, get a fix. Consult the Decca radar, no large blips nearby. Good. Now, set ourselves a course. There. Southeast at one-three-eight degrees should bring us nicely between the mainland and the Isle of Man.' Drawing a deep breath, Ace threw the two longest levers forward, then taking the helm, he turned it hard. 'Nev, check the Armour Brown, that's the compass there, behind you. When the number one-three-eight degrees comes to the top, sing out.' Twice in quick succession Ace blew the ship's horn.

'One-three-eight coming up...now,' said Neville.

Alec Ace glowed. 'England, here we come. And if there were a way for me old Mum to see me now, I'd sail this babe right into her garage.'

'Alec, I thought you said your Mum passed on.'

'So she has, so she has. But I'm still her son.' Ace sounded the horn again.

'Sorry, man,' said Neville after a moment's time.

'For what?'

'Doubting you.'

'Doubting me? Hell, Neville, the only person you ever really doubt is *you*.'

447-989. His mother used to make him repeat the number often when he was a child. Very good, she'd say, now, again, until he learned to rattle it off in his sleep. 447-989.

Brew Moray entered the crowded forward lounge. All faces turned to him — all except the small community of black hats in over-sized prayer shawls off in one corner. Their Rebbe, Felix Frankelstein, the young Hassid from New York, led them in their morning prayers. Frankelstein was loud in his devotions. His head rocked with a chopping action that beat his wispy nut-brown beard against his breast. In his fervour his eyes were closed to the world.

447-989. Remember the number, his mother taught him, and if ever you get lost, call home right away. 447-989.

Naomi broke away from Sophie's hand. She came running to Brew. 'When are we going home, Uncle Brew?' she asked.

The Rabbi dropped to one knee. 'My mother always used to say to me when I was your age, if ever I got lost, call home. We're calling home, Naomi, right now. Tell me something, love—'

'Yes—' she answered, her dimpled face confused about what was coming next.

'What should we call our ship? Have you got a good name for her?'

The child saw that people were listening. She looked up to her mother, who shrugged sympathetically. Brew couldn't resist touching her cheek. Her lips puckered. 'Praise. Is *Praise* a good name?'

Brew Moray announced, '*Praise*— Our ferry, from now on, is called *Praise*. Absolutely perfect, dear.' There was clapping. Naomi beamed, then leapt into Sophie's arms, 'Mummy, I named Uncle Brew's ship!'

447-989. Once as a little boy of seven, Brew Moray got separated on a school outing. He wandered away from his class without the teacher noticing. When Brew saw he was alone, he said the number. It felt good to say it out loud. 447-989.

Reb Frankelstein sidled up to the Rabbi, and introduced himself. He asked what special accommodations and provisions would be made for Orthodox Jews. Rabbi Moray said simply that he was leader of the whole community. Frankelstein raised a finger, but Guriat excused Brew and brought him to the front of the lounge.

Guriat called for calm and quiet. She asked for volunteers to form six search parties, one for each deck. They were to systematically comb the ship, take stock, and report back in an hour. She put Dr Avigdor Ross in charge of the sick bay. Jonathan Brodie and his half-sister Judith Levitt offered to make a complete list of names and work out a fair system of daily watches. Deborah and Anna Moray stepped forward to help organise food and drink. Mr Sinclair volunteered to supervise the dietary laws in the galley. Izzy Sofer signed to his wife from his wheelchair. Pearl nodded affirmatively, and threw up her hand. Brew Moray applauded the old couple's willingness to help. Izzy was a retired baker, and Pearl an accountant.

447-989. He found a red telephone box. No one inside. He managed to pull open the hard-sprung door, but the phone was high up, out of his reach. Not to fash yourself in a tight spot — his father used to say — look, see, think. Six fat phone books luckily, through use, had come unfixed, and lay on the shelf, not too high. He piled one on top of another, climbed up on them straightening himself to his full height, and called home for the first time in his young life. It rang the familiar double ring. He rehearsed his statement: I'm lost, Mummy, come fetch me. 447-989—

Within half an hour the search parties began to return with their reports, written on whatever bits of paper came to hand.

The ferry's main and upper vehicle decks were fully packed with two hundred and seventy-two passenger cars, six lorries and two semi-trailers, one an oil tanker. A smaller, brightly painted van, a travelling "New Age" chemist's shop, carried a large inventory of potions and powders. Brew made a note for Dr Ross. As he wrote, a hunch, a long shot came over him. He felt drawn to take a closer look for himself at the "cures".

One search team brought in a leaflet with a plan of the ferry. On it they marked the lockers where hundreds of orange life jackets and inflatable life rafts were stored. Each of the four remaining lifeboats contained a supply of emergency flares and some provisions.

Other searchers found reserves of blankets and linens, tools, acetylene torches and the ubiquitous hand-held radios. The ship's few crew cabins were inspected and their contents listed: uniforms, shaving tackle, cosmetics, books and magazines.

Guriat, herself, checked out the weapons locker in the captain's cabin. The contents were disappointing: one old single-barrelled shotgun, two semi-automatic hunting rifles and a pair of P1 pistols of the type used by British army officers, plus a few boxes of ammunition for each.

Brodie and Levitt came back with a rough figure of about a thousand passengers. Brew said, 'We need to know exactly how many people we are.' They gave him a quizzical look. 'Call it my weakness, but it's the numbers that count.'

Pearl made a preliminary list of food stores. The ferry's provisions in commercial quantities sounded ample, but with around a thousand mouths to feed three times a day, supplies would not last long. Also, Brew ordered that all the meat, mostly bacon and breakfast sausages, be thrown over the side. At this, the Rabbi's first direct order, came the first murmurings of discontent.[98]

447-989. The phone rang, but nobody answered. Brew waited. At last he hung up the receiver and his coins came back. He was sure he'd dialled the right number. He tried again. He slipped his two coins in the slot and dialled, this time more deliberately. 4-4-7-9-8-9. Again, there was no answer. He hung up. But one of his five-pence coins jumped out. Desperately, he looked everywhere, but it was nowhere to be found. Now, he did not have enough money left for a bus. 447-989.

Deborah came in with black coffee in paper cups. 'Don't throw away the cups,' she said as she was being thanked. 'They're in limited supply. We're going to have to recycle the plastic things as long as we can, because we can't use the crockery.'[99]

'Debs, you look absolutely exhausted,' said Brew.

'Aren't we all? It's a nightmare. The kitchen's impossible. So many of our Jews here haven't the *faintest* clue about keeping kosher. Mr Sinclair and I have to explain and justify everything. Why must people be so, so negative?'

Brew shook his head. 'I know, I know. Our real battle is not with our enemies or the elements; it's with ourselves.'

'I'm sorry, Brew, I can't stop thinking about Tsippi.'

'I'm sure she's thinking of you, too. I can almost hear her calling out your name. You two are meeting in each other's thoughts.' Brew clasped her hands together in his. 'Debs, you're winning.'

Turning to Guriat, he said, 'Ms Gaoni, I must check out something.'

'But I need to talk to you about a press release—'

'I won't be long.'

A few moments after Brew and Deborah left, three people presented themselves to Guriat. A tall young man, pock-faced with dark red hair swept back into a short ponytail, spoke first. 'You're the Israeli, right?' he asked in a thick Glasgow accent. Guriat nodded. 'My name's Todd Harrison. This is Lindy, my partner—' She was thin, nervous with sleepy eyes. 'And that's our lad.' In her arms, she was cradling a small baby. Todd then shot a glance at the man standing between them. He had the cringing look of a beaten hound. 'We found him...skulking about in some sort of control room near the engines. He gave no trouble when we asked him to come with.'

'Like I told them,' he said, glancing at Todd, 'name's William Warboys, chief engineer's mate. I'd like to see Rabbi Moray.' He wore a blue-denim work shirt with his laminated ID card pinned to the pocket. The man's thin, orangy-blond hair and pale skin made his small blue eyes stand out.

Guriat was short. 'Rabbi's not here now, mate. Why didn't you just leave with the others?'

'Well, if you really want to know— No, you won't believe me.'

'Try us, mate.' She took off her sunglasses, and let her pale eyes bore into him.

'I happened to come up on the vehicle deck — you know, before we got under way, for a little breather. I heard someone — they couldn't see me — whispering-like to his kids. "Don't talk anybody, an' not to say Rabbi Moray's name, not to anyone." I take a good look about and see folk, more than we seen in years on this floating plank. I put two an' two

---

[98]From Biblical times only certain cuts of meat from specific animals, humanely killed and prepared in the prescribed way, may be eaten by Jews. However, not all Jews share the same sensitivities concerning the minutiae of the dietary laws.

[99]Because of its porosity, used ceramic crockery cannot be rendered fit (kosher) for observant Jews to eat off.

together an' I says to myself, "Rabbi?" This whole lot's Jews. I'm back down below, an' I don't breathe anything to anybody. Keep myself to myself. Then come the hijack, an' I says, hey, this is it... my ticket to the Promised Land. I stayed. Impulse. That's all.'

Guriat capped his story with a sharp 'Jeez.'

Just then Brew Moray came rushing in. He was holding two very large apothecary jars filled with bright yellow powder.

'What's that?' asked the Israeli.

'Quite possibly the antidote to the Prime Minister's handshake.' Guriat would have followed him up, but just then Deborah reappeared. She was back to collect the plastic cups. 'And who have we here?' asked the Rabbi. Guriat quickly filled him in on Warboys' story.

'Rabbi Moray, I can be a lot of help. I know this old shit bucket inside out.' Warboys had a puppy's voice, high-pitched and pleading.

'Brew, he's right,' said Deborah. 'We need help, and anyway we can't just toss him into the sea.'

'That's exactly what we ought to do,' said Guriat.

Deborah reassured the stranger, 'You've got nothing to be afraid of.'

Even though Warboys' calling his ship an 'old shit bucket' set him on edge, Brew felt the fervour in Deborah's voice and could not reverse her. 'If he wants to join us, he can.' Deborah and the Harrisons left satisfied.

Brew's decision bothered the Israeli agent. But seeing no easy way out, Guriat closely interrogated Warboys. Her questions, voiced with professional distrust, concentrated on the ship — its fuel capacity, range, and cruising speed. He answered crisply and to the point. 'He sounds kosher,' she said to the Rabbi, then to Warboys, 'but you're going to show us every inch of this tub.'

'Mr Warboys? asked Brew, still gripping the jars in his arms. 'Are there any long planks aboard?'

'Long planks—?' Warboys thought for a moment, '...of wood? Don't know. But there's plenty of aluminium tubing in different profiles in the repair shop. Would that do?'

'Even better,' said Brew. 'Let's have a look.'

'What are you thinking, Rabbi?' asked Guriat, craning to read the jars' quaint, black-framed labels. "LYCOPODIUM" was handwritten in large capital letters. A red flame sticker on each jar showed the contents were highly inflammable.

'Just an idea—'

447-989. *Mummy's out. Brew must find his own way home.* He began his hike. It happened to be a very warm day, and he was miles from home. He followed the bus stops with the numbers of the lines he knew that led to the city centre. At the other end of Princes Street, he followed other bus numbers that led him out again. All that walking made him very thirsty. His little legs ached. But he knew each step he took brought him closer to Canaan Lane. Over and over, he said the telephone number to himself like a comforting mantra. It kept up his spirits. And it brought him home. 447-989.

* * *

For some strange reason, not clear to me, I ran the name Warboys through several computerised genealogical nets. To my delight I turned up a Warboys, who was a permanent resident in Jerusalem. Cpl W Warboys, Serial No 592927, London Irish Rifles, fell May Second, Nineteen eighteen, in Palestine in the closing days of the Great War. He lies in the British Military Cemetery on Mt Scopus overlooking the Holy City. Perhaps Chief Engineer's mate William Warboys' sudden decision to see the Promised Land was not an "impulse", but rather the voice of an ancestor calling him from the grave. E.T.

Chapter LIX

'Many Happy Returns'

[Monday morning, November 30, 2009]
Hamish found Montrose slumped over his desk. The butler gently woke him. He then discreetly retired to the "en suite" to give Hamish and his crew a few minutes to tidy up the office. He switched on the radio to drown out the flushing sounds.

Angus Montrose was seventy-one years old. The inescapable office birthday party yesterday evening had been admirably orchestrated. Mrs Jamieson invited all the right people. Hamish, with his usual efficiency, saw to the food and drink. Gareth Gunn brought in the candle-lit cake at the proper moment. Party Secretary Kenneth Keller dutifully headed a small, select circle of moneyed supporters. The Cabinet, minus the resigned Justice Minister Judith Levitt, stood closest to him in a supportive circle. A few kilted old cronies and retired hangers-on lent the occasion the decorum and respect due to a head of state. And there were toasts, handshakes, songs, presents and adulatory speeches — all freely given as sincere expressions of loyalty and devotion.

Yet on reflection something was wrong with yesterday. He finished shaving, and studied his mirror image. That was it. No one, not one of them, really spoke to *him*.

Had everyone fallen under the pall of the media pundits? It seemed that no word, written or spoken, did not have 'rabbi' overtones. Every day brought more news, comment, opinion, analysis, and controversy. The English Parliament was set to vote on a partial embargo on Scotland. The US State Department had made another public "diplomatic" statement. The European Union was calling for economic sanctions, and in the UN General Assembly, delegates came out with a resolution of condemnation. Signed op-ed pieces in the warring local press were becoming more hysterical in their attacks and praises of the government's performance. There were dark allusions to alcoholism in coded phrases like 'a growing loss of control'. Leaks and denials of 'divisions in the ruling party' and a rumoured Prime Ministerial 'visit' to the Chief Rabbi's wife were also making their way into print and newsnet sites.

Montrose turned off the radio and, hearing nothing outside, decided that it was safe to re-enter his office. He abstractedly panned the panelled walls. He had sacrificed life, love, and the family he never had for Scotland. He said it out loud. 'For Scotland'.

It was not even eight. Montrose clicked open the on-screen diary. Another full hour before his first meeting of the new week. He picked up the hammer—

A speck of memory had been lost. Lately, he was obsessed with trying to retrieve it. He was convinced, if he could only remember what it was, it would clarify his crumbling hold on reality.

There was a knock. Immediately, the double doors opened wide. Thomas Butterstone, bowler hat in hand, burst in unannounced. Hamish followed behind, looking flustered.

'That'll be all, Hamish. Thank you,' said Montrose, dismissing his bowing butler. 'Mr Police Commissioner—' The man irritated him; no, not the man — his voice: he was relatively young, but his voice somehow sounded like an old woman's. 'What brings you here so early? It must be a matter of some urgency.'

Butterstone ignored the sarcasm. 'Urgency and confidentiality. Sir— May I wish you many happy returns of the day?' The Commissioner had not been invited to the Prime Minister's birthday gathering.

'Do, do sit down. A drink? You look like you're in need of one.' Montrose waved his hand in the direction of the sideboard.

Butterstone excused himself. 'A bit too early in the day, sir. My reason for coming—' He sat. 'Within the last quarter of an hour two lifeboats with one hundred and twenty passengers and crew have come ashore at Portpatrick, the Thinns. It appears, sir, that the car ferry out of Cairnryan, the *Duchess of Galloway*, has been...hijacked.'

'Hijacked?'

'That's right, Prime Minister. Hijacked at sea.'

'Moray? The Rabbi. Don't tell me—' Montrose's staring expression begged for a denial.

'Just so.'

'Bloody hell!'

'The ship's master, one Captain Hugh Gordon, confirmed his identity. Apparently, Moray audaciously introduced himself and his brother. Gordon's descriptions fit them perfectly. There was also a third operative — a young Australian woman, good-looking, short, dark-complexioned. Perhaps Aboriginal. But no other description. She wore dark glasses and called herself Gloria.'

Montrose sat rigid, while he waited for the raging in his skull to subside. He'd been outmanoeuvred...again. When he was finally able to speak, it came out as a croak. 'Butterstone, I'm holding you personally responsible for that man's recapture.'

'No one could have foreseen such an eventuality.'

'Where are they? How can we stop him?' Montrose reached for the red phone.

The commissioner continued his report: 'They took no hostages. Apparently, though, Gordon's wife was held at gunpoint during the operation. My men are checking that one out now. The captain, his crew, the ship's catering staff and all passengers were freed. However, one member of the crew, an engineer's mate by the name of William Warboys, is apparently still aboard. In any case, he's unaccounted for.'

Montrose found his full voice. 'Christ Almighty! I want that ship stopped. This is piracy, terrorism. Scotland cannot permit such an affront to go unanswered.'

'One more thing,' Butterstone sidestepped. 'The captain's statement indicates that the ship is carrying her maximum load of passengers, maybe a thousand, eleven hundred, possibly even more. As yet we have still not received the final tally from Caledonian's head office.'

'Where are they now?' asked Montrose again.

'You'll have to get the navy in on that one, Mr Prime Minister. Not my area of jurisdiction.' Butterstone went on cautiously, 'But speaking as a completely non-maritime man, I'd reckon — if they had their wits about them, and judging from the careful planning and execution of this operation, they do — they'll be doing a runner straight for English territorial waters, where essentially we cannot touch them.'

Montrose, hearing only deep-voiced femininity, slammed down the receiver. He rolled back his chair, got up and began to pace. Butterstone's head, swivelling like an owl's, followed him. 'He's only one man, for Chrissakes, one man, and he's destroying this entire nation. We have to stop him—'

Not to antagonise, Butterstone's reply was measured and thoughtful. 'Perhaps, if I may say so, Prime Minister, this calls for a policy reassessment. We' — respectfully substituted for the thought "you"—

Montrose wasn't listening. 'A thousand, you say?'

'Maybe more, with dependents.'

Montrose briefly lapsed into himself, and as quickly came out again. 'How many people know about this?'

'The absolute minimum. For the time being, all the ferry passengers and crew who came ashore have been sequestered at the Fernhill Hotel outside Portpatrick for further questioning and medical care.'

'Excellent. Keep it airtight. For as long as possible. We need every minute. It may be already too fucking late.' Angus Montrose went to the sideboard.

'As you say, Mr Prime Minister,' said Butterstone, as he considered what motives the hijackers might have for not blowing the whistle to the media.

The old man took out a fresh bottle — one of the many he'd received for his birthday — and a square glass. One thick hand held the brown bottle while the other twisted out the cork. He poured to the brim, and drank deeply, but not to the bottom. Montrose brought the glass and bottle back to his desk. The old bear slumped heavily into his chair, head down. When he again raised his face, it was transformed: warmer, calmer, and resigned—

Butterstone felt a certain pity for the man; but that he would have felt for any man trapped in a confused situation not of his own making. Pity, yes, respect, no. He should have resigned as Police Commissioner that day — the day of the Escape, the day of the Great Gale. Instead, he stood on Castle Hill watching the rainfall as too many citizens of Edinburgh needlessly lost their lives.

In his changed mood, Montrose said without rancour, 'You know what I say? I say, let him go. Let them all go—'

* * *

The day following the hijack, a neighbourhood London paper, The Strand, carried an exclusive angle on the nation's top story. An anonymous caller had tipped off the paper before the story was confirmed. The receptionist who took the call characterised the man's accent as 'English, with a strong smattering of Scottish in it'. He refused to identify himself or state his affiliation with any terrorist organisation, but he curiously wished her an 'early Merry Christmas'. E.T.

Chapter LX

'Vegetable Brimstone'

[Monday morning, November 30, 2009]
'I'll tell you what I'm thinking,' said Brew. '"...ram's-horn trumpets, empty clay pots, with torches in the pots"'[100] — the Biblical version of improvisation and deception. Only for us it'll be cardboard, a little wood, aluminium pipes, and a mixture of flare powder and these lycopodium spores—' He patted the jars.

The Rabbi's cool unnerved Guriat. 'Lyco...what?' she said, exasperated.

'Lycopodium or, if you prefer, vegetable brimstone—'

On the bridge Neville contemplated the empty sea, while Alec Ace concentrated on the main console dials and displays. Something wasn't adding up. Ace double-checked the GSL monitor. 'Can't be,' he muttered. He left the wheel to confirm the compass bearing. Spinning back to the console, the little man broke into lathered sweat. 'Damn and blast!'

Neville looked at him. 'What is it?'

'We've been going the wrong *effing* way. One-eight-three degrees *south* instead of one-three-eight *southeast*.'

Neville sickened. He hated himself; being Neville made him want to cry. Useless in every way. Bruised and beaten, unlovable, and now fumbling numbers. All his life he been a numerical dyslexic: the polar opposite of his brother.

Ace's eyes burned with idol-like concentration, as he punched buttons, reversed levers and flung the helm around to the new heading. All Neville could say was 'Is there anything I can do?' The little man, through rapid, shallow breaths, slurred, 'Just keep your eyes open. You see something, anything; you let us know, fast. It's my fault. I should have realised sooner...we've gone out of our way, that's all. Maybe lost half an hour.'

Neville gratefully escaped outside to the bridge wing. Though told to watch the sea and the sky, his eyes kept coming back to Guriat and the frenzied activity on the forecastle deck. One team of men and women were feverishly sawing wooden slats and cutting cardboard and plywood into odd shapes. A second group nailed the slats together to make two huge, multi-sided frames. When the skeletons were finished, the workers tacked the siding in place, leaving the front open. Others slapped on navy grey paint. Guriat and Brew, hands flailing, hurried on the workers. Two men Neville hadn't seen before — one blond, the other pony-tailed — appeared on deck. Each was carrying a long metal tube. Putting these down, they left but soon returned with two more tubes — shorter, narrower with three fins, and nosed-off at one end. Neville watched Ponytail and Blondy muzzle-load the finned tubes into the hollow outer casings. The assemblies looked like two huge mortars. Together with Brew and Guriat, the two men easily dragged the grey-painted outer structures a few

---

[100]The Rabbi alludes to the defeat of the Midianites by Gideon the Judge at the head of a small force equipped with only cacophony, fire and bluff. See Judg. 7.16.

feet forward to cover the tubes. From above, the two installations on the forecastle deck appeared aggressively poised for action.

The morning sky was arctic blue. A pair of seagulls swooped and dived in wide arcs around the ferry.

With the defence preparations completed, the Rabbi and Guriat returned to the lounge. Guriat expressed her uneasiness about the ship's isolation and vulnerability. She wanted to alert the media. If, she argued, Montrose knew that the world was watching the ferry, he'd think twice before trying anything.

Brew opposed a media feeding frenzy. Before he could explain himself, Jon Brodie and Judith Levitt came in to report that they had set the first watch. Each lookout had a hand-held radio set. Levitt said that the work on the bow had made people skittish. Rumours needed to be dampened. Guriat opposed Levitt's idea of ordering people below as counter-productive. Cramming everybody into the lower, more secure decks was bound to set off a wave of fear and defeatism, or worse, cause panic. Guriat suggested a practice lifeboat drill to establish a shipboard routine. Brew backed the idea as a "vaccine" against the real thing—

Brew went to the bridge to brief Neville and Ace on the current state of play. When asked about the ship's progress, Neville hedged, 'Compass says we're sailing as straight as a curved line on a curved surface.' He saw no benefit in confessing the delay he'd caused. Ace's silence made him an accessory.

The Rabbi joked, 'Mr Ace, open hailing frequencies, if you will.'[101] Ace flicked on the PA system. The Rabbi, his voice resonating with warmth, praised everyone aboard for choosing life for themselves and for their children. He cheerfully announced that the ferry would soon reach English waters, that the weather forecast was good, and that in an hour's time there would be a *dry-run* lifeboat drill. Until further instructions, he advised everybody to relax. To conclude, he read the traditional travellers' prayer for peace on their voyage—

Brew left the wheelhouse to join Guriat on the forecastle deck. Neville resumed his watch on the bridge wing. The sky was strangely quiet. The shrill cry of the gulls was gone. Visoring his eyes, he searched the horizon. He locked on to something moving. Two black specks were coming in fast and low over the water. Neville pointed. The blur of the powerful rotors was fast becoming a distinct grey circle against the blue of the sky. Neville's shouted warning stuck in his throat. The two helicopters flew straight at the ferry. Neville heard panicked shrieks from the decks below. At the last moment the attackers swept sharply upward, passing just metres from the bridge. Neville staggered back, plugging his ears against the engines' turbo-driven scream. Marked with the blue and white St Andrew's flag, the war-drabbed aircraft carried black fangs of heavy cannon and rockets.

The helicopters looped for another run.

Ace pushed the ship's engines to their limit. At full speed, the hull vibrated alarmingly. Frantic voices on the forecastle called out final orders.

The second pass was slower. The two helicopters hovered off the bow. A loudhailer warning was issued. The engine noise drowned out the message, but its thrust was clear: turn back or suffer the consequences. Brew Moray shouted with all his might to the bridge, 'Do not change course! Do not slow down!'

On watch, Jonathan Brodie panicked and fired off a harmless smoke flare. In retaliation the lead helicopter unleashed a brief burst of cannon fire. The shells ripped through the top deck into the crowded club lounge.

---

[101] A catch phrase from *Star Trek*, a popular television series of the late 20th and early 21st centuries.

Deborah had come up to the club lounge only moments before to collect cups. The storm of jagged metal and flying glass exploded all around her. Terror-stricken, she held herself in her arms and shut her eyes. Her ears rang. In less than a second it was over. Out of the grotesque shrieking emerged sobs and moans. Deborah opened her eyes to a hideous scene of bloodied, writhing bodies. Her stomach turned. She buckled, and puked.

One anguished cry, 'My baby, my boy,' rose hysterically above all the others. As the force drained out of her voice, 'My baby, my boy,' began to sound like a pitiable lullaby. People nearest her who could crawl or creep shied away. On her knees, clutching the lifeless body to her breast, the woman rocked as though her child slept. Sticky and dark red, his head drooped limply like a dead rose bud. A long glass blade lodged in the back of his neck. And tugging relentlessly at the crazed mother's sleeve, a terrified little girl half cried, half screamed, 'Mummy, Mummy, Mummy.'

Deborah's sickness on the carpet stared back at her. The sight and smell of it hit her like a slap in the face. She pulled herself up, and went to comfort Sophie. The child in her arms was Benny—

Neville peered inside the wheelhouse. Unflinching, Alec Ace craned forward over the helm, as if pushing the ship forward by willpower alone.

Brew Moray took up position at the tip end of the forecastle, facing forward. Guriat stood between the two grey boxes, as they were being slowly pushed back from within. From above, the mechanical effect looked real. When fully exposed, the tubes appeared as ominous weapons of war. Brew, his beard bent sideways in the breeze, stretched both arms over his head.

Meanwhile, the two marauders circled for another sortie. As their shrill roar built up behind him, Brew jerked his arms even higher. Guriat, after looking from side to side at the boxes, nodded affirmatively. The helicopters swooped and dived. The first flew low, beating the ocean into a white froth; the second followed close behind, flying higher. They came straight in over the bow, aiming to knock out the bridge.

The first attacker opened up with rattling cannon fire. Neville gaped at the arrows of flame throwing up ivory teeth of sea water. At the last moment, he crouched and covered his head.

Brew threw down his left arm. Guriat yelled: *'WARBOYS!'* Almost instantaneously, a roaring whoosh cleared the portside tube. The rocket trailed a bright yellow plume of fire and smoke. Brew's right arm came down. *'HARRISON!'* shouted Guriat. The second launch, like the first, shot out, cutting another erratic path across the sky.

A deep-throated shock wave split the air. Where the two helicopters collided, a cloud of black smoke and flame spewed charred metal in all directions. When the fireball hit the water, it exploded again. The sea sizzled.

The whole ship rocked violently. The force of the blast threw Brew and Guriat to the safety of the deck. The flimsy box-covers were blown away. The rocket tubes, twisted from the launch, sprawled on the deck like dead insects. The operators, Warboys and Harrison, scrambled for cover along the bulwarks. Fiery, flying debris hit the ferry as Ace took evasive action to avoid ploughing into the boiling crash site. Neville, keeping low, dived headlong into the wheelhouse, gasping, 'What the hell! What the hell happened?'

'Didn't you see it, man? What a pair of duds—' cried Ace. 'Spectacular fireworks! Extravaganza of the century!' Neville shook his head stupidly as Ace went on, 'Copter No One bought the missiles for the real thing. He evaded, pulled up straight into the path of No Two. And BOOM! Nothing!' Ace was beaming.

'Damn nothing!' cried Neville, panting wildly. 'Those pilots...are dead. It could have been us!'

'But it wasn't us. Big difference,' answered Ace. Before he could say anything more, a roar — a lusty, great cheer — erupted from below. It seemed everyone was on deck.

Ace pointed out towards the horizon, 'It's over. You can relax. Here come the Royal Navy.' Two English destroyers were fast approaching.

Neville stumbled outside again. On the forecastle deck below he saw men and women dancing in circles, and leaping on each other like footballers celebrating a winning goal. His brother was wrapped in Guriat's arms. She was whirling around with him, and shouting at the top of her voice, 'It worked! It worked! Just like you said it would!'

* * *

Chapter LXI

Prime Minister's Question Time

[Monday-Tuesday, November 30/December 1, 2009]
'That last question, Sir—?' asked Keller, catching up.

As usual Montrose had dispatched the opposition with his tried-and-tested formula of bombast and ridicule. He was striding along the portrait-lined corridor, back to his office at the far end of Parliament House.

'Sir—'

'Remind me, Kenneth, which question would that be?'

'The very last, Sir, the question about the two missing helicopters—'

Montrose had couched his short opening statement on the hijacking to the Scottish Parliament, the Estates, in the studied language of diplomacy: Scotland demanded that England return the ferry and that the hijackers be punished. He saved his sharpest barbs for parliamentary question time.

'As I said, a training accident...over the North Sea—'

Keller questioned, 'An accident...in the clearest weather we've had all winter?'

Montrose stopped short. With the formidable, dark portrait of the Abbot of Cambuskenneth looking over his shoulder, the Prime Minister's bulk appeared diminished. In a dry voice, he asked, 'What are you implying, Mr Keller?'

'I'm not implying, Prime Minister. I'm asking—'

'Once more—' The PM's two bodyguards, sensing that privacy was called for, moved back to a discreet distance, out of earshot. 'A regrettable mishap, a collision during a routine training exercise, pilots missing, families informed, and the deceaseds' names to be withheld pending an enquiry.'

'However, Sir, there's the timing—'

'Unfortunate. Pure coincidence.'

Keller went on. 'Don't you see, Prime Minister? Such a coincidence has already led to speculation. The question, as asked, insinuated that the loss of the two helicopter gunships is somehow connected with the hijacking incident. How will the government answer these charges if the media or some independent body were to follow up—?'

'There were no witnesses. No one to ask—'

'I'm afraid, Prime Minister, there's no easy way to say this. I believe there's a cover-up going on. The evidence—' Keller's voice melted. He looked to Montrose for an honest answer.

'Absurd! And now, Mr Party Chairman, if that's all — it's getting late—' The Abbot's cairngorm grey eyes stared in a downward line that fell on the old man.

Keller persisted, 'Then deny it, please.'

'Keller, your remarks here could be construed to constitute either rank insubordination or a pathological inclination to political self-destruction—'

'I am perfectly aware of what I am saying, and what I am thinking. For once, Sir, they're the same.'

'Kenneth, perhaps a rest, a break—'

A pair of deputies deep in whispered conversation were approaching. Keller waited for them to pass. For their benefit Montrose took the Party Chairman's hand in a warm, fatherly handshake. When let go, Keller looked up, past the old man and saw the Abbot. There was stern, uncompromising reproach in his smoky eyes, but also a certain painful regret. Keller kept his voice low. 'I'm thinking things, terrible things, that I am not wanting to think. I'm thinking that there was shooting this morning, that people died. Women—? Children—?'

Montrose spoke evenly, convincingly. 'My orders were "to turn the ship back, no shooting". There was no shooting, no killing, and no gunships. A spotter plane located the vessel in Scottish waters, but by the time a naval cutter arrived on the scene, it was too late. The ferry had made English territorial waters and two Royal Navy destroyers turned the cutter back. That's all.'

'Prime Minister, I want to believe you—'

'Keller—'

'I called Air Force Command— Admiralty House— The Secretary of Defence— Everybody says the same thing, "Speak to Montrose." I am now speaking to Montrose. I am asking—'

'You're overstepping your office—'

'Did some trigger-happy pilot fire on that ship? Was there any shooting?'

Through tightly rounded lips, Montrose hissed a voiceless 'No!'

'Then what happened to those two helicopters?'

'For the last time, there was an unfortunate accident — yes — which occurred in a coincidental time frame. But — it took place on the other side of the country, two hundred miles away. An Air Force enquiry committee is already investigating the cause of the crash.' Montrose shifted from one leg to another, blocking out the Abbot's righteous gaze.

'For your sake, Sir, I dearly hope the press don't start stirring up the coals. With all the hullabaloo over the hijacking, it's likely nobody will miss a couple of helicopters. As for me, you'll be relieved to know that I'll be keeping my reservations to myself. Not out of respect for you, nor out of party loyalty, but because I'm a Scotsman, a Scotsman who is too afraid to face the truth about his own country.' Montrose retreated half a step, placing his head between the Abbot's ears. Keller went on. 'And for some twisted, crazy reason that I cannot fathom, Moray — according to all reports — is refusing to allow anyone on board, or even near that ferry. I can't help thinking, he's saving our souls. Dear Christ, he's saving *our* souls.' Finished, Keller let his head hang, turned and walked away.

Unable to move, Montrose called down the corridor, 'Keller, I'm not done with you yet.' The call left his throat a dry croak. The bodyguards pretended not to hear. People were coming. Montrose turned to the wall and, feigning admiration of the portrait, met Cambuskenneth's smoking glare. He pondered the brooding visage longer than he intended. His eye settled on the monk's tightly pressed lips. And on the hairline cracks of time in the pinkness of their painted flesh.

*

Returning to his office, Montrose cut himself off. He cancelled his last meetings of the day and let Mrs Jamieson go. He uncorked a fresh bottle. Between drinks, the copper hammer beat time as pandemonium raged in his skull. At last Montrose passed out. He came to after midnight, knowing what he had to do. As he punched in the red-phone code for the Admiral of the Navy, he vowed, 'No, I'm not done with you yet.' His call was automatically diverted. The Admiral was at home, asleep. Montrose skipped the pleasantries. 'I need an entirely private, highly confidential meeting with you, tonight—'

* * *

Chapter LXII

'This Much'

[Monday-Tuesday, November 30/December 1, 2009]

Sophie sat on the floor behind the bar. Her ankles were crossed, her knees folded up. Her hands like ivory, cold and white, covered her face. Brew gently clasped one wrist. 'Soph, show me your eyes.'

'There's nothing in them to see.'

He began to ramble: 'You know, when we were in hiding, in the Landis's old shop, I went out once. The Sabbath was barely over. I didn't tell Debs where I was going; I just left. She still doesn't know where I went. Soph, I need to tell you this—

'I saw Jemima Roscoe...Rev Roscoe's daughter. I had to see her, to say something. Her dad died in Edinburgh Castle. Jemima has a boy, a baby called Roy, like his grandfather. Jemima...she's...a wee touch slow.

'On the walk over I worked out what I wanted to say, but the moment she let me in, everything flew straight out of my head. I couldn't even her look in the face.

'She sat me down, and asked me if I'd come to see "the Reverend", because if I had, she said, "He's dead". I said, "I'm very sorry". Then I sat, that's all. I don't know quite how long it took me to tell her who I was. "Oh," she said like she'd been expecting me, "the Scottish rabbi. Father told me so many lovely things about you—" I simply had no words. She said it so honestly, like a child. I didn't know what to say. Then she said, "Look at me." I did — for the first time that evening. Before, I'd been too afraid. She knew it, too. She knew so much. I...I can't explain it, Soph, but she knew who I was, I mean really was, inside. And what's more important, she knew that I was fooling myself. I thought I'd come to offer her my sympathies. I really came, because I needed something from her.

'Anyway, I looked into her eyes. She was beautiful. She beamed every time little Roy gurgled. She began to tell me her stories. "Jemima and the Two Roys" she called them. Through them, I discovered wisdom in her. She taught me new and deeper meanings for love and dignity. But more than anything else, she understood loss. "Loss is gain," she said, "as long as you don't forget the loss, there's always gain." Then for an hour more she did nothing but rock the baby, while I wrestled with Roy's memory.

'Her place was in a mess. I could see she was trying. But alone, without any outside help, she wasn't coping. I could see that. And she, herself, without Roy, had no one to love her and care for her.

'All of a sudden she put the baby down, and stood up. I got up too, thinking she was wanting me to go. She knew I still didn't understand. She came straight over to me, and put her arms around me and held me.

'You see, Soph, what I'm trying to say is I needed her to forgive me—

'We sat down again. And I started telling her about the Highlands. You know, she'd never been there. What she couldn't imagine were the colours, the purple of the heather, the green meadows, blue lakes and sea, golden summer sunsets, and white snow. All she'd ever known was Murrayfield, and Edinburgh grey stone. I told her that she didn't have to imagine the Highlands, that I could take her and the baby there. And if she liked it, she could stay.

'I have to tell you, Soph, I was lying through my teeth when I said that, I mean the staying part.

'"Take us, now," she said. "In the middle of the night?" I asked. "Yes, now." We got her and the baby in Roy's old banger, and all the way up, I was so scared. After all my promises. She trusted me, and I was leading her on.

'Who else did I know in the Highlands but the Frasers? Soph, they were the people who took us in. Alan and Becky had enough with three kids of their own, and a herd of sheep, and here I was bringing them two more mouths to feed. When I think about it, when I hear myself telling you this, it was crazy— What I was asking those poor, good folk to do—'

Sophie slowly let her hands slip into her skirt. Her eyes were red and shiny moist.

Brew cleared his throat. 'Dr Ross needs you. There's a man injured. Badly. Jon Brodie. If he doesn't have surgery, and soon, he'll die.'

'I can't. Look at me, Brew, I'm in no state. You know—'

'You can. I know you can. You're a nurse.'

'Why me? Are there no other nurses—?'

'I have no right, Soph, to ask you to do this, no right at all. But Dr Ross is old, and afraid. He doesn't want to operate. He's afraid to lose another life. He wants me to stop the ship. To get Jon off to a hospital on land. I can't do that. I can't. Because I'm forcing *him* to operate, he's demanding that *you* assist. He thinks, well, he thinks you won't do it.'

'But, I...I never did any real nursing.'

'Ross refuses to operate unless *you* assist. Jon will die if you don't help. With your help he has a chance. You've got to try. If there were any other way—'

Sophie gave her hands to her brother. He came to his feet, and then raised her. She said gravely, 'There've been too many funerals already.'

Guriat Gaoni left her specially set-up radio room on the bridge deck for a breath of air. Though it was getting dark, and the weather was turning heavier and colder, her face was, as usual, masked behind shaded glasses.

She saw the Harrisons. The ponytailed man who'd fired one of the rockets and his puppy-eyed partner with their baby stood leaning against a rail. Their wind-blown outlines were black against the grey mist. Guriat went over, and together all three talked quietly about the day.

Lulls in the conversation were filled by dreary blasts and clangs coming from the sea all around. The constellation of twinkling green and red lights, visible between clouds of rolling dampness, seemed to be growing. Guriat moved to the rail for a better look. The ferry, sailing between two Royal Navy destroyer escorts, had become the nucleus of a flotilla of curiosity seekers and seaborne media.

'A tower—' said Lindy Harrison dreamily, without any particular cause. 'Rabbi Moray might be small, but he's a tower of strength.' She kissed her baby's forehead. Guriat wondered that the infant didn't seem to mind the cold and damp one bit. Todd picked up the thread, 'Cor! The way he conducted those funerals this morning— To stand up before that poor, weeping mother, his own sister, like he did — with her wee, dead kid lying between him and her — Cor! That was the toughest thing I ever saw in my life. Did ya see her face? I could hardly bear to look — but the Rabbi, he wipes her tears with his handkerchief, then — unbelievable! — he folds it into the wee body's sheet. I'll never forget that as long as I live—'

'What I don't understand,' said the woman, 'is why this boat's got to keep going.'

Guriat related the incident in her radio room — how the Rabbi persuaded a Royal Navy commander that theirs was no act of piracy, and that the ferry and her passengers must be allowed to proceed through English waters, unhindered. The captain was dubious, but agreed to consult his superiors. The Israeli agent went on, 'The question must have gone straight to the Prime Minister, because half an hour later, the destroyer captain was back on the horn. Blunt as a kangaroo's bottom, he says, "Seems you're in luck, Rabbi. Prime Minister Blakemore and His Majesty's Government are apparently prepared to do anything to rattle Montrose. You're on your way. Good luck."'

'By now the whole world must know about what happened to us this morning,' said Lindy, proudly.

'Not a bit of it,' returned Guriat, prickling with exasperation. 'You saw! He had us cover the damage on the top deck with that tarpaulin. The Royal Navy offered every assistance. Not that they really know what happened, either. Just a couple of blips disappearing off a radar screen. Anyway, he refused their help. Neither will our Rabbi allow any media people aboard. He asked the Navy to keep all planes, helicopters and ships at least a mile away. And nobody leaves this ship...except the dead.' Guriat's sardonic tone sent a shiver through Lindy. 'The doctor, Ross, begged him to at least let off the wounded. And somehow, Moray got his own sister to help the old man save Brodie's life.'

Todd whistled through his teeth, then asked, 'But I still don't understand, why the quarantine? Think what the publicity would do for our cause.'

'I regret to say it, mate,' said the Israeli agent, 'but I think our Rabbi's direct line to the ON HIGH has developed some static.' They shook their heads. 'Why? you ask. "Because" — he says — "*we* fired first." A couple of lousy smoke flares, and it's all *our* fault. If anyone got off this boat, he believes that they would either be silenced, permanently, before they could talk to the press, or if they did manage to talk, they'd be putting the lives of those who stayed behind in Scotland on the line.'

'How so?' asked the young mother.

'Anti-Semitic backlash, ultra-nationalist violence, police roundups, arrests in the night—'

He came up from behind, slid a hand under Guriat's arm and sharply spun her round. She spat, 'Hey! You crazy sonuva—!' Neville released her, but shot her a hard glare rabid with anger. Flushed, she said to the young couple, 'This is Rabbi Moray's brother, Neville,' and to him, 'Lindy Berman and Todd Harrison, from Dundee.' Todd played with the baby's blanket as Lindy's eyes swept the deck with embarrassment.

Neville ignored the introduction. 'Dance with my brother again, and— You leave *him* alone. Understand? Leave him *alone*.'

Deborah's first day at sea had lasted well into the night. When she finally got to bed, her body switched off, falling into a deep, concentrated sleep. But her disturbed mind played on. After a couple of hours, she woke up shaking. Brew wrapped her in his arms, stroking and soothing her. Her trembling subsided. 'Brew— I can't stop thinking: what if he'd been our child?'

'You mean, how could you have forgiven me.'

'No, Brew. Don't say that. Please. That's not what I mean. I mean Sophie, her anguish, it'll be with her for the rest of her life, day and night, forever.'

'Debs, they cheered me today. And I danced. I danced, while you were taking Benny from her arms. That took far more courage than anything I did. What's it like to hold a lifeless two-year old boy, Debs? Tell me.'

'Brew, you're punishing us both.'

'He was a baby. What did Benny Banks do? Eat and sleep. For that he was made to bleed and die? And be dropped into the sea? No grave, no marker, no nothing. Just a ripple—' Anger spilled into self-recrimination. 'What right, what authority did I, Brew Moray, have to sacrifice a child on the altar of "we, the Jewish people"?' Deborah could not answer his pain. 'And what was my answer to death? The empty ritual of a Jewish funeral. Soph's eyes were begging me to say something, anything to heal her hurt. Mother, too. I wanted to say, Benny would still be alive, if it hadn't been for me and my dream. That was the truth. But I was too much of a coward for the truth. So I puffed air, the ancient rituals.'

'Brew, you mustn't blame yourself. *She* doesn't. Somebody asked her to appeal to you to stop the ship. Right after the funeral. Can you believe it? The insensitivity! She refused. She told me herself, this evening. She's your sister. She put herself through Brodie's surgery only for *your* sake. And the operation was a success! You didn't kill Benny, and you helped to save Mr Brodie.'

'Still, I am responsible. I can't shake it. And you feel responsible, too. Don't deny it. Didn't you stay with Soph this evening, only because you're my wife?'

'I wanted to see her sleep. That's all. I stayed until she fell asleep.'

'And tomorrow when she wakes up?'

'I'll go to her again.'

'Debs, there's a phrase from the Sages that's gone through my head, and won't go away. "Dreams are unripe fruit..."[102] Why unripe fruit? I never understood why until today. It's sour! Three dead and twelve wounded. Our enemies also — dead, incinerated. And it's only the first day. Why must Jewish survival always have to feed on death and suffering? What kind of CREATOR is it WHO makes a woman a wife and a mother, then takes away her husband, and then her child? WHO hands down the death sentence to a little boy even before he knows who he is—'

'Brew—' cut in Deborah, 'how much do you love me?' She had never asked him before.

Brew pulled her close to his body, caressed her and kissed her. When love was over, he said only, 'This much.'

* * *

The tarpaulin used to cover the top deck was most certainly the ship's emergency signal sheet. Fabricated from a special reflective material, the sheet was designed to enable navigational satellites to detect and pinpoint a vessel in distress. However, the intense reflectivity "blind-spotted" or "burned out" the centre of every computer-enhanced eye-in-the-sky image taken of the Praise. *In other words, the damage inflicted on the hijacked ferry by the Scottish helicopters was blotted out from every high-resolution photograph of the ship, whether generated from high-altitude planes or spacecraft. The tarpaulin, in this instance, became yet another in the small, seemingly insignificant accidents of destiny that came together to forge Rabbi Brew Moray's dream into a Twenty-first century miracle. E.T.*

---

[102]The complete sentence is "Dreams are the unripe fruit of prophecy" from the Midrashic commentary *Bereshit Rabba*, 17.

Chapter LXIII

Bonar Bridge

[Tuesday pre-dawn, December 1, 2009]
By the time he put the phone down, the Admiral was wide awake. The pale-lit digits on the radio-clock by his bedside flashed one-twenty-one. His wife murmured, 'What is it?' and immediately rolled over back to sleep. He got up, dressed — though not in his white uniform — and went to the lounge to wait.

Montrose, after a short battle with his security team, drove himself. Driving was no longer habitual for him. He had to concentrate on the mechanics. But in the dark hours of the morning there was virtually no traffic. The five-mile run out to Cramond tempted him to speed. He resisted.

The Admiral understood why the Prime Minister cut the mandarins from Ministry of Defence out of the decision-making process: Bureaucrats only delay, while sometimes politicians have to make on-spot decisions in accordance with which the military must act. He'd been following the crisis minutely. His mind was awash with contingencies. The Navy man reviewed the first pages of his notepad:

> Duchess of Galloway, short-run, roll-on/roll-off ferry
>> a) Total fuel capacity, 180 tonnes including reserves
>> b) Maximum range at full fuel, +/-1,500 miles
>> c) Service speed, 19 knots
> Chart and Navigation Department report
>> a) Cairnryan-to-Gibraltar (Atlantic leg), 1,407 miles; 3 days' sailing time non-stop, full speed
>> b) Gibraltar-to-Haifa, Israel (Mediterranean leg), 2,310 miles; +4 days' sailing time non-stop, full speed
>> c) Cairnryan-to-Haifa, Israel, total distance 3,717 miles; +/-7 days' sailing time non-stop, full speed
>> NOTE: All calculations based on optimal weather, course and shipboard conditions; estimated sailing time of complete voyage likely to be *in excess* of 7 days; long-range weather forecast, average for time of year
> Intelligence reports
>> a) Present fuel on board 90 tonnes; ship's manifest shows fuel tanker truck aboard carrying diesel oil good for approximately another +/-190 miles
>> b) English/Zionist interests able to ensure the ferry will reach the Royal Navy base at Gibraltar for refuelling and revictualling (civilian car ferry services at Gibraltar are owned/operated by a North African state inimical to Zionist immigration policy)
>> c) Middle Eastern (Islamic) forces to prevent any further attempts to refuel the ferry en route throughout the Med leg
>> d) +1,000 people aboard; food and water supplies will be stretched beyond their limits during the Med leg

<u>Conclusions</u>
  a) The ferry's present range with added tanker truck oil is a maximum of 1,690 miles, against the Gibraltar-Haifa voyage of 2,310 miles
  b) Hijacked vessel's ultimate destination is, therefore, +/-620 miles beyond the ship's range unless additional fuel oil can be taken on during the Med leg →
  HIGHLY UNLIKELY

Yes, whatever the question, he was primed to answer it. The only thing he couldn't know was exactly what the 'old boy' expected of the Navy.

The moment he heard Montrose's car, he opened the door, and ushered his guest through to the study. Angus Montrose declined all hospitality. The Admiral picked up his notepad again.

Montrose came straight to the point. 'What have we got to stop them?'

The Admiral repeated, 'To stop them reaching their destination—' As he started to turn over the pages of his pad, Montrose gently removed it from him, saying, 'You know you don't need this.' The pad shook in the old man's hand.

'No, Sir,' answered the Admiral. 'The way intelligence reckons it, they will have to swim the last six hundred miles.'

'I haven't made myself clear,' said Montrose. 'I mean, *stop them*.'

The Admiral's features hardened. 'Stop them— That calls for an undetected silent strike capability. The *Bonar Bridge*—'

For Montrose, the *Bonar Bridge* needed no introduction. At the time of independence, H.M.S. *Mars* was in a Clydebank dry dock, undergoing a refit. His Majesty's government were infuriated when Scotland 'appropriated' the vessel. At the time of her acquisition, naval officials advised the Scottish government that she was 'old but serviceable'. During the protracted negotiations for the return of the craft to England, she was 'temporarily' commissioned into the newly formed Scottish Navy and renamed—

'The *Bonar Bridge*,' the Admiral went on, 'is currently in the Red Sea, officially on manoeuvres.'

Montrose reflected. Officially on manoeuvres, unofficially delivering the first instalment of Dounreay uranium, weapons grade, to Scotland's Middle East arms dealer. He said, 'Red Sea— Far from home. Admiral— How long would take to bring her into the Mediterranean?'

'Through the Suez Canal, on a good day, twelve to fifteen hours.'

Montrose laid down the pad, and asked, 'What really happened?'

'Sir—?'

'To the two helicopters we sent—'

'Really happened—? I don't know. Nobody knows. Nobody was there.'

'Except them—' The shaking in Montrose's large hands was growing stronger.

The Admiral went on, 'Maybe they have weapons, surface-to-air missiles, hand-held, possibly Israeli-made. Or, it was an accident. We'll never know—'

'An accident...a training accident— Isn't that what I said?' The Admiral looked at his hands. 'Yes, they're shaking—' said Montrose, '...for the first time in my life. Our submarine. How long did you say? Twelve to fifteen hours through the canal?'

'That's right, Sir.'

'Do it.'

* * *

Chapter LXIV

'Brew's Jews'

[Friday afternoon, December 11, 2009]

Brew's daily briefings with Guriat outside the radio room followed a pattern. First he said the Afternoon Service alone on deck, and then allowed himself a few quiet moments to commune with his thoughts. Or let his mind blank out to the rhythm of the waves slapping against the ship's side.

Guriat maintained a twenty-four hour watch, eating and sleeping next to the radio. He knew she was waiting for his knock. But he needed a few extra moments before the Sabbath began to wrestle with events—

The voyage was taking longer, much longer than anyone expected. For one thing, the stopover at Gibraltar for fuel and food took seventy-two hours instead of the planned thirty-six. At the insistence of Rebbe Frankelstein and his small band of Hassidic Jews, the *Praise* stayed on at the Royal Navy installation for an Orthodox Sabbath. Anchored offshore in "crisis quarantine", no one was allowed on or off. Moments after dark on Saturday evening, as soon as the Sabbath was over, tugs nosed the hijacked vessel out to sea. In the opinion of most aboard ship, the added thirty-six hours' stopover amounted to a unforgivable waste of time.

To bring the ferry through the Mediterranean, Guriat put engineer's mate William Warboys in charge of fuel management. Warboys immediately reduced engine speed to three-quarters to conserve fuel. He pumped out the diesel oil from the articulated tanker truck into the ship's reserves. He also siphoned off diesel from the fuel tanks of the other lorries on board. But Warboys said that it was still not enough to make up the difference between the ferry's maximum range and the distance she had to cover. He remembered that it was possible to extend crude diesel fuel with motor oil and antifreeze drained from the cars. At Guriat's request he removed the petrol, too, storing it in the empty tanker truck. As each vehicle was emptied, it was dumped overboard to lighten the ship. As a last resort, Warboys declared that the alcohol content in the ferry's generous inventory of spirits was also a suitable fuel ingredient. The ship's engines coughed and spluttered on the unorthodox mixture but, nevertheless, continued to produce motive power.

Yet for all the good he did, Warboys was despised. He was peculiar looking, he made himself obnoxious, and he abused the power he was given. And at every opportunity he reminded people of the heroic courage he'd shown in launching one of the decoy rockets. It was a one-off. The man was scared of his own shadow. Brew distrusted Warboys. It troubled his soul to think ill of an outsider just because he was an outsider,[103] but like many others, could not help his feelings. Still, Warboys was not universally shunned. He appeared to have at least one important friend and ally: Rabbi Felix Frankelstein. The two were often seen together.

On the bridge, Alec Ace piloted the ship with skill and devotion. The little man left the helm only to relieve himself. Short bursts of sleep on a blanket on the floor were all he allowed himself. He spent hours patiently poring over charts and instruments to plot the

---

[103] "Do not hurt the feelings of the foreigner, nor oppress him, for you were foreigners in Egypt." Ex. 22.20.

most fuel-efficient course. In his role as mate, Neville stayed with 'Acey' at all times, as much to avoid *her* as to help him. Though Brew was drawn to Alec Ace, anything he said to him seemed to come out tainted and insensitive, in the way of the great patronising the small. So Brew only came up to the bridge when absolutely necessary.

A motley fleet dogged the hijacked ferry. Civilian craft of all descriptions carried the media and the just plain curious. The naval vessels of five nations — Scotland, England, the US, Israel and a broadly backed Islamic "suicide ship" — created a standoff. The circle of ships maintained a "safe distance" from the *Praise*. Brew likened the situation to 'a fluid chess game in which each piece on the liquid board holds every other piece in check.' Guriat Gaoni used a different, more disturbing metaphor. 'It's like we're floating at the centre of a delicate, protective bubble, and only a perfect balance of forces, inside and out, keeps the thin film of our bubble intact.'

If there were to be another attack, given the circumstances it could only come by stealth. Guriat's answer to stealth was surprise. She devised a terrible weapon of destruction. Like the rockets that defeated the helicopters, her "unit" had to work the first time; there would be no second chance. Brew's mind replayed what he told her more than once, 'As loose canons go, this idea of yours is at least as dangerous to us as it is them. Whoever *they* may be—' Brew shuddered at the vision of himself behind the wheel. For the driver it was practically suicide.

Thank HEAVEN, he thought, that since the helicopter attack, there'd been no further loss of life. *Praise* was coming through. Their ordeal was nearly over. The end was almost in sight — only a hundred and sixty miles to go, less than a day's sailing. But, with Friday night and the beginning of their second Sabbath at sea fast approaching, the final stretch of their voyage would have to wait twenty-five hours longer, for the Day of Rest to pass. Again, Rebbe Felix Frankelstein would not bend. With no immediate danger threatening them, the ship had to stop for the Sabbath day—[104]

Brew looked over a grey and choppy Mediterranean. Cold came with the dusk. He was ready to hear her news, and to deliver his. He knocked on the radio room door.

'Rabbi—?' she asked from inside.

'Yes—' He had no easy name for her. Guriat was too familiar; Ms Gaoni, too formal. So he usually didn't call her anything.

She came out on deck, and began with, 'I have a confession to make.'

'A confession—?'

Guriat slowly took off her sunglasses, and stared at him shamelessly, as she began, 'This won't be easy for me to say, but here goes. There've been times, when I felt like I could have thrown you off this bloody boat. I was arrogant, and thought the worse of you. I see now I was wrong. Each and every one of your decisions has proven itself. You seem to see just that little bit further than us mortal souls. I'm saying this now, because I might not get another chance after we land.'

Brew's eyes did not flinch from hers. He was the first man she ever met who made her turn her gaze away. She lost herself in some undefined point in space. The ocean's surface seemed to be boiling under the solid grey of the sky.

Brew followed her line of vision. 'The sea is angry with me.'

'Why?' she asked, unable to look at him. 'Why do you say that? Angry with *me*.'

---

[104] A consensus of opinion among the Talmudic Sages gave Jewish sailors the liberty to violate the Sabbath in order to save the ship from the immediate danger of storms or enemies in accordance with the principle "that the duty of saving life supersedes the Sabbath laws". However in practice, what constitutes "immediate danger", and at what point the Sabbath may be violated is left up to the individuals concerned (Cf. Tractate *Eruvim* 4.8 and *Mishna Yoma* 3.6).

'Because something's telling me, I'm not going to make it. I'm not obeying my instincts. I should have overruled Frankelstein. Sabbath or no Sabbath, we should be going full steam ahead. Instead, we're stopping.'

Guriat raised her face to his. 'I was hoping—' she said tenderly, daring to think he might— The Rabbi was elsewhere. 'I was hoping...to be home for Hanukkah. First candle, this evening.'[105]

Planting both hands on the railing and fixing on the horizon, Brew asked, 'Do you remember when you brought me paper to the shop, you told us about a mountain you saw in the wilderness? Tell me, now, what did it look like?'

'Like a pile of rocks. A low pile at that. Not really very impressive—'

'No, I need to know. How did the mountain appear, exactly? What shape did it have?'

Guriat wasn't sure where to begin. 'Well, if you ask, like a giant, broken tree trunk. The top was incredibly jagged, and the rubble swept down the sides in ridges like old roots.'

'Yes, that's it. Please, go on.'

'There's not much more to say. Other than it's completely alone, just a big lump on the desert floor. Some Bedouin believe it's the remains of a colossal tower surrounded by the ruins of an ancient city. Others will tell you there's a legend—'

'The legend the doctor told you, yes—'

'All the legend says is that ALLAH brought the remains of Mussa, Moses, across the Jordan from the heights where he was buried to the mountain, so that his tomb might never be found.'

'And you said you climbed it, this mountain?' He asked as if the answer meant everything.

'Yes—'

'And—'

'And nothing, nothing there. Certainly, no tomb of Moses.'

Brew displayed no emotion. 'I see. And the name of the mountain, you said it was something like the Mountain of the Salt Land.'

'Yes, that's right. In Arabic, it's called Jebel el Sabha. Why all this interest in a lonely old mountain, anyway?'

Brew answered tonelessly, 'Let's just say, I think I've been there, too, and leave it at that.'

The subject was closed, so Guriat said, 'Better be getting back inside. Oh, by the way,' she said holding him a moment longer, 'my informants tell me that the world's got a name for us.'

The Rabbi flashed her his wryest smile.

'They're calling us "Brew's Jews."'

* * *

---

[105]The Hanukkah holiday commemorates the re-dedication of the Temple in Jerusalem after it had been desecrated by the Hellenistic Syrians. Only a single vial of untouched consecrated oil was found in the Temple after the Syrians were driven out (Tractate *Shabbat* 21b). The amount of oil it contained was only enough to burn for one day in the Temple's Menorah, yet it lasted for eight days until more pure, consecrated oil could be produced. To celebrate the miracle, Jews light a single flame (candles or oil lamps) on the first night, and then another flame is added every evening over the next seven days for a total of eight flames. The lights are kindled at sunset, except on Friday when, in order not to transgress the Sabbath ban on lighting a fire, the lights are lit before sunset. In 2009 (Jewish year 5770) the festival began on the evening of Friday, December 11.

Chapter LXV

Operation Lone Wolf

[Friday-Saturday night, December 11-12, 2009]
The red phone brought the Admiral to attention. He stared at the receiver, clicked open a pen. The hot line burbled three times before he picked up, stating his name clearly into the receiver. The phone fell dead a few seconds for voice/number verification. He'd been expecting the call, but hoping it would not happen. The line opened again. 'Operation Lone Wolf. Proceed. Tonight.' The dial tone returned. The Admiral held the receiver a long second before putting it down. Montrose's five clipped words buzzed in his ears.

The Admiral pushed back his chair, and rose with military precision. He never thought the ferry would make it as far as she had. It had been easy to follow the hijacked vessel. The tarpaulin that covered the strafed sundeck was impregnated with a reflective substance that enabled ships at sea to be found and tracked from space. Tonight, satellite reports indicated that the ferry was standing at rest. For the Jewish Sabbath. Radio news reports confirmed it. A thousand souls bobbing on an open sea—

The Admiral left his office, walking briskly. Montrose had repeated several times during the last week that his orders were 'to cripple the ferry, not to sink it'. The Admiral tried to impress on the Scottish leader that torpedoes were 'ship killers', and that a passenger ferry had little or no chance of surviving a submarine attack. 'My orders, my responsibility,' Montrose kept saying. 'They must not reach their destination.'

The Navy's chief officer passed the desk outside the Operations Room door without acknowledging the guard. Inside, the graveyard watch sitting at their consoles shifted their gazes up. The Admiral looked straight ahead, intent, preoccupied, impenetrable. At the far end of the room was a grey metal door. He punched in a numbered code on the access panel. Lights and ventilation came on, the door clicked open. Entering, he sealed himself inside. It was no more than a cubicle. He sat down at the bank of wall-mounted electronics, and studied the permanent on-screen display

COMMUNICATIONS SYSTEMS OPEN AND FUNCTIONING
He keyed in his password and waited. Red nonsense symbols danced across the monitor. He stretched his fingers, then typed a number/letter call sign. Crunching noises, and

SCOTCOM<>SATELLITE CONTROL
PASSWORD:>
flashed up in response. His fingers tapped again, with care. Waiting for the new log-on prompt to come up, he ran through the call-up procedure in his head. Next there followed an extended exchange of coded ciphers in a series, including the date and exact time; asterisks appeared on a second monitor. Again there was a wait

SCOTCOM<>BAND AND FREQUENCY
He removed a pad from his shirt pocket, rifled through its ruled pages of symbols and numbers. Double-checking, he punched in the information corresponding to the date. The machine verified his signal

SCOTCOM>0.986@COLIN.END

One more crosscheck and he was in. From his pad he typed on the next line
     COLIN>RESUME\8271.89.BEGIN-LINK
The second monitor began flashing urgently in red
     READY!
The Admiral released a breath and messaged
     BONAR BRIDGE LONE WOLF PROCEED
He pressed the "send" button, and the screen instantly responded
     MESSAGE SENT/RECEPTION VERIFIED
He then typed
     >DELETE PREVIOUS FUNCTION/MESSAGE<
and the machine answered
     >PREVIOUS FUNCTION/MESSAGE DELETED FROM MEMORY<
The Admiral logged off. The
     COMMUNICATIONS SYSTEMS OPEN AND FUNCTIONING
message returned to the first screen — as if nothing had happened. Still sitting, he said it aloud, so that they might hear: 'Good luck, lads.'

* * *

Chapter LXVI

'It's Not Over Till It's Over'

[Friday-Saturday night, December 11-12, 2009]

BONAR BRIDGE
LONE WOLF
PROCEED

The Admiral's transmission came through in three-line format. The submarine drove forward, all engines full. Estimated pursuit time: one hour, thirty-seven minutes. The *Bonar Bridge* had slipped into the Mediterranean from the Suez Canal under cover of darkness on December Two. The ferry's tarpaulin had made it simple to home in on satellite-transmitted coordinates, but the submarine kept a safe distance to avoid detection. Under strict orders to maintain total radio silence, the *Bridge's* mission was known only to Montrose, the Admiral of the Navy, her captain and sixty-eight crewmen.

*

Guriat looked at the dry Sabbath bread and cold food. She had no appetite. Deborah had brought up the plate hours ago, and was in an unusually chatty mood. As she was leaving, she said, 'Seeing that first Hanukkah candle burn so brightly...it really looks like the end's in sight. Why, even Neville seems to be coming out of his depression.' Guriat couldn't help her response. 'In Israel we have a saying— It's not over till it's over.'

In the quiet moments when Deborah had left, the Rabbi's brother played on her mind. Neville brought unwanted feelings to the surface. She actually liked him. He made her laugh. She hadn't seen him since the day of the helicopter attack. Until last night: He came to her to apologise for his outburst in front of Lindy and Todd. She pitied him. Then, somehow, in a perverse moment of absurd weakness that she could neither fathom nor forgive herself for, she allowed him in her bed. Inside she was tight, dry and when it was over, she simply told him that liking a man had never been enough.

The radio came alive. The signal was weak against loud background noise. Guriat tried the squelch. For a few seconds it helped. She was able to copy the speed and bearing. Sudden new interference — jamming — squealed out of the receiver. She slammed her palm against the set. She caught 'Estimated contact time—' but the figures that followed were lost in high-frequency screech. She turned down the volume and switched to transmit. 'Repeat, urgent, repeat message. Over.' She flipped back to receive. Nothing. She cursed the set. Sweat broke out under her arms. Emergency band and frequencies — useless. She gave up with a black word, exploded from the radio room and dashed along the short gangway to the bridge. Ace was asleep on the floor. Guriat sounded the emergency signal — three short, sharp blasts of the ship's horn. The little man woke up with a shock. Guriat uttered one word: 'Submarine.'

Ace leapt to his feet. He furiously threw levers and flipped switches. The ship's idling power plant juddered. The twin screws turned, churning the sea. The ferry slowly accelerated. Guriat gave him the sub's speed and heading. The *Praise* zigzagged, turning south. Ace also flicked off a bank of switches, blacking out the ship except for the lower car deck. He sounded the ship's horn frequently. Collision was now a real danger.

Guriat delayed only long enough to instruct Ace. Just as she was finishing with '...you got all that, Acey?' Neville showed up. He took one look at her and said, 'This isn't an exercise, is it?' She brushed by him, saying to Ace alone, 'I'm heading for the car deck, *now*.' In a single breath, 'Bitch—' Neville registered his defiance, his frustration, his anger, and his darkness.

Ace said to him, 'Screw her, man, there's a fuckin' sub out there. The second you see a blip on the echo screen, sing out. They've got some sort of crazy strategy — "a chance in a thousand", she says—' As he took up his position at the echo sounder screen, Neville asked, 'Who's "they"?'

'Her and your brother—'

In near panic the ferry people ran to their assigned emergency stations. A thousand pairs of eyes combed the blackness of night for signs of approaching danger.

*

The *Bonar Bridge* blew out her ballast tanks; the black hull hovered at a shallow depth. The gurgling sounds of many screws told the sonar officer that the whole convoy of ships was moving. The sub had been detected. The flotilla made a perfect cover. A depth charge attack was too risky with all those boats close by. Onboard computers revised target intercept time down to forty-seven minutes.

*

The little man's eyebrows knit together in thought. Ace saw no reason to hide from Neville what he knew of Guriat's 'depth charge on wheels'.

'Who's driving? Him or her?' asked Neville.

'Don't know,' came the answer.

Neville's face puckered in the eerie green light of the echo screen. He thought, either way—

The Rabbi pulled himself up into the driver's cab. The door had been removed for a quick getaway. Following the string of emergency lighting, he stared hard down the cavernous length of the empty car deck. Sweat rolled off his forehead. He buckled up. The makeshift safety harness and lifeline arrangement gave him little comfort. He imagined the rig hitting the sea, the shock of cold water clamping his body. He tried to build a picture of Deborah's face in his mind. He couldn't. She knew nothing of the plan.

Guriat was kneeling on top of the articulated tanker truck. She checked her improvised detonator — an alarm clock taped to a heavy-duty battery and wired to one of the ship's signal flares. The assembly fitted neatly into a large watertight glass jar. The heat from the exploding flare blows the jar apart, ignites the petrol fumes, and—

*

The *Bonar Bridge's* acoustic analysis system clearly indicated that the ferry led, and the fleet followed some two miles behind. The ferry's isolation meant that the stalemate situation on the surface held fast. The suicide ship loaded with ammonium perchlorate threatened to blow up the entire flotilla within the radius of a mile, if any vessel tried to defend the hijackers. The submarine, now running just below periscope depth, resumed full speed to outflank her target.

*

Alec Ace began to whistle. Oddly, in all his life he had never felt quite so alive, relaxed and concentrated as now.

Neville monitored the radar screen and the echo sounder. He said nothing.

Rebbe Frankelstein burst into the wheelhouse. With fat fists clenched, his blazing eyes ping-ponged off the walls and floor. It was his first time on the bridge. The Hassid was wearing his long black Sabbath coat.

'And a good *Shabbes* to you, too, Rebbe,' said Neville deadpan.

'He's not here— Where *is* Moray?' demanded Frankelstein.

Neville mocked him, 'Oh, you're here to see the Chief Rabbi—?'

'He's no rabbi. A man who desecrates the sanctity of the Shabbos is not even a Jew.' Frankelstein's Brooklyn accent rippled with righteousness.

'For you,' said Neville, flipping imaginary pages, 'let me check his appointments book— No, sorry, the Chief's in conference with the Devil-woman.'

Ace stopped whistling. 'Stuff it, Nev, this is no time for a bloody comedy routine.'

'What—?' said Neville. 'Just when the audience is eating out of my hand?' He turned back to the echo sounder. 'Rebbe, Rebbe, come here, quick.' In spite of himself, Frankelstein looked into the scope as Neville went on, 'You see that blip on the edge? There—' He plunged his finger into the green light. 'Yes, that blip. That blip wants to sink us. If that happens, there'll be nobody left to desecrate the Sabbath, or to keep it—'

Ace calmly radioed the news of the submarine down to the car deck.

Neville fixed Frankelstein in his gaze. 'Keep an eye on that blip, Rebbe, and save our souls.'

Frankelstein looked into the scope. 'It's gone.'

'Hey, Acey, the Rebbe, here, made it go away.' Ace looked at Neville as though he'd gone barking mad. 'I just remembered,' said Neville, 'I've got a great joke to tell my brother. In case you see that blip again, Reb Frankenstein, just let my good friend here Mr Ace in on it. He'll know what to do.'

Neville left the bridge.

Ace shouted after him, 'Where the hell 're you *going*? I need you, I need you *here*—'

* * *

Chapter LXVII

'Last Touch'

[Friday-Saturday night, December 11-12, 2009]
As the *Bonar Bridge* pulled ahead of the weaving ferry, the commander ordered a new heading. The submarine's long, black hull hung motionless in watery space until the rudder and planing fins bit again. After three minutes on a bending course, the sub's periscope broke the surface. Her quarry appeared in the cross hairs as a highly visible infrared silhouette.

Range and speed, confirmed.

Torpedo guidance systems, set.

Tubes, flooded.

*

Neville's heart and mind raced to the beat of his feet on the metal stairs down to the lower vehicle deck. Throwing open the watertight door with a dull clang, he took in the dim-lit tanker truck at the bow end of the ship. All one hundred and thirty meters of deck were as clear as a runway. As Neville closed the gap, he saw *her* on top of the rig's tank and Brew in the driver's seat.

Neville came alongside and said to Brew, 'What the hell are you doing? What's this all about?'

'Get out of here, Neville!' It was Guriat.

Brew stared. 'Stay out of this, Neville. Please. It's my responsibility—'

'Are you out of your mind? This rig's a death trap.'

'Neville, Rabbi—' shouted Guriat.

'Look, Nev, it was *me*, Brew Moray. *I* got us into this. It's up to *me* to get us out.'

Neville climbed up on to the step of the cab, and started to unhitch his brother. 'If anyone's going to be a bloody human depth charge, it's me.' Their hands fought over the harness buckles. Eyes locked. Neville gently pulled Brew's hands away, and said, 'You have to let me do this thing for you. You're needed. The people, they need you, they need your leadership.'

Guriat's voice was shrill. 'Neville, ya crazy bastard, get the hell out of here. You're going to get us all blown up!'

The Rabbi's brother went on, 'You have Deborah. She wants you to live— Who have I got?' Neville was begging. 'Let me do this thing for us. Tell me what I have to do—'

There was no arguing. Brew finished unbuckling the harness. The brothers changed places. Brew said, 'Just drive as fast as you can, like the Red Sea was opening up and the whole Egyptian army was behind you—'

'Like go down, Moses, eh, Brewsy—?'

Brew smiled at his childhood name. 'Something like that. And when you hit the water, jump free. We'll winch you in. There's a seven-minute delay on the clock before this thing goes. Are you sure you want to do this, Nev?'

Neville was perfectly calm. 'Never been surer. I know what I have to do.' The brothers hugged, and Brew blessed Neville, 'May HASHEM be with you and watch over you.' Neville broke their clasp with a light tap on Brew's shoulder.

Guriat came running along the top of the tank to the cab. There was nothing she could say or do to stop them.

*

The *Bonar Bridge* fired torpedoes one and two at short range.

*

The torpedoes streaked towards the *Praise*. The night was clear and starlit. Two bubbly white wakes scarred the ocean's surface. At screams of 'Torpedoes! Torpedoes!' coming from the ship's starboard side, Ace kicked in the bow thrusters and threw the helm over, directly into the path of the torpedoes. If the *Praise* could intercept the torpedoes before their homing systems could lock on, she would have a chance. He shouted into the radio, 'Car deck, torpedoes!'

Frankelstein began blubbering prayers.

As the *Praise* slowly lurched round to the new bearing, Ace urged, 'C'mon, you beautiful bitch, c'mon.'

The ferry people on deck watched in hushed horror. The torpedoes' phosphorescent wakes curved in a wide arc. The *Praise* was still turning as the lead torpedo harmlessly passed by. The second warhead smashed home. The ferry reeled. People plugged their ears, clasped each other, and waited for the explosion. It didn't happen. The torpedo lodged itself between the portside screw and rudder.

*

The crew of the *Bonar Bridge* braced themselves. When nothing happened, the commander raised the periscope for another look.

*

On the car deck, the torpedo's impact was sharp. Guriat only just managed to save herself and the timing device from falling off the top of the tanker truck. Brew fell against a wheel. Ace's voice, coming out of the handheld radio, was shouting, 'Car deck, port screw and rudder, frozen; the ship's loosing steerage.'

*

The submarine commander reared back from the periscope, flipping up the handles. He roared, 'Down scope—' The ferry's forward momentum was silently carrying her straight at them. 'Right full rudder—' Already she was too close for the *Bonar Bridge* to fire another torpedo. 'Take her down, fast—'

*

'There's that blip!' Frankelstein cried out.

Ace had a look. Frankelstein's pointing finger was shivering over the centre of the screen. Ace radioed the car deck again, 'We're running over that iron coffin *now*. Hammer home the nails.'

Brew ran down the deck. At the ramp-operating panel, he stabbed the green "open" button. The hydraulic ramp started to lower. 'Ready!' he yelled down the length of the ship.

Guriat called out, 'Neville, start the engine.'

He turned the key. The power train burst into life, filling the car deck with a loud roar and a blast of blue-grey exhaust.

Guriat set the alarm clock at seven minutes to twelve, and inserted a battery to start the countdown. She placed the activated detonator in the jar, and screwed the lid tightly shut. The tanker was half full of petrol siphoned off from the cars. The fumes were overpowering. She dropped the detonating jar in. Hearing it splash on the surface, she sealed the intake port, and climbed down the ladder.

- 221 -

Neville revved the engine. He sat on the edge of his seat, staring through the windscreen. His hands gripped the wheel so tightly, they were white. Wild, unconnected thoughts stumbled through his head: *the Edinburgh sewers rushing with water, the capsized sailboat at Joppa, Brew's turtle sinking in the mud, his father lying cold in the grave—*

Guriat jumped onto the step of the cab, holding on to the mirror. He turned to her, put his hand on her arm and said, 'Last touch, lassie.' She said, 'Neville, be good tonight—' then jumped backwards onto the deck. The ramp was completely open, making a square target. Pumping both arms forward, Guriat yelled over the engine noise, 'Go! Go!'

Neville released the handbrake. The truck jerked. Ramming the fourteen-wheeler into gear, the engine engaged with a jolt. He slammed his foot to the accelerator, flooring it. The roar filled the huge emptiness. The wheels started to roll. The rig soon hit ten, twenty, thirty miles an hour. Neville had the horn blaring. The artic flew off the end of the ramp in a graceful dive, splashed into the sea, and was swallowed up whole, all in seeming slow motion.

Brew waited a few seconds, and then turned on the winch. The spool took up the slack, neatly winding up the rope like a fishing reel. At the appearance of the yellow ribbon Brew stopped the winch. He ran out to the edge of the ramp to haul Neville in and give him a hand up. The harness came in empty.

Guriat came running. Seeing what the Rabbi saw, she said in a low voice, 'Be good.'

Twice, three times, Brew shouted his brother's name. No answer came back from the blackness.

'He's gone,' cried Guriat. 'Get inside. Now!'

Brew was standing frozen. Guriat ran out on the ramp, shook him to his senses. He whispered, 'Blessed be the TRUE JUDGE.'

As soon as they were back inside, Guriat hit the red "close" button on the control panel. The ramp did not come up. Jammed. Guriat pushed the button again. 'Why the hell won't you bloody close?' she pleaded. Brew tried. Nothing. It would not budge. 'The hydraulics must be frozen,' he said. 'Is there a manual crank?'

'Probably, but there's no time for that. We've got to get away from here before that thing blows.' They started running together for the watertight door amidships that Neville had come through.

First came a low, thundering rumble. Then, the explosion in a fusion of fire and water shot a luminescent column a hundred metres up into the night sky. The blast set off a slow-rolling ridge of water. The wave crest swept up the *Praise*, and carried her like a surfboard on a swell. When the ferry finally dropped back into the trough, the open ramp scooped up the sea. Seeing the water flood in, Brew and Guriat leapt through the door that Neville had left open. Brew closed it behind them just in time.

As the water sloshed out again, the ship rolled violently. Brew and Guriat were thrown to the deck. The Rabbi got to his feet first. He turned his face away from her and pounded his fist into the ship. He was crying.

* * *

Chapter LXVIII

'It's Land'

[Saturday pre-dawn, December 12, 2009]

Guriat put her hand on Brew's shoulder. He turned to her. Two tiny reflections of her face swam in his moist eyes. She had an angry welt on her forehead. 'Will you hold me?' she asked, laying her head on his shoulder. Brew lightly put his arms around her. She said, 'Neville did it...because of me, because he loved me, and I—'

'No,' he said softly, 'Neville did it because of Neville.'

William Warboys, up from the engine control room, stumbled on Guriat and Brew. From the shadows in the stairwell where he stood, he watched. Their entwined bodies did not move. Brew gently turned Guriat's face to the light. 'Better have that cut seen to...who's there?' The presence in the shadow stepped forward, snapping them apart. 'What are you staring at? Warboys—' Brew spat his name as though it were a curse. Guriat glared. Warboys dropped his leering eyes.

At that moment a deep-throated grating noise from below wrenched the ship. The hull shuddered. The light flickered, and went out.

'It's one of the shaft bearings! It'll tear the ship apart!' cried Warboys. 'We have to shut down the drive engine—' Warboys buckled to his knees, whimpering, 'I don't want to die, not like this—' Brew slapped him hard across the face. The engineer's mate felt the heat on his cheek. A stinging mixture of surprise and glowering suffused his fixed glare.

On the bridge the wrenching from the bowels of the ship ended Rebbe Frankelstein's prayers with a jolt. He babbled, 'The sea is swallowing us up. This is our punishment for breaking the Sabbath peace.' Lunging at Ace from behind, he tried to tear him from the helm. The little man ended the struggle with a single blow.

Halfway between the *Praise* and the horizon, the suicide ship lit up the night. A great storm of fire curled over the surface of the sea in all directions, engulfing the silhouettes of distant ships large and small. Only the invisible aftershock hit the *Praise* and, like a blast of hot desert wind, pitched the ferry deeply to one side. Another surge of panic shot through the people on deck. To cries of 'the ship is sinking', three lifeboats were lowered into the sea. One hysterical passenger, seeing the empty boats drift away, first pushed his wife overboard then jumped himself. Both were lost.

Shaken but holding on, Mr Sinclair and 'the missus' — *his* Miriam for fifty years — together with Pearl and Izzy Sofer, watched the blazing fires from the stern of the ferry. In the bizarre light of the burning sea, the two old couples caught a glimpse of what seemed to be huge bubbles of air bursting on the surface. Miriam asked, 'Could that be the submarine?' Mr Sinclair said to the sea, 'Now will you leave us in peace?'

The Rabbi forced William Warboys back down to the engine control room. The fire-protection system filled the air with vapours. It was steamy hot, and the alarms were ear piercing. Through small windows, they could see the power plant enveloped in white smoke. 'Electrical fire. Shit!' exclaimed Warboys. Brew, shaking his head, did not understand. Warboys spoke fast. 'The whole electrical system is fucked—'

'What can we do?' asked Brew.

'Nothing, at sea. Let it smoulder, and hope it doesn't spread too fast. We can't stay here—' Warboys turned to run. Brew caught him by the shoulder, spun him around, and said, 'You're a coward—'

'Damn your eyes—' Warboys shot back.

Brew looked around. 'Can't we shut it down? Disconnect the generator? There must be something—'

Warboys' eyes opened wide. 'Other side of that door, inside the engine room' — he nodded in the direction — 'a lever. Pull it down. But cutting off the current won't help,' he shouted over the noise. 'There's no flame. The smoke's a bitch. It's electrical, man. Fumes 'll kill you. And it's going to be hot as hellfire in there.'

'*You* do what you have to do to keep the second engine running,' said Brew. He waited a few seconds to see that Warboys went to the control panel. Then taking a deep breath, Brew put a handkerchief to his nose and mouth. He plunged through the door into the main engine room. The intense heat and noise threw him back. Acrid fumes forced him to shut his eyes. He felt the wall. The lever handle was there, but it would not come down with one hand. Brew dropped the handkerchief from his face to pull with both hands and the whole weight of his body. It gave way, and as the lights went out, strips of emergency lighting cut in. At the same time, the engine wound down. Gasping and coughing, his eyes smarting as if rubbed with salt, Brew called out Warboys' name. There was no answer. The ship lurched, throwing Brew through the door back into the control room. Again, he shouted out for Warboys, then collapsed.

When Brew opened his eyes after some minutes, he could see again. The ferry no longer shook. He dragged himself to the lower car deck level, where he found the engineer's mate curled up in a corner of the stairway. He was shivering. 'Don't think you've beat it,' said Warboys looking up, surprised to see Brew. 'I'm here to tell you, I've seen electrical fires before. It's down but not out. Bloody wires are still smouldering like hay. It can't be put out, not at sea—'

Brew looked at him with pity. '"Though our way is through water and fire, we cannot die."'[106]

'Save your preaching,' said Warboys with contempt. 'You think I'm a scared dog. I am. That torpedo is wedged into our screw. It could blow any time. While you, *Rabbi*, dance...with the black woman.'

On his way to the bridge, angry voices damned him. 'There he is. Madman! Murderer! He's sinking the ship.' Someone spat in his face. Slowly, Brew raised his eyes to the sky.

'What are you looking for up there?' asked the spitter.

The stars twinkled and winked in the dark wells of Brew's eyes. The constellations re-form themselves into the outline of the desert mountain. A small stone of light detaches itself and rolls down the mountain, bouncing off larger stones, rolling, bouncing, jumping into the air, landing, spinning, turning, loosening more little stones—

'What are you looking at, I asked you?'

---

[106]Moray is paraphrasing the poet Uri Zvi Greenberg from the ship's plaque (see endnote, Chapter 53).

Brew wiped the spittle from his face. 'What am I looking at? At the source of that spot of rain that fell on my face.' The ferry lurched. 'Tell everybody to move to the front of the ship. If anybody needs me, I'm on the bridge.'

'Mr Ace,' said Brew, 'I saw the North Star. We're moving away from it. Going south. Why? We are meant to be heading east.'

'Rabbi, we're running for the nearest landfall. That's south, man, not east.'

'But—' said Brew desperately.

Ace kept his voice even. 'On one screw, one lifeboat, next to no fuel, ship's on fire and taking in water, a torpedo that could blow any time— It's our best hope.'

Brew looked away and saw Frankelstein slumped in the corner. 'What happened to him?'

'He went berserk,' said Ace, explaining what happened. 'I didn't mean to hurt him. Is he dead?' Brew put the back of his hand to Frankelstein's forehead. 'No. He's warm. Too much Kiddish wine. Knocked him out, right?' Ace smiled with relief. Brew propped up Frankelstein's body into a more comfortable sitting position.

The Rabbi asked Ace when they would reach land.

'The good news is that the wind and current are both coming from the north, helping to push us south. Tell me one thing, Rabbi. Did Neville—?'

Brew went onto the bridge wing. He spoke to his brother, 'Nev, I never told you how I envied you. You were so miserable inside, but you made everyone around you laugh. People liked you; only you would never believe it. You know something, you were closer to people than I'll ever be. And now, you're gone, and I can't tell you how much I miss you.'

'Brew—?' It was Deborah.

'Debs—'

'Thank goodness I found you. I thought maybe something terrible happened to you—' She felt his living face. He was rigid to her touch. 'Something's wrong,' she said.

'Yes, Neville's— Poor Neville's...not coming back. He...he took my place.'

'I don't understand,' she said.

'I know.' He could not say it straight out, 'Neville did it for me, for us. He saved the ship.' In the darkness Deborah held his face in her hands. 'Oh, my G— I'm so sorry. How—? B...but I still don't understand—'

'Neither do I. Why I was born? To kill the people I love? To destroy lives? I'm supposed to know all the answers. I don't. And to be in control. I'm not.' Deborah began crying. 'Nev's taught me something very important tonight. Before anything more happens to us — Debs, please, don't cry — I want to say it. I love you. I love you so very much. I love you and I've hurt you so many times that I don't have the right to ask you to forgive me.'

'You shouldn't say that.' Her tears flowed. 'All I want is for us to be happy, together.' Deborah looked up into the distance. The eastern sky was starting to turn grey.

At that moment Alec Ace came out. 'I didn't mean to interrupt, but—'

'Yes, Mr Ace.'

'I think some of the plates underwater must have buckled with the impact of the torpedo. We're taking in water fast, and she's beginning to list.'

Brew looked back along the ferry. The angle was perceptible. A column of thick, ash-white smoke was rising high into the air from the stern. Brew said, 'Mr Ace, as long as there's more water outside than inside, we're not sunk yet.'

'Maybe not,' answered Ace. 'But with one alternator down, we only have half the pumps working. If the ship lists too far over, she'll start taking in water through the stern ramp.'

The day was brightening fast; calm, wintry seas mirrored the sky's streaky dullness. Brew observed, 'It seems we've lost our escort.'

'The suicide ship,' said Ace. 'Whoever's left is picking up survivors, way too busy to think about us.'

'The Israelis?' asked Brew.

'We've entered enemy territorial waters. They can't follow us without starting World War III.'

'Then where exactly are we, Mr Ace?'

'In pretty deep water.'

Brew smiled. 'Now I see why Nev liked you so much—'

Before Ace could comment, Deborah cried out, 'Brew! Look!' Craning over the rail, she pointed to the faint horizon, 'It's land!'

* * *

The plane, unofficially called "the big, black bird", was among the last of an ageing breed of reconnaissance aircraft. A super-wide wingspan enabled it to fly into the stratosphere. Home base was a large Mediterranean island.

With no spy satellite overflying the southern Mediterranean in the early hours of Saturday, December Twelfth, the Americans authorised an extraordinary U-2 mission. The surveillance data recorded at first light that morning are now in the public domain, available to anyone on netcom. In the image coded MA-102, three heads are clearly visible on the bridge wing; one arm, Deborah's, is fully extended. E.T.

Chapter LXIX

'Fish Out of Water'

[Saturday morning, December 12, 2009]

He left without turning off *Good Morning, Scotland.* The set stayed on day and night, but however much he watched, there was no way of knowing if *his* family were alive or dead. News, comment, analysis — he couldn't stand it any more. He had to get away, go for a walk.

Jake Banks had not meant to come as far as Salisbury Road. He just kept going, possessed by some homing instinct.

The signboard still said "Edinburgh Hebrew Congregation". The doors were locked, the windows boarded up. Jake stared at the walls, red-stained, where the graffiti had been blotted out. He hummed, trying to bring on the Sabbath morning. But the spirit of the place was gone. Nothing was left, not an echo, not even the silence after the echo. The evening before, Friday, he had jammed the first candle into the Hanukkah menorah. He struck a match. But he knew he couldn't bring himself to say the holiday blessings without Sophie and Naomi and Benny to watch and sing with him. The match flame singed his fingers. The first candle went unlit—

'Mr Banks? Is that you?' Startled, he turned around. Her eyes were red-rimmed, her lipstick smeared.

'Ms Landis—'

'She ran away from me, never came home from school.'

'Ms Landis, Eve— You look tired. Here, let's sit down.' Together, Jake and Eve seated themselves on the low wall, their backs to the synagogue.

Jake, staring into nothingness, let her ramble on. 'I called her teacher. She said she never assigned any geography project to anybody—' He was only half listening. Sophie's fierce anger, when she'd dropped one of her African violets on the kitchen floor, suddenly filled his head.

Eve went on: '"Aunt" she called me. She said she'd be going along to the public library to look at maps for a school geography project— She's gone. I gave her ten pounds, she took it and went away.'

Jake suddenly understood. His chest constricted. But to say something, anything, he said, 'So you don't know where she went.'

'No,' answered Eve. 'She went to the library, all right. The librarian remembered her. He told me that he showed her a road atlas of Scotland. She took it away to photocopy a couple of pages.'

'Did he see which pages?'

Eve sat still, as if what was coming next was important. 'No. But he said the girl had a beautiful Highland accent.'

'The Highlands— Could be anywhere—' Sophie had never told Jake anything. She didn't know. Nor did Neville. No one knew where Brew and Deborah had stopped during their disappearance. They never told anyone, did they? Never had the opportunity. Brew was arrested. Deborah had no reason to say. All Jake had heard was the girl's name, Fraser, as common as a penny. She'd been registered in school with the promise that her previous records would be forthcoming. They never arrived. She came from nowhere, and now had returned to nowhere. All that was known of her home was the Rabbi's parable of the turtle. There must be ten thousand broken-down croft houses in the Highlands—

Eve's voice now spoke in tears, though her eyes were dry. 'I've lost everything. In a matter of weeks, everything. My profession, my beautiful things, my little Elen. I wanted to keep her so badly. I couldn't bear to give her up. And now she's gone. Who's going to hold my hand when I'm dying?' She turned to the synagogue. 'Look at this place. Boarded up. Those boards. Can't you feel them? Nailed across our eyes, our mouths. They've boarded us up. Shut us up. Jake Banks, what you are doing here? Why aren't you with your beautiful family?'

'I was on the ferry. I walked off. Left them there. I couldn't go. I left them. I thought I couldn't leave Scotland.' In his heart, Jake begged Sophie to forgive him; in his arms, he held the kids. He steadied himself. He couldn't face Eve. He talked to the street. 'Ms Landis, Eve, there's something...there's something you have to know about me, and you—'

Eve cut him off: 'There's nothing I don't already know about myself, Mr Banks. All my life I've been teaching children to peel away the words, to dig hard for meaning, to desire truth. And when they have found a truth that works for them in their own lives, I taught them not to be afraid of it. The truth about me is I'm a selfish old spinster who tried to force a child to give me a new lease of life. I failed. That's the whole truth about me. What more can you tell me?'

He slowly looked at her. 'That it was me. I sent the police to your house. I told them about the Highland girl stopping with you.'

'You?'

'They hauled me in. Threatened me. I was afraid. I was flapping around like a fish out of water. I'm sorry, so sorry.'

Eve thought. No reproach came to her face. 'Some cliche — "like a fish out of water". I shouldn't be concerned if I were you, Mr Banks. Not now. Not any more.'

Jake's mouth dropped. 'But—'

Again, Eve stopped him. 'Aren't we both fish out of water? You and me? Your children are far away, and mine, mine were never born. What does the past matter when you cut yourself off from your future?'

* * *

Chapter LXX

'I Will Not Be Defeated'

[Saturday morning, December 12, 2009]

Angus Montrose woke up with the radio; pre-set, it came on at seven fifty-five every morning. He liked to hear the five-minute sermon. Words of faith from men and women who truly believed fascinated him. Montrose *wanted* to believe.

The old man's hands prickled with the sudden rush of blood. As he started to rub out the numbness, it came back — that lost speck of memory! Moray, the Rabbi...rubbing his hand...after the handshake. He said *something*, but Montrose could not remember.

The radio babbled in the background. He only half-heard. The speaker finished on a high: 'And today, Saturday, the Seventh Day, the LORD rested.' Ads and trailers before the news—

He stared at the red phone. Its redness appeared to be throbbing. Montrose stood. His head began ringing. Operation Lone Wolf...proceed...tonight. A decision of state, he told himself. Without malice. The dizziness passed off. He looked again; the red phone no longer pulsed.

His stiffness couldn't wait for the news headlines. The need to urinate was overpowering. He rushed into the private washroom attached to his office, and brought down his zipper in a hurry. The pressure on his bladder produced a straight, dark yellow rush. Not a bad flow for an old man, he thought to himself. His stream muffled the pips and the news headlines. As Montrose was finishing, the newscaster took a pause, then read:

'First, to the ferry hijacking. Unconfirmed reports speak of a powerful underwater explosion immediately followed by a massive fire storm in the early hours of this morning—'

Just then the red, hot line telephone gave a loud burble. He ran in to grab the call. 'Montrose—'

'Prime Minister—' It was the Admiral. The line clicked dead, the electronic voice verification and security checks cutting in.

'...small boats swamped...few survivors plucked from calm seas at dawn—'

Montrose sat down and nuzzled the receiver between cheek and shoulder. He picked up the brewer's hammer.

'...unidentified bodies were also recovered. The fate of the ferry—'

He snapped off the radio, and started loudly tapping the hammer in the palm of his hand.

The Admiral came on again, 'Prime Minister—'

'Yes, what have you got for me—?'

'When may I see you, Sir? It's vital.'

'You may not see me. Just report what happened.'

'This is not a conversation for the telephone. The news is highly confi—'

'Talk. I'm in no condition to be seen.'

'I— We have had no radio contact from the probe.'

'...no contact— What do you mean, no radio contact? You didn't stop the ferry boat—?'

'It seems not. Haven't you heard the news this morning? Most of our surface vessels in the area were blasted to cinders by that damned suicide ship. We have lost contact with the ferry. Last reports indicate that the ferry appears to have escaped...that she's still afloat—'

'Lord Jesus in Heaven. And our submarine?'

'The probe, Sir, appears to be...lost.'

'What? What do you mean, "lost"?'

Montrose thought he heard a gulp.

'The p-probe—' The Admiral steadied his voice, 'the probe must be assumed dead.'

'Dead—?'

'On the bottom of the sea.'

Now Montrose swallowed deeply. The hammering stopped.

'Sir? Mr Montrose? Are you there?'

'I'm here. How many?'

'Men? Sixty-nine. Some of the best lads in the Navy.'

'Oh, my Go—! Are you sure?'

'Sure, Sir? No, Sir. Not until there's verification.'

'Find her. She has to sink that godforsaken enemy ferry. It's vital. She must—' Breaking off, Montrose said, 'I can't believe this is happening to me—'

The Admiral's tone turned sombre. 'Those men are gone. What do I tell the families?'

'Nothing, nothing yet. Give them time to come home.'

'Sir, they are not coming home—'

Montrose let the phone drop from the squeeze between cheek and shoulder.

'Prime Minister— Prime Minister— Are you there—?' shouted the detached voice at the end of the curled wire. Letting the hammer fall from his grip, Montrose slowly lifted the receiver, put it down on the base unit, and then took it off again. He took off all his phones. The dial tones hummed. He got up, shambled to the sideboard, took out a fresh bottle and uncorked it. In the few steps back to his desk, he half-emptied the contents. Montrose put the whisky down next the empty bottle from the night before. He stood — looking at the hammer. "Take it, lad, so when you get to the top, you don't forget how far you've come." Thick fingers curled around the handle, and squeezed the wood so hard the knuckles turned white. His shaking hand lifted the hammer to his eyes. He crashed it into the empty bottle. The noise of the shattering glass exploded in his ears. 'I will not be defeated.' He hit the half-full bottle, splashing glass and whisky everywhere over himself and the desk. 'I will not be defeated—'

The hammer felt red-hot. He let it fall, and swore as he shook his right fist. 'By this hand that won the freedom of Scotland, I will not be defeated—' The back of his tongue constricted, choking off his breath. Teetering, he leaned heavily on both hands over his desk. The poison from his gut spewed onto the humming phones. His great white head hung between his shoulders. There was fire on his tongue. His breathing came in deep gasps. His wild gaze fell on the mallet lying in a pool of vomit and whisky. The copper head, dented and scarred by a thousand blows, came into sharp focus.

He wound the fingers of his left hand around the thick, short handle. Slowly, by degrees, he raised his arm high. Above his head, the copperhead hammer orbited in a tight circle. From the corners of his lips, a coffee-brown ooze dribbled down his chattering chin. 'I...will...not...be...defeated.' Fixing on the splayed paw that anchored him to his desk, the old man steadied himself. And in a white, flashing arc, Angus Montrose brought the hammer down on his right hand.

* * *

End Part Three

PART FOUR: SPRING MORNING

Chapter LXXI

Night and Day

[Saturday, December 12, 2009]

NIGHT The funeral procession left from the edge of the sea after the Sabbath.[107] As the mourners slowly filed along the beach, many looked to the sea. The *Praise* still glowed in the darkness—

DAY Alec Ace, Guriat Gaoni and Brew Moray left the ship last. As they reached shore in the brilliant morning sunshine, the ferry settled in the ebbing tide and the torpedo exploded.

NIGHT The bier that led the funeral was an improvised stretcher made from a deflated life raft stretched between two oars. Alec Ace's white shirt, tied off at the waist and stuffed with round beach stones, served as the body—

DAY Alec Ace spent the whole morning combing the beach. He carried his lumpy shirt like a sack. By the time Brew saw him, his back was on fire. Brew took off his jacket, and gently placed it over the little man's wide shoulders. 'What are you doing?' Brew asked him.

'Collecting stones.'

'Why?'

Ace's back stung under the Rabbi's coat. 'I had to do something. I couldn't just sit in the sun. So I started collecting stones. I soon found more than I could carry in my hands and pockets, so I took off my shirt.'

Again Brew asked him, 'But what are you going to do with them?'

'At first, I didn't know. But it came to me. Neville won't have a funeral, a grave, a place to rest. Can we, I mean, can *you* bury these stones from the sea instead of Neville? For his body.'

The Rabbi saw Ace's simple sincerity. 'There's no reason I can think of why not. We'll do it this evening, after the Sabbath. It will be a good and fitting memorial to Neville, and to all the souls we lost at sea.'

'But not everybody will want to come...to the funeral...they're only stones, stones collected on the Sabbath—' Ace's search had brought him near Rebbe Frankelstein and his band of bearded men in black hats and coats. They were huddled over the Torah scroll that Mr Sinclair had saved from the burning ferry. When Frankelstein saw Ace bend over to pick up a stone, he interrupted his service to scream 'Sabbath-breaker!' Ace quickly moved on.

The Rabbi simply answered him, 'We'll worry about the objections — after the funeral.' Ace went on collecting.

NIGHT The Rabbi walked behind the stretcher, reciting Psalms. Anna Moray walked by his side—

---

[107]The Sabbath Day ends at sundown.

DAY It hurt Brew to look at her. His mother's eyes were swollen and red. 'Couldn't you have stopped him?' Anna asked. 'He was your brother.'

'No. He was determined.'

'Haven't we sacrificed enough for one family? First your father dying, Jake — some husband — abandoning your sister, then my only grandson, and now one of my boys. Who's next?'

Brew placed an uneasy hand around her shoulders. She wore her winter coat. 'Nev took my place,' he said.

'They even took away my dog,' she said, quivering under his touch. 'Why did you let him? If you had driven, you would have lived.'

'No one can know that.'

'You want to live. Neville wanted to die.'

Brew looked away. Everywhere, the ferry people were milling about, some exploring the desolate sandbar, or playing at the water's edge, or staring at the burning ferry.

'He loved that Israeli woman. She was driving him to distraction—' Anna's wispy white hairs fluttered in the breeze. So quickly, she'd become an old woman, small and shrivelled. 'He never told me straight out, but a mother knows these things. Given half a chance, Neville would have lavished his love on her—' She couldn't finish. Tears were rolling down her cheeks.

NIGHT Even as the funeral procession wound its way along the sandy reef, the grave diggers were shovelling out a last resting place with oars and paddles. Others piled a stone mound at the head of the pit for a simple memorial. The stones came from the Crusader ruins at the top of the hill—

DAY Rabbi Moray was taking his turn at lookout from the ruins at the top of the hill when Felix Frankelstein and a group of his followers came up to him. It was noon, the hottest hour of the day. One of the Hassidim began, 'Gut Shabbes, Reb Moray. We come to offer you our sympathies on the loss of your dear brother. May his memory be blessed, and may you enjoy long life.'

Brew had never found a workable formula for accepting sounds of sympathy. Loss is a sickness of the soul, which perfunctory expressions cannot cure. 'Thank you,' he said, 'I miss him.'

The delegation ignored the Rabbi's shortness. 'You and I have to talk,' said Frankelstein.

'No,' answered the Rabbi. 'You have to talk, and I have to listen.'

'We hear you are planning a funeral tonight,' said one of Rebbe's lieutenants.

The word had spread quickly. 'Yes, I approved the idea. Otherwise our brothers and sisters lost at sea will not have a marker.'

The Hassidim all spoke at once. 'But a funeral?' 'There are no bodies to bury.' 'How can we have a funeral without a body?' 'There's no precedent.' 'We must first study the laws of burial—'

Brew defended himself, 'Study the Law, conclude nothing, do nothing. You just finished reading this week's portion of the Law?[108] Now open your hearts to what it said: how our Father Jacob grieved for his son Joseph. 'He tore his clothes in grief...he refused to be comforted. And he said, *"I will go down to my son, a mourner, even into the grave."'*[109]

---

[108]Every Sabbath morning (Saturday) one complete portion (and some weeks, two) from the Five Books of Moses is read aloud to the congregation. The reading of all 54 portions completes the yearly cycle, which begins and ends on the same day, Simchat Torah, or the Rejoicing of the Law, which immediately follows the Festival of Booths (Sukkoth), and completes the autumn New Year (Rosh Hashanah) festival season .

[109]Gen. 37.35.

'But Jacob didn't dig a grave and bury stones in it.'

'Try to understand. We need to grieve. My mother needs to grieve, I need to grieve.'

'But the stones are being gathered on the Sabbath. Surely you cannot sanction sacrilege.'

'The stones were gathered long before we landed here.'

'The man who collects the stones is a criminal; he beat our Rebbe,' said one of the younger men.

The Rabbi spoke directly to Frankelstein, 'You tried to put the Sabbath before a thousand Jewish lives. He would have been justified in killing you. Consider yourself fortunate, Rabbi.'

'We can see there's no talking to you. You're no rabbi,' said another hotly.

'Don't you think you've said enough?'

'No,' said the hothead, 'We came to tell you that none of us will join you in your abomination this evening.'

'What makes you think that any of us will even see this evening?' said Brew.

The faces of Frankelstein and his delegation went blank with consternation.

'Yes, that's right, look before you speak.' Brew pointed to three open boats coming over the inland sea.

NIGHT When the procession reached the pit's edge, the Rabbi jumped in. 'Gently,' he said, and he slipped Ace's shirt into the grave. The stones made a hollow clunk as they came to rest at the bottom. Alec Ace said, 'He knew how to be a friend,' then gave Brew a hand up. No one spoke while the bereaved took turns refilling the grave. When the work was finished, the Rabbi entreated the souls of the dead to forgive those who had wronged them in life. He ended the short service with the Orphan's Kaddish.[110] With his final 'Amen', the sighs of restless waves and quiet sobbing filled the cool night air—

DAY Brew's eyes stung as he watched the boats land in the dazzle of the golden afternoon sun. The commander of the small force leapt from the bow of the lead boat and scanned the crowded beach. His men, wearing beige uniforms piped into tightly laced-up black boots, were armed with assault rifles. The officer, motioning his soldiers to stay back, came forward to parley.

Two feet from the Rabbi, he marched to a halt and saluted. Guriat shadowed Brew, and in his name greeted the officer in an extended Arabic formula.

He answered in guttural bursts. Brew looked to Guriat for interpretation. 'Colonel Raoul Abed as-Mansura, Officer Commanding, Northern Sinai Military District.' Then she added in an aside, 'My Arabic is fairly basic, learned mostly from the Bedouin when I lived on kibbutz.'

The Rabbi bowed slightly but respectfully. 'I am Rabbi Brew Moray. We've been driven ashore here—' Guriat interpreted. The Colonel stood motionless. Brew tried again. 'We have little food, almost no water and no shelter,' he said with the appropriate gestures, then waited for Guriat's Arabic. Brew continued, motioning behind him, 'My people and I expect nothing from you, but we would *appreciate* help. We've lost everything.' He pointed to the smouldering remains of the ferry.

---

[110]In the face of death, the Jew repeats Kaddish, a prayer that reaffirms life. No mention of death or resurrection is made in the prayer. The irresistible rhythm of the prayer's words sweeps forward and upward, lifting the souls of both the bereaved and the deceased. The version of the prayer recited for the dead is sometimes also known as the Orphan's Kaddish (*Kaddish Yatom*), expressing the profound, childlike abandonment felt by the mourner when a loved one has departed.

'Rabbi,' Guriat whispered to him, 'we are talking to the Egyptian army here. The present Egyptian government is ideologically and fundamentally opposed to the Jewish State.'

'Please, just let him hear what I have to say.' Guriat suddenly felt the sun hammering at the back of her neck. She strained to make the soldier understand.

He asked how many people they were.

Guriat answered him directly. Brew said to her, 'I'll handle the negotiations. Speak to me. Now ask him to tell us exactly where we are.'

Guriat put the question to him. As-Mansura answered: 'Sabkhet el-Bardawil'. Brew turned to Guriat, looking sour-faced in her role of intermediary. 'The Bardawil Lagoon,' she said without elaboration.

The Colonel then launched into a long speech. Nothing but his mouth, little more than a thin-lipped, moustache-lined crease, moved. Despite the Rabbi's concerned glances in her direction, Guriat let the Egyptian talk without interruption. As soon as he finished, he turned to rejoin his troops.

Brew asked her what he'd said. Instead of answering him, Guriat called out to the Egyptian. His answer, tossed over his shoulder, was brief and merged into laughter.

The soldiers departed.

Guriat kicked at the sand. 'I didn't get it all, but the good Colonel was full of fatherly advice for you, Rabbi. He said, your people are a mob. You'd do better to organise them like the military. He said, that if we were a thousand, then you should divide us into hundreds with heads over each hundred. Make the ten heads responsible to you, their re'is, their leader.'

'That's what he had to say?'

'Bastard. You should have let me talk to him.' The Rabbi shook his head. Guriat added, 'What I shouted to him, my last question, I asked him when he was coming back.'

'And—'

'He said, "When the tombs are turned upside down—"'

'What's that supposed to mean?' asked Brew.

'A quote from the Koran, I believe. In other words, he'll be back, but not before he's bloody well ready.'

The ferry people groaned and started to disperse in knots, some angry, others hopeless. Brew watched them go, then said to Guriat, 'What the Colonel lacks in manners, he makes up for in a certain amount of truth and wisdom. It's an old lesson, one we've learned before, from an ancient ancestor of his.'[111]

NIGHT After the funeral, the Rabbi produced three small wax candles and a box of matches. He melted the bottoms of two of candles to the top stone of the memorial mound. The third candle, he melted onto a small rock chip, which could be lifted to light the other two candles—

DAY In the late afternoon when the heat had begun to subside, the Rabbi chose ten men and women to represent him and lead the hundreds. These were former Justice Minister Judith Levitt, the advocate Jonathan Brodie, Dr Avigdor Ross, the beadle Mr Sinclair, Alec Ace, the Reform Rabbi from Glasgow Vivienne Falk, Rebbe Felix Frankelstein, young Todd Harrison, Brew's sister Sophie Banks, and Deborah Moray volunteered to be the tenth. 'Divide the people into equal groups,' he told them. 'It is important that like-minded individuals and families stay together.'

---

[111]The Rabbi refers to Moses' father-in-law, Jethro, and the good advice he gave the Law-Giver (Ex. 18.13-26).

The ten men and women asked many questions. After half an hour of listening to their grumblings and complaints, especially concerning the water shortage, Brew pointed out to sea. The sleeve of his white shirt fluttered in the freshening breeze. A dark cloud bank was climbing over the western horizon.

NIGHT The Rabbi called on Guriat Gaoni to come forward. He lit the candle on the stone chip and gave it to her. Shielding the flame from the wind, she said the blessings for the second night of the Feast of Lights, and kindled the two candles on the stone mound. Everyone sang out at the top of their voices.[112] Guriat alone stayed to see the three tiny flames burn out—

DAY The Harrisons — Todd and Lindy with their baby — came to the Rabbi as soon as the sun set. Lindy gave Brew a box of many-coloured Hanukkah candles, which they'd salvaged from the ferry. Brew thanked them, then asked, 'Have you two thought about what I said earlier?'

'We've talked about it, Rabbi,' answered Lindy. 'But Todd, doesn't think it's that important—'

* * *

---

[112]The song they sang was the Hymn of Hanukkah, 'O FORTRESS, ROCK of my deliverance,' a rousing tune of victory and joy.

Chapter LXXII

Baby Brew

[Sunday, December 13, 2009]
The desert night was cold and rainy. With no shelter and few blankets, the ferry people lay awake, shivering. The first rays of light were greeted with relief.

Deborah's sleepless body came alive unexpectedly refreshed in the quiet morning greyness. She stirred to a strange feeling; a sense of fullness and well-being that was wholly new to her. 'Brew, there's something...it's—'

'Can't it wait, Debs? We have a long day ahead, and I have to be there for everybody—'

Brew found Guriat. 'Where exactly are we?' he asked.

She drew him an upside-down harp-shaped triangle in the sand. 'The Sinai.' She added a crescent in the lefthand corner. 'We're out here on a sandbar. Between us and the mainland, the Bardawil Sea. Actually, it's a shallow lagoon.' She X-ed a spot to the north. 'The border crossing is up here — Nitzana. The quickest route is across the lagoon, much quicker than going around the sandbar.'

'Then "there" is where we must go.'

'With this lot? They're tired, and some are very weak. It's about a hundred miles.'

'We can't stay here. And we can't expect help. We've got to get away...now, this morning, before the clouds break up. We must cross over before it gets too hot—'

Guriat took off her sunglasses and stared into his eyes. 'You mean it, don't you? Why didn't you let me talk to him yesterday? That bloody bastard of a colonel spoke to us alone. He was angling for sling back.' Brew gestured communication breakdown. 'You mean a shmeer, a bribe.' Guriat said, 'Only they call it baksheesh. You know, Rabbi, if we go now, you could be taking us for a fall.'

Brew called for the ten leaders. He gave the order to prepare themselves and their hundreds to cross the flat lagoon. Overnight, the rain had left a few millimetres of fresh water in the bottoms of the inflatables and the one lifeboat. Everyone was allowed a few mouthfuls of water before starting out.

The youngest and strongest dragged the lifeboat, cork rafts and inflatables across the sandbar to the lagoon. Without enough boats and rafts to ferry everyone over the inland sea at once, the crossing took two relays.

The mainland shore was marshy. Tall, dense thickets of reeds and bulrushes grew right to the water's edge to form an impenetrable wall of vegetation. Tangled roots and slimy, dead stalks floated on the lapping tide. The atmosphere reeked of salinity and rot. Flies and mosquitoes swarmed. The heat and humidity of the day magnified with every passing minute. Few people had hats. The ones not on rafts had to stand in the brackish water up to their waists.

Brew Moray dispatched two rafts to scout out the coast. In less than an hour the parties returned with their report. The ferry people had landed at the tip end of a wide spit of land, jutting maybe ten or twelve miles out into the lagoon. The scouts argued among themselves that even if they could get through the swamps to dry land, a march across the desert dunes would be impossible. Hearing of the bitter conditions surrounding them, many cried to go back to the sandbar, and wait for the Egyptian Army to return.

Two of the scouts — Alec Ace and Todd Harrison — differed. Ace said, 'We must go on. We can make it.' Todd suggested that they split up. 'Let the weakest, the youngest and the oldest go by sea. The lifeboat with its motor can pull the rafts. The stronger, younger men and women can wade through the water around the spit to drier land.'

Brew agreed. Most of the women, children and old people went in the rafts and inflatables with Guriat commanding the lifeboat. Brew sent Sophie, Naomi and Anna in the boats. To Brew's surprise Deborah also asked to go by sea.

To those going on foot, Brew shouted encouragement. 'We've come too far to give up now. We've *seen* miracles, we've *made* miracles, we *are* miracles. Don't you see? The moment *we* stop fighting to move forward, we are lost.' The Rabbi started off, wading through the shallows. His wild hair and beard were matted with sweat. Deep ridges, the troughs scored with thin black lines of grime, furrowed his forehead. Sullen looks followed him as he walked along the line. Nobody moved. Brew stopped when he came to Mr Sinclair, who insisted on walking with the Edinburgh Torah Scroll despite his years. Brew asked the old caretaker for the Scroll of the Law. With the Torah, Brew splashed ahead to Lindy and Todd Harrison, who was holding his baby boy. The Rabbi held out his free arm, and said, 'Trust me.' Todd looked at his wife, and Lindy nodded. He placed their son into Brew's care.

With the Torah Scroll in one arm and the child cradled in the other, Brew Moray said for all to hear, 'Trust me. Walk with me.' Slowly, the Rabbi moved forward. Todd and Lindy and Mr Sinclair walked with him. And gradually the line edged ahead, churning up silt and turning the water yellow.

After a while, Todd said to Brew, 'Your arms must getting tired. Let me take him back.' Brew said that the Torah was heavier, and put the Scroll across Todd's shoulder.

'I've never held a Torah before,' said the young father. 'Here I am plunging knee-deep through water, holding a Torah. What if I trip and fall?'

'You won't,' said Brew. 'The Torah won't let you. I...I could say the same thing about your wee fine boy. If I were to fall— You know something, this is the first time in my life that I've ever held a baby—' Somehow he'd never held Naomi and Benny when they were babies. The child's heart beat in his arms. It made Brew feel so alive. 'I like holding him,' said the Rabbi. 'He's a good little lad. How old is he?'

His parents beamed. 'Almost six months,' said Lindy. 'You don't remember, do you, Rabbi?'

'Remember what?'

'You picked up his dummy when it fell out of his mouth. Remember? On the march, crossing Dean Bridge. He was six weeks then.'

'Of course—' recalled Brew. To the baby he said, 'You were crying your poor little lungs out, weren't you?'

'I'll tell you something, Rabbi Moray,' said Lindy. 'He's been a different little boy ever since, ever so good. We've both noticed it, haven't we, Toddy?' Her partner agreed, 'You have a way with kids, you know that?'

Brew asked Lindy why she and the child had not gone in the boats. She answered, 'Todd can't bear to be away from his son, so we stay together.'

Again, the Rabbi brought up his proposal. Todd said, 'I just don't see the need for a Jewish ceremony. We love each other. Cor, isn't that enough?' Lindy's mournful eyes floated to their child in the Rabbi's arms.

Brew changed the subject, 'By the way, I don't think I ever asked' — the couple looked worried — 'what's your little man here called?'

'Why, Brewster, of course,' said his mother proudly.

Todd joined in, 'We'd never given much thought to being Jewish, Lindy and I. But the day before our little one came along was the day you spoke on the radio. We said if he's a boy, we wanted him to be the answer to your dream, Rabbi. We both liked the idea, so we named our son after you — Brew.'

As Brew was sorting out his tangled emotions, a fat-bellied military helicopter came roaring out of the sky. Its shadow blackened the water like a huge monster lurking just below the surface. The thrashing rotor blades beat the sea into froth. The line froze. The Rabbi held little Brew's downy head close to his chest, and stroked his cheek. The baby did not cry. Then, as the helicopter lifted, the Rabbi — straight-armed — raised Brew high into the air, and slowly turned with him in a full circle for all to see. The baby boy grinned and gurgled at the attention. The march restarted.

The reed swamps ended suddenly. The vastness of the Sinai desert stretched out into the distance. Palms and clumps of scrub hugged the troughs between the dunes. On the horizon a violet-hued mountain range rose up to form an almost seamless join with the dark blue sky. Keeping their distance, black-clad women, and men in keffiyehs, sometimes with a donkey, sometimes without, stood, looked, then vanished.

Brew Moray did not stop. He went up and down the line, coaxing and encouraging his flock to keep going a little further, a little longer. He pointed to the diminishing afternoon sun, and gave praise for the cool breeze coming off the sea. The tired and despairing complained bitterly of thirst and headaches. To take their minds off their misery, Brew left groups of marchers with riddles from the Talmud, and later returned to discuss their solutions.

The sight of telephone poles raised new hope. A few broke into a run, shouting, 'There must be a road there—' They were disappointed. The blacktop was dusted with a thick film of dust, and there was not a vehicle in sight. On the beach, nearby they spotted the rafts and the lifeboat, empty. The only signs of those who came by water were their tracks in the sand leading up to the road.

At the roadside people dropped with exhaustion. Their eyes were riddled with questions, with reproach, with despair. Brew Moray walked among them, and told them that they would stay here for the night.

Evening closed in fast. The ferry people lay down and slept.

* * *

Chapter LXXIII

Hobbled

[Sunday, December 13, 2009]
'Lights! Headlights!' People shocked out of deep sleep moaned, 'What now?' The night watch excitedly pointed down the road. The lights quickly grew larger and brighter. A jeep leading three ramshackle military trucks pulled up, brakes squealing.

A starch-uniformed sergeant stepped out of the jeep. Helmeted troops, wielding assault rifles, leapt down from the lorries and fanned out along the road.

By then all the people were on their feet. Brew Moray pushed forward to greet the Egyptians.

'Salaam.'

The Sergeant in command pumped his side-arm menacingly high overhead. His troops fired into the air. Screams of dread shattered the night as people fell over each other to get back. The soldiers used impatient grunts, boots and rifle butts to herd everyone on to the road.

From behind, two men hoisted the Rabbi by his arms. As he struggled, he demanded, 'What have you done with our people? Where are they? The ones who came in the boats? Where are you taking us?' The Sergeant, who had started to turn away, spun back and slapped the Rabbi across the mouth. He then spat on his "contaminated" hand and wiped it off on Brew's shirt. At the Sergeant's command, one of the soldiers hobbled Brew's feet with a cord at the ankle.

The jeep and lorries turned around. Their headlight beams swept across dull shocked faces. The jeep and one lorry went to the front of the convoy, the other two lorries to the rear. In between, the troops spaced themselves out along both sides of the road, sandwiching the Scottish Jews in the middle. As a monosyllabic command passed down the line, each soldier gave the nearest person a shove to start.

Brew was forced to march at the head of the column. Separated by the jeep and a lorry from the rest, he kept looking back at first. He saw the Sergeant asleep next to the jeep driver, and a trooper sitting high in the back with his weapon ready.

The night march did not stop to rest. It held up only long enough for the occasional taxi or over-loaded truck to pass. To hold up for short pauses was more painful than not to stop at all.

In the illumination of the headlights, the ferry people watched with black envy as the Egyptians drank water from their canteens. Fresh troops from the lorries replaced tired men. At all times soldiers slept peacefully on the floors and benches of the open vehicles.

The asphalt was hard, bone-jarring. Tramping feet beat out a steady, dull rhythm. Brew's normal rolling stride was hampered; the hobble bit into the flesh of his ankles.

Frankelstein collapsed first. Warboys tried to help him. Soldiers kicked him away, signalling other black-coated Hassidim to carry their Rebbe. These men, too, soon flagged. The soldiers then prodded them to take their leader, broken and babbling, to the last lorry. Hefting him over their heads, Frankelstein's followers unceremoniously rolled him into the truck like a bag of rubbish. As the night wore on, many others followed.

In the light thrown out by the jeep Brew counted telephone poles. At six hundred and thirteen,[113] he stopped and began all over again. Counting kept his mind off the pain around his ankles—

Dawn brought no relief. The sands of the interior looked grey in the pale light. Strips of stringy, blown-out bits of tyre rubber and large, square tins dotted the roadside. Half buried under the sands, turret tops and cannon snouts from rusted tanks looked like the remains of prehistoric beasts. In the far distance, the fronds of scattered date palms waved in the sharp winter airs that blew off the sea.

Later in the morning, an oasis and the outskirts of a town on the horizon raised hopes for an end to the ordeal. But the jeep led the column off the main coastal highway onto a narrower road that descended into the desert.

Burning feet and numbed legs now moved without any connection to the humanity they were part of. Periodically, a bored or nervous soldier fired off a round. With a life of its own, the column ploughed on, as if in perpetual motion since the beginning of time.

Again, the road forked, turning the convoy away from the rising sun, and deeper into the boundless waste. The Sergeant ordered his jeep to stop. Dulled by the rhythm of the march, Brew kept walking. The Sergeant fired a round from his revolver. Brew Moray tripped over his hobbled feet, and fell into the sand. Looking back, he saw the Egyptian standing tall in his jeep, angrily motioning him with the gun to get up. From where he lay, nearly senseless from exhaustion, he could see no sign of traffic, no destination, no reason for stopping. The Sergeant took aim and shot again, kicking up a puff of dust by Brew's head. The Rabbi pulled himself up.

The Sergeant holstered his weapon. His driver and guard watched him survey the surrounding wilderness, as though he were seeking some sign. At last, he reached into the jeep's foot well, and stepped down carrying a small rolled carpet under his arm. He limped slightly. At a leisurely pace, he unfurled the red carpet on the desert floor and removed his boots and cap. He was bald. In his stocking feet, he stepped onto the fringed prayer rug. Eyes closed, mouthing words, he first looked to the sky, and then kneeled with hands cupped upward on his thighs. Often he brought his forehead forward to the carpet. Not moving a muscle, Brew watched the Moslem at prayer, while his driver and the back seat soldier enjoyed their morning bread, and long, cool drinks of water from a jerrycan.

After half an hour, during which no Jew was allowed to sit, the soldiers' break for prayer and sustenance was over. The jeep sputtered to life. The Egyptians now quickened the pace. The desert track rounded a bend, then climbed a long slope. The heat of the mid-morning sun grazed heads and shoulders.

From the brow of the ridge, the Rabbi was first to take in the installation spread out on the flats below. Coils of razor wire glinted in the sun. Close to the entrance was a low, hexagonal tower supported by two concrete wings. Some distance from the tower stood a single large structure of corrugated metal walls topped by a sloping roof with many missing panels. The compound's other salient feature was a V-shaped outline barely visible under a thick film of wind-blown sand.

The final descent was done on the run, double-time. Stragglers were pushed, kicked or rolled down the slope.

The convoy halted at the entrance to the compound. The trooper in the Sergeant's jeep hopped down and exchanged words with the two guards at the gate. The guards opened up. With shouts and waves, the Sergeant made Brew stand aside. The jeep and lorry drove through first. The Rabbi, under close guard at gunpoint, was forced to watch the splintered

---

[113]613 is equivalent to the number of commandments in the Five Books of Moses.

humanity file past. Most of the wretched faces did not have the strength to look at him. Those who did had rage in their eyes. Brew was pushed in last.

Guriat came rushing up to him. She said something in Arabic to the guards, then to Brew, 'Let's get you to some shade.'

'Is everyone with you all right?' asked Brew, his voice thick and croaking.

'Yes, why, yes, but you look—'

'Where's Deborah?'

'With Sophie, and your mother. Your mother, she...she... keeled over last night. Doctor Ross tells her it's nothing serious, but—'

'You better take me to see her,' said Brew. In his hurry, he forgot the hobble around his bruised and bloodied ankles, and almost fell over again.

* * *

Chapter LXXIV

Difficult Delivery

[Sunday morning, January 10, 2010]
Elen watched her father stroke the sheep's black face. The big ewe lay stiff-legged on the hay floor. Alan Fraser was in his Sunday suit; there'd been no time to change. Becky ran her fingers lightly along the animal's flank. She pressed slightly — Liquorice jerked. Flinging off her straw hat and rolling up the frilly sleeves of her cotton blouse, she put an ear to the sheep's belly. Strands of greying hair fell over her eyes. She lifted her face, nodding negatively.

The animal stretched her neck and convulsed. Her bleating was mournful. 'You're not to worry, Liquorice. Mother 'n' I'll get you right as rain, old girl.'

'If Deborah—' began Elen.

'Enough of Deborah,' said Fraser sharply.

Fraser seemed changed since Elen had come back from Edinburgh. Some of the love between father and daughter had gone missing in her absence. The man was less patient, and tired-looking. He worked harder than ever. Together with the twins, he was building a simple but liveable extension to the house — the 'new wing' — for Jemima and the baby. And he was forever harping on at Becky. Said she was worrying herself sick over people and things she couldn't control.

'So what do you say, Mother?'

'Multiple birth, for sure. I can hear two heartbeats.' The Frasers had seen it before, many times. The position of the lead lamb had to be changed. It was going to hurt the mother.

Shifting places, Alan locked Liquorice's twitching feet in an iron grip. He started sweating. Birthing, when things went wrong, was the one part of shepherding he'd never liked. 'Elen,' he said, 'take the hair out your ma's eyes, and hold Liquorice's head.'

Elen had spent hours on end telling and retelling her mother about her time in Edinburgh: the Sabbath in "school", the Rabbi's sermon and his arrest; the march and the events at Dean Bridge; the raid on Ms Landis's house, and how the same policemen who took Brew in smashed all her beautiful things. But above all, it was Deborah this and Deborah that— And when Becky was too busy or too tired to listen any more, Elen brooded.

'Ready, Fraser?'

'I'm ready. Go.'

Becky firmly manipulated the swollen belly. The ewe thrashed violently. 'There, there, girl.' Becky patted the sheep's quivering flank. 'I think that'll do it. The rest's up to you and HIM. Fraser, Elen, hang on to her a few minutes longer, till she settles down. I'm going up to the house to wash up, and change. Must check on Jemima and wee Boy Roy.'

The twins, Ross and Crom, invented the name 'wee Boy Roy', and it stuck. Even Jemima seemed to like it.

- 242 -

Before going upstairs, Becky peeked into the lounge. Jemima was feeding little Roy by the fire. Roy's hands were wrapped around hers and the bottle, and his mouth worked hard. In a strange way, it often seemed to Becky that Jemima was the sanest, most uncomplicated human being left in a Scotland gone mad. And her father must have been a saint. In the two hours of his second visit, Brew Moray had told many wonderful stories about Roy Roscoe. But what rang in Becky's mind was the Rabbi saying, 'Reverend Roscoe didn't *lose* his life helping me escape from the Castle, he *gave* his life for mine.' Brew now owed it to Roy to risk everything to help his daughter and grandson. He promised the Frasers that their stay would be temporary, and that he and Deborah, when they were safe again, would find Jemima and Roy a permanent home. He also insisted on paying for their board and lodging as soon as he could.

Fraser wanted to deny the Rabbi, but Elen's eyes would not let him. 'Deborah would take them in,' she said at the time.

Liquorice gave a shudder under their hands. Elen had spotted her black face lying in the snow from the Land Rover on their way home from the kirk. 'Father, why don't you say "our Elen" any more?'

Alan's jaw quivered. 'Maybe, it's sometimes, I don't feel you're "our Elen" any more. The way you go on to your mother, it sounds like you're "their Elen", you're Deborah Moray's "Tsippi". I feel like we've lost you.'

'Father, I'll always be yours first, "your Elen", your daughter.'

Alan looked up. Becky was back. 'Jem and the baby are fine. El, I'll take over here, you go in, get washed up and start seeing to some lunch. Let Jem help. An' get the twins to peel the potatoes. Tell them your Father said so.' Becky gave her husband her sly look. Her hands were behind her back.

'Right, Mother, what is it? I know when you want to talk to me alone.'

'First, let Liquorice go. Let's see what she does.' The ewe raised her head, kicked the stiffness out of her legs, rolled over and stood up.

'Good girl,' said Alan.

'Fraser, sometimes I think you love sheep more than you love folk.'

'Why not? Sheep treat each other a good deal kinder than folk do. Mother, be sensible. For the hundredth time, what do you think we could do for them over there? We're building the annex, because, well, we both know the Rabbi might not be able to keep his promise about Jem and Roy. What more can we do? We haven't got a lot of spare cash. I don't have to tell you that.'

Becky knew that Fraser would not sell even a single acre. The land had been in his family for over two hundred years. The lambing season was just beginning, and shearing was far off. Nothing was coming in for months. In any case, money in Scotland, and especially in the Highlands, was tight.

'I honestly don't know what we could do for them,' said Becky, 'but at least we'd be closer—'

'Closer—' he repeated.

'Closer. They've been in the desert for almost a whole month now, and the world couldn't care a damn. It's all jabber, jabber. The international community this, the international community that. But does anybody *do* anything? No, not even the Israelis. Is everybody powerless these days? Can nobody pull chestnuts out of the fire any more? This is the Twenty-first century.'

'And what about Jemima and little Roy? Who'll take care of them if we go away?'

'I've thought about that.'

'You have, have you?' He mockingly lifted a lock of his hair.

'Fraser, I'm trying to be serious.'

'I know you are. That's what scares me. One thing's for sure. You 'n' Elen aren't going without me. Sometimes I think you two forget who's the guardian angel of this establishment. It's twice now the Rabbi turns up in the middle of the night, an' twice *I* dinna deny him.'

'Guardian angel—' echoed Becky. 'In your dreams, Alan Fraser, in your dreams.' They both laughed.

'Becky. I'm a hand-t'-mouth Highland sheepman. Sheep are all I know. Politics, religion, national security are big words for me. What can one family do, what can we do? As it is, I think we're doing more than our share.'

'We can always do more—'

'What, with Jem and Roy? They're no trouble, but—'

'Fraser, she might not know how to say it — but she *is* mighty grateful to us. An' Jem's not afraid of hard work, and she's a good mother to her baby. And wee Roy's as quiet as a Highland breeze.'

'Mother, I'm not arguing with you. I'm only asking you to tell me something I haven't heard you say a thousand times before.'

'Right, then. Mrs Dougal-Christmas—'

'Now, who in HEAVEN'S name is Mrs Dougal-Christmas?'

'She's a bonny brave lady. Demonstrates every day outside Parliament House. She was the Moray family's housekeeper for the better part of her life, and now she's all alone in the world. Her husband's left her, and her daughter's in England, struggling to be a musician.'

'How do you know so much about her?'

'She was on the radio. They interviewed her.'

Liquorice had found herself a quiet corner in the shadows. A sign that her time was very near. Fraser went to have a closer look. Not too close. Animals about to give birth seek seclusion. 'I'm still with you, Mother. Go on—'

'I've invited her up here.'

'No! Where are we to put her? Here, in the sheep shed? We're already building the extension for Jem and Roy with money we haven't got. Mother, sometimes—'

'Just listen a minute—'

'I knew it. I knew it.'

Becky went on, fast: 'She takes care of the house and the boys. Jem looks after the baby and does some of the cooking. We'll go around Easter, no school. Ross and Crom can mind the sheep. It's all so neat.'

'Who says she'll agree t' come?'

'She already has. I wrote to her; she's coming.'

'Crikey! I should have known!' yelled Alan. 'And what about cash? Three airline tickets. And where do we stop out there? Under some palm tree?'

'That's the miracle. Settle down, and I'll tell you—'

'I'm settled, so tell me.'

'It's all in these letters.' Becky held out the pack of envelopes she'd brought down from the house. 'Before she left Scotland, Anna Moray — Rabbi Brew's mother — left her house and a good sum of money to pay for the bomb damage to Agnes Dougal-Christmas. Of course I didn't know that when I wrote to her. But she's only willing to come up here if she can pay for our trip.'

'We're not taking advantage of some poor old woman—'

'She's not poor, and she says that we're not to feel obliged to her. The money Anna left her is more than enough to pay for repair of the house. Don't you see, Fraser? This way we'll be going out there for Mrs Christmas, too.'

Alan made a doubting face. 'So where do we stay when we get there?'

'Well, Jemima says her father was in the Holy Land once, and he had a dream to go back someday. He always said he could stay in Church o' Scotland hostels out there, in Jerusalem and on the Sea of Galilee. So I contacted Church headquarters in Edinburgh. We're booked in — if we can get there—'

Alan took Becky in his hands. 'That's my Mother. Thinks of everything.'

In quick succession, Liquorice gave birth to two healthy lambs. 'Now look what you've done, Mother,' said Alan. Even in the dimness of the shed, Alan could see Becky looked happier than she had in months. He gave her a big swinging hug.

'The only thing I haven't told you, Fraser...it's the reason why El's been so moody, lately. She was terribly afraid — even if I got it all sorted — you'd still find a reason to say no.'

'C'mon, then, let's tell our Elen the good news.'

* * *

Chapter LXXV

Delirium

[Wednesday-Tuesday, March 3-9, 2010]

Guriat Gaoni stumbled over the last quarter mile alone. It was the coldest hour of the desert night. She moaned like a lost spectre.

As commander of the Mossad's "Morning Star" division to save endangered Diaspora communities, Amos Lev-Ari had come under increasing pressure to devise a rescue plan. Operation Snatch had gone wildly wrong. The hostages were most likely suffering severe reprisals. But without precise intelligence, nothing could be done. The decision came down from the very top: bring out Guriat Gaoni at once, and pray the Egyptians do not find out.

**

For hours Amos Lev-Ari and Rafael "Pete" Petrovski lay hidden in silence behind a huge concrete, anti-tank barrier at Kilometre Fifty-six on the Egyptian side of Sinai-Israel frontier. In the quietness of their wait, both men had almost given up hope. At the same time neither expected her to be so weak. She fell into their hands. 'They're dying—'

During the sixty hours it took her to reach the border, Guriat went with almost no sleep. Whenever it was safe to move, her Bedouin guides shunted her on foot or donkeyback from one encampment to the next. The Egyptian army patrolled everywhere. In the daytime heat and dust, the veil suffocated her. At night she shivered and convulsed in the desert cold. For months, she'd been sleeping on concrete between the dying and the dead. As soon as the camp gates were out of sight, Guriat bit off two strips from her heavy Arab dress and wrapped them around her painfully raw hands.

**

The open jeep rumbled along a military track. Petrovski drove. Lev-Ari sat in the back next to Guriat. She kept saying, her voice weak and wheezing, 'Amos, they're dying. We've got to get them out of there—' Her head fell back. She'd blacked out. Lev-Ari splashed water on his hands to wet Guriat's face. She came to, scarcely able to speak, 'They're killing them. Working them to death. We can't let them die— Rabbi Moray, save him—' From the driver's seat, Petrovski spoke over his shoulder, 'Guri, we need facts, facts on the ground, if we're to help those people. Facts, not speeches.' Again, she fell unconscious.

From Enhanced Satellite Surveillance Imaging (ESSI) and unmanned drones overflying the Sinai, the intelligence community knew that the Scottish Jews were confined at Nakash, a former Israeli air force base — twelve miles south of El-Arish, and thirty-nine miles from the Nitzana border crossing to the east.

Coils of razor wire topped the chain-link fence around the facility's perimeter road. All indications pointed to mine fields planted around the compound at strategic points. The main gate, serviced by a single narrow track, was the only safe way in and out.

The Egyptians deployed eight mobile SAM-Six anti-aircraft missile batteries on hilltops around the makeshift detention camp. The SAMs were camouflaged and frequently moved to prevent a satellite fix.

Other than military vehicles, only local Bedouin women came and went freely. The guards welcomed their trade in pita bread and fresh desert-grown dates. In the camp, the tribeswomen took the opportunity to pick over the rubbish tips for discarded plastic and metal. From the women the Mossad's well-paid Bedouin informants learned that the active guard within the installation never numbered more than twenty-four men, and two cooks. The security road inside the fence was jeep-patrolled every two to three hours. The camp guards were headquartered in the air-control tower near the main gate. The hostages slept in the hangar.

It was clear, the Mossad concluded, that Egypt was more concerned about keeping Israeli rescuers out than keeping the Scottish Jews in. The camp was too far inland to mount a workable commando raid from the sea. The missiles, though Chinese-made and antiquated, deterred any airborne rescue attempt. And even if the hostages overpowered the small camp guard, the thirty-nine mile run through the desert to the border was out of the question.

Getting a picture of the installation's physical setup was no obstacle. But the Mossad had no reliable, first-hand information about the fate of the thousand captives. Whether out of Arab pride or shame, Israel's Bedouin allies politely avoided questions concerning camp conditions or the treatment of the hostages.

**

Petrovski raced through the sleeping outskirts of Eilat. A helicopter was waiting on the old airfield at the northern end of the Red Sea town. As Petrovski stopped the jeep under the rotor blades, Lev-Ari swore, 'Damn! She keeps passing out.' Petrovski said, 'She needs a hospital. She's been through some kind of hell.'

'Sorry, Pete,' she murmured, 'was I asleep? What's the date?'

'March third, two days after Purim—'[114]

'That late. Where are we now?'

'About to fly you to a warm bed, Guri. Up you go.' The two agents gently guided Guriat into the rear of the four-seater. Lev-Ari took the controls, while Petrovski sat next to Guriat. Her body and dress gave off a sharp stench in the closed cockpit.

'Here, Guri, drink some of this,' said Petrovski, pouring a cup of strong hot coffee from a flask. He held the cup to her lips.

'Elite. Forgot how good it tasted—'

Lousy instant coffee, thought Petrovski. She must be in a bad way.

Petrovski sat at her bedside. Guriat was fevered, exhausted, dehydrated. The bandages around the weeping sores on her hands and knees yellowed within hours and had to be changed often. The doctors kept her on a constant drip. She babbled endlessly.

'Rice...buggy rice...smelly water...half litre a day...every drop...trucked in...no regular pattern...tried to figure out timing, but I had to sleep—

---

[114]Purim or the Feast of Lots commemorates Persian Jewry's successful repelling of attempted genocide, as narrated in the Book of Esther. Esther is the only book in the Hebrew Scriptural canon which does not once explicitly mention the Name of God. The Jewish Sages teach that the omission is the lesson. "Scripture implies that Heaven above rewarded [with success] what the Jews took upon themselves [to fight their enemies] on the earth below" (Tractate *Megillah* 7a). Purim is also early spring "carnival". In addition to eating, drinking spirits and exchanging gifts of food, celebrants are encouraged to wear fancy dress.

'Need sleep...let me sleep...after sleep...hangar...concrete floor—

'Work... sweep runways... men, women, children... days... hot, so hot... freezing at night...no let-up... keep two runways free of sand... day and night... wind... never stops blowing... more sand... one detail finishes, the next starts—

'On our knees... for hours... no brushes, no brooms... sweep runway... bare hands... they tear out their hair to make brushes... no scissors, knives to cut with...they catch you with a brush, they take it away, beat you—'

'Work... inspection every four hours, round the clock...whole camp must turn out... surprises... punishment... beatings... no exceptions... everybody up... to witness beatings... even the sickest... Rabbi's mother... so sick—'

'Parade... every morning at dawn, every evening before sundown... parade... standing... at attention... count off...one...two...three—

'Bastards!' gasped Pete.

**

Over the noise of the helicopter, Pete said, 'It's all right, Guri. You're safe now.'

'Parade!' she blurted wildly. 'Everyone, up. Parade!'

Guriat remained delirious for days. Everything she said, all her raving, was recorded and analysed. The Mossad pieced her story together, and began to work out a rescue plan.

**

Lev-Ari brought the helicopter down at Tel Aviv's Sde Dov Airport, near Mossad Headquarters.

'People are dying. Bodies lie where they die. Smell of death all around.'

After a week in hospital, Guriat was sitting up, eating solid foods and starting to walk. She repeated much of what she had said in her delirium, but in more detail.

'The dead couldn't be buried until a local doctor signed the death certificate. Sometimes, it took days for the doc to show up. Bodies just lay waiting—

'Colonel Raoul Abed as-Mansura, Officer Commanding, Northern Sinai Military District. Smooth-talking, bloody son of bitch used false hope to keep people slaving. Blah-blah about negotiations with the 'Zionist enemy' and humanitarian flights. Promises day in, day out, that the planes were coming. Said they were coming today, tomorrow, any day now, but no plane could land on sandy runways. So the landing strip had to be kept sand-free at all times—

'It was all bullshit. Lies. And excuses when nothing happened. I knew it. I overheard the guards talk and I listened to their radios. I knew there were no negotiations, no planes. But I kept it to myself. The truth would have been too heartbreaking for any of them to know—

'The Rabbi? He's trying to hold things together. But he's one man, essentially alone. His wife's a great help, absolutely beautiful under stress. His mother is dying there on the concrete floor—

'They blame him for everything. And his only answer is that he dreamed a dream. What dream? He won't tell anybody for sure. Only that it's some verse from the Bible which he can't-won't repeat, and something about a mountain—'

**

The ambulance screamed through the sparse dawn traffic to Tel HaShomer Hospital.

'He doesn't know that the Bedouin girl took my place, that I'm gone—'

'Who, Guri?' asked Amos.

'Brew— Oh, shit— He doesn't know — the two good ones—' and she started to pass out again.

- 248 -

'Guri, Guri,' said Petrovski, gently shaking her, 'Guri, talk to me. The two para-blanks? Your handgun, your weapon—?'

'Colonel. Ditched KTL, had to, before they searched us — first time. Bastards found it...buried in the sand. Metal detector picked up the bullets. All hell broke loose. Double shifts, public execution. Nobody talked. Nobody knew to talk. Oh, my G— Colonel carries my KTL—'

* * *

At the time throughout the crisis, there was no breaching the wall of silence surrounding the hostages. Israel was resoundingly unsuccessful in its attempts to introduce the International Red Cross, or any other impartial body into the "internment facility". Repeated calls for economic sanctions in the United Nations and other world forums had no impact on the conservative Islamic regime. Nothing could stop the ruling Moslem Brotherhood from exacting its revenge. The abortive arms deal with Scotland had not only lost Egypt millions in revenue, but also the opportunity to acquire enough fissionable material to build a nuclear warhead. E.T.

Chapter LXXVI

Mummy

Brew welcomed the late afternoon breeze. The cool air whistled through the hangar roof's many missing panels blown away by time and the desert wind. He stole a moment to contemplate the patches of broken sky. But here, even his vision of heaven was barred. The network of steel supports under the roof splintered the blue rectangles into sharp kaleidoscopic patterns.

Brew held his mother's hand. Her fingers twitched. He looked at her face. Her eyes had become slits of sticky yellow butter.

The breeze blew into a wind. Walls of corrugated metal began to rattle. The hangar's vast concrete floor seethed with bodies that moved in patches like cloud shadows passing over the earth. The atmosphere was thick with moaning, snoring, coughing and quiet crying.

Anna was past speaking any more. Before, her speech had been slurred, and she kept saying the same thing over and over: 'Manny— Is that you? You know... our son... Neville... is gone. Manny—'

Dr Ross said that even if she couldn't speak any more, she could still hear. Sophie and Deborah whispered to her. Brew followed the teaching of his mentor Rabbi Rozanski: Words are nothing but shadows of thoughts — the purest speech is unspoken—

Mummy, you're breathing easier today. Good.

She rested under her winter coat. For two days her jaw was locked, open slightly as though ready to let her soul go. Sometimes she would squirm, trying to touch parts of her body she couldn't feel. At other times she lay disturbingly still for hours. With a jerk her hand pulled his—

You, too, want to know the verse I dreamt. What brought us to this place. Please don't ask. It would be more terrible for you to know than not to know.

Somehow, Anna Moray had managed to save the little book Dr Ross had given her when Manny died. Emily Dickinson, she said, comforted her. Deborah read the poems to her—

Deborah? She's not feeling so well again today. It's the food, she says. Still she carries on. Mummy, she's marvellous. I don't deserve such a blessing as her. I know you wanted me to have children. But I could never have left her. She's at work now, sweeping. The longer we're here, the less sleep she seems to need. And yet she glows. From within. Her spirit touches everyone. Everything she says and does is a lesson in kindness and goodness. I learn more from her than I ever did from study. Mummy, even the Bedouins are moved by her love, they give her pita bread. And she gives it to the sick and weakest among us.

She coughed. It was an ugly unnatural rattle. Dark amber fluid bubbled up between her lips, and oozed down her chin. There was nothing to clean her with, no cloths, no tissues. His fingers wiped her, and smeared it on the floor. The amber fluid had the smell of death—

What was I telling you, Mummy? Deborah— Yes. Mostly, she seems, well, elsewhere, in a happier place. There's a bloom in her face I've never seen before — like she's bursting to tell the world some great good news, only she's decided to keep it hidden from the evil of this place. But this morning her mouth was twitching like it does when she's concentrating or upset. I asked her what was bothering her. She told me that she overheard them talking. They said my name. She stopped to listen, but around a corner so they didn't see her. One said to the other that he saw "the whoor" in my arms, that I kissed her. I asked her what the other one said. Her answer was, that if Brew Moray is false and unfaithful to his wife, then his dream is also a lie. Deborah asked me if it was true — the kiss. No, I told her, it was not true. Mummy, it happened when Neville died. She — Guriat — needed to put her arms around me and cry. That was all. Deborah said that she was sorry she listened to them, and that she believes me. And now I tell you, Mummy, what I told her: If I have to choose between being a rabbi and a mensch, I'll be a mensch. If I can't let a person hold me when they need to, then what am I?

Brew looked away.

You blame me for what happened to Neville. You blame her. She never meant to hurt him. She was sent to help us. She saved my life, more than once. She's gone, now. She left a Bedouin woman instead. They exchanged clothes. So far the Egyptians haven't discovered the switch.

Her skin was white, her hair hung in strands like dried cucumber stems. The muscles and veins of the one arm that tried to touch were stringy and twisted.

She looked serene—

Mummy, seeing you like this, living on air alone—

Against the strengthening wind, Brew pulled up her coat, under her chin—

The Colonel's here today. I demanded an interview with him, and he saw me. I asked him through his Adjutant — he speaks some English — if he knew who Moses was. He stared at me like I was crazy, said something private to the Adjutant, and they both laughed. I asked the Colonel why Pharaoh let Moses live. After all, Moses was a dangerous man, and Pharaoh could have had him killed at any time. The Colonel looked at me and said that Pharaoh let Moses live, because he was intrigued to know what he would do next. Then he laughed even louder, and asked me what I wanted. Thirty minutes, I said. Give us half an hour to be all together, to celebrate a wedding.

Anna turned feverish, pulled her working hand free from Brew's fingertips, and rubbed her forehead. The arm fell back over her coat like a broken twig. Brew stroked her brow and arranged her hair. To soothe her he silently started to read a poem from Anna's little book. The last lines of the poem...

> *Who is to blame? The weaver?*
> *Ah! The bewildering thread!*
> *The tapestries of paradise*
> *So notelessly are made!*[115]

> > > > > ...finished in a flash of insight—

They are the thread of that tapestry! It was for them that I had my dream!
Brew cried—

---

[115]Emily Dickinson (1830-86). Untitled poem, first line, "A shady friend for torrid days".

Lindy and Todd, Mummy, they asked me to marry them. They want a Jewish wedding. They said to me, 'Marry us, here, today.' They came to me this morning, only hours after their little baby died. Mummy, they named him Brew, after me. He was the first child I ever held in my arms.

Brew cried, and the people around him saw—

The Colonel refused. I asked him why. He told me — through the Adjutant — that he appointed Rabbi Frankelstein his 'official adviser on Jewish affairs'. In return for his services, he and his family and followers are given time off for prayers, and double water rations for 'ritual washing'. He could marry the couple. The Colonel enjoyed telling me this news. I could see it in his face. He had that same look in his eye that Montrose had when he shook my hand.

Brew sensed a change. She relaxed. Her sleep was deepening—

447-989...Mummy wasn't home...when Brew called her... Mummy...Mummy didn't love him any more. Brew was a good boy; he didn't forget the number Mummy taught him. Mummy was angry with Brew because he walked home alone.

She stopped trying to touch herself. Her arm went limp. Brew took her hand again in his—

Say something, so I know...

Her mouth clamped shut. She squeezed his hand—

Mummy, I know you can hear me.

Her eyes opened. Her lips parted—

Say you love me.

After how long — a minute? an hour? — the wind whistling through the roof brought him back. He pulled the coat over her face—

Mummy's out. Brew must find his own way home.

He said to the sky, 'Blessed be the TRUE JUDGE.' Brew tore his shirt,[116] and sat quietly—

'Parade! Evening parade!' The call spread across the hangar floor. 'Parade! The Colonel is here!' Weary people groaned, as they came to their feet. 'Evening parade!' Brew Moray left his mother. Alone.

* * *

---

[116] The rending of garments is an ancient sign of mourning, observed when a close relative (parent, child, sibling or spouse) dies. When a garment is rent for a deceased parent, the child may never repair it.

Chapter LXXVII

KTL

[Tuesday afternoon, March 16, 2010]

Deborah detoured past the hangar. She was coming from her shift. 'Brew—?'

'She's gone.'

Her face crumpled. She looked into the hangar's empty space. 'I'm going in to say goodbye.'

Brew said, 'Parade. And the Colonel's here. There's no time for goodbyes. You know it's a double shift for anyone who's late. If As-Mansura's come from El-Arish, something could be up.' Everyone was hurrying; no one wanted to be last.

'But we can't leave her alone—'[117]

'Debs— The Law is for the living. Let's go, before we're late.'

Deborah put her arms around him, and held him. Her tears wet his cheek. They separated and looked into each other's eyes. Brew said, 'I don't know where your strength comes from, but mine comes from you, from your love.' His expression turned dark. 'Whatever happens in the next few minutes, don't be afraid.'

'What's going to happen?'

'I'm not sure—'

They walked quickly to the open ground in front of the tower building. The evening parade was in its final stages of formation. Spaces were left for anyone who was missing. Deborah fell in. The place between her and Sophie remained empty. Deborah's tears fell onto the sand. Sophie saw them form little round pebbles, and she knew her mother was dead.

The Colonel, the Adjutant, the Sergeant and the Rabbi came to attention in a line before the assembly. As-Mansura recited, his Adjutant interpreted, and Brew Moray was forced to repeat the Colonel's opening formula loudly in English for all to hear: 'In the name of the Prophet, peace and blessings upon his name, fall in and be counted.'

Under the Sergeant's watchful gaze, armed guards passed between the rows, checking and double-checking the numbers. The count was brought to the Sergeant, who in turn presented the final figure to the Colonel. Announcements and news of the day came next. The Colonel began, 'The Zionist interloper, the plunderers of Jerusalem—' as the Adjutant interpreted in the background.

Brew started, 'The sovereign State of Israel, the builders of Jerusalem—' The Adjutant whispered into his Colonel's ear. As-Mansura reddened, and shouted one word. The Sergeant smashed Brew across the mouth. He spat blood. The Colonel continued, but instead of repeating what the Adjutant said, Brew slowly began to recite Kaddish for his mother, 'Yis-ga-dal v'yis-ka-dash sh'may ra-ba — Magnified and sanctified is HIS great name in the world that HE created as HE wills—' Steadily, the Rabbi's voice rose. Others

---

[117]According to the Code of Jewish Law (*Shulchan Aruch* 194.10), an unbroken vigil must be kept over the body until it is buried.

picked up the familiar cadence, and joined in. The Sergeant beat the Rabbi, one blow at a time, to the ground. And still Brew carried his prayer to its climax: 'Oh, the PEACE-MAKER in HIS high places, HE will shower peace on us and on all Israel, and let us say, Amen.'[118]

Deborah started to break ranks, but Sophie and Alec Ace held her back. One of the guards levelled his weapon at her belly.

People shied like a jittery herd. The lines became ragged. The Colonel nodded to the Sergeant. He fired into the air. The burst of gunfire restored order.

Pulling himself up from the dust, the Rabbi shimmied like a desert mirage. But his voice was steady, 'And now we will have our wedding.'

The Adjutant laughed, then spoke to his superior, pointing to the Rabbi. The Colonel pulled Guriat's KTL automatic from his belt, and crashed it into Brew's face. Again he fell. Painfully, he came to his hands and knees, and said again, slowly, 'We will have our wedding.'

As-Mansura handed the belly-barrelled KTL to the Sergeant with a sharp order. The Sergeant lowered his arm. The Rabbi rose to his knees. Stiffening, the Sergeant took aim at the side of Brew Moray's head. The handgun followed Brew as he slowly came to his feet. The range was point-blank.

The assembly were horrified into silence. Most turned away, or shut their eyes. But others could not stop themselves looking on in terrified fascination. Mothers blindfolded their children with their hands. Deborah struggled in Ace's arms. The howl of horror in her was so huge that she could not bring it out. The blood drained from her head, but she refused to let herself faint.

Brew cried out, 'Our Debs—'

As-Mansura angrily repeated his order.

Brew's lips quivered in prayer.[119]

The Sergeant's wide forehead glistened. He pulled the trigger. The action sprang noiselessly. He squeezed off two rounds in quick succession. The shots boomed out, and echoed back from the hills with a sharp double clap. The crowd reeled back.

To everyone's amazement, the Rabbi did not fall.

As the reverberations died around him, Brew brought up his hands to ease the thunder ringing in his ears. Then realising he was alive, he looked at himself in disbelief.

As-Mansura snatched the gun from the Sergeant's shaking hand. He looked down the muzzle, took out the clip, inspected it, rammed it back and again trained the KTL on the Rabbi. He brought up his second hand to steady his aim. There were loud gasps. At the last minute the Colonel jerked round, and fired a silent shot into the assembly—

* * *

---

[118] See Chapter 71, fn. 4.

[119] Though not made explicit, my rabbinical sources strongly suggest that the Rabbi is praying the Shema ("Hear, O Israel..." Deut. 6.4). As the central affirmation of Jewish life on earth, it is repeated even at the very moment of death.

Chapter LXXVIII

Wedding in the Wilderness

[Tuesday evening, March 16, 2010]
Warboys twitched to attention — his mouth a gaping black hollow. The bullet struck in his throat. A low gurgling rose from deep inside him, as he toppled to the ground like a felled tree.

The Colonel, glassy-eyed and uncomprehending, shook the gun from his grasp, as though it were a hot ember. The live third round, silent and deadly, had delivered only the slightest kick.

Brew picked the KTL out of the dust. In low voice he said, 'Enough,' and threw the weapon away. 'Enough,' he repeated more loudly. To the Adjutant, Brew said, 'Tell your Colonel, two people want to marry. And that *we* are going out into the desert to witness their wedding according to the Law of Moses.' The Adjutant interpreted. His words seemed to make no impression on the stunned Colonel.

Without orders, the camp guards began to fidget. Among too many targets, too close, the rifles in their hands suddenly became things without purpose or meaning.

Brew said, 'Tell them to lay down their arms. And open the gate.' The Adjutant looked to his superior, who wagged his head dumbly. The commands came in short, guttural bursts. The men obeyed, and dropped their weapons. The Sergeant went to open the gate. More orders. Two lines formed up. As-Mansura, leaning heavily on his Adjutant's shoulder, followed the men back to barracks.

Brew announced, 'We leave without delay. No one, no matter how weak or ill, must be left behind. Once we are over the first hill, there' — he pointed beyond the gate — 'we will celebrate our wedding.'

People rushed about in all directions, calling out desperately for each other. There was frenzy in the twilight.

Brew came over to Felix Frankelstein, kneeling at Warboys' side. The Hassid said in a smouldering voice, '*Ro-tze'ach!* Murderer! You killed him.' Frankelstein closed Warboys' eyes.

'No, he was dead, already. For the lie he told about me. I never kissed her.'

'How do you know what he said to me? You put spies among us, is that it?' Frankelstein announced, 'My people are not coming to your wedding. It's an abomination, a desecration of the HOLY NAME—' He paused. 'We're taking the jeep and the two camp trucks.'

'Take them, but at your own risk.'

Frankelstein said defiantly, 'We need transport for the sick, for people who can't walk. You don't expect us to carry them. How far can we get without vehicles?'

'A way will open up, I know it.'

'But if we leave the trucks, the Egyptians can use them to hunt us down,' countered Frankelstein.

'Then disable them.'

The hangar hummed with commotion. Friends and relatives rallied the weak and the sick, while the rest grabbed what few belongings they still had.

Frankelstein came in for his phylacteries and prayer shawl bag. He passed Brew and his family on the way out. The Rabbi was arranging his mother in her coat. The Hassidic Rebbe was indignant, 'You're not bringing a corpse to a Jewish wedding. There are priests[120] among us.'

Bruised and sad-looking, Brew answered without looking up, 'This is my mother. And if my mother wishes to attend a wedding with her son and daughter-in-law, then by HEAVEN'S NAME, she'll go.' He lifted her tiny wasted body in his arms. 'My poor mother.' Together with Deborah, Sophie and Naomi, he walked away from Frankelstein.

The Hassid shook with anger. 'You call yourself a Jew? A rabbi? You're mad,' he shouted, as he ran to catch up. 'You'll all die in the desert.'

At that moment, there was a crack of gunfire from the barracks.

'That was the Colonel, coming to his senses—' said Brew.

Frankelstein was wide-eyed, flabbergasted. 'The Colonel... shot himself—? How do you know?'

Brew bowed his head. 'Reb Frankelstein—' He searched a moment before going on, 'Will you lend us your prayer shawl? I...lost mine a long time ago.'

'My *tallis*—? What for—?'

'To make the wedding canopy.'[121]

'Please,' added Deborah, 'it will lift your spirit.'

The Hassid considered, then asked, 'Is the couple Jewish? According to Torah Law?'

Brew and Deborah nodded.

'It's soiled. It should be white for a wedding canopy.' Frankelstein held out his *tallis* bag for Brew to take.

'Thank you,' said the Rabbi. 'If you don't mind giving it to my wife...my hands...are full.'

The Hassid placed the bag like a little child in Deborah's hands, saying only, 'Let the bridegroom keep it.' He walked away into the darkening grey.

Rebbe Frankelstein and his followers left in the three vehicles. The Egyptians made no attempt to stop them. They quickly disappeared over the ridge, leaving only a cloud of dust hanging in the air.

Night took hold in stealth. No moon.[122]

Mr Sinclair carried the Edinburgh Torah Scroll high on his shoulder. Behind him, the Rabbi carried his mother. Deborah walked beside him. The young Bedouin woman in Guriat's clothes dashed ahead up the steep road.

The column slowly threaded its way over the first hill. The weakest and sickest had to be carried, or limped with an arm over a stronger shoulder. It wasn't long before the Rabbi stopped. 'Here,' he said.

The fearful babble of the people carried far on the crystalline air, and ricocheted off the hills. 'Can anybody tell us when this insanity is going to end?' asked someone.

---

[120]Jews descended from the Temple priesthood (Heb. *Kohanim*) are forbidden to come in contact with the dead.

[121]The Jewish wedding ceremony is traditionally performed under a canopy without walls, and a fringed prayer cloth, or tallis, is perfectly adequate for the purpose. The canopy, or *Chuppah* in Hebrew, may be held up on four poles, or as high as arms' length. Commentators suggest that it represents the formation of a new home, into which the couple enter together for the first time. Others say that it symbolises the Heavenly presence hovering over the bride and groom.

[122]It was the night of the new moon, and first day of the Hebrew month of Nisan during which the Freedom Festival of Passover is celebrated.

'That day none of us know,' answered another. 'We only know the day it began.'
'What day was that?'
'The day we were born.'

The four tallest young men held the four corners of Rebbe Frankelstein's fringed shawl above their heads. The wedding canopy fluttered in the wind. The Rabbi was under the canopy, alone, waiting. Few were in any mood to celebrate.

The wedding started with only the light of the stars to see by. A small circle of men, led by Mr Sinclair and the Torah Scroll, brought the bridegroom to his place under the canopy. Rabbi Vivienne Falk and a few women ushered in the bride. Izzy Sofer nearest the canopy in his wheelchair shushed the assembly for silence.

The Rabbi began, 'Lindy and Todd...Oh my...Lindy and Todd asked me to say something tonight. "What can *I* say?" I asked them. "Comfort us, comfort us all," they answered. I said, "I can't. There are no words. We hurt too much. So many of us have lost a parent, a child, a brother or a sister." I said, "Lindy and Todd, your son, your only—" Brew choked, and had to wait before he could begin again. 'Lindy said, "Remind us about the joy we have all forgotten." I asked her, "How can there be any joy? How? After all the terrible things we have seen and suffered, even tonight. To be joyous when our hearts are sick, and tired, and broken. How?" Todd said it, "But we're alive. That's joy—"' Again, Brew's voice lapsed into silence. 'Lindy and Todd,' he started again, 'your wedding here, tonight, is not a sign, or a wonder, or a miracle. It was your choice. Your choosing to be married under the canopy is nothing less than an ancient Jewish response to all those who would wish to destroy us. Your wedding will always be a reminder to us all — to love liberty...to fight for freedom...and never, never to use our independence to deny others theirs. Lindy and Todd, your wedding, this night, in this wilderness, affirms our destiny. Thank you for giving us this gift.'

Rabbi Brew Moray took off his own wedding ring and gave it to the bridegroom. Todd put the ring on Lindy's right forefinger, and repeated after the Rabbi to her, word by word, '*Ha'rei*— Behold...you...become holy...to me...by this ring...according to the Law...of Moses...and of Israel.' Brew ended the ceremony with the Seven Wedding Benedictions.[123] Todd stamped on an imaginary glass. The bride and groom clasped hands, and the canopy holders let the fringed prayer shawl fall around the couple's shoulders. Todd and Lindy kissed with a loud smack. Cheers of *Mazel Tov! Mazel Tov u'Siman Tov!*[124] erupted. And at the top of their voices, Mr Sinclair and Izzy Sofer led the Scottish Jews in a rousing "Auld Lang Syne". There was dancing, too. And tears, so many tears.

* * *

---

[123]The smashing of a glass underfoot (among many interpretations of the tradition) is best said to symbolise Jewish continuity even as the sounds of destruction and violence are heard.
[124]Hebrew, loosely meaning "Congratulations and felicitations".

Chapter LXXIX

Ebbing Back

[Tuesday evening, March 16, 2010]

A lone voice ended the wedding.

'Listen!'

Low but distinct rumblings came from the hills. With each passing second, the formless sounds grew louder, closer, more ominous. *They* came lumbering in from a hundred directions at once. There were no lights.

No one moved. There was no place to run.

'What is it?' asked someone.

Voices of fear, despair and hopelessness bubbled up into calls to go back to the camp. At once.

All around echoes hit high pitch, ready for the final descent. People hugged each other. Eyes strained to see something, anything through the dark.

Then as suddenly as it had begun, the roaring died away. And the empty silence of the desert ebbed back.

'Rabbi—?'

'Mr Sinclair—?'

'Rabbi,' said the old beadle, 'you take the Torah. If this is the end—'

'No, Mr Sinclair,' whispered Brew, 'I can't. My hands are not clean—'

'Then will you give us your blessing? There's nothing wrong with your tongue.'

Brew whispered, even lower, 'Mr Sinclair—'

The old Scottish Jew would hear none of it. 'Everyone, everyone hold hands,' he trumpeted. 'Our Rabbi is giving us his blessing.'

Now that the wedding was over, there was no more direction. Brew was lost. He felt dry inside. Who am I to be giving blessings? I know nothing, I am nothing, he told himself. Brew then heard Mr Sinclair give quiet voice to the opening word of the ancient Hebrew blessing: '"*Yivarech'cha*—"'. The Rabbi repeated after him, one phrase at a time, his voice pure and ringing:

> May HE bless you...and watch over you.
> May HE shine HIS radiance upon you...and delight you.
> May HE lift up HIS face to you...and give you peace.[125]

> Mr Sinclair breathed, 'Amen.'

In the next hushed moments, every mind descended into its own separate world. With the return of the cold quiet, Brew felt the stinging around his mouth, the powder burns on his temple, the places where he'd been kicked and beaten. He felt tired, incredibly tired and weak. The chilly desert air clung to his skin and hair. In seconds a full-blown headache hit

---

[125]Num. 6.24-6.

him with a ringing in his ears that vibrated like wires. He braced his head between curved hands. Then came a flash of living light. It lit up the night in his eyes. The starburst transformed itself into Deborah's round and contented face. Her eyes quickly dissolved into two twinkling brilliances. The smaller, a tiny spark, flew up and out of his vision. The second radiance immediately grew larger, and streaked down like a meteorite. It landed in a green cleft between barren rocks, and glowed. And out of the glow came fire, and out of the fire came THE VOICE, and out of THE VOICE came the verse he'd dreamed so long ago. It was over in a second. Brew released his hands from his temples. The darkness of the moonless night was back, and his headache, gone.

The stillness ended when a child dared hope aloud, 'Maybe it's our army coming.' As fresh excitement broke out, Brew picked his way through the dark, back to the spot where he left his mother. There, too, he found Deborah, and Sophie clutching Naomi.

'Debs— Are you all right?' he asked. Before Deborah could answer him, Naomi piped up, 'Uncle Brew, is Grandma cold? I'm cold.'

'No,' he said, 'she's not cold any more. She's lovely and warm now. But if you're feeling cold...have you tried hugging yourself?' The little girl giggled. 'Here, let me show you.' He bent down, wrapped his arms around her, and sweeping her up, he wheeled around. She squealed.

'Brew—' said Deborah, her voice loaded with urgency.

'Young lady,' Brew said to his niece, 'you go to your Mummy now. And take good care of her for me. Right?'

Naomi asked, 'Can I give you a kiss before I go?'

Brew held her close to his face, 'Now let's see, we have to find you a spot here with some skin.' His beard had grown wild. Brew took her little hand and placed it high on his cheek, so she could feel first. Her kiss was wet and ticklish. 'Thank you,' he said, 'that was a very sweet kiss. Now, Mummy will take you.' Sophie hugged Naomi without words. She was careful not to let her feel the tears running down her cheeks.

'Brew Moray,' said Deborah again.

'I know what you're going to say, I know it, I saw it,' he said quietly.

'You did—?'

Brew found her ear, and spoke into it like a child so no one else could hear, 'I saw inside you. Just now, a beautiful vision. It's wonderful, our Debs—' Then he asked her again, 'Are you really all right?'

'Yes,' she said, 'I think so. I was so afraid, so afraid I'd lost you when...when they put that gun—' Deborah did not know what else to say to him. How could he know? How could she be sure he knew? But there was a certainty, and a serenity in his voice.

'I thought I was lost, too,' he said, 'but I've just seen the way—'

At that moment, a piercing, ululating howl split the air. The assembly divided and a wide path opened straight to the Rabbi.

* * *

Chapter LXXX

Dr Othman

[Tuesday-Wednesday, March 16-17, 2010]

Two came.

The young Bedouin woman in Guriat's clothes did not stop her shrill cry until she reached the Rabbi. The huge man who walked before her wore a generous moustache, keffiyeh and flowing robes. He kissed Brew on both cheeks, Arab-style. 'Rabbi Moray, it is a pleasure to meet you.' His English was cultured. 'I am called Dr Othman. My tribe of Bedouin is here — on behalf of the Israeli authorities — to bring you and your people to safety.'

Brew looked up and said, 'I do *believe*—'

Dr Othman quietly cut him off. 'There's transport for everyone...up the road, over the hill. Everyone must go, now, without delay. There isn't a minute to spare. The Egyptian Army will soon be swarming like locusts.'

'Transportation for everyone, over the hill here,' Brew cried out. His message rippled out through the numbed crowd. Fresh hope gripped hearts and minds. 'How can we thank you?' said Brew, turning. But their deliverers had dissolved into the night.

There was no panic. The discipline of the last few months conditioned the Scottish Jews to walk briskly, not run.

Brew lifted his mother. He talked to her like a child, explaining that they had to go. In that moment Deborah wondered if his ordeal, his brush with death, had not pushed him over some dark edge.

The flats over the rise were clogged with trucks, vans, jeeps and cars. Everywhere engines came alive, wheezing and throbbing.

People quietly distributed themselves among the vehicles. Brew carried his mother onto an open safari truck. There was room, too, for Deborah, Sophie and Naomi. Deborah wrapped her arms around him. No words. The driver started the engine. But at the sounds of footsteps and cries in the moonless dark, Brew loosened Deborah's grip. 'Please don't go,' she said.

'I have to see to them, Debs.' He jumped down as the truck rolled away. She stifled a cry.

Every few minutes, full vehicles raced off into the wastes of the Northern Sinai.

'Mr Ace, if you can hear me—?' called Brew.

'Rabbi?' It was him.

'Will you help? Children and old folk are lost out here.'

'I'm your man,' said Ace.

Together, Ace and the Rabbi united families and squeezed the last stragglers into already packed cars and vans. When their offers of help brought no more responses, Ace said, 'Seems that leaves just us.'

Brew sat down on a rock to catch his breath. After a while, he said, 'Mr Ace—'

'Alec—'

'Alec, could I ask you something?'

'Ask away, Rabbi. Anything. Nobody's listening.'

'Alec, why did you come?'

'Tomatoes.'

'Be serious.'

'I am.'

'Nev told me you retired early. And that you had a nice little cottage on an island with your own garden. You had peace and quiet. Why would you leave all that? To follow a mad-hatter Scottish rabbi?'

'Tomatoes. I never could grow tomatoes as red as they grow them in Israel.'

'That's it?'

'I suppose if you really want to know, Rabbi, I'm a coward. It was easy to hide under my shell. Then you came along. I knew I had to go. To leave my shell. And something else, I like you, Rabbi, and I loved your brother. It's good to be with people you really like, isn't it?'

'Alec—' said Brew with a smile in his voice, 'stick to tomatoes.'

'Tomatoes,' said Alec, with a sniff of laughter—

After another short lull, Brew said, 'Will you take care of Deborah for me while I'm gone?'

'I don't understand,' said Ace, completely puzzled.

'I can't come with you. My parents, my brother are gone. They're gone because of me, because I broke faith with them.'

'Whatever you say, Rabbi—' said the tubby little man worriedly, like he'd missed something, or like the Rabbi was missing something.

'Thank Ms Gaoni for me— Somehow, I believe, she'll be able explain why my head is still on my shoulders—'

Again, the small Bedouin woman popped up from nowhere. Pointing and pulling, she made them follow her to a ramshackle Mercedes. Brew looked in. Dr Othman was at the wheel. He threw open the passenger door: 'Rabbi—' Brew took the front seat, while Ace hopped in the back next to the woman. All three doors slammed at once.

Othman zigzagged between dunes, or hugged the stratified walls of deep wadis. The car creaked and groaned. As they bumped along the rough desert floor, the steering wheel jerked back and forth like a ship's tiller in a tempest. Brew marvelled at how the Bedouin found his way in the wilderness without headlights on so black a night.

No one was saying anything. Brew looked at the back seat. The steady rocking motion had put the girl to sleep. Ace, too, seemed on the verge of succumbing. The Rabbi sank back, thinking about his vision. It was so clear, so strong. The mountain must be near.

Suddenly, Othman stopped the car, and cut the engine. The passengers were instantly wide awake. 'What is it?' asked Brew.

'Quiet!' hissed the Bedouin doctor.

Cat's eyes, the dim lights of an armoured personnel carrier, blinked on the hillcrest in front of them. The vehicle lumbered past without stopping. Alec breathed out.

'Egyptian patrol,' said Othman as he restarted the engine. Brew asked, 'Why are you and your people you doing this for us?' The car hit a deep rut. 'Ask the Little Lioness, she will tell you,' answered the doctor, as the wheel jerked sharply. 'This is no time for long explanations.'

Brew's mind raced— It's him...the Bedouin sheikh...the doctor...who befriended her in the desert...who gave her her name Guriat, the Little Lioness...who brought her to the mountain of Moses' tomb. The same mountain he saw in his dream, and again, just now, in his vision. Brew broke out in a sweat of realisation. It was no accident that Dr Othman was his driver—

The night flight carried on in utter silence until, without warning, Othman braked and drew to a final stop. 'This is as far as I and my sister go,' he said. 'From the top of the ridge just ahead you will see the border crossing and beyond it the Israeli village of Nitzana.'

'Alec, you go ahead,' said Brew, 'I need to have a quick word with the doctor.'

Ace jumped out of the car. The nippy desert air on his face flushed the drowsiness out his head.

'Dr Othman,' Brew stammered, 'you, you once brought Guriat to the mountain where your legends say the tomb of Moses our Prophet lies. She said you climbed to the top together.'

'How could I forget. You speak of the Mountain of the Salt Land that we call Jebel el Sabha.'

The Rabbi began to recall in a dreamy voice, 'Even though the mountain is not high, the ascent is steep and rugged and long.' Othman concurred with a nod as Brew Moray went on, 'From the plain below, the tomb, the tomb your teachings say was brought by ALLAH to this place, is hidden from sight. But it's there, hidden in a narrow gorge on the mountain. A bubbling spring feeds the green trees and grasses. The letters on the sepulchre burn in everlasting fire.'

'Rabbi, how could you know all this?' asked Othman, astounded. 'No one has ever been able to find the tomb.'

'I have been there,' said Brew entranced. 'Is the mountain far?'

'No,' said Othman, 'from here, about ten or twelve kilometres away.'

'Will you take me there?'

'Now?'

'Yes, now.'

'If that is your wish—'

'That is my wish. I cannot ignore my dreams.'

'And your wife. Will you ignore her—?'

Brew did not answer. All around, he heard car doors slamming. In the morning darkness he imagined them running, walking, limping, like phantom shadows escaping the fires of hell.

Dr Othman pressed his point with humour. 'The Jews have many prophets. We Moslems have but one Prophet, but he had many wives. We know about wives.'

Brew asked, 'Can you wait five minutes?'

'Five minutes, but no more. It will soon be light.'

After a few steps, swept forward by the crowd, Brew heard his name called. It was Deborah. He followed her voice, and found her kneeling by his mother. Sophie was next to her holding Naomi who was shivering wildly in the damp, dewy air.

Deborah and Brew hugged without words. He knew the hands that held her lied to her—

'Brew,' said Sophie, 'can you bring Naomi? She's freezing, and I've not got the strength to carry her any more.'

Given an excuse to let Deborah go, Brew slipped his arm around the five-year old and picked her up. The two women, supporting each other, limped ahead.

Alec Ace came back. He said to Brew, 'I shouldn't have left you. Go on. I'll take her.' Ace gathered up Anna Moray's lifeless body. He swung her over his shoulder like a duffel bag.

As each huddled group emerged over the crest, another young Israeli soldier seemed to be there to guide them through a minefield, then around the concrete anti-tank barriers and under several banks of electrified fences laced with razor wire. The final dash passed in a blur—

* * *

The two Egyptian army trucks and a jeep commandeered by Rebbe Felix Frankelstein and his Hassidim vanished in the desert. No amount of pleading or pressure by the international community produced any information. The Egyptians denied that the vehicles were missing or that their passengers ever existed. E.T.

Chapter LXXXI

On the Mountain

[Wednesday-Thursday, March 17-18, 2010]

With Naomi in his arms Brew glided towards the border crossing. Ahead of him Deborah kept stopping to look back. Each time she did so, her soldier prodded her on. The gate in the last fence was no wider than an ordinary door. Deborah and Sophie went through. Ace followed, sweating under Anna Moray's dead weight.

Ten feet from the final gate, Brew stopped. He dismissed his young soldier girl with polite thanks and a firm, 'We can go on from here.' The flow of people seethed around him. He put the child down. 'Go through, Naomi. Go.' He gave her a gentle push with his fingertips, but she stubbornly planted her feet. Her child's voice piped up, 'But what about you, Uncle Brew? Aren't you coming?'

'Before I can come home with you, I first have to climb a very special mountain.' Brew glanced over his shoulder. A faint orange glow tinged the eastern sky.

'Why?'

'So I can learn first to be a good man. One day, Naomi, you'll understand, but now you must go home with Mummy and Auntie Deborah.' Brew took a step back. Naomi couldn't move. She turned one way, then the other. Brew backed away. He soothed her. 'Uncle Brew has to go, now. You will like your new home.' He shooed her away. 'Go on, Mummy's there already. Go on.' After one last look in Brew's direction, Naomi ran away as fast as her short legs would carry her, shouting, 'Mummy! Mummy! Wait! Wait for me!' The little girl raised her arms and balled fists in the air to make herself as tall as possible.

Brew watched her vanish through the gate. On the other side more soldiers, police and medics absorbed the Scottish Jews. He saw, beyond the frontier he would not cross, the far faint plains and hills he would not enter into.

Homing in on the child's calls, Sophie turned back. Deborah stumbled after her. Not wanting to lose the Morays, Alec Ace also went back.

Just then a familiar voice called out, 'Rabbi Moray!' Alec Ace almost dropped his burden. 'Rabbi Moray!' It was Guriat.

Sophie caught Naomi in her arms. When Deborah heard the little girl stammering that Brew had not come across, she screamed out a thin wail, more infant than adult. There were words in her appeal, but the shriek of her voice obliterated them. Guriat held her from going back. Deborah's cry dissolved into broken sobs.

Guriat summoned the army medics and a stretcher for Deborah. She stared at Ace. He said looking at his shoulder, 'The Rabbi's mother—' Guriat called out for a second stretcher crew. Other workers threw blankets over Sophie and Naomi and bundled them off to safety.

'Where is the Rabbi? What happened to him?' Guriat asked Ace. His face fell. 'He was right behind us—'

Guriat closed her eyes. Her mental picture of Brew Moray assembled in bits. She saw the Edinburgh rabbi she saw for the first time, lifting his face to the congregation, radiating the light of his dreams. But when her picture of him was complete, it was missing the one thing that made him Brew. It had no voice.

In short, excited breaths, Ace told Guriat what the Rabbi had asked of him, to thank *her* for his life and to take care of Deborah for him.

'Anything else?' asked Guriat.

'Only that the doctor called you "the Little Lioness" and said you would be able to explain everything.'

In a white flash the riddle became clear. Guriat remembered telling the Rabbi about Othman in the butcher's shop, and about the mountain on the ferry. Brew was on his way to the Mountain of the Salt Land, and Othman was taking him there—

*

Shortly after sunrise Guriat went into the Sinai to search for Dr Othman. She wore a Bedouin woman's black robes and drove a small flock of sheep and goats in the way of the desert nomad. It was a windy spring morning.

Several times Egyptian Army patrols stopped and questioned her. Had she seen 'infidels'? She shrugged her shoulders as if to say, here? Guriat reasoned that the Egyptians would not have asked her if they'd found him.

She arrived at the encampment of Othman's Tza-va'e-ra clan in the early afternoon. The doctor had just woken up. He confirmed her suspicion about Brew. 'You're both mad,' she angrily told him.

Though it was late in the day, Othman drove Guriat and two Bedouin trackers to Jebel el Sabha. From miles away, the solitary low mountain could be seen dominating the vast plain around it. In the last hour of daylight, the mountain's steep, sun-fired slopes of flinty rock and rubble seemed to pulsate like dying coals.

Guriat and the Bedouins camped at the foot of the mountain. The night was cold. At first light, they began their search. The two trackers led the climb. They found no sign of the Rabbi. Nothing. They passed off the heat of the day sleeping and eating under the shade of an overhanging rock. At two in the afternoon, the sun's rays were already slanting from the west. The four resumed the search. An hour before sunset, they gave up.

The Bedouin trackers shook their heads, asking, 'How can any man who walks not leave his footprints?'

* * *

Chapter LXXXII

Elijah's Cup

[Monday evening, March 29, 2010]

What a difference twelve days made. From her hidden vantage point, Guriat delighted in their radiant faces. They could not stop staring at each other. Their expressions were saying, it's almost impossible to believe. We are alive!

And sweet irony, thought Guriat. They were celebrating their first Passover in Jerusalem under the gleaming chandeliers of the great hall of a transplanted Scottish castle![126]

Long banquet tables groaned under the weight of more than nine hundred settings. The small sound of clinking glass soon silenced the buzz of excitement. Everyone faced the head table.

'Ladies and gentlemen, welcome to Dunhoorn Castle. I am Donald Muriel, *the former* Scottish Ambassador—' Muriel's stress on "the former" sparked off raucous laughter and applause. The tall diplomat, who wore an ill-fitting skullcap for the occasion, waved for quiet and raised his voice to begin again. 'You will notice that there are vacant seats at our table tonight—' The central mystery of the Passover Seder meal, Elijah's Cup, stood before the empty place setting between Deborah and Mr Muriel. Carefully lifting the cup filled to the brim with wine, the ambassador said, 'Rabbi Moray,' — and the whole hall rose up as one — 'wherever you are tonight...know that you will always have a place waiting for you among us.'

As everyone sat down after a minute's silence, Alec Ace who was next to Deborah, gave her a tattered paper folded in four. 'I found this in the pocket of his coat, the jacket the Rabbi lent me. You should have it.' Carefully, Deborah unfolded the crumpled note. She instantly recognised Brew's tiny handwriting. Deborah simply said, 'Alec, thank you. It means so much to me.' And to stave off her tears, she asked him, 'Where is Guriat? And who are all these places for?' There were four more empty chairs next to Alec.

'You'll see,' whistled Ace with a cheeky half-smile. Sophie, further down the head table with Naomi, understood from the glint in Alec's eye that Deborah had no inkling of the surprise in store for her.

Once more Muriel tapped his glass. 'Given that the evening is short and the Passover Seder service is long, this is no time for speeches. But I would like to thank the Foreign Office for being so tardy in sending out my replacement— Seems nobody wants this job—' More uproarious laughter and applause. 'I and my wife and our children are very, very proud to be in your presence this evening. We have been here for almost three years now. I was free Scotland's first ambassador to Israel. I was honoured to serve and represent my country. I was a Scot, who was proud of Scotland.

'But reborn Scotland lost her way, when Rabbi Brew Moray courageously called on us to claim our vision of freedom, to pursue our destiny and to be who we are. You risked

---

[126]See the endnote of Chapter 3.

your lives to follow his dream. And many of you lost loved ones and dear friends along the way.

'We who are here tonight are the happy ones. Your children and their children will remember you, and what you did. Whoever chose to stay behind, they are the ones who are writing themselves out of our history. Here, in Jerusalem, the final chapters of *our* story will be written, indeed, are being written. Here is where the Book of Books began and here is where it will end.' Muriel bowed his head. 'As I said, our celebration tonight is flawed. Your ordeal is still very fresh. But even in the face of suffering and loss, it is an ancient tradition for us to take delight in our blessings, and share our Seder table with guests. Especially for you, dear Deborah,' he brightened, pointing to the empty places next to Ace, 'we have three very special guests this evening. Guriat, if you will—'

As soon as Deborah saw Tsippi, she was on her feet. She could not hold back her tears. Tsippi broke into a run. Clapping wildly, everyone sprang up to see the reunion. Eyes were streaming. Tsippi and Deborah rocked and turned and cried in each other's arms. It seemed as if they would never let go, now that they were together again. At last, Deborah said, 'How you've grown. Thirteen, and already a young woman.' Tsippi looked back. Deborah saw Becky, Alan and Guriat and hugged and kissed them, too.

When Mr Sinclair pointed to his watch, Muriel announced, 'Let's begin our Seder!' Another cheer went up.

Mr Sinclair and Rabbi Vivienne Falk shared the honours in leading the festive meal's opening benedictions and telling the Passover story. There were no clear eyes as Mr Sinclair read the lines, '"HE brought us from slavery to freedom, from sorrow to joy, from mourning to festivity, from darkness to bright light and from bondage to redemption—"'

During the meal, Deborah and Tsippi talked. Deborah explained that the cup of wine in Brew's place was for the Prophet Elijah to drink. Deborah said with a sudden touch of pain, 'Every year at Passover Jews hope for Elijah to return again, and announce the coming of the Messiah.' Tsippi told Deborah that the Frasers had arrived only yesterday, the day before Passover, via London after much difficulty. Somehow everything they said skirted what was closest to their hearts. Tsippi sensed something other than Brew's disappearance was troubling Deborah. She glowed, but uneasily like a small flame in a sooty lantern.

After the meal, before the recitation of Grace and the Psalms, Alec Ace got up and aimlessly peered out of a window. Just below the castle he saw St Andrew's Scottish Church, handsomely illuminated, as were David's Tower and the outer walls of the Old City of Jerusalem a bit further away. Guriat joined him.

After a short while, she said, 'It's all so beautiful at night.'

He slowly faced her. 'I was just thinking about Neville.'

'So was I.'

'You were?'

'Don't sound so surprised.'

His face fell. 'I didn't mean it the way it sounded.'

'I know. It's just that...it's all so mysterious. A man loves a woman. She can't find love for him. He kills himself to prove his love for her and, in the bargain, that man saves her and a whole shipload of people. If I had loved Neville, maybe we'd all be dead. I don't understand how these things work—'

'No word on the Rabbi,' offered Ace as an escape.

'Nothing. Vanished without a trace.'

'It's what he must have wanted. Could be, it's better that way.'

'Not for her, it isn't,' said Guriat, slightly twisting her head towards Deborah. 'She really hasn't got anyone now.'

'Ms Gaoni? Guriat? Could I talk to you, sometime?'

'Sure, Acey, I'd like that.'

'You would?'

'You can start by calling me Guri.' She pecked him on the cheek. 'I hear Mr Muriel calling us back to the table.'

After the last cup of wine and a rousing shout of '*L'Shanah haBa'ah b'Yerushelayim haB'nuyah* — Next Year in Rebuilt Jerusalem', Muriel had a word in Deborah's ear. He rose. 'Ladies and gentlemen, quiet, please. Quiet. Deborah Moray would like to say a word.'

Deborah stood up, erect, steady, dry-eyed. 'Thank you, Mr Muriel, Mrs Muriel. And to all of you. You have all been so wonderful to me. And to see Tsippi and the Frasers here tonight—' She waved aside any interruption. 'I...I apologise, I'm not much of a speaker. I don't have the voice or the words. But Brew did. He is the Rabbi in our family. Earlier this evening Mr Ace gave me Brew's radio talk. I'd like to read it again to you. Try to imagine, as I will, *his* voice. It seems like only yesterday I watched him dashing it off, on the back of my shopping list—'

She turned over the paper. Her mind recovered the snapshot of him in their bedroom, writing furiously. Then, he was a man, her husband, the incorrigible dreamer. Those were the ways she remembered him. Now, she saw him as no less alive, but a shimmering image, temporarily incorporeal, called to work in a higher place. That call of a verse from the Torah was her only explanation for his disappearance. She often found herself trying to imagine what verse he heard that morning, where he was now, what he was doing, and if he really did know— She turned the paper over again and began to read:

Good morning.

For Jews today, the little town of Chelm in Poland was never real. Like Gotham in England, Chelm was an imaginary place inhabited by fools and simpletons, who in their own narrow world thought themselves wise, indeed, the wisest of the wise.

There are many stories about the Wise Men of Chelm, like the day they all started walking into trees and bumping into each other. They became alarmed, and turned to the City Fathers for leadership. The Mayor suggested the Wise Men go to the Physician. His eyes, too, had grown filmy. 'How can I examine you if I, too, cannot see?' he asked woefully. 'This is a matter for our revered Rabbi.' So everyone shouted at once, 'To the Rabbi. He is a great sage and a holy man. He will know what to do.'

The Wise Men went off to see their old, long-bearded Rabbi in his little study hall next to the synagogue. 'Rabbi, Rabbi,' they cried as one, 'the whole town is going blind. What shall we do?'

He stroked his white beard and said, 'I, too, had begun to suffer. On the Sabbath the words of our beloved Torah swam before my eyes, and in the week the lines in the Books of our Sages became as waves in the sea. But this morning I woke up with a dream, and following my dream, I walked out of town. And miracle of miracles, my vision was restored to that of a youth. But when I came back again my eyes were once more fogged.'

'So what does it mean, Rabbi?' asked the Wise Men with deep concern.

'It means that your eyes are clear.'

'But if our eyes are clear, why can't we see?' asked the Wise Men.

'Why?' answered their Rabbi. 'Because the air of Chelm has become clouded and grey.'

'But if we have to leave our lovely little Chelm in order to see again, we lose our homes and our livelihoods.'

And the old Rabbi said, 'But if we do not leave and soon, the air here will get so thick and black that we'll never be able to find our way out. And the promise of our future will be lost to us.'

End of story.

I ask the indulgence of all our listeners to speak a moment directly to the Jews of Scotland. To you, I say Chelm is no fable. Chelm is real. Chelm is any place where our eyes are clear-sighted, but the atmosphere is dull and dreich.

Leaving our homes is no joke. But leave we must. And soon, before 'the air gets too thick and too black for us to be able to find our way out'. We must go before the promise of our future is lost to us. If we stay here, we will become like the Wise Men of Chelm, nothing but a fable.

I fear that many of you, my fellow Jews, who hear me this morning will resist my call to leave Scotland. But the dreams we dream, the visions we see, are not just markers to be passed by, but signs to be followed. The path marked out for us in life of "doing justice, and loving kindness, and walking upright in humbleness"[127] does not permit us the luxury of shortsightedness.

To you, the good Scottish people who hear me this morning, do not be alarmed by what I have just said. Do not forget that only two years ago you won back your own independence. Now I ask you, as Scots, to regard our longing for life with the sympathy and understanding of a free people living in a free nation.

Good morning to all, and thank you.

Folding the paper, Deborah said, 'One last thing, I know. Brew isn't lost. He's in the wilderness finding himself, and when his search is over, he'll be back. And when he comes back, I'll be by his side. In the meantime, Brew is with me. His spirit is sitting in this chair beside me. He is with us all in our hearts and souls. I know it, I see it—'

A long and deep stillness gripped the gathering. Tsippi took Deborah's hands between hers. A soft warm current flowed out of Deborah that confirmed it for Tsippi. She leaned very close and whispered into Deborah's ear, 'You're going to have a baby—' Deborah said nothing. Maybe she hadn't heard. Tsippi said it again, a little louder, 'I see it in your eyes. I can feel it in your hands. You're going to have Brew's baby—'

Becky, overhearing, said it aloud, 'A baby—? Deborah—?' In seconds, the news burst over the great hall.

Pearl signed to Izzy in his wheelchair. He signed back mouthing aloud for all to hear, 'She said, "Deborah's-going-to-have-the-Rabbi's-baby."' Mr Sinclair began dancing in a little circle. Others joined him clapping and singing at the top of their voices. Lynn and Todd Harrison toasted each other. They, too, would have another child, lots more children. Guriat gently closed Alec Ace's speechless, gaping jaw, and smiled, 'So that's what this was all about, eh, mate?'

Sophie had left before Deborah's news escaped. Naomi fell fast asleep, and when Sophie looked into her little face, she saw all those she'd lost — her son, her brothers, her mother and father, and even her husband. As she quietly slipped out of the hall with the soft swells of Naomi's breath on her neck, Sophie cried bitterly inside.

The good cheer carried on late into the night. One by one they came to say goodbye to the Rabbi's wife. In the end Deborah was left by herself, sitting alone, looking at the undrunk Cup of Elijah. Tsippi saw her, but first looked to her mother. Becky let her go with a wink. Tsippi folded Deborah in her arms. And three hearts beat as one.

---

[127]See Micah 6.8.

Tsippi wept.

'Why am I crying?'

Deborah's eyes shone.

'Our tears, too, are a blessing from the hand of God.'

* * *

Deborah's baby, a boy, was born on Thursday, September Second, Twenty-ten. In the Jewish calendar, it was the twenty-third day of the month of Elul, exactly one year after his father related his vision of the turtle in Edinburgh. The brit milah circumcision ceremony that welcomed the child into the world was celebrated on Rosh Hashanah, the Jewish New Year. In memory of his father the child was named Chalam-ish, "the dreamer". E.T.

End Part Four

Epilogue

The late Scottish philosopher John Malcolm Campbell wrote, 'Good books are like batteries — charged in the writing, and recharged in the reading. The ultimate worth of a book should not be measured just in its ability to withstand time, but also in its capability to point to a better time.' I often pondered these truths during the last three years while editing the book that you are now about to close.

In my Prologue I referred to an envelope with my name on it. It was placed under the loose leaves of the manuscript. The note inside was short, unsigned, undated.

> Prof Evlyn Tennet, Shalom,
>
> I am a distant admirer of your work. I particularly appreciated the humane conclusions you reached in your recent paper on Edinburgh's ancient sewer system.
>
> I am old and dying. Before leaving this world, I am attempting to put my affairs in order. I feel fortunate that I am given the time and strength to perform my task. That is why I am writing to you.
>
> The enclosed manuscript was willed to me by a dear friend. Her grandfather, like mine, played a role in the events recounted within its pages. First she, then I tried to trace the source of the manuscript, but our resources and time proved too meagre to discover its true author.
>
> Now that I am reaching the end of my days, I have decided that you, a highly esteemed scholar living in Edinburgh, are the only person in Scotland worthy of taking on the task of determining the provenance of the manuscript.
>
> I believe the interpretation of the events written therein to be true and faithful, and deserving of a wide audience. But I leave it entirely for you to determine the fate of the story enclosed with this letter. I only ask that you bury the original manuscript in a Jewish cemetery in Scotland.
>
> Gratefully yours,
> The son of a Scottish Jew who never saw Scotland

The task laid before me remains uncompleted. I was unable, despite all my research, to determine for certain who authored the manuscript. However, I have turned the work into a publishable book.

In accordance with the dying wish of my anonymous admirer, I have laid the manuscript to rest in the hallowed precincts of a old Jewish burial ground. The location of the site will remain a secret that will go with me to the grave.

Since committing the manuscript to the earth, I have learned that Jews traditionally bury worn-out holy books in which the Name of God is written. Our manuscript mentions the Name of God only once. It is the final word.

And one last note. The manuscript arrived without a title. That sweet duty of finding a fitting appellation fell to me. I would like to believe that the title I have chosen for our book comes from the verse that woke the Rabbi, Deuteronomy 4.34, '...and take HIM a nation out of a nation by trials, by signs, and with wonders and war, and with a strong hand and an outstretched arm...'

Prof Evlyn Tennet
Edinburgh, Twenty ninety-six

Appendix I
The Rabbi's Responsum

The question of resorting to transgression in order to save life is first discussed in the Gemara,[128] Tractate Bava Kamma.[129] Rav Huna says, "King David is fighting the Philistines,[130] who are hiding in a barley field, which belongs to a private citizen. So David sends to the highest law court in the land, the Great Sanhedrin, 'Is it permissible for me to burn down the field in order to flush out the Philistines?'" "What goes on here?" asks the Gemara. Jewish soldiers are in the middle of battle. Their lives and the life of a whole people are at stake. And their king sends to the highest court in the land for a ruling... So the Gemara asks, "Is it permissible to save life at the expense of someone else's belongings?"

In order to save a life as long as we are not forced to commit idolatry, murder or incest, we may transgress all other commandments including those of the Sabbath. So it would stand to reason that we can burn a field for the sake of saving a life... The Torah was given to us to live by.[131]

The Sanhedrin answers David, "You are the king and the king can go and confiscate someone else's field and build a road." But *we* are not kings...

Now when the Rambam[132] brings down *Halacha* [rabbinic law], he sidesteps the main issue, that is, if one may or may not steal in order to save life. Instead, he tells us: If one did steal, one must compensate the owner for his loss. So, the question remains: Is one allowed to steal in the first place? The Rambam does not rule.

In the Tractate Ketubot,[133] the Gemara deals with the case of witnesses who confessed that they falsely signed a document saying that someone owed someone else money. They claimed that they did so under duress, at gunpoint, so to speak. Nevertheless, the Gemara argues that their testimonies are unacceptable, because by admitting that they lied they are unreliable witnesses. But their lives were at stake.

The Gemara now injects into its argument the principle of *midat chassidut*, that is, "strictest performance" of the law. Here the distinction is made between what is right and what is required. It may be right to sacrifice one's life rather than to steal, but is it required? The answer is "no". The Gemara goes a step further and asks: "By not accepting *midat chassidut* does one turn oneself into a *ra'sha*, an 'evil-doer'?" The Gemara's declaration is an emphatic "no". Therefore, a witness who admits to the non-performance of *midat chassidut* is not a false witness.

---

[128]Talmudic commentary. Called Gomorrah in Ashkenazic Hebrew.

[129]"The First Gate", the tractate that deals mainly with the civil law of damages.

[130]A reference to 1Chron. 11.13. An apparent amalgam of two battles from 2Sam. 23.9-10 and 23.11-12.

[131]Lev. 18.5.

[132]Rabbi Moshe ben Maimon (Moses Maimonides, 1138-1204), Halachist, philosopher, physician and commentator on the Torah and Talmud (Mishnah).

[133]"Marriage deeds", the tractate that deals with marriage contracts, and also the laws of rape and seduction.

Before reaching a conclusion, one more obstacle has to be overcome. As already established, one has to surrender life rather than to submit to any one of three cardinal prohibitions — idolatry, murder and incest.[134] In a Berei'ita[135] Rav Meir adds a fourth, *gezel*, that is, theft, plunder. According to the Rambam the beginning of the Gemara agreed with Rav Meir and the end of the Gemara argues against Rav Meir. But since *midat chassidut* is desirable but not required, and since the transgression of stealing is not irreversible, indicated by the fact that compensation must be paid, stealing is, therefore, not on the same level as the other three. In other words Rav Meir's opinion is rejected...

But the question goes a little further. If one is saving himself, he may decide to do *midat chassidut*, the right and proper thing. But when other people's lives are at risk, it is unlawful to adopt the line of *midat chassidut*, the strict interpretation...

That there is nothing more important than human life, and that stealing is forbidden, we know. One does not steal, possibly not even to save one's own life...

However, if one decides that stealing will save others' lives...and asks the opinion of a rabbi, "Am I allowed to steal to save an endangered life?" that rabbi must say, "Yes" with all his heart on condition that restitution will be made. If it is a matter of saving someone else's life, we are not only permitted but required to steal, but we are also required to repay.

---

[134]Talmud, Tractate *Sanhedrin* 74a.
[135]A non-Mishnaic source.

Appendix II
Scottish Money

Within six months of independence the Bank of Scotland issued new currency, which matched neither English nor European denominations. The government allowed the public eight weeks to exchange all old notes and coins circulated by the former United Kingdom and the four banks of Scotland. All new Scottish notes carried the "taloned lion of Scotland" watermark and a silver bar. The pound Scots (£Sc) paper money was printed in six denominations as follows:

DENOMINATION	OBVERSE	REVERSE
£Sc1	Robert Burns	Golf
5	Sir Walter Scott	Curling
10	David Hume	Caber tossing
20	R L Stevenson	Highland reels
50	Susan Ferrier	Salmon fishing
100	Hugh MacDiarmid	Pheasant shooting

The Estates divided the pound Scots (£Sc) into one hundred pence. The new coinage was minted in five denominations as follows:

DENOMINATION	OBVERSE	REVERSE
1 penny	Thistle	Saltire
5 pence	Leach's petrel	Saltire
10 pence	Scottish terrier	Saltire
25 pence	Shetland pony	Saltire
50 pence	Highland cattle	Saltire

The coins carried the Latin mottoes "Nemo me impune lacessit" ('No one provokes me with impunity' — motto of the ancient Order of the Thistle) and "In Defens", dates of minting and their denominations in numbers and letters.

Slang terms for notes and coins quickly arose. Single pound notes were called "golfs", fives "curls", tens "cabers", and twenties "reels". Fifties were either "salmons" or "fishers" and hundreds, either "pheasants" or "shooters". The five-penny coin became known by the ancient designation "bawbee". The Scottish public adopted the American custom of calling twenty-five and fifty pence coins a "quarter" and a "half", respectively.

Keep updated with the latest novels from
Iumix.
Join our mailing list.
Simply register as a member online at:

http://www.iumix.com

Or send your name and address to:

Mailing List,
Iumix Ltd.,
P.O. Box 179,
Totton, SO40 8YD,
U.K.

Printed in the United Kingdom
by Lightning Source UK Ltd.
288